# GIRLS LOST

## A Parker McLeod Thriller™

Hi Julius,
you have a cute girlfriend
in the book — Enjoy!
come Fish with Marty and
me this summer
Love you,
Grandpa

**By**

**A. Hardy Roper**

West Bay Publishing
Houston, Texas
www.facebook.com/TheGarholeBar


Cover Graphic by Luis Pruneda
Edited by: Chris O'Shea Roper

A Parker McLeod Thriller Series Book Five


ISBN: 979-8-218-15180-5

FIRST EDITION
1 2 3 4 5 6 7 8 9 10

# Acknowledgements

This book could not have been completed without the help of many friends and associates to whom I owe an endearing sense of gratitude.

At the top of the list is Chris Roper, for her herculean efforts in editing and re-editing the manuscript. Chris's advice was invaluable in all aspects of the book including grammar and sentence structure and clarifying areas that might have been confusing for the reader. Thank you, Chris. I owe you more than I can repay.

I also want to thank my writers' group members Diane Teichman and Anne Sloan both authors of distinction in their own right. Dianne helped me get started and was a great assist getting me on track. Diane is a heck of a positive critic. And thank you, Anne, for your time consuming and thoughtful reading of the manuscript pointing out phrasing adjustments and plot enhancements. Thanks again to Diane and Anne.

And many thanks and gratitude to my lovely wife and friend of 30 years, Winkie. Couldn't have done this without your love and support. Thank you, dearest.

I want to thank Bruce Moran for his invaluable assistance in constructing and formatting the book. Bruce, you are a real pro. I couldn't have accomplished the final product without your help.

Photo credit of the author goes to John Leech Photographers, Houston, Texas

Photo credit for the rifle goes to Kolanowski Studios, Houston, Texas

And the beautiful cover is the result of graphic artist Luis Prunela. Luis is one terrific artist, whose knowledge and creativity goes beyond way beyond the norm. Thank you, Luis, for your extraordinary talent. Luis may be contacted at Theartist21.com and Louieprun@gmail.com.

# Chapter One

---

Akemi noticed the girl in front of her in the lunch line because of her long black hair, carefully braided into two strands that fell below her shoulders. Colorful red ribbons adorned each braid.

The girl wore a white shirt with a green collar, a matching green-and-white plaid skirt and white knee stockings. Akemi's school friend in California had worn a similar outfit, only it was red and white. Akemi knew that the style was a traditional part of a girl's school uniform in Mexico. She thought this girl's dark skin meant she had some indigenous Indian blood, like the people she had studied in her Social Studies class.

This was the first day at a new school for Akemi. She knew no one and she needed a friend. Just as Akemi stepped up to meet her, the boy standing behind the girl yanked one of her braids. The boy was several inches taller and much heavier.

The girl let out a yelp and turned. She immediately slapped at the boy's face, but he pulled back and the slap missed. Then the boy edged closer, his chest puffed out.

Akemi was small for her age, but it didn't bother her. She didn't like bullies. She quickly stepped in front of the girl and blocked the boy. She stood defiant, with her back arched and hands ready at her sides.

"Back off," she said to the boy, her eyes steeled on his.

The boy sneered. "What? Who are you, little girl?"

"My name is Akemi Aoki." She said nothing more, her eyes riveted on his.

Suddenly, another boy whispered into the bully's ear. The bully broke his stare at Akemi and turned to the boy who had stepped up. The boy nodded. The bully eased back a step.

A teacher arrived and bent down to the girl with the braids until their eyes were level.

"Are you okay?" she asked.

The girl nodded yes, then took a tissue from her purse and wiped moisture from her eyes.

The teacher turned to the bully. She shook her finger in his face. "I saw what you did, young man. You go to the principal's office right now and wait for me."

When the teacher left, the girl turned back in line and gently rested a palm against the side of her cheek that faced the student tables. Probably trying to hide her embarrassment, Akemi thought.

Akemi spoke softly, "This is my first day at this school and I don't know anyone. Is it okay if I sit with you at lunch?"

The girl dropped her hand from her cheek. She lifted her chin and said, "My name is Maria Santos and I am new here too. I would very much like to have lunch with you, Akemi."

The bully was quickly forgotten as Akemi and Maria giggled all the way through that first lunch together, each excited about making a new friend on her first day of school.

At the end of the lunch break Maria said, "Akemi, it was so brave of you to face that boy. He was much bigger than you."

"I'm not afraid of that boy, Maria."

"Really? Why do you think he backed off when that other boy whispered to him?"

"My grandfather, Jiichan, teaches jujitsu classes at the high school gym. A lot of the boys go. I think that other boy heard me say my name and he knew about the classes."

"You think he was afraid of your grandfather?"

"Well, maybe. But he should have been afraid of me. Jiichan has been teaching me. I could have put that fat jerk down in a second, and I would have if he had touched you again."

Akemi and Maria laughed all the way back to class.

Later, at Akemi's nightly bedtime chat with her Nana Maggie, she told her about meeting Maria and how much she liked her new friend.

"I just know we will be BFFs," she said.

When Nana raised her eyebrows in a question, Akemi said, "You know, BFF…, Best Friends Forever."

Nana smiled.

"We are so much alike, even the same height. I measured again last week and I'm still not sixty inches." She looked expectingly at Nana. "Do you think I will ever grow? All the other girls in my grade are taller, except Maria."

"Of course you will grow, Akemi," Nana replied. She reached out and softly touched Akemi's cheek. "You just turned fourteen. You will probably hit a growth spurt very soon."

"Maria told me she was almost fifteen. She has breasts and wears a bra. Why hasn't she grown?"

Nana paused. "Well," she said, "people from different parts of the world grow to different heights. Perhaps all the people in her village were small."

When Nana pulled the blanket up around Akemi's chin,

she noticed moisture forming in her eyes.

Nana said, “What are you thinking about, Akemi?”

Akemi closed her eyes as if gathering her feelings. After a moment she opened them again.

“I miss my mom and dad so much. I think about them all the time. Why did they leave me?”

Nana Maggie focused on Akemi’s eyes. “They didn’t want to leave you, Akemi. Sometimes things happen we don’t understand. But you must believe this: your mom and dad loved you very much. They will always be with you. When you want to see them, just close your eyes and remember their love for you. Remember the little things. Sometimes it’s the little expressions of love that we remember the most. A smile, a hug. You will always have those special memories, Akemi. No one can take them away from you.”

Akemi closed her eyes. Maggie kissed her forehead and turned off the light.

***

The next day at school, Akemi noticed Maria didn’t have her hair fixed in braids. Maria’s long black hair now looked like hers, parted in the middle, with the strands pushed behind her ears and falling past her shoulders.

During the next several weeks, Akemi felt she’d found the sister she had always wanted. Every morning before school they met for a chat in front of the flagpole and then had lunch together in the cafeteria. They discovered they both liked mathematics and science. They also enjoyed art and music.

Akemi wanted to attend a top university and was thrilled when Maria shared the same hope. They both knew scholarships were the only way their dreams would come true, so keeping straight-A report cards was more important than peer pressure to be popular. They didn’t need to see who could have the most friends on Facebook: they had each other.

Each one had enjoyed the other's house for Friday night sleepovers. Maria's *mamá* always made delicious bean-and-cheese burritos for breakfast and homemade sopapillas with honey. And both girls loved Nana Maggie's special blueberry pancakes. Akemi was happy that Nana had met Maria's mother and said how nice she was.

One sleepover they stayed up late practicing kissing on each other's cheek. Akemi pursed her lips and said, "This is the way you do it—pucker your lips and touch his." She kissed Maria on the cheek. "How did that feel, Maria?"

"Ok, I guess," Maria said. "Is that all you do? I heard two girls talking in the bathroom and one said you were supposed to stick your tongue into the boy's mouth."

"Ewww…gross," Akemi said.

"I know," Maria shot back.

# Chapter Two

## Wednesday Afternoon

---

On Wednesday in the second week of October, Akemi and Maria made plans to go to the first girls' volleyball game of the season, scheduled for that afternoon in the gym. Nana Maggie had agreed to pick up a few cosmetics so the girls could practice applying makeup before the game. She picked them up at 3:00 pm and a few minutes later they sat side by side, giggling and making funny faces at each other in Nana's big mirror.

"This is so much fun," Maria said. "Before we start, let's compare faces."

Akemi studied her friend's face in the mirror. "Look at yourself, Maria. You are beautiful."

"You really think so? My nose is too big. I don't like it."

"Your eyes are prettier than mine, Maria. Yours are big and round and dark. Mine are shaped like almonds, slanted down at the ends."

"I bet the boys think your eyes are cool," said Maria. "And anyway, my skin is so much darker than yours."

"I wish I had your dark skin."

"Really?"

"Really! My dad said that my skin is pale because his grandfather came from one of the northern Japanese islands where the winters are cold with not much sun. He said people from those islands always have lighter skin."

Akemi turned to their makeup, "Why don't we try

mascara first?"

When Akemi applied some on her eyelashes, Maria said, "Oh my gosh, Akemi. Look at the way it makes your lashes stand out."

Then both girls added blush to their cheeks and applied lip gloss. When they were all made up, Nana Maggie came in.

"My, who are these beautiful movie stars sitting in front of my mirror?"

After Akemi and Maria finished giggling, Nana told them it was time to go to the game. She said she would drop them off and Jiichan would pick them up when the game was over.

Akemi said, "Jiichan promised we could walk to McDonald's for a hot fudge sundae after the game. He said he would pick us up there."

Even though Akemi had told her grandfather the four-block route was through one of the nicer areas of Galveston and that the game would be over before dark, she had still had a difficult time convincing him to pick them up at McDonald's rather than the gym. But with a big smile and a little cajoling, Akemi usually got what she wanted from her Jiichan. And today was no exception.

Nana Maggie thought for a moment and said, "I don't think it's a good idea, sweetie."

"But Jiichan said…."

Nana pursed her lips, thinking hard. "Well, if Jiichan said it was okay. But you must promise me you will go straight to McDonald's and stay there until he comes for you."

***

While walking to McDonald's after the game, Akemi noticed Maria nervously glancing around. She said, "Are you okay, Maria?"

"It's just getting dark so quick. Maybe we should have left earlier."

"I know," Akemi agreed. "But the game was so close. I hated losing in the last few seconds."

Akemi took Maria's hand and noticed she seemed to relax.

"I hope I get tall enough to play on the volleyball team," Akemi said.

"Me too," Maria added.

"Who was that cute boy who sat next to you?" Akemi asked.

"His name is Carlos. He said his mother named him after a famous Mexican author. But I don't know who he was talking about."

"Maybe we could ask the school librarian if she ever heard of a famous Mexican author named Carlos."

"Good idea, Akemi," Maria said, breaking into a smile.

"I think he likes you," Akemi said, giggling.

Akemi continued to hold Maria's hand as they prattled along, laughing and jabbering about everything from the fun of taking their makeup off with a glob of Nana's cleanser to wondering when they would get their first kisses.

With only a couple of blocks to go, they could see the lights at McDonald's and the cars zipping along on Broadway, the heavily traveled boulevard that split the city and carried traffic from the end of the causeway to the East End beaches.

With Maria and Akemi constantly chattering, they hardly noticed the dark van that passed them, cut across to their side of the street and parked next to the curb. Later, Akemi remembered thinking it was strange that the van was facing the wrong way on the street and its engine was still running.

When they were even with the van, the side door slid

open and two men, one short and one tall, leaped out. The short man wrapped his arm around Akemi's body and placed a rough hand over her mouth before she could scream. The taller man grabbed Maria.

The men quickly shoved the girls into the open side door of the van and jumped in behind them. When Akemi started screaming and kicking her feet wildly, the short man put her down on the floor of the van and flipped her onto her stomach. He quickly zip-tied her hands behind her and pulled a cloth hood over her head. Akemi fought back. She kicked out again and her heavy platform shoes hit something hard. Probably the man's leg, she thought. The straps broke and the shoes flew off her feet.

Akemi heard one of the men jump out of the van and slam the door. Since the short man had never taken his hands off her, Akemi knew the tall man had gotten out. She heard the gears shift, then felt the van swerve into the right lane and speed toward Broadway.

Even with the hood pulled over her face, Akemi heard Maria whimpering beside her. She wanted to reach out and touch her friend, but the zip tie held her hands tight behind her. With her hands losing feeling, she wiggled her fingers to keep the blood flowing.

Akemi almost retched when she felt the hot breath of the man on her neck. He was close—too close. She smelled the raunchy odor of burritos and stale cigarettes. Then a fat hand slipped between her thighs. She squeezed her legs tightly together and flipped on her side, dislodging the hand.

The man gave out a hard laugh.

A few seconds later, Maria wailed, "No, please! Don't touch me."

Akemi heard Maria cry out beside her and cringed at the

thought of what the man was doing to her friend.

Akemi turned on her other side to face Maria. Hoping Maria could hear her, she repeated softly, "Jiichan, Jiichan, Jiichan."

# Chapter Three

---

My name is Parker McLeod, proprietor of The Garhole Bar on the far west end of Galveston Island out among the prickly pear, cord grass and coyotes. My little piece of heaven sits on the edge of West Bay, the body of water that separates the island from the mainland.

Two types of regulars frequent my watering hole: fishermen who come in for a bowl of gumbo and a cold beer after a few hours on the water, and older ex-fishermen with too much arthritis to climb in and out of boats. But the latter still like to hang out, drink beer and harass the younger guys about the good old days when the trout were larger and more plentiful.

When I returned to the island after twenty years in the army, I decided to turn the old, cedar-planked bait camp into a bar. I added a serving counter, a beer box and a small kitchen. I picked up some tables and chairs at the Salvation Army, installed a couple of ceiling fans and hung some beer signs on the wall. I also cut out part of the front wall and put it on hinges. On good days, I raise the wall with the rope and pulleys I'd attached and latch it to the ceiling to capture the breeze off the gulf.

I needed a name for the bar so when I found a huge alligator gar washed up in the neighboring marsh, I cut off its head, boiled and bleached it white, and hung the skeleton from the ceiling over the counter. The gar's rows of gleaming white teeth glare down at the customers.

A tradition at the bar is to toast the gar's head with the first beer, showing respect for its successful traverse across thousands of years of environmental disasters. While a million species have come and gone, the lonely gar fish hangs on. Such tenacity well deserves the nod we give it.

The spoil bank of the Intracoastal Canal frames the other side of the bay a couple of miles across the water. Beyond the canal's berm, large, diesel-powered tugboats push strings of barges laden with everything from petroleum products to sand and gravel.

I have spent many evenings sitting on the top deck in my favorite Adirondack chair with my trusty army-issued binoculars, watching the red and green navigation lights atop the masts of the tugs as they trudge along the heavily traveled waterway.

I like the stillness of the bay when the water lays flat like a wide sheet of glass. I like the early-season cold fronts that bring a lazy breeze sweeping across from the mainland. I like the fall—after the weekend crowds disappear from the beaches—that provides the opportunity for a quiet walk on the sand. I like the occasional yipping of a lonesome coyote somewhere on the prairie. And I like the alone time.

It's why I came back here after Kuwait—hurting and drinking too much, trying to ease the pain from the war. I have good memories from growing up on the island. Well… mostly good memories.

***

Bully Stout helps run the bar when I'm not around. Bully was married to my mother's sister, my Aunt Norma. I guess that made the cantankerous old warrior my uncle, more or less.

On June 6, 1944, Bully landed on Omaha Beach in the third wave and fought his way through France. During the last days of the war, he'd gone into a minefield to help his wounded lieutenant. A misplaced step killed his friend and severely injured Bully.

He returned home with a prosthetic leg below his left knee, three fingers missing off his left hand and a destroyed left eye. Along with a new leg, the VA had also fitted Bully with a glass eyeball, but he complained it itched all the time and drove him crazy, so he took it out and resorted to a black eyepatch. He also never liked the leg the VA gave him so, as soon as he got back to Galveston, he found a piece of driftwood on the beach and hand-carved a new leg for himself.

After my Aunt Norma died, Bully harassed me day and night to live at The Garhole. He had no place to go, so I finally relented. He bought a used camper and moved it behind the bar. He lived in that camper for several years until he met Molly Putts, a frosty, wheelchair-ridden rancher's widow who lived in an old house on the prairie across the causeway from Galveston. They did nothing but argue and complain to each other, but he sold the camper and moved in with her anyway.

At that time, he was in pretty good shape for an eighty-year-old. Then a stroke left him partially incapacitated. They were quite a sight: Both wheelchair bound, sitting on the front porch of her dilapidated farmhouse watching grasshoppers devour what was left of her peach trees. When Molly's passing left Bully homeless again, he called about moving back to The Garhole.

We found a used oil-field trailer and moved it behind the bar. The trailer had a small kitchen, bedroom and bath. I spent a week renovating the inside to make it handicap accessible, which meant widening the doors and redoing the bathroom. It took several more days to build a wooden ramp with a low enough angle that Bully could run his motorized wheelchair up the incline.

Several years ago, Bully and his octogenarian friends organized a group they called the Dead Peckers' Club. The charter members were all Bully's school friends from Ball High in Galveston, class of 1940. During the past few years, several members had gone on to that big fishing hole in the sky. As of a few months ago, only four originals remained: Bully, Neddie Lemmon, Harry Stein and Marvin Klaus.

Then Marvin, a retired deputy sheriff, expired at a donut shop on Broadway while attending his daily coffee clutch with several fellow law enforcement officers. While laughing at one of the group's old jokes with a mouthful of sausage kolache, a piece of the sausage got stuck in his trachea. Even the trained officers couldn't get the Heimlich Maneuver to dislodge the obstruction. The medical examiner later said the attempts probably failed because of Marvin's size. It seems Marvin had gained a few pounds since retiring. That left three members.

# Chapter Four

---

Fortunately for the club, a few weeks ago Bully met a new candidate when the prospect came out to The Garhole to eat lunch with his granddaughter and let her fish off the back dock. The group felt a tinge of excitement—as much as octogenarians can—when Bully called a special meeting to discuss the promising new member.

For that meeting, I fried a batch of speckled trout I'd caught off the dock the night before. The beer and food for these meetings were always on me as a small token of appreciation for these old WWII war horses who'd been through so much. None of them talked about their war experiences. Like all veterans who'd experienced heavy combat, the more hell they'd experienced, the less they cared to discuss it. Still too painful after all these years.

I'd seen some of that hell myself, like hundreds of decaying Iraqi soldiers being bulldozed into trenches for burial. The smell was so horrible, I still occasionally awaken in the night with the stench in my nostrils. All tragedies of war are horrible, but at least the Gulf War was over quick, not like the months and even years guys endured in Bully's war or Korea or Vietnam.

That night, when the Dead Peckers chowed down, I left for a quiet dinner with my lady friend, Kathy Landry. Kathy is an ER nurse at the University of Texas Medical Branch or UTMB, a teaching hospital in downtown Galveston. We had been seeing each other for about a year, only spending the night together when her daughter Julie was off with her father, an orthopedic surgeon in Houston.

After I left for Kathy's, Bully and the remaining Dead Peckers discussed the new prospect. Bully told me later the meeting went something like this:

"Rudy Aoki didn't go to Ball High," Neddie Lemmon complained. "He's not even B.O.I." (Born on the Island).

"Right," Bully interjected, cutting off his friend. "But he's got his *bona fides*. Distinguished Service Cross, second highest award in the army, plus a Purple Heart and a bunch of unit citations."

"Where did he serve?" Harry Stein broke in.

"Italy."

"Those boys had some tough going," Harry added.

Harry's poor eyesight had kept him out of the fight. He had told me, as he had watched his friends march off to war, he'd deeply regretted not being able to give more, like Bully and Neddie. But by the time the war ended in 1945, Harry was a top-of-his-class, second-year law student. He was totally surprised but thrilled when Leon Jaworski, a lead prosecutor in the Nuremburg War Trials, recruited him as a researcher. Harry had spent several months in Germany helping Jaworski make sure top Nazis like Herman Göring and Rudolph Hess faced their sins.

After a successful law career in Galveston, Harry now spent his time doing *pro bono* legal work for local police officers and volunteering as president of the Galveston Historical Society.

"Was he at Monte Cassino?" Harry asked. "We lost a lot of good Texas boys trying to cross the Rapido River."

"No," Bully said to Harry. "That was the Texas 36$^{th}$ Division. Rudy was in the 34$^{th}$ Division, 442nd Regimental

Combat Group."

"Damn," Harry said, about as close to profanity as he ever got.

"Holy Mackerel," Neddie exclaimed. "He's a fu—Ja—."

Before Neddie could finish, Bully somehow reached over the table and punched Neddie's shoulder, rocking him back in his chair.

"Good Lord, Bully," Neddie cried out, while regaining his balance.

Bully yelled at his friend, "Don't let Rudy hear you use that word. He'll kick your ass. And when he's through, I'll do it too. The man's a genuine hero. He spent six weeks in an army field hospital in Italy trying to survive the German shrapnel eating away at his stomach."

Neddie straightened, rubbing his shoulder. "Sorry," he said.

Bully told me later he'd felt bad about punching his old friend. Rudy had had it rough, but so had Neddie. He'd experienced his own brush with death as the only survivor when a German panzer obliterated his Sherman tank somewhere in the North African desert.

"So, he's a *Nisei,*" Harry said.

"Yes," Bully added, "Second-generation Japanese American. His parents immigrated to Hawaii in 1915 when the planters brought a wave of immigrants to the islands to work the sugar cane fields. Rudy Aoki is a U.S. citizen, born on the island of Maui. He was nineteen years old on December 7, 1941, when the Japanese bombed Pearl Harbor."

At that point, with all due reverence, the group voted Rudy in by acclimation.

# Chapter Five

## Wednesday Afternoon

---

Rudy's initiation meeting had happened a couple of weeks ago. Today, Neddie had called a meeting because he said he had something special he wanted to show everyone. It didn't take much of a reason for the old friends to get together.

For today's meeting, I whipped up a pot of crab gumbo. We all knew this would probably be the last decent catch of the season before cold weather sent the tasty crustaceans into the mud for the winter.

I kept the gumbo and cold beer coming until the last of the French bread had sopped up the dregs. I hand-washed the bowls then sat on a stool at the back counter with a cold Shiner Bock to listen to Neddie's agenda.

The meeting began with everyone formally welcoming Rudy as a new member and then Harry, with a big smile, said to Rudy, "I've been reading about the *Nisei* and I have a question."

"Sure Harry," Rudy said. "What is it?"

"Why are so many *Nisei* named George?"

Rudy chuckled. "Only the eldest boy," he said. "My older brother was named George. Back in the day, Japanese immigrants wanted to show reverence for their adopted country, so they named their first-born boy after George Washington." He smiled. "True story."

That brought a good laugh from everyone.

Then Neddie held up a rifle and introduced the reason for

the meeting. He said, "My Cousin Doug was on the cruiser *New Orleans*. He always said they were damned lucky the kamikaze didn't hit them at Okinawa. When the war ended, the *New Orleans* brought some of the G.I.s back to the states. Doug said he won this rifle in a poker game on the ship. When Doug passed, the family gave the rifle to me. I'm the only WWII veteran left in the family."

Everyone noticed the Japanese characters hand-printed on a piece of faded yellowed paper taped to the stock.

Neddie said, "This rifle has been in the family for fifty years and no one has attempted to decipher the writing." He held the rifle out toward Rudy.

I hadn't known many Japanese, but I assumed Rudy was typical. He stood about five-foot-seven with a slender build, probably hadn't gained a pound since he got out of the army. Damned good for eighty-plus. He had a light complexion and close-cut, graying hair. His long, wide face looked slightly out of proportion to his height. Dark, penetrating pupils seemed too large for his eyes, but they helped light up his face when he smiled. His friendly bearing was easy to warm up to.

Rudy racked the bolt back and forth a couple of times and set the rifle in his lap.

"I can tell you anything you want to know about the M-1 Garand we used in Italy," Rudy said with a grin. "But I don't know a damned thing about Japanese rifles. This is the first one I've seen. I wonder if the old relic will even fire."

Rudy aimed the rifle out the back door. "I hate to brag," he said. "But I was the best shot in the 442nd Combat Team with an M-1. Qualified as Expert, *w*hich as you guys know is the highest level of marksmanship. My CO wanted me to go to sniper school, but I turned it down because I didn't want to leave my buddies."

"Sniper school, huh? Woulda been pretty cool," Neddie said.

Rudy shrugged. "I didn't mean to be so cocky. It was a long time ago."

Harry asked, "Can you tell us what those figures on the stock say?"

Rudy removed a pair of reading glasses from his shirt pocket and studied the faded writing.

"Well..., my parents spoke Japanese at home, so it was my first language. I used to be okay at it, but not so much anymore. And I never was good at reading the stuff. Too many crazy characters to remember."

Rudy studied the writing for a few moments. Then he paused and looked out at the bay. His eyes said he was somewhere else. When he refocused on the group, a tinge of irritation came to his voice.

"Hell's bells, I am an American," he said. "Growing up, my buddies and I did the same things you guys did. We worked on old jalopies, played baseball, ate burgers and fries, studied American history and eyed pretty girls. The difference was, after Pearl Harbor, your parents went about their daily jobs carrying on semi-normal lives, while ours...well...our parents lost their jobs, sometimes their businesses. They were forced to sell their property at reduced prices and were hauled off to relocation camps."

Rudy caught the eye of each man in turn as if he wanted to make damned sure everyone understood the grief and suffering his parents and those like them had endured because of their treatment during the war.

No one spoke. It was as though Rudy had buried the resentment he felt over his parents' treatment, but at times like these, all that anger surfaced. Then just as quickly,

Rudy's demeanor changed. As though an internal switch had flipped, he broke into a half-smile and his eyes resumed their sparkle. Gregarious Rudy was back.

"Anyway," Rudy continued, "the Japanese vernacular changed over the years. And there are many dialects throughout the country." He squeezed his eyes to focus on the characters. "I'm not sure I can make these out. Let me take the rifle home and I'll report back at the next meeting."

When everyone nodded agreement, Rudy stood and said, "Sorry guys, I have to go. I promised Akemi and her friend I'd pick them up after the volleyball game. And it's a thirty-minute drive back to town."

# Chapter Six

## Wednesday Night

---

Several years ago, I installed two large stadium lights just below the top railing of my boat dock. The powerful lights throw a healthy beam about forty yards out over West Bay. The lights attract shrimp, and bait fish and trout follow in their search for a tasty snack.

Out on the dock, a night heron's shrill squawk pierced the quiet night. The bird paced as usual, demanding its nightly ration of shrimp tossed by Bully from his wheelchair. Bully feeds as many of the tasty morsels to his buddy as he does to the fish he tries to snare with his trusty rod.

After the Dead Peckers' meeting, Bully had draped an old woolen afghan over his stump and one good leg and motored out to the dock in his wheelchair to fish and feed his buddy. Molly Putts had crocheted the afghan for her late husband and Bully had commandeered it when he moved in with her.

At least Bully said he was going to fish. In reality, he sat in his wheelchair with a line out in the water, alternating between dozing and occasionally slapping his neck to fight off mosquitos. I envisioned a swarm of the pesky critters buzzing around his body like a flight of WWII fighters attacking a carrier. The mosquitos were no doubt attracted by the $CO_2$ coming from his relentless snoring and the beer-infused sweat seeping from his pores.

Weary from cooking and cleaning, I retired to my Adirondack chair on the upper deck to drink a Shiner and watch fireflies light up the darkness.

After a while, the mosquitos made it from Bully's neck to the upper deck. I had decided to call it a night and was tucked in bed with the latest issue of *Texas Parks and Wildlife* magazine when the phone in the bar rang.

The only calls we got at The Garhole at this time of night were Houston fishermen wanting to know if the weather would be good enough in the morning to make the hour-and-a-half trek down to the beach. Knowing Bully couldn't hear the ring, I stumbled down the stairs through the back door of the bar and reached for the wall phone by the beer box.

"Garhole."

A frantic voice said, "Parker, it's Kathy. I've been calling your cell phone."

"Sorry, I guess the battery ran down again."

"Two girls are missing from Julie's school and she is home alone scared to death. We've got emergencies at the ER and I can't get off. Can you go to her?"

"What? What happened?"

"The girls disappeared walking to McDonald's after a volleyball game."

"I'm on my way."

I grabbed my cell phone, left Bully dozing on the dock, hopped in my rusty pickup and raced up the sand lane to the highway. The Garhole Bar sits twenty miles out West Beach from the city, so I'd asked Kathy to call Julie and let her know I was coming.

Any metropolitan area is dangerous at night, but two young girls missing off the street is not a regular occurrence in the laid-back City of Galveston.

As I raced along the darkened West Beach highway, I popped open the glove compartment, removed my Colt 911 and checked the magazine. I'd grown fond of the .45 caliber's stopping power during army training and decided it would be my handgun of choice.

But what was I thinking? I stuck the weapon back in the glove box.

A few minutes later, I knocked on the front door of Kathy's 1940's bungalow, shouting to Julie. The door opened to a frightened fourteen-year-old with long dark hair past her shoulders. A normally pretty face was now puffed and red. Tear-filled eyes radiated fear.

"Oh, Parker…."

I gave her a quick hug and we moved to the living room.

"Any news?"

"No," she said, swallowing hard. "I know a girl whose dad is a policeman. He picked her up at school and told her that Akemi and Maria were missing. She called me and I phoned Mom. She won't be home 'til after eleven when her shift's over."

"Don't worry sweetheart, I'm here."

As I tried to reassure Julie, I kept thinking this can't happen. Chances are those girls had detoured to one of their friends' houses and were busy drinking cokes and talking about boys. When they didn't come home, one of their parents probably panicked and called the police.

Then it hit me! Rudy had left earlier to pick up his granddaughter.

"Julie, what did you say the girls' names were?"

"Maria Santos and Akemi Aoki."

I turned my head, trying not to show the shock on my

face. The last thing Julie needed now was more alarm.

While Julie took calls from her frantic friends, I slipped out to the truck and called Harry Stein on my now-charged-up cell phone. Harry kept a police radio by his bed and heard every 911 call.

"Harry, you hear anything about two girls—?"

His frantic voice interrupted, "Oh, Parker. This is terrible, one of the girls is Rudy's granddaughter."

"I know."

"McDonald's is only a few blocks from the school.... Several people noticed the girls leaving the gym and walking in that direction, but there's no sign of them.... Police are knocking on doors along the way, looking for anyone who might have seen them."

Harry's panting told me he could barely get the words out. He moaned over the phone, a sound I'd heard before when his angina acted up.

"Harry, calm yourself. You're gonna stroke out."

He took a big breath and let it out slowly. When his breathing slowed, he said, "Some of the parents of the kids in Rudy's class are also driving the neighborhoods. This is not good, Parker."

"Rudy's class?"

"Rudy volunteers to teach jujitsu at Ball High. They say his class is pretty popular. Where are you?"

"At Kathy's house with Julie. Kathy's trying to get off work early."

"Can you take me to Rudy's house? I don't like to drive at night."

"I'll take you when Kathy gets home, and then I'm going to hit the streets myself."

Back inside, Julie sat at the kitchen table with tears

streaking down her cheeks. Her reddened face and quivering bottom lip were almost unbearable. We sat silently, glaring past one another, each with our own thoughts. After a moment, she lowered her head into her arms on the table and cried softly. I sat like a stump trying to think of something to say but had no clue how to comfort a teenaged girl. The best I could do was set a glass of cool water in front of her with a box of tissues.

Kathy had encouraged me to strengthen my relationship with Julie by spending more time with the two of them. But Julie's mind always seemed to be somewhere else, caught up with the usual teenage self-confidence angst and worries about peer acceptance. As with most kids her age, her life revolved around her friends and school.

"So Julie," I said, trying to break the tension, "tell me about the girls. How well do you know them?"

Julie blotted her eyes with a tissue and sipped some water. Her lips widened and turned slightly upward: not a smile, but at least a break from total despair.

"They are both new to the school. Akemi's mom and dad were killed in a car accident in California. She came here last summer to live with her grandfather, who she calls Jiichan, and her Nana Maggie. Akemi doesn't talk about her mom and dad much. She only says she misses them terribly."

Julie looked at me as though she'd finished so I asked, "What about Maria?"

"She came up from Mexico with her mother. They got here last summer also. She talks about how hot it was and almost running out of water on the long walk from the border."

"So Maria and her mother are not legal?"

Julie shrugged, as if ignoring my question. She said,

"Maria's really smart. She already speaks pretty good English. She says she loves it here and is so glad they came."

Julie blew her nose with a tissue and sipped more water. When she sat back in her chair, her shoulders slumped as she seemed to relax a little.

"We have some classes together," she continued. "Sometimes I join them for lunch, but mostly they go off by themselves. They're kinda quiet, but I like them a lot. A couple of times Maria invited me to her house. Her mother makes great tacos. I would have gone to the game tonight and probably walked to McDonald's with them, but Mom wanted me to stay home because she was working. I guess...I...I was the lucky one."

Hers eyes teared again. She dropped her chin to her chest. I wanted to hug her again but didn't feel we shared that level of intimacy. I sat across from her and stared at a photo of her and her mother that was sitting on the kitchen counter.

It was then I thought: If two missing friends could affect Julie like this, what were Akemi and Maria going through. My gut was telling me something was wrong, that these weren't the type of girls who joy ride on the beach with boys, especially when Akemi knew her grandfather was coming to pick them up. It didn't fit. Something bad was going down, and I didn't like the feel of it.

I felt my adrenalin firing up, the same as when I was in the army in Germany. As an Intel officer, I was involved in several cases where soldiers—both male and female—became unknowingly involved with enemy agents. If a soldier went missing, the end was usually not good.

The front door opened and Kathy hurried in. Even with her forehead wrinkled in concern, she looked good. Her hazel eyes turned green against her scrubs. Her skin was smooth and she wore no makeup that I could tell. She wore her light-brown hair pulled back over her ears. She gave me a quick nod and said, "Thank you, Parker. The ER cleared and I got off earlier than I expected."

When Julie lifted her head, Kathy's expression instantly went to something soft, her moist eyes brimming with concern. And then Julie stood and folded into her mother's arms for a long, silent embrace.

The loving, intimate scene between mother and daughter made me feel like an intruder. While they were still wound together, I nodded to Kathy I was leaving. I went out to my truck to put together what I knew about the missing girls.

Twenty years of army intelligence training gave me certain investigative skills, most of all how to think through a problem and not get lost in emotion. Julie had given me directions to Maria Santos' house, and that was as good a place to start as any. I decided I would pick Harry up as he requested, drop him at Rudy's house, and head over to Maria's.

# Chapter Seven

## Wednesday Night

---

Harry Stein liked to brag that his one-story, 1850's Greek Revival home was unique among the stately Victorians that dotted his neighborhood. He told every visitor about the home's original slate roof and the hand-blown glass that covered the three gabled bay windows. The front porch stretched across the entire width of the house. A plaque on the porch read "Texas Historical Commission." Harry had spent months tracing the house's history before finally obtaining the state's approval for the designation.

I pulled up to find every light in the house lit up like the field of a football stadium and Harry pacing nervously on his porch. At five-six, Harry's stature was smaller than most, but he made up for it in his dress. His friends called him "Harry the Clothes Horse."

Tonight Harry was decked out in smart gray slacks, matching suede shoes, a neatly pressed blue shirt and a lightweight navy windbreaker. His full head of white hair was perfectly coiffed and swept back along the sides, and his Colonel Sanders look-a-like goatee and mustache were trimmed to perfection.

He opened the passenger door to my truck, spread a white towel on the seat and climbed in on top of it. Worry lines in his brow telegraphed his stress level. He said nothing, not like the usually expressive friend I had known for forty years.

He fidgeted around in the seat, tweaking his goatee and strumming the dashboard with his fingers. I glanced over, concerned his reddened cheeks meant his blood pressure was up and he was about to stroke. I didn't say anything as he took several deep breaths with long measured exhales. By the time we turned onto Rudy's street, he seemed to have calmed himself.

He looked at me. "You probably don't know Maggie, do you?"

I shook my head.

"Margaret Thompson was a year behind me at Ball High. I actually had a date with her to the Valentine's Day dance as a junior."

"No kidding."

"Yes, but sadly it was our only date. She liked one of the football players better. Go figure."

I made a sound in my throat like I was sorry for his troubles.

"After Ball High, she went to nursing school in New Orleans…married someone she met there. I lost track until I caught up with her fifty years later living with Rudy. I don't think they are married."

"Why do you say that?"

"She still uses her married name, Peterson."

"Sounds like you still have some interest."

"She's just as lovely now as she was in high school. I'll tell you this, Parker. If I had known that Maggie's husband was deceased, I damned sure would have attempted to find her."

"So Rudy beat you to it. Wonder where they met?"

"During the war."

"Really?"

"That's all I know. I haven't had the courage to ask for

details."

I felt the wistfulness in Harry's voice as he trailed off.

A group of eight or nine people stood together on the front lawn of Rudy and Maggie's house, their focus on the highly animated discussion between Rudy and a Galveston police detective.

The detective's nameplate read "W. Kroton." I nodded to Harry. He shook his head, indicating he didn't know him. That was unusual, as Harry knew almost everyone on the force, including the chief.

Kroton wore jeans and a light jacket with the word "Police" imprinted in large white letters on the back. He appeared mid-thirties, maybe six-two and well-built, with a hawkish face, heavy eyebrows and glaring eyes. He stood erect with his ample chest puffed out.

I noticed Harry catch the eye of the uniformed officer standing beside Kroton. His name tag read K. Pulley. Several hash marks on Pulley's sleeve designated him as a sergeant. He was mid-fifties, shorter than Kroton, with a slight pudge to his midsection. Pulley grimaced and bit his lip as though something was amiss.

Harry pointed out a petite, gray-haired lady holding hands with Rudy. He was right. Maggie looked good, trim, well groomed, with a touch of makeup that highlighted her cheekbones. The whites of her eyes were reddened with concern, but the pupils were still bright. Even with excellent posture, she was only a little over five feet.

Harry moved beside Rudy and I stopped slightly behind them. The rest of the group closed in a circle around us.

The frown on Maggie's face signaled the conversation wasn't going well. Kroton moved closer, obviously invading their personal space. Not good. The detective's voice grew louder, swelling with arrogance.

"The department's policy is to wait twenty-four hours before initiating a search. We have a lot of runaways at this age, especially girls. Maybe a wanna-be boyfriend coaxed them into a joyride or maybe there's some unhappiness at home. Most cases, they'll be back when they get hungry or when the toke wears off. I told the chief to wait, but he jumped the gun and sent officers to the streets anyway. Good waste of resources, if you ask me."

That's when Maggie released Rudy's hand and stepped in front of Kroton, her head tilted upward toward the detective's chin, eyes defiant.

"Well, nobody asked you," she said. "Goddamit, will you just listen? Our granddaughter is not like that. Akemi is a straight-A student. She is responsible and would never do anything you're suggesting. We demand that you put out a maximum alert now and organize this search. Find our granddaughter!"

Then Kroton made a big mistake. He eased his hand onto Maggie's shoulder. One might think it a friendly touch, but I spotted the grimace on her face and knew better. Maggie pushed his hand off. I started toward Kroton, but Rudy beat me to him. In a blur, Rudy stepped around Maggie, grabbed Kroton's opposite shoulder with his left hand, then slipped his foot behind Kroton's knee and shoved him to the ground, falling on top of him. Rudy ended with his forearm pressed against Kroton's neck, immobilizing the detective.

If someone blinked, they missed it. The scene stunned the crowd. Sergeant Pulley reached for his baton but stopped short when Rudy rose quickly. Kroton got to his feet with his hand on his weapon, then glimpsed the faces gathered around and seemed to think better of pulling it.

He backed away a step and yelled, his voice up an octave. "You are under arrest!" Pointing to Pulley, he added, "Cuff him."

Pulley didn't move. Kroton bellowed, "Did you hear me?"

"On what charge?" Pulley asked.

"Assaulting a police officer. Now do it!"

Pulley didn't respond.

I stepped in. "Did anyone see an assault?"

No one spoke or moved.

"I'll have your badge for this," Kroton shouted to Pulley. He brushed his pants and stormed off.

Harry motioned for Pulley to walk with him. A few steps away but close enough for me to hear, Harry said, "Don't worry, Ken. I've got your back."

Pulley smiled. "I'm not worried, Harry. Nobody likes that SOB. His name is Willie Kroton, but behind his back, everyone calls him 'Woolly,' like woolly croton, the plant farmers call 'goat weed.' Sounds like a fit, doesn't it? A pest plant that is difficult to get rid of."

They both laughed.

Harry and I shook hands with Rudy and expressed our concern about Akemi. Harry hugged Maggie and introduced me. She spoke softly and asked us inside, then turned to the knot of people in the yard. "Rudy and I sincerely appreciate your concern. Please pray for Akemi and Maria. Thank you so much. We'll keep you updated."

In the small living room, Harry and I stood by the couch while Maggie went to make coffee. Rudy paced the floor, rubbing his hands together in a constant motion. He stopped and turned to Harry and me.

"I know damned well someone took Akemi and Maria. Akemi and I have had many conversations about her safety.

She sure as hell wouldn't get into a car when she knew I was coming to pick her up."

Harry and I realized Rudy's statements were rhetorical: No comment was expected and we didn't offer one. He wasn't the kind of man who needed or wanted to be patronized.

"I can't just stay here and do nothing," he said.

As he started for the door, Maggie came in with a tray and set it on the small table in front of the couch. She saw Rudy at the door. "Where are you going?" she asked.

Rudy stepped back and pulled her close. "Akemi's in trouble," he said softly. "I have to find her."

Maggie held him tight. "Please don't go," she said.

A knock sounded and Rudy opened the door.

A tall, attractive female stood on the stoop wearing the same type of jacket as Woolly Kroton. The porch light highlighted a gold badge that hung from a lanyard on her neck. The nameplate on her jacket said, "Sumner." She was slim but well-proportioned, as though she worked out and took care of herself. Thirty-something, with medium brown hair cut to her shoulders and deep brown eyes that brimmed with concern.

"Mr. Aoki?" she asked.

"Yes."

"I am Detective Donna Sumner with the Galveston Police Department. May I come in?"

Rudy stammered, "The cops are doing nothing. I'm going out to find Akemi myself."

Sumner stepped inside and said, "You will do more good staying here and talking to me."

Maggie shook her fist at Sumner. "Those girls wouldn't do that!" she blurted out. "That prick cop that was here—."

Sumner moved another step inside. "I am very sorry about your missing granddaughter and can only imagine what you are going through."

Sumner's calm voice was almost a monotone. When she spoke, I knew she was the right person for the case, obviously trained to diffuse tense situations. She'd also smartly chosen to disassociate herself from Woolly Kroton by ignoring Maggie's outburst.

"I am the lead detective now," she continued, "and have worked many missing children's cases. Sergeant Pulley and some of your neighbors spoke with me outside. I understand the situation and agree with you that the girls wouldn't have done anything out of character. Sergeant Pulley told me the other detective said our policy was to wait twenty-four hours. I can assure you that this is incorrect. Right now, every available officer is on the streets searching. We will work night and day and will not rest until the girls are safely home."

It was good to see some of the lines disappear from Maggie's face as relief seemed to course through her.

Sumner glanced at the small table and then back at Maggie. "The coffee looks good," she said.

At that point, Harry and I knew we were not needed. We eased into the connecting dining room but stood close enough to the door to hear the conversation.

Maggie motioned the detective closer and poured coffee. She and Rudy sat on the couch while Sumner pulled a chair up close. She picked up the cup and sipped the coffee.

"Thank you," she said.

Maggie asked, "Is it true the first forty-eight hours are critical?"

I could almost read Sumner's expression when she looked at Maggie. It was as if she wanted to say something about

Maggie watching too many police shows on TV.

But instead, Sumner said, "That's statistics that some departments have gathered. My thoughts are that every hour is important and, as I mentioned, we are doing everything we can. In my experience—and I have a lot—there is no particular connection to the forty-eight-hour period you refer to.

She took another sip from her cup and set it down on the coffee table. Then, shifting her eyes between Maggie and Rudy, she said, "Now, please," she said. "Tell me about Akemi."

# Chapter Eight

## Wednesday Night

---

Akemi's face itched like crazy. But with her hands zip-tied behind her and the hood over her face, all she could do was lower her head and try to rub the hood against the sleeve of her cotton blouse. Nothing worked.

When the man had pushed her into the van, he forced her across the floor to the other side. Sitting on the metal floor of the van with the cold seeping through her pants, Akemi tried hard to stay in the present like her grandfather Jiichan had taught her. Be mindful: Stay focused.

She heard Maria whimpering beside her and spoke softly, "It's okay, Maria. I am here with you."

Knowing she was against the right-hand side of the van's interior, she could tell which direction the van turned by either forward or backward pressure.

When the driver sped off, he took the first left-hand turn fast, without slowing. She noticed they had also stopped for several traffic lights. That, plus the frequent whooshing sound of passing vehicles, probably meant they were traveling on a busy street. And because the van had only turned once since they were kidnapped, they had to be on Broadway.

Then the engine ramped up, the van gathered speed and moved onto an incline. She felt a slight tilt toward Maria, who was closer to the rear. Where could that happen on an island as flat as Galveston?

The driver gunned the engine again, gathering more power and speed. Wind noises cantered off vehicles as they passed them. Then she felt herself tilting toward the front of the van as though they were moving downhill.

And then it hit her. They had made only the initial turn onto Broadway. The driver had accelerated, and they had traveled up an incline and now down. They had to be on the causeway bridge, leaving Galveston. For the first time, she felt the absence of hope.

Her body quivered as she realized the farther they traveled, the less chance they would ever be found. Going off the island meant the men could be taking them anywhere. She hoped it wasn't to the big city of Houston to the north, the city with thousands of places to hide someone….

Maria whispered, "Akemi? Akemi, are you there? The man is not here. He must have moved to the front of the van."

"Did he hurt you, Maria?"

"Oh God, Akemi, the way he…touched me…I…I am so ashamed."

Shocked at her friend's words, Akemi didn't know what to say. But she knew she had to stay brave for both of them. She tried hard to keep her voice strong, as if she wasn't worried.

"Try not to cry," she said. "We don't want to show fear."

Akemi moved her leg and touched Maria's leg. She kept her leg close to Maria's so they could share their warmth.

Akemi thought about Jiichan, the way he worked out and kept his body sturdy and tough. He also did the same with his mind. She would be strong too.

The van slowed and she felt the slight pressure of her back pushed against the wall of the van, which meant they were turning left. Strange, she thought. They had gone off the causeway only moments ago and now they were taking a left-hand exit from the freeway. Where would that be? She couldn't put it together.

A few minutes more, she heard the ticking sound of the turn signal and the van's engine slow. She felt a turn to the right, then a zigzag through streets before slowing again. She heard the crunch of gravel under the tires as the van came to a stop.

The man on the passenger side got out. Then there was the ratchetting sound of a garage door opening. The driver eased the van forward. The garage door closed behind them. She heard the driver get out and open the sliding side door. Since it was the driver, Akemi thought it must be the tall man, the one who had grabbed Maria. It had all happened so quickly, she hadn't seen either of their faces. She knew only that one was tall and the other short. The driver carefully eased Akemi and Maria out of the van. Akemi felt the cold from the cement floor of the garage seeping into her feet. She wanted her shoes but realized with the straps broken, they wouldn't work anymore.

As close as Akemi could figure, they had only traveled for five to ten minutes after leaving the causeway. At least they were close to Galveston and not on their way to someplace far away. She prayed this was the final stop.

The man pushed them out of the garage and across a yard, up a few steps and into a house. Akemi smelled food. From her times at Maria's house, she thought it might be beans. Since they had walked from the garage to the rear of the house, it made sense they were in the kitchen.

One of the men put his hand on Akemi's back, moved her a few steps and removed the bag from her head. He told her to sit. Akemi inhaled a deep breath and blew it out, the first fresh air she'd breathed since being thrown into the van. It felt good.

Her eyes slowly adjusted to the dim light of a single bulb hanging from the ceiling over a wooden table. Akemi quickly focused on Maria sitting in a chair across from her. When the man removed the bag from Maria's head, she also gasped for air.

But when Akemi noticed the quiver in Maria's bottom lip, cold chills raced along her spine. Maria was still suffering from the shock of the man touching her in the van, and Akemi knew then she would have to pay close attention to her friend.

Two Hispanic men, both young, stood by the sink gulping beer and mumbling to one another in Spanish.

Akemi easily identified the one who had grabbed her on the street and put his hand between her legs. He was short with a pudgy face and close-cut hair. A heavy black beard covered his face with a bushy moustache on his top lip. He slumped his shoulders, which made his midsection resemble a volleyball. His tee shirt depicted a bull with wide horns, snorting, with steam coming out of its nostrils. Tattoos, imbued with orange and red and black colors and depicting intertwined snakes, covered both arms. A tattoo encircling his neck resembled a barbed wire fence.

The other man, the driver, was tall and thin, skinny as a butter knife. Clean shaven, with black hair pulled tightly against his head in a ponytail. He wore a brightly colored tee shirt that pictured a Hispanic man with a large moustache, wearing a large sombrero and playing a guitar. There were no tattoos Akemi could see.

Maria had been teaching Akemi Spanish. She could now carry on a brief conversation with Maria if she spoke slowly, but the men spoke so rapidly she only understood a few words. She hoped Maria was paying attention and could follow the conversation.

Akemi shouted at the men in English, "Water! We need water." She nodded toward Maria hoping the men would notice her condition. The tall man with the ponytail filled two paper cups from a plastic jug and placed them on the table in front of the girls. He unfolded a large knife from his pocket and cut the zip ties holding the girls' wrists.

Akemi and Maria gulped the water and asked for more. The man moved the jug to the table and the girls quickly refilled their cups.

"The beans are almost done," the tall man said in English. "We will eat soon."

Akemi took his statement as a sign she could speak to him. "Could you please tell us why we are here?"

The tall man turned away without answering. He filled two bowls with beans, slipped in spoons and set them in front of the girls. The beans smelled of cumin and pepper.

Akemi whispered to Maria to eat the beans because they didn't know when they would be fed again. When they finished, Akemi forced herself to thank the tall man. He told them to get up, then fastened their hands behind their backs with new zip ties and marched them through a door into a dark room. The light from the kitchen allowed Akemi a quick glance around the space. She observed no furniture, only several sleeping mats rolled out by the walls.

The man opened another door off to the side and showed the girls the bathroom. It was hard to see in the dark, but Akemi did notice iron bars on the outside of the window. The man ordered Akemi and Maria to sit against the wall in the bedroom. He unlocked a door across the room, went in and returned with two more mats. He locked the door behind him then gave the mats to the girls and went into the kitchen and locked that door. Akemi scooted the mats together so they could feel the warmth of each other's body.

Akemi remembered what Nana had told her. She focused hard to find her mother's smile and the tenderness in her eyes. She tried to sleep but couldn't, her heart pounding too much. Where were they? What was going to happen to them?

Late in the night, the kitchen door opened, stirring Akemi. A girl dressed in leggings and a low-cut blouse shuffled into the room. The girl glanced in Akemi's direction, as though she knew Akemi and Maria were there. Akemi doubted the girl could see her in the darkness.

Backlit by the kitchen light, Akemi glimpsed the girl's blond hair and light complexion. She was tall with slumped shoulders. At first Akemi thought she was just tired, but as she plodded to a mat at the end of the room, Akemi felt an air of hopeless resignation arise from the girl with every step.

Two more girls followed the first girl in. Akemi only caught a glance as they padded by. They were younger and shorter than the first girl, with darker skin.

Someone pulled the kitchen door shut and the lock clicked. The room went dark again.

When Maria broke down and started to weep, one of the girls spoke in English. "We heard they got two new girls. Cry all you want to," the voice said. "It will do no good."

Thank God, Akemi thought. Someone we can talk to, who can maybe help us. "My name is Akemi," she said. "What is yours?"

After a long pause, the woman replied, "Sarah."

"These men kidnapped us, Sarah. Why are we here?"

"You are in a house no one knows about. And you are here to make money for El Tigre."

Akemi said, "What do you mean 'make money'?"

"El Tigre will take you to a place where you will give your bodies to the men."

"We will not do this!" Akemi stated defiantly.

Sarah laughed. "You will," she said. "Wait and see. He will give you pills to make you feel good. You will be with many men every night. To do what they want."

Akemi said, "Who is El Tigre?"

"The man who owns us."

"No one owns me," Akemi replied, her voice strong. "Your hands aren't tied, why don't you run?"

"Once was enough," Sarah answered. "El Tigre caught me. Beat me in the stomach so the bruises wouldn't show. I coughed up much blood. I had much pain. He gave me pills for the pain. Now I can't leave…I need the pills."

"Why are the lights off, not even one in the bathroom?"

"Hector keeps it that way. You will even pee in the dark."

"Why?"

"You'll see," Sarah replied.

The room went quiet. After a while, Akemi whispered to Maria, "Did you understand what the men were saying to each other in the kitchen?"

"Yes," Maria whispered back. "They said their names. I remember their voices. The tall one is Juan and the short one is Hector. Hector told Juan they had done the right thing getting us."

Akemi's blood rose hearing Hector's statement. She blurted out, "The right thing…the right thing for who?"

She took a deep breath, thinking it would give her extra strength. She twisted her hands violently, trying to break the ties behind her back. It would be her first attempt at freedom.

# Chapter Nine

## Wednesday Night

---

A friend of mine in high school, Johnny Klepper, drove a 1950 black Ford convertible—one cool car. He worked hard sacking groceries to pay for it. He told me he'd named the car "The Mayflower," hoping the girls would come across. Don't know if he had any luck.

On Saturday nights we would park in front of a liquor store, wait for a person who looked as if he could use an extra buck or two and bribe him to go in and buy us a couple of six packs. Then we'd drive the streets, mostly looking for girls. In the course of one summer, I was sure we had traveled every possible area of the city. But I was wrong.

Harry and I had eased out of Maggie's house when Rudy started talking about Akemi. I dropped him at his home, circled back to Broadway and turned on Forty-Sixth Street toward the docks. After a few streets, the area faded into a warren of old warehouses that took up entire blocks, many with rusted corrugated iron siding and weeds stretching to the curbs, where once there may have been manicured grass. Some of the buildings appeared empty, ghosts of a bygone era. Abandoned rail tracks, partially covered with asphalt, ran alongside the storage facilities.

Past the warehouses were a couple of blocks of small homes filled with people too poor to have any influence with City Hall. The down-and-out lived here, eking out a day-today existence well below the radar of the *American Dream.* Where rent was due weekly or the local slum lord cut off electricity.

The houses were paint-bare, with sagging front porches and rusty tin roofs. A couple of homes stood empty with waist-high weeds in the front yards.

There were no streetlights. A few yellow porch lights provided a ghostly feel to the neighborhood. Supposedly, yellow lights dispelled insects, but nobody had told the bugs. Hordes of moths and nits hovered around each light.

I turned into a dirt alley just before the last street, carefully dodging mud holes probably filled with mosquito larvae. Two mobile homes were set back so they couldn't be seen from the side streets.

Kathy's daughter Julie had told me she had been to Maria's house and Maria and her mother lived in the one on the right. Next to their mobile home, a house faced the street behind them. In the house's backyard, maybe thirty feet from me, a pit bull stretched to the end of its chain and began a ferocious growl, its cheeks pulled back showing more teeth than I wanted to see up close. There was no fence. If the dog broke the chain or pulled the stanchion from the ground, it could have my leg for supper in a manner of seconds.

I had read that keeping a dog on a chain made it mean. But this was a pit bull, the breed infamously used for dogfighting in certain areas of Louisiana and South Texas. I had always assumed malice was inherent in their genes, but a vet once told me that this breed of canine was naturally loving, and only brutal training changed their character. I wondered about the back story of this poor animal.

I felt for the dog but still had to protect myself. I grabbed a tire tool from the bed of the truck, slapped the iron rod in my hand a few times and met the creature's stare with my own. The dog only got more determined. So much for intimidation. I dropped the tool back in the truck bed and moved toward the front door of Maria's house, hoping the stake would hold.

A ten-year-old Chevrolet sedan bathed in dust sat in front of the mobile home to the left of Maria's. A well-worn dirt path connected the two trailers. The area was dark, lit only by a faint bulb on Maria's porch. A dim light showed though a sheet-covered window.

On the wooden deck, a lone plant stood in a colorful Talavera pot. The healthy green leaves of the plant and bright shades of yellow, blue and green of the pot were the only signs of hope in the neighborhood. Not wanting to surprise Maria's mother, I made as much noise as I could stomping onto the wooden porch.

A voice from inside shouted in Spanish as I knocked.

*"Quién es?"*

I spoke in English to test her knowledge of the language. "Señora Santos, my name is Parker McLeod. I am a friend of Akemi's grandfather and Nana Maggie. I am here about Maria. May I speak with you for a moment?"

A soft voice answered, *"No habla Inglés."*

I grew up speaking some Spanish among Latino friends in Galveston and later honed my ability in Army language schools. I repeated my request in Spanish. A moment later a diminutive, mid-thirties, Hispanic woman wearing a faded house dress opened the door. Straight, nicely combed black hair hung to her waist. She stared at me through moisture-filled eyes.

I continued in Spanish, assuming she was Maria's mother. "Señora Santos, I am here to help if I can. You can call Maggie if you want to check on me."

Another Hispanic woman, maybe ten years older, moved beside her and wrapped her arm around the shorter woman's waist. After a moment, the shorter woman removed the older woman's arm from her waist. She stepped back from the doorway and motioned me into the small living area. A threadbare rug partially covered the floor.

A light across the room drew my eyes to a card table set against the wall underneath a cardboard painting of Our Lady of Guadalupe, the patron saint of Mexico. Several candles flickered on the table.

The shorter woman introduced herself as Alicia Santos, Maria's mother, and the other woman as Patricia Gonzalez, her cousin who lived in the mobile home next door. Señora Santos motioned me to a small folding chair and she and Patricia moved to a sagging couch with a small plastic table in front. Maria's mother lowered her head and began a quiet sobbing. I wanted to say something comforting but held back and waited for her to compose herself. When she was ready, we continued in her native tongue.

"Señora Santos, I am sorry Maria appears to be missing. A lot of people are trying to find her. The police were at Akemi's house when I left, and I am sure they will be here soon. Can you tell me anything? Does Maria have a boyfriend?"

Alicia lifted her eyes to mine. "Maria is only fourteen. It is not permitted."

"Is it possible she would have gotten into a car with some girls she knew, or a boy?"

"Absolutely not. She is a good girl."

"Have you noticed anyone new in the neighborhood, maybe driving by?"

Both women shook their heads.

"Is there a gang in this neighborhood or any drug users?"

Patricia spoke, "Alicia is new here, but I moved into my mobile home a year ago. The people are poor, but honest. There are no drugs in this *barrio.*"

She spoke with such a knowing firmness that I believed her: two proud, independent women trying desperately to make a go of it in an unfamiliar and unwelcoming new land.

Just then, car headlights flashed from outside. I moved to the window and pulled back the sheet. Detective Sumner parked beside my truck, stepped out and turned to Sergeant Pulley, who'd stopped behind her in a patrol car.

Behind me, Alicia moved to a chair at the shrine. She clasped her hands in front, raised her face to the painting and began to pray. I nodded to Patricia, stepped out to the porch and closed the door.

I stood on the porch contemplating the mistake I'd made by invading the privacy of a mother in terrible pain. I am not the police, a relative or a friend. Damn.

Sumner yelled up from the yard. "Parker McLeod, what the hell are you doing here?"

I wondered how she knew my name. "Good question," I replied. I walked down to face her. She waited with hands on her hips. Pulley stood beside her.

"I thought it was you at the Aoki house," she said. "So I called Kathy. She described you well, about six-foot, dark hair and eyes. Good looking…at least she thinks so." The sarcasm dripped off her tongue.

"Glad to hear 'at least she thinks so,'" I replied, smirking. "How do you know Kathy?"

"She's drawn a lot of sketches of perps and missing children for me. She's a hell of an artist. But I guess you know that."

Kathy worked part-time for the department. I'd seen her work and knew her talent.

Rather than reply to Sumner, I nodded, stalling to form the best choice of words. It was time to get on the right page with the detective.

"Okay," I said. "My coming here tonight was inappropriate. I apologize for jumping ahead of you."

Sumner scowled, "Ahead of me? What the hell does that mean? You damned well shouldn't be here at all."

An awkward silence followed. Then she chewed her lip as if trying to decide something. I squeezed out a big breath and held my eyes away from hers.

"But" she continued, "you saved Dr. Lang at the Gulf Coast Laboratory from that gang of assassins. Maybe the Secretary of Homeland Security, as well. I guess that counts for something."

Hearing that made me feel uneasy. I never wanted a spotlight from the terrorist episode. I am basically a loner. I like being anonymous, invisible. But as much as I hated the exposure, it was a small price to pay if it helped me connect with Sumner. Anything to find Akemi and Maria.

"Anyway," she observed, "you may have hit it lucky, McLeod. My partner's out on medical leave and the department is already short two detectives. I work the day shift and wouldn't be here at all if Harry Stein hadn't called Chief Puryear and read him the riot act about that a-hole, Woolly Kroton. Puryear woke me up at home, told me to get my ass out of bed and over to the Aoki house."

There wasn't anything I could say to that.

She took a breath and said, "And according to what I know about you from Kathy, you're going to stick your nose in this case whether I want you to or not. So you can go around like the Lone Ranger or you can work with me. Unofficially, of course. Hell, for all I know, Harry's already cleared it with the chief. But don't go stepping on my toes and don't go off half-cocked on some wild goose chase. The last thing I need when I find these girls is for you to have screwed up the perp's rights so the piece of scum gets off on a technicality."

I held up three fingers and said, "Scout's honor. And just so we're clear, you already think these girls are in trouble?"

"Yes, sadly, I do. Now what did you learn from Señora Santos?"

I related my conversation with Maria's mother.

She turned toward the porch, then stopped and shifted back to me. "Okay, listen. I haven't eaten and I'm starving. Meet me at the Waffle House on Sixty-First Street in about an hour."

She motioned to Pulley and the two of them walked up to Señora Santos' porch.

***

Not ready to quit, I drove the streets in desperation looking for the girls, but got nothing except a few hard looks from others also out searching. I considered going by Kathy's, but figured mother and daughter needed some alone time. I called her instead.

"So how's Julie?" I asked.

"Worried, frantic. Texting her girlfriends back and forth."

"Anything from any of the girls I can use?"

"Probably not, but I'll check. I assume you met Donna?"

"Donna?"

"Detective Sumner."

"Yes, tough broad."

"Really, Parker. That's uncalled for. Give her some slack.

She's seen a lot of God-awful sights searching for missing kids."

"How about if I say 'dedicated broad.' That better?"

***

Rudy's house was not out of the way, so I drove by on the way to the Waffle House. Maggie was in the yard with the same group of neighbors, who were probably doing their best to support her. Rudy's car was gone. No doubt he was out searching for his granddaughter.

I drove on to the Waffle House and grabbed one of the booths across the back. The place was empty except for a tat-covered cook about thirty with long, greasy hair hanging out from his ball cap. Two waitresses, one gray-haired and the other a peroxided blond, stood behind the counter. The gray-haired waitress shuffled a glass of water in front of me and slapped a menu on the table.

Her sagging cheeks and tired eyes took a chip out of my heart. What life story had pushed an older woman into working for minimum wage on the late-night shift at a Waffle House? Just thinking about the possibilities saddened me. But who was I to judge? I learned a long time ago everyone has their own brand of baggage. The best I could do was smile and leave a fat tip.

Just as I sipped my coffee refill, Detective Sumner pulled into the parking lot. A minute later, she hustled to my booth and sat across from me.

"Waiting long?" she asked.

"Second cup," I said.

The waitress came. Sumner asked for coffee and we both ordered hamburgers.

"Learn anything more at the Santos home?"

"Unfortunately, no," she said. "I don't speak Spanish and

Sergeant Pulley only knew enough to stumble through the interview. I'll have to go back in the morning with an interpreter."

I raised my hand.

"Damn, the gallant Parker McLeod. I should have known." She paused, sipped her coffee.

She said that without a smile, so I didn't know if she was kidding me or simply continuing her brand of sarcasm. Either way, I ignored the dig and said, "So I have a question. Why did you give Maggie Peterson the 'Ali shuffle' about the first forty-eight hours?"

Sumner set her coffee cup down and caught my eyes with a steady stare. "If I told her she was right, that the first forty-eight were critical, what would happen when we reach that point and haven't found the girls or maybe don't even have a viable lead? Do Mrs. Peterson and Mr Aoki crater, lose all hope?"

"Okay," I said. "I understand. But what do you really think? What does your experience tell you?"

"It's critical."

I sat back in the booth and blew out a big breath. I chewed my lip, looked around the empty Waffle House and focused back on her. Said nothing.

The gray-haired waitress brought the burgers and refilled our cups. Sumner eagerly bit into the burger, chewed and swallowed, and sipped more coffee.

"Another question," I said. "How do we know for sure the girls went missing on the way to McDonalds? I mean, hell, as far as we know, they could have set up a rendezvous with some boys."

Sumner set her hamburger on her plate and wiped her mouth with a napkin. She gave me a smirk like the question was so stupid, she couldn't believe I asked it.

"Two reasons," she said. "Because Akemi knew her grandfather was picking them up at McDonald's after the game, and they didn't have time for a 'rendezvous' as you put it. My God, McLeod they're not even fifteen years old. Give me a break. You've met Maria's mother and Akemi's nana and grandfather. Did any of them strike you as a parent who didn't have the respect of their children?"

She paused and shook her head as if totally disgusted. She sipped her coffee and gazed out the window to the street. I leaned back in the booth, sufficiently chastised and thinking, wow, this *is* one tough broad. The kind I need to be teamed with who could see this thing through.

She looked at me again and said, "And the second reason, if you really need it, is that the father of one of the students called in and said his son Carlos sat with Maria at the game. She asked him if he'd like to go to McDonald's with them. He couldn't because his father was picking him up at the school."

She paused, exhaled a long breath, then took in another and said, "Now think about this if you can. If Carlos had gone with them, would they be missing?"

Oh, man," I said. "How things turn on a dime."

"No kidding," Sumner responded. She took another bite of hamburger and swallowed. She touched her mouth again with her napkin and said, "I observed enough at the Santos home to drop the kidnapping-for-money motive. Which means I go to the basics. I've confirmed my thoughts on the first part of the triangle." She took another bite.

"Triangle?"

"I've been working Juvie for eight years. I equate missing-person cases to the Bermuda Triangle: both full of mystery and tragedy. The cases usually boil down to one of three possibilities with some variations. The first leg of the triangle is that the girls decided to run away because of an argument at home or parental abuse. Or maybe a boyfriend talked them into it."

"Doesn't sound like any of that fits here."

"Right. After speaking with Rudy Aoki, Margaret Peterson and Señora Santos, I'm convinced these girls didn't run off. They're both top-of-their-class kids with level heads on their shoulders. And there is certainly no abuse and no boyfriends. I eliminated that part of the triangle."

"So what are the other two parts?"

"Well, the second leg is the pedophile angle. But both of these girls have been warned about strangers who ask for help looking for a lost dog and all those come-ons. And neither one is foolish enough to have gotten into a stranger's car. So I've discounted that one too. But just to be safe, we are getting updates on every known child molester in Galveston County. Detective Moss is in charge of that team. They are running the sickos down as we speak."

"That leaves the third leg, and I'm not sure I want to hear you say it."

Sumner lowered her head as if in prayer. Then with a furrowed brow, she raised her eyes, filled with moisture and worry, and said, "They were snatched."

# Chapter Ten

## Wednesday Night

---

Detective Sumner left the Waffle House saying she needed to go by the station and check updates for the missing girls. Since I thought she could have done that on her radio, it left me wondering if our arrangement was going to be a one-way street.

My phone read 11:00 pm. I decided to drive the seawall. I hung a right out of the Waffle House and turned left on the boulevard. The restaurants were closed and their parking lots empty, but people were still coming and going from the bars. Even at this late hour people strolled atop the seawall. Not unusual for a tourist city.

Just ahead, two teenage girls on the seawall laughed and giggled as they moved casually along, seemingly ignorant of their surroundings. I wanted to caution them about the dangers of the night and the missing girls but thought an older man pulling beside them in a rusty pickup might frighten them more than my warning would.

Past Gaido's Seafood Restaurant, I turned left and drove toward Rudy's house, thinking they would still be up. The crowd of neighbors had dispersed from the yard and Rudy's porch light was off. I parked in front and noticed someone on the front stoop.

Rudy sat in the dark in the lotus position, with his hands on his lap, palms up, and his feet crisscrossed beneath his body. Not wanting to disturb his meditation, I remained in the truck. Ten minutes later he unfolded his body and walked toward me.

"I could feel a presence," he said. "Hoped it was someone bringing news…."

"Sorry, nothing to report."

"Maggie's inside with a couple of friends that came over when they heard. I couldn't handle the negative vibes, so I came out to meditate. Want to make a run with me?"

I thought about the Colt 911 in my glove compartment and asked Rudy to ride with me.

When he climbed in, I said, "We can drive the seawall to where the road dead-ends at the ship channel and then cross over and come back on the beach."

Galveston P.D. had probably run this course, but it was better than driving around in circles. The trip gave me the chance to learn more about the enigma riding beside me. Rudy Aoki, son of an immigrant, war hero and now a father figure to a displaced teen-aged granddaughter.

A slow drive along the seawall gave me time to consider what questions to ask. And then I almost blurted out, "How was it growing up in Hawaii?"

Rudy gave me a surprised stare, probably trying to determine my intent. Then he smiled.

"I think you mean did I feel discriminated against as the son of a Japanese immigrant growing up in an Anglo-oriented country."

"Well, I—"

"Of course, you meant that, Parker. That kind of innuendo has been thrown at me my entire life. Listen…my father was tough, the most tenacious man I've ever known, determined to carve a better life for his family. For the first ten years, he worked daylight to dark under a broiling sun in the pineapple fields. He saved his money, what little there was of it. By the time I was in Junior High, he owned his own grocery store catering mostly to Japanese neighbors. You probably don't know this, but in 1940 at least a third of the Hawaiian population were people with Japanese heritage.

"I may have felt some condescending behavior from some of the people, but I sure as hell wasn't about to let them know it. My father taught me two things I will be forever grateful for: a martial art to defend myself and the practice of Zazen."

"Zazen?"

"It's the meditation you watched me doing on my doorstep. Buddhist monks brought the art to Japan hundreds of years ago."

"How does it work?"

"The goal is to empty the mind of all thought, to suspend all judgmental thinking, letting words, ideas and even images pass by without getting involved in them. To be truly in the present. It takes practice.

"The martial arts gave me confidence," Rudy added. "And meditation provided peace. A hell of a foundation if you think about it. I'm so damned glad I've been teaching both to my granddaughter. If any fourteen-year-old girl can take care of herself, it's Akemi."

I didn't know Rudy that well and wondered if he truly believed Akemi was that confident in herself or if he was just awash in his own hopeful rhetoric

Then I remembered his momentary loss of composure at The Garhole when he talked about his parents' plight during the war. Despite his confidence in meditation, it didn't appear he had total control of his serenity. Still, since Rudy had opened up, I decided to push to learn more about him.

"So how did you come to join the army?" I asked.

"I was an American and my country was attacked. I dropped out of school and joined up, along with most of my buddies. After training in Mississippi, the army sent us to Italy as an all Japanese-American battalion. Guess they didn't trust us for Admiral Nimitz' island-hopping campaign. Although some of the boys did serve as interpreters in the Pacific."

"Bully said you received the Distinguished Service Cross. They don't just hand those out to anyone."

"I lost a lot of good friends in Italy."

It was obvious Rudy dodged the intent of my statement. He had clammed up not wanting to get into details and I didn't press. We were on the far eastern part of the island approaching the barricade where the road dead-ended at the edge of the ship channel. Out in the channel a tanker, riding high and empty, steamed toward Houston to pick up a load of oil.

It was late and we had passed no cars. At the road's end we turned right onto a narrow asphalt lane. In front of us, jetties made from huge blocks of granite stretched out into the gulf, protecting the ship channel. The road veered right before we reached the jetties and cut across the low part of the island, ending at a county park. The gate-arm to the park was down, closing the entrance. I managed to skirt around the barrier and drive across the sand to the beach. The low tide left a wide ribbon of wet, packed sand.

We rode close to the water, listening to broken seashells and washed-up debris smack the underside of the tire wells. I knew my old pickup was in for more rust from the salt, but that was safer than sinking to the running boards in the dry, powdery sand higher on the beach. The smell of sea life cast ashore by the tide drifted in through the open windows.

After a few blocks, we came up on an old Chevy Suburban parked at the water's edge. I flashed the high beams, but the lights reflected off dark tinted windows so we couldn't see inside. I thought it was a late-night fisherman trying to snare a shark or a bull red, but there were no fishing poles in holders stuck in the sand. That left either an illicit rendezvous between married folks or teenagers necking.

Before I could say anything, Rudy jumped out of the truck and raced toward the Suburban's driver's side. He yanked open the door, pulled a surprised teenager out and, in a flash, had the terrified boy flat on the sand. A girl's screams roared from the Suburban.

Holly crap, what has he done? I barreled into Rudy with a side body block, knocked him off the boy and tumbled past them onto the beach.

I yelled, "Stop, goddammit, Rudy! Stop! What the hell are you doing?"

The girl's screams from the Suburban caught Rudy's attention. He shifted to the girl and realized it wasn't Akemi. He stopped in mid-stride, pressed his hands to his head and moaned softly.

"Oh, my God," he said.

The boy stood and ran back to the Suburban. He pushed the girl to the other side, climbed in and cranked the engine.

"Wait!" I yelled.

The boy narrowed his eyes toward Rudy. "Oh, Jesus," he cried out. "Is that you, Mr. Aoki?"

Rudy's eyes went blank as though staring into an empty space.

The boy said, "Mr. Aoki, it's me, Kevin. I'm in your jujitsu class at school. We heard about Akemi and Maria. We are praying for them."

Rudy regained his self-control and took a step toward the Suburban. "Kevin, I am so sorry. Please forgive me. I thought it might be…."

Kevin put the Suburban into reverse and backed up, the girl still crying, her head on his shoulder.

"Don't worry, Mr. Aoki. We'll find her." He turned and sand spit from his tires as he roared down the beach toward town.

Witnessing Rudy's breakdown set me on edge. The pressure of finding Akemi must have affected him more than he could handle. Now I had two tasks to worry about: finding the girls and keeping Rudy's behavior from exploding into something he would regret.

I could only imagine his exasperation and sense of guilt. He had been drinking beer at The Garhole instead of insisting the girls wait at the school. And now he had attacked an innocent kid on the beach.

I took a deep breath and exhaled slowly, trying to calm my own emotions. I didn't like curve balls thrown at me. First, Sumner said she had to go back to the station to check on developments when she could have handled that with a simple radio call. And now Rudy losing it, acting out his frustrations on a kid. Thank God the kid knew him.

I wanted to keep going into the early hours, but my lower spine ached from too much riding around. I was bone-tired and needed sleep. Plus, I wanted to get Rudy off the streets before something worse happened. With little conversation between us, I dropped him off at his house and drove to The Garhole.

Since witnessing the burned and blown-apart bodies of innocent civilians during the Gulf War, I hadn't been particularly religious. How could a loving God allow that? Alone in my dark bedroom, I pushed my doubts aside and offered a short prayer that Akemi and Maria would make it through the night.

# Chapter Eleven

## Thursday Morning

---

Akemi heard coarse voices vibrating through the wall. She put her ear to the sheetrock. She understood a few words, mostly the profanity Maria had taught her. Maria had said if Akemi knew the vulgar words, she could tell what manners people were raised with. And that would be important in finding "the right boy."

Akemi needed Maria to listen. They couldn't afford to miss the conversation. The room was so dark she couldn't see her palm held in front of her face. She couldn't feel Maria next to her. She swallowed hard and rolled, her head bumped Maria's cheek.

She whispered, "It is me, Maria. If you are awake, don't say anything, just listen. I don't know what time it is or even if it's morning or night. The men who took us are arguing in the kitchen. Put your ear to the wall and tell me everything they say."

Akemi told her to remember their voices from when they were talking to each other before in the kitchen. Try to put a name to each face. The conversation on the other side of the wall became even more heated. Akemi whispered the name 'Hector' to Maria. She could tell by his voice he was the short one with the hair on his face. Then Maria identified Juan, the tall one with the ponytail who had helped them out of the van and given them water and beans.

Juan called out, "Damn it, man. You are loco. Taking two girls. Only needed one."

"They were together," Hector groused. "We had no choice."

"Don't know anything about them," Juan added.

"Don't have to. Caught them young, easy to coach."

"Woulda done better at the bus station or the mall," Juan continued. "There're easy to spot—the lone ones, abandoned. Neglected or abused, sitting around with dead eyes, maybe already on drugs."

"These were too easy to pass up," Hector argued. "At the mall, we had to risk being seen. But last night—"

Juan interrupted, "You just need to tell El Tigre the truth about Juanita."

"That we found her in a tub of bloody water with her wrists slashed? No way. My job was to watch all the girls and I screwed up," Hector said. "This way I can tell El Tigre that Juanita left her spot one night, disappeared. No one's seen her since. He will think she ran away or was killed by a customer."

"What if one of the other girls squeals and Tigre learns you lied to him?"

"They won't," Hector barked. "They know I'll beat them. They'll think they'll end up like Juanita," Hector snickered. "And they might."

"Why take a chance?" Juan countered. "Wouldn't it be better if you just left before Tigre comes back?"

"Hey man…what you think? I like it here, *mucho coño*. The new ones are special, cherries. I hope Tigre will let me train them. The Asian girl is okay, but I really like *la niña,* so innocent. I will have much fun with her. If anyone should leave it's you. Why are you here anyway?"

"I had to leave Honduras. Cartel forced my family to pay money weekly or they would burn our roadside cafe. *Papá* refused. They murdered him. I had no money. Someone who worked for El Tigre came through my village and said he would loan me money to pay the coyote if I would work for Tigre here. I would be dead in Choloma."

"How long you been here?"

"A year, I think. I coulda paid off the loan but he keeps adding more so I can't get away from here. If I leave, he will find me and kill me for sure."

"I think you're right," Hector said. "I'm nervous myself. Tigre will not be happy when he finds Juanita missing. She always made her quota."

"We have to get rid of her body before Tigre gets here tonight."

When the conversation ended, Maria translated. Akemi was glad Maria couldn't see the tears welling in her eyes and her heart beating out of her chest. She wanted to immediately meditate to calm her soul, but first she had to somehow reassure Maria. She couldn't see but she knew Maria was looking at her. She laid her cheek gently against her friend's and felt the trembling in Maria's body.

Maria whispered, "Hector said he wanted me. He would have fun with me. I can't do this, Akemi. We must get free."

Maria's statement lifted Akemi. Pride welled in her chest at her friend's newfound courage. She knew it would take both working together to escape.

Then she said, "Did you hear the frustration in Juan's voice? He's the one who gave us water and beans. We must try to talk to him. Maybe he will help us."

A loud voice speaking English blared from across the room. "Hey, shut the hell up over there. We just got in a couple hours ago. We need sleep."

"Is that you, Sarah?" Akemi asked.

"Yes."

"Are your hands tied behind your back?"

"No," Sarah answered. "Once they trust you, they untie you. Now leave me alone."

Akemi's zip tie cut into her skin. She'd had no luck trying to break the tie, but she kept trying. She twisted and pulled her wrists trying to break free. The harder she worked, the deeper the indentions in her wrists. Finally, the tie broke. She pumped her wrists trying to increase circulation, then brought her wrists to her nose to see if she could smell blood. So far so good.

When she thought all the girls were asleep, she stood and edged along the wall toward the kitchen door. Last night when Hector had opened the door and the light momentarily flashed across the room, she had seen the other mats at the end of the room by the window.

A tiny stream of light seeped underneath the kitchen door. Akemi realized no matter where she was in the room that light would keep her oriented back to Maria.

She worked her way to the kitchen door, then past the bathroom door to the other side of the room. At the door Juan had gone through to get the mats, the knob turned but nothing happened. Akemi realized this must be the room where Juan and Hector slept and where they'd found the girl named Juanita in the bathtub with her wrists slashed.

Somehow, she had to check the window in the far wall without disturbing the girls lying close by. The room was about twenty feet wide. Ten small steps out to the middle of the room and a turn toward the outer wall. Extended arms acted as a guide. Her foot hit something soft, a small, cloth roller bag with wheels, the handle sticking up. Two more bags between her and the window.

She flinched, wondering if the other girls were moving out. She hoped not. That would leave Maria and her there alone. No please, she thought. Not alone with that terrible Hector.

She moved around the bags, stopping when her hand hit the paper covering the window. Light snoring came from the left and the slight movement of a body to the right as if someone was turning over. Good, she thought. None of the girls were in front of the window.

She ran her hand across the heavy dark paper covering the glass and wondered if the outside was boarded up. She worked her hand to the edge of the window, tore a small piece of the paper and was able by the light of the moon to see heavy boards fixed to the outside. Her heart sank. Tears welled in her eyes as she crept back to her mat.

# Chapter Twelve

## Thursday Morning

---

After tossing and turning, not sure if I had slept at all, I gave up at daybreak. Sumner's words haunted me all night—the girls had been snatched. Taken. But by whom, a sicko child molester? She didn't think so, but as backup she had a team running the traps on all known pedophiles and sex perverts.

I threw on my usual Garhole ensemble of shorts and tee shirt, stumbled down the stairs and put coffee on to brew. Scattered rays of light cracked the eastern sky. I had seen hundreds of sunrises over the gulf since my return to the beach. During my darkest days of constant pain from the war, seeing that great orange ball break the horizon gave me hope. On many days it was only the sunrise and a generous supply of scotch that had kept me going.

Hopefully, Akemi and Maria had been found unharmed during the night and Sumner had been too busy to call. Was it possible the perpetrator had listened to the TV broadcasts, gotten scared and dropped the girls off somewhere? A comforting thought, but I knew better. Whatever the kidnapper's motive, his damaged mind wouldn't allow it.

Out front, I heard a vehicle blowing down the sand lane racing like a fire truck en route to a scene. I hurried to the front of the bar and opened the door. The pickup slid to a stop just shot of the bar's wall.

Bully pulled his old double-barreled twelve-gauge close

to the steering wheel. Then he flipped a switch and a crane in the back brought his wheelchair to the driver's side. He reached down, opened the chair and maneuvered into the seat using his powerful arms. He reached back for the shotgun and put it across his lap.

The stub of an unlit cigar hung from his lips and a black patch covered his bad eye. The oyster shells covering the parking area crunched beneath his weight as he motored toward the front door.

He snorted, "Damn it, Parker. When you gonna get rid of these forkin' shells? They rattle my teeth every forkin' time I roll over 'em."

I started to tell him he'd better get his brakes checked before he crashed through The Garhole wall, but I decided not to waste my breath. Instead, I ignored his whining and stepped aside as he rumbled past me into the bar.

The dust from Bully's truck still hovered over the lane when Harry drove down from the highway. He parked and got out, grimacing at the layer of dirt covering his newly washed Cadillac.

Then Neddie Lemmon arrived, smacking nicotine gum as usual, his tee shirt filled with the dregs of cigarette smoke. I don't know who Neddie thought he was fooling. Everyone knew he still smoked, a habit he'd started during the war when GIs received free Lucky Strikes in their ration kits. Neddie told me he'd tried to quit because everyone he knew from the war who hadn't stopped smoking was dead. Sounded like a good incentive to me.

But according to Neddie, the nicotine gum didn't do jack, except maybe help his breath for the ladies. He said he'd given up sex until Viagra came along. Now he picked up most of his girlfriends at his part-time job at the San Louis

Pass toll bridge. His provocative tee shirts said things like "Free Mammograms" and "Rehab is For Quitters." He told Bully the shirts either got him laid or pissed the women off. He said his success rate ran 50/50 which, of course, no one believed.

It appeared the Dead Peckers were gathering for a meeting. Their harried faces and bloodshot eyes told me they'd been out all night.

I unlatched the wall, raised it with the ropes and pulleys and hooked it to the ceiling rafters. A batch of fresh air off the gulf blew the stale reek of Bully's cigars, Neddie's cigarettes, and the smell of spilled beer out the back door of the bar. The high Gulf Coast humidity created condensation on the cement floor. Hopefully the breeze coming through the front opening would dry the floor before someone slipped and fell. Everyone got coffee and settled at a table.

Harry sipped his coffee, then put it down. "What a night," he said. "We split up the West End and each drove a section. Hit all the subdivisions and back roads looking for anything suspicious. Nothing."

"Damn it, we had to do something," Neddie added. He dropped his head into his arms on the table.

Bully removed his eye patch, rubbed his vacant eye socket and squinted at me through his one good eye.

"The socket still bothers me," he said. "I thought the glass eyeball was causing the problem, so I quit using it. Damned itching still drives me crazy."

He rubbed the socket again, put the patch back on and said, "What did you do, Parker?"

"Got some rest. It's going to be a long day."

A vision of these old guys toting shotguns and looking for trouble hit my mind. I had already decided not to share everything I knew or would learn during the hunt for the girls. No telling what the Peckers would do. I sure wasn't going to mention Rudy's confrontation with the high school kid.

I went behind the bar, scrambled some eggs and jalapeños and stuffed the concoction into tortillas. The guys refilled their coffee cups and quickly scarfed down the breakfast tacos.

Harry's cell phone rang. "Thanks for calling back, Ryan. Any news?"

Harry held the phone away from his ear as Chief Puryear's voice boomed across the table.

"Damn it, Harry. I don't have time to be checking in with you...but...no, nothing new." When the chief clicked off, Harry studied his phone as if it had bit him. He must have felt chastised by his old friend but was magnanimous enough to recognize the load Puryear was carrying.

"Never seen the chief that worried," he said.

I agreed with Harry about Puryear's distress, but I heard more helplessness in his voice than worry. If the Chief of the Galveston Police Department felt powerless, where did that leave us?

I took my coffee to the dock and watched a flock of pelicans feeding out on the water. One after another, a bird would fold its wings back like a jet fighter and turn into a dive. At the last minute, the bird brought its wings tight against its body and sleeked down to a minimum profile, hitting the water—bill first—at forty mph. Wham! One less bait fish. What a performance! I wanted to applaud.

Then my mind saw the analogy. Folding its wings was a normal plan of attack for the big birds but folding my wings would be a sign of surrender. And that sure as hell wasn't going to happen. It was time to redouble my efforts: Buck up and find the girls.

I went back inside and suggested that the guys get some rest. I would call if any news broke. After Harry and Neddie left and Bully motored up the ramp to his bedroom, I lowered the ropes to close the wall opening and tacked a "Closed for the Day" sign on the front door.

I stopped for gas at Red's, a convenience store on the road to town. A flyer taped to each pump showed a photo of the missing girls and a plea to call Galveston Police with any information. The local Crime Stoppers had posted a $50,000 reward. Hopefully a cash incentive would motivate someone to turn in the abductor. But the downside meant it would create a lot of false leads, taking the task force's time away from the search. Catch Twenty-Two.

Before I could pull out to the highway, my phone buzzed. Sumner's name popped up from my contact list. I only had three names in my phone—Kathy, Harry and Sumner—so the phone didn't labor much finding Sumner's name.

I answered saying, "Please tell me you have something."

"Good morning to you too. Although I guess it isn't. I have a meeting in an hour with Atticus Lott. Can you make it? He lives over the causeway in Bayou Vista."

"Who is he?"

"A retired Galveston Police lieutenant."

# Chapter Thirteen

## Thursday Morning

---

Before I could ask what a retired cop had to do with the search, Sumner added we were going back to Señora Santos' mobile home after the meeting in Bayou Vista. She quickly gave me the lieutenant's address and ended the call. I went back to Red's and picked up a treat for the pit bull next to the Santos' mobile home.

Thirty minutes later I crossed over the Galveston Causeway and took a left-hand exit toward Highway 6 and Bayou Vista, an older development with homes built on canals. Lott lived on Blue Heron, the last street in the subdivision. The street fronted a large marsh bordered by the freeway on one side and the railroad track into Galveston on the other.

Out in the marsh, a blue heron stood still as a Greek statue waiting for an unlucky baitfish to meander past his laser eyes. Wham! Faster than a speeding bullet, the heron's head and long neck struck the shallow water and came up with a mullet in its bill. Survival of the fittest.

Halfway down the street, I pulled in beside Sumner's black sedan. A beat-up pickup—worse than my rust bucket—sat on the driveway next to her car.

Lott's house was one of the older, smaller homes on the street. I knew that the higher the pilings under a house, the more recently the structure had been built. After every hurricane, the federal flood insurance program raised the height requirement for coverage. Judging from Lott's pilings, I figured the house was built in the 1970's. It needed paint and a new roof, but neither of those conditions seemed to bother the owner.

A man standing on the bulkhead across from the house worked a fish on a bent pole. Sumner hovered next to him with a net. Just as I got out of the truck, she swooped the net down into the water and pulled it back up with a flopping fish. "Wow, Atti. You got him!" she yelled.

Lott unhooked a good-sized redfish. He put the catch in a doughnut net, dropped the net into the marsh, and tied it to the bulkhead.

"Supper tonight," he said.

Lott appeared mid-fifties, stocky, five-nine or -ten, with dark wavy hair, black eyes and a several-day-old beard speckled with gray. He ambled toward me with a slight bend in his back as though it was painful to fully straighten.

"Atticus Lott," he said as he pushed his hand toward mine.

I said my name and noticed his firm grip.

Lott motioned Sumner and me to three folding chairs set up among the pilings that held up his house.

"I would invite you in," he said. "But my air's been out all summer. Doesn't bother me, I like the heat."

Lott winced as he eased down into one of the chairs. He picked up his beer can off the concrete. He didn't offer us one. After a swig, he focused on Sumner.

"So you want to know about the girls who went missing during my time, huh, Donna?"

"You were in charge of the Galveston task force at the time. You know a hell of a lot more than I do and Parker wasn't here then."

"You're working Juveniles," Lott said. "Does this have to do with the missing girls from last night?"

Sumner nodded. "I thought a refresher of those older cases might give us some insight into what we are up against now. There may even be a connection."

"Damn," Lott said. He grimaced as he put his hands on the chair's arms to push himself up. He stood, arched his back and then slumped back down in the chair. He narrowed his eyes and stared out at the marsh.

After a moment, he lowered his head and wiped his eyes with the bottom of his shirt. He took in a breath and blew out a slow stream of air.

"Sorry," he confided. "I just saw so much, the bodies…."

"Take your time," Sumner said, her voice soft.

Lott looked at me. "When did you go into the army, Parker?"

"1971. I didn't come back to Galveston until my discharge after the Gulf War in '91."

"Understood," Lott continued. "You were out of the country when the disappearances began. I'll give you the Cliff Notes' version. During the seventies and eighties, sixteen young girls went missing in Galveston and along the I-45 freeway south of Houston. In those days, before computers, there wasn't a lot of communication between the small-town police departments along the route. Without the staff or experience to handle the situations, they didn't know what to do.

"Runaways were common in those days. The country was awash with the anti-Vietnam movement, drugs and rebellious teenagers. Police departments had different protocols for how long to wait to see if the missing kids came home or were heard from before they started to investigate.

Some used twenty-four hours, others forty-eight. We didn't know it then, but it turned out those first forty-eight hours are critical."

I said to Sumner. "Sounds like the conversation we had in Galveston last night with Woolly Kroton."

"I know about him," Lott said, frowning. "I think he came over from one of those departments. From what I hear, he won't be around long. Seems to have the presence of a snarling dog."

Lott paused, sipped his beer. He chewed his bottom lip and narrowed his eyes again. I wondered if he was remembering a specific murder investigation. I could only imagine the gruesome scenes he'd been involved in. I looked away and waited patiently for him to continue.

He said, "Things really hit the fan when four bodies were discovered in shallow graves in an abandoned oil field off the freeway. The newspapers put it together with the missing girls and dubbed it the 'Killing Field Murders.'

"Several more bodies turned up, some in ditches, some buried, one in a marsh. Several of the missing girls were never found. People thought some kind of monster was roaming the streets. It was during this time that the serial killer Ted Bundy was on his murder spree. He confessed to killing thirty girls, but the FBI thought more."

"Did they consider him for any of these murders?" I asked.

"Oh, sure. He murdered girls in several states from Washington to Florida, but authorities could never put him in Texas. He was finally caught in 1978 and sentenced to death for the brutal murder of three college girls in their dorm. It took ten years after his trial, but Florida finally fried him in 1989.

"Back then, the FBI told us there may be as many as 600 serial killers in the U.S. maybe half of them active at any one time. No telling how many are out there now. The FBI behavioral unit said the men they'd compared had a few genetic similarities, something in their physiological makeup. Also, possible early childhood linkage between sex and violence."

"Holy Christ," I said.

"But," Lott continued, "I never bought into the serial killer scenario back then. It's possible a killer may have been responsible for more than one murder. But there were too many different MO's for one killer to have done them all. The causes of death varied: blunt trauma to the head, strangulation, shot at close range. Some bodies were found with their wrists and ankles tied, some not. And no two girls went missing the same way. One was waiting for a ride. Another was last seen walking to a Quick Stop.

"One girl's car was found abandoned on the side of the freeway. Two girls hitchhiked into Galveston and were never heard from again. One girl skipped school that day. One vanished walking to her grandparents' house. It was clear to me there was more than one monster out there."

"Did the police catch any of the perps?" I asked.

"We didn't have DNA in those days. Several suspects passed lie detector tests. Finally, good old-fashioned police work put several of the perps behind bars for life. Another one was killed trying to escape."

Lott paused. He turned his beer up and drained it. Then he crushed the can with his hands and dropped it at his feet. He looked past me with vacant eyes.

Sumner said, "Sorry to have to get into this Atti, but...."

Lott blinked. "No, it's okay, Donna. I want to. Anything I

can do to help."

She nodded.

"How quickly life can turn," Lott mused. "If one of those girls had not played hooky from work or taken another road or refused a ride from a stranger...."

Lott paused. His eyes said he was searching for an answer, but neither Sumner nor I could offer one. Who was I to judge how a parent raised a child? Or why some teenagers were so full of rebellion? My first thought, which I didn't say, was 'Just shoot the perp when they find him. Say he was reaching for a weapon.' I'd like to be on the jury for the accused cop if it got that far.

Lott continued, "The sad part was every one of the killers we caught blamed the victims: 'If they hadn't made themselves so accessible. What were they doing out alone at night? They shouldn't have smiled at me, got into my car. It was their fault, after all.'"

Lott rubbed his face with both hands. "Unbelievable," he said. "The twisted minds of psychopaths."

"But you were right," I added. "There was more than one killer out there."

"Sadly, yes," he said, chewing his lip again. "And then in the nineties, four more girls went missing. It's like this," he said, pointing across the marsh toward Galveston. "People pass through. No record of them ever being here. They stay on the beach or get a room for cash. Come and go. A small town that balloons during the summer and holidays. Thousands of visitors on the weekends. Then, workers migrate in for jobs in the oil patch or processing seafood, in chemical plants and cruise ships. Galveston's a beautiful city but with an extremely transient population.

"When you add that Galveston County has seventy miles

of beachfront and vast underused tracts of land on the mainland with bayous running through them, it makes for a lot of handy places to dispose of a body."

Lott grimaced again as he rose from his chair. He put his hands on his lower back and grunted.

It was time to go. Detective Sumner and I got up, but I had one more question for the retired lieutenant.

"Is it possible some psychopath has been laying low since his last kill and is now out of his spider hole and taking young girls again? Or maybe he left town and returned?"

Sumner broke in, "We have to consider the possibility. Or maybe a copycat, someone who recently got into the act. It's why I wanted you to meet Lieutenant Lott and hear what he knows."

"I can tell you this," Lott offered, staring off into the marsh again. "Evil exists in this world and it has visited Galveston. Maybe it's back, maybe it never left. If there is a monster out there, I'd like to get my hands around the bastard's neck myself."

I took Atticus Lott's hand again. His grip seemed stronger than the first time. We caught each other's eyes with solemn purpose. He said to me, "If there is anything I can do to help catch this scumbag, call me. I mean it."

# Chapter Fourteen

## Thursday Morning

---

Sumner called on my cell before we'd even left Bayou Vista.

"What do you think?" she asked.

"I think I'd like to find whoever has the girls and rip his eyes out."

"I get it," she said. "Except I have to play nice, go by the rules."

"Then be sure I go in first when we find this guy."

"Did you notice the way Atticus moved?" she asked. "Like he was in a lot of pain?"

"I couldn't help but see the hurt in his face."

"You remember he said one of the perps was killed trying to escape?"

I knew where she was going. "Lott shot him?"

"At the arrest, the officer assisting Atticus hadn't put the handcuffs on the suspect tight enough. He slipped a hand out and grabbed a gun off the officer's hip. Atti was walking in front toward the car. The perp killed the officer and shot Atti in the back."

"Damn."

"The bullet's still in his back, too close to the spinal column to risk surgery. He retired on full disability. Doesn't do much now but fish off his dock and drink beer."

"And the suspect?"

"Somehow Atti was able to get to his gun and shoot the

perp as he was coming toward him."

"Dead?"

"Eight times dead."

"Damn good," I said. "You called him Atti, seem pretty tight. Are you—"

"No," she said, abruptly ending the thought. She told me to follow her to Señora Santos' home and terminated the call.

The smell of salt air drifted through the window of my truck as I drove back over the causeway into Galveston. On the water below, a shrimper had stopped trawling and was pulling in his nets. A dozen seagulls hovered over the boat's stern, flapping and squawking, constantly repositioning themselves, impatient for the captain to empty the dregs from his catch. I caught the scent of seaweed mixed with the pungent smell of an old net that had a thousand tiny organisms captured in the tangle.

The last time I had left Galveston was more than a year ago for an appointment with Colonel Ben Kennon, my doctor at the VA in Houston. Kennon had been treating me for the mysterious condition the VA termed Gulf War Syndrome. Thousands of us came home from Kuwait struggling with symptoms the doctors couldn't explain. Blurred vision, nerve and joint pain, liver damage and even memory loss. Mine were sleepless nights and joint pain in the shoulders, arms and back. Doctors treated us with antibiotics and anxiety meds, but nothing worked for me except booze.

That was before I met Doc Kennon. After almost a year of visits, he finally straightened me out. Mostly with holistic stuff like exercise and a better diet. I still drink beer, of course, but he got me off the heavy stuff. I have a half-bottle of Famous Grouse sitting on the shelf under the bar. As long as that bottle is half full, I know I'm okay.

After my last meeting with Kennon, I joyfully said goodbye to Houston. Adios to traffic, noise, pollution and getting the bird shot at me for driving too slow. Not my kind of life.

As I cleared the causeway, my blood pressure eased a notch. Back to Island Time.

Sumner took the first exit over the causeway and turned under the overpass. Harborside Drive paralleled Galveston's industrial area and seaport. Off to the left, huge cranes transferred cargo from ships to the docks. Further ahead, towering high in the sky, steam poured from the stack of a massive cruise ship.

I followed as she turned right on the Fifty-First Street viaduct heading away from the dock area. She drove several blocks and turned left into the warehouse area I'd driven through last night during my visit with Maria's mother. This was my first time on these streets during daylight. On the left, we passed a small store where several grown men loitered outside, smoking and drinking beer. The stares I got made me think this was not the place to have one of my old tires blow out.

Down the block, a young woman, maybe still a teenager, wearing tight shorts and too much makeup, leaned against a post. She gave me an accommodating stare and a small wave as I drove by. Past her, a woman who looked sixty but was probably forty, with stringy gray hair, a winkled face and dirty tennis shoes, pushed a rusted grocery cart filled with old clothes and rags. She shuffled along with downcast eyes, never bothering to look up.

Two women not that far apart in age, trapped in a cycle of poverty and despair. I wondered if the gray-haired woman had once walked this same block with too much makeup.

Sumner missed the alley. She drove another block and stopped where the street dead-ended at a water-filled ditch. I stopped behind her. Past the ditch was a two-block area full of old cars, the largest junkyard I'd ever seen, at least a thousand steel carcasses crammed into the lot. I'd witnessed none of this in the dark last night.

On the far side of the junkyard lay several sets of parallel railroad tracks. The deserted tracks had once been the switching area for trains coming to and from the mainland. An abandoned caboose, probably fifty years old, sat at the end of the tracks.

Sumner looked back, saw me behind her and called my cell.

"Where the hell am I?" she spouted, frustration obvious in her voice.

"It's okay," I said. "You just missed the alley. Follow me."

I backed up a half-block, turned into the alley and parked in Santos' back yard.

I sat in my truck until Sumner parked behind me. What was I thinking? This trauma wasn't mine. I could be at The Garhole right now, cooking up today's lunch.

But then I pictured an evening out to dinner with Kathy and Julie, and the innocent eyes and bright smile of a lovely young teenager full of hope and future. And just as quickly, the image switched to the face of the grieving, hurting little girl I had witnessed last night. Then the photos of Akemi and Maria on the flyer flashed before me. I clenched my teeth, knowing I had to try.

When Sumner slammed the car door, the pit bull next door awoke from his slumber and raced to the end of its chain, barking and spitting saliva. I unwrapped the pork chop I'd gotten at Red's and tossed it at the canine's feet. The barking stopped as the dog smelled the chop and then hungrily devoured the tasty treat.

Sumner nodded at my benevolence to the animal, but it didn't change her frown. She stuck a finger at my chest.

"I took a chance today, bringing you as my interpreter after the stunt you pulled last night. Showing up at her door like that, you could have been a kidnapper demanding money for all she knew."

"Really," I said. "One look at this neighborhood, any kidnapper would know better than to try and extort money from these folks."

"Don't kid yourself," she said. "Mexico, and in fact all of Central America, is saturated with gangs kidnapping people and demanding ransom. The people find ways to pay. Sadly, it's becoming the national heritage for some of those countries."

As we approached the steps, Señora Santos opened the door and stepped out to the porch. She wore the same brightly flowered housedress as last night, but with her hair fixed in two long columns of braids that reached to her waist.

Julie had told me Maria used to wear her hair like that. I wondered if the Señora was trying for a psychic connection with her missing daughter. Some type of ancient mental telepathy practiced by her Indian tribe in Mexico. I hoped it was and that it would work. We needed all the help we could get.

"I saw you through the window," she said in Spanish. "Have you found my Maria?"

I answered in her language, "We are trying very hard, Señora. Detective Sumner would like to ask you some questions."

Santos put a hand on the door frame and steadied herself.

She removed a red cloth from her pocket and wiped her eyes. "You must help me," she said, her voice barely audible. "You must find my Maria."

We followed her inside. At the Señora's shrine, a photo of Maria leaned against the wall below the painting of Our Lady of Guadalupe. The candles on the table beneath the painting were burning close to their ends. I could only imagine the praying that had gone on there last night.

Sumner began the conversation in English and I translated into Spanish.

"Señora Santos, thank you for seeing us again this morning," she said. "We want you to know we are doing everything possible to find Maria and Akemi."

"*Muchas gracias,*" she said.

"I see your cousin's car is gone. Is Patricia working today?"

"Yes, we were up all night praying to our patron saint. Patricia wanted to stay with me today, but she can't afford not to work."

"And what type of work do you do, Señora?"

"The same as Patricia, cleaning houses. She got me a job in the neighborhood where she works. I usually ride with her."

"Señora, if you are here illegally, do not worry. We are only interested in finding Maria."

She nodded.

"Are you from Mexico?"

"Yes, Tlacotepec, a small village in the mountains near Veracruz. My father and his brother, Patricia's father, owned a coffee farm. The farm had been their father's and his father's before him. A long time in the family. My husband, José, worked the farm with my *padre* and *tío*."

When the Señora paused, Sumner asked, "Did your father and uncle do well with the coffee farm, make much money?"

After her interview last night with the Señora, Sumner had decided kidnapping for money was not a viable motive. But the fact that her father had owned a coffee plantation could change that perspective.

"They did good," Señora Santos said, "until the drug cartel came. They forced my *padre* to sell the coffee to them at low prices. José resisted. Maria and I begged him to go along but he would not. The cartel murdered my José. It was horrible. They…they cut off his…head and put it on a post. Thank God Maria never saw it."

Santos crossed herself and broke into tears. She pressed the cloth to her eyes. Sumner got her a glass of water from the kitchen. We waited. After a moment, the Señora began again.

"José was a good man. Maria still cries at night for her *papà*. We could not keep the farm going at the lower prices. The cartel forced us to sell to them. They burned the coffee plants and planted the poppy flower.

"There was no other work where we lived. Even the dishwasher jobs were taken over by immigrants from Guatemala and Salvador. It was all bad. My *padre* and *tío* had no choice but to work for the cartel. They were paid very little. We needed money to live so I cleaned the drug *jefe's* house.

She paused, wiped her eyes again and continued, "We had to leave. My *padre* knew a coyote he trusted. Enrique would take us to *el norte*. We were all planning to go, but $3,000 American money for each of us was too much. Enrique told us the price was high because it was getting harder to cross. More fences, more border patrol trucks, more electronic sensors and more thieves preying on the desperate.

"Our *padres* told Patricia and me to go with Enrique, make some money and send it home by Western Union. Anything would help, they said. To get us out, they saved every *peso* they could. Patricia came last year. Then Maria and I followed several months later."

When Santos paused again to wipe her eyes, Sumner said, "Señora Santos, this is important. Do you still owe your coyote money for the trip?"

"No, no. I see what you think," she exclaimed. "Maybe Enrique had some men kidnap my Maria for payment? No, no, we paid everything up front or he would not do it."

"Where did your father get $6,000 for two of you?"

"He saved for a long time. And then he borrowed some too."

"Who would loan money to a poor farmer?"

"There are people who do it. They charge much extra money. *Padre* will be paying the loan back for a long time. I send him what I can. He said he borrowed the money because it was his duty to keep Maria and me safe. Maria is his only grandchild."

"How did you get here?"

"We rode on top of a train with many people trying to leave. We spent one night at the border before crossing. Enrique told us this night would be the most dangerous part of the trip because local gangs often rob the travelers. He gave us food and water, put us in a small room and told us not to go out. The next day, he took us in a van for several hours to where the river was shallow. We crossed on foot and traveled only at night.

"Our home in Mexico was in the mountains. We were not

used to the heat in the desert. Enrique said it could kill us. He said people had been dying out there for hundreds of years. He said we would, too, if we didn't pay attention.

"Night creatures came out after dark—scorpions, snakes. It was frightful. We had to follow him closely to stay on the right path. One morning two wild dogs came to our camp. They were mean, snarling with big teeth. Enrique scared them away with a large stick.

"We also found a body along the way. The dead man's mouth was open, formed in an odd way, like it was his last gasp of breath. He was naked and burned red by the sun. It…it was horrible."

The Señora paused and averted her eyes as if trying to discard the memories. We waited for her to continue.

"We rested during the day, but we did not sleep. We heard many stories of thieves out in the desert with guns and knives, robbing people, even…*la violación*."

The Señora went quiet again. She closed her eyes and tears streamed down her cheeks. I wondered if the rape had happened to her. After a moment, she wiped her cheeks and continued.

"But it was good we had Enrique. He said some coyotes deserted the migrants in the middle of the desert. Sometimes with no water. Only God knows what happened to them.

"When men passed us, Enrique knew when we were safe or not. He said many of the men were going to the chicken farms to work. Some have worked at the farms for years. They earn much money. They marry Mexican girls. The children are born in Texas and are U.S. citizens.

"We were in the desert three nights. When we traveled, the last one in our group walked backward with a branch of mesquite to brush the trail clean to keep thieves and the

American *policía* away from us."

"What about water?" Sumner asked.

"Enrique gave us two large bottles each to carry in our backpacks. He said it was enough if we were careful. We had nothing to eat but stale tortillas and a few scraps of meat. When that ran out, we were very hungry. We heard stories of people eating the cactus, but we did not know which ones were safe.

"Our lips cracked and our hair stiffened from the sweat. Thank God, Enrique knew the desert signs. A flight of doves flew over us and Enrique said they were going to water. We followed their path to a windmill and concrete tank. The water was cooled by the morning air. We refilled our water jugs and washed our faces and hands. It felt good. We left quickly, still covering our tracks. Enrique said some of the ranchers hired men to patrol their land. He said if they found us there, they might kill us.

"On the morning of the fourth day, we reached a sand road. Enrique called someone and two hours later a truck came. Enrique and the driver shook hands and laughed. Enrique gave him money. Six hours later we were in Houston."

Señora Santos raised her finger and thumb to her forehead and began the sign of the cross again. She prayed, "In the name of the Father, and of the Son, and of the Holy Spirit. Amen." She kissed her thumb at the finish and then rose and went to her shrine where she sat and repeated the gesture. We waited for her to finish.

When she returned to her chair, Sumner asked, "Señora Santos, is it possible that the man your father borrowed money from may have taken Maria to force you to pay the loan?"

The Señora's eyes tightened. Her forehead winkled, as if trying to understand the question.

"No, no, not possible," she said waving a hand in front of her for emphasis. "The man did not know me or Maria. He does not know where we are."

"Your coyote, Enrique, knows."

"No, he doesn't. The man who took us to Houston dropped us off at a small store in a Hispanic *barrio*. I paid to use the phone and called Patricia. She came from Galveston and picked us up. The man my father owes money to has no idea where we live. Neither does Enrique. What you say about this man is not right. And my father would not allow it to happen. He will find a way to pay the man."

The room went silent. We stood and thanked Señora Santos for the information.

But then she said, "Wait, please. I want to show you something."

She went to another room and returned holding a red dress. She held it up in front of us. The dress was puffy at the bottom with bright sequins sewed into it.

Sumner said, "What a beautiful dress. Are you going to a special dance?"

When I translated the words, Señora Santos cocked her head as though she didn't understand.

Then she said, "No, this is for Maria. Patricia and I have been working on it for weeks. I wanted her to wear white like I did, but she demanded red."

"When is her birthday?" I asked, a lump in my throat.

"She will be fifteen on Saturday."

Sumner said to me in English, "Is that what I think it is?"

"Afraid so," I said. "Maria's *quinceañera* dress. Saturday, Maria will officially pass from girl to womanhood. In

Mexican culture, it used to mean the girl was eligible for marriage. These days it's all about the party."

Señora Santos took the dress back into the other room and returned holding a white cardboard box. She reached into the box and removed a silver tiara, recently cleaned and polished. She held it up for us to see.

"My *padre* gave me this for my *quinceañera,*" she said. "He had it made in Taxco, the silver city. I saved it all these years for Maria. I will be so proud when she wears it."

The Señora replaced the tiara in the box and retreated to her bedroom. The sound of her weeping filled the trailer. We left quietly.

Outside by the vehicles, I turned to Sumner, "What do you think?"

"I think I'm pretty tough," she answered. "But I almost lost it in there."

I nodded, noticing her teary eyes, knowing mine must look the same.

"I'm getting desperate for a lead, even a clue, a direction." She said, shaking off the sadness. "I need to find the reason, the motive for taking those girls."

"It doesn't appear it revolves around Señora Santos or her family," I said. "We need to find another track to follow."

# Chapter Fifteen

## Thursday Morning

---

After leaving Señora Santos' mobile home, I crossed over Broadway and looped around to Kathy's house. As I parked in front, she came around the side of the building with a garden shovel in one hand and a tray of pansies in the other. Loose-fitting jeans and a long-sleeved shirt hid her still-slim figure at age forty-five. She wore a wide-brimmed straw hat to keep off the sun, but her cheeks were bright red from working the flower bed.

"I gave up on you," she said, obviously upset.

Not waiting for our usual hug, she bent to plant the last of the fall flowers, then patted around the plant with her shovel.

"Sorry, Kathy. I should have called that I was running late. Sumner had me hopping with interviews."

She stood and faced me. "It's okay, Parker. I know how important finding Akemi and Maria is. It's just that I have the afternoon shift today and have to leave at 2:30."

I felt the disappointment in her voice and saw more in her eyes. I gave her a big hug. Not feeling a return squeeze, I couldn't tell if her reticence was real or imagined but, either way, the warmth from her body felt good.

I said, "Kathy, I don't know which outfit I like best, the straw hat and jeans or your flowered nurse's uniform. Both are damned sexy on you."

I had my arms around her as I spoke. I gently turned us

both toward her front door. "It's not even noon," I said. "We have plenty of time."

Her eyes crinkled, body relaxed and the corners of her mouth turned up.

"I guess I'll have to shower twice," she said, a wry smile on her face.

I gave her a sideways hug and said, "Mind if I join you?"

An hour later, we lay in bed totally spent but still wrapped around each other like the rapture was near and this was going to be our last moment together. No doubt we had both needed the release that intimacy brought. She was tied in knots over her daughter's close brush with being kidnapped, and I couldn't get my mind away from Akemi and Maria.

Kathy rolled on her side to face me with her head propped on her arm. I scooted up with my back on the headboard.

Kathy mused, "Life is so damned fragile, Parker. There are no simple decisions. We don't realize it, but everything we do is fraught with risk."

I ran my hand through her hair and caressed her cheek. "What do you mean?"

"If I hadn't been on the night shift last night, Julie would have gone with Akemi and Maria and—"

I stopped her in mid-sentence. "Thinking like that will drive you crazy, Kathy. You're right, everything we do has risk. We must accept that and do the best we can. Life is short enough without adding more worry than we need to."

She moved her head to my mid-section and looked up. Our eyes met. She grasped my hand and squeezed.

"I'm sorry I acted like a twit earlier. I'm just so uptight about all this."

I leaned down and kissed her forehead. I glanced at the clock and was thinking about initiating another round of frenzied ecstasy when my cell phone buzzed. Normally I would have ignored a call in a situation like this, but this was not normal times. I gently moved Kathy's head and reached to the nightstand for my phone.

I pressed "send" and before I could say anything a frantic voice boomed through the receiver loud enough for Kathy to hear.

"Parker, it's Harry. I'm at Rudy and Maggie's house. Where are you?"

"Kathy's"

"Maggie's beside herself with worry. Can you come here?"

I glanced at Kathy sitting beside me and nodding yes.

# Chapter Sixteen

## Thursday Afternoon

---

Five minutes later I jammed my truck into park in front of Rudy's house and hurried to the front steps. Harry opened the door. My pulse quickened when I spotted the worry lines on his face.

"What's wrong, Harry?"

He motioned me in without answering.

Maggie sat on the couch with her head in her hands. She looked at me with reddened and puffy eyes. "Rudy's been gone all morning," she said. "I have no idea where he is."

I sat in a chair close to Maggie and leaned forward. "He's probably out driving around like he did last night, searching for Akemi. Sitting at home would make him feel helpless."

"Parker, you don't understand," she said.

Her bottom lip quivered as she spoke. She bit her lip to make it quit. I noticed the redness in her cheeks and hoped her blood pressure was under control. We didn't need a heart attack.

She took a breath and exhaled slowly as if trying to compose herself. Finally, in a voice so low I had to lean in to understand, she said, "He took the rifle."

Oh God, I thought but didn't say. What the hell is Rudy doing? I leaned back in the chair and blew out a quiet breath.

Harry said, "What do you think, Parker?

"The question is...what is Rudy thinking? He has no

ammunition."

"No," Maggie said, her voice stronger now. "He searched the internet and found a supply here in Galveston."

"Do you know the name of the dealer?" Harry asked.

"No, I.... Wait, I'll check his computer." She got up and went into another room. After a couple of minutes, she came back with a piece of paper. "A place called Bubba's Ammo. I know this street," she added. "No commercial buildings on that block. He must be working out of his house."

"Against the law," Harry added. "Licensed gun dealers are required to have a storefront presence."

I pulled my phone out and called the number she gave me. A husky male voice answered, "This is Bubba."

"Hi, Bubba," I said, using my friendly Parker voice. "I've got an old rifle and I'm looking for ammunition. Think you might have some?"

"No sweat, man. You need it, I got it. Give me the info, I'll have it ready for you."

"Thanks, I'll just come by."

I terminated the call quickly not wanting Bubba to ask any more questions about the rifle. If Harry was right about Bubba breaking the law by not having a storefront, there was a good chance he was doing even more on the shady side. And if I told him the gun's caliber, he might remember Rudy's purchase and shut me down thinking I was ATF.

Bubba's house sat in the middle of the block in a neighborhood where the front yards were more weeds and dirt than grass. Every house needed paint. The roof on Bubba's house had been patched with different-colored shingles.

At the front door, a huge man, well over six feet and breaking 300 pounds, stepped out to the porch. He appeared mid-thirties with a round puffy face, long greasy hair combed straight back and a wisp of hair on his chin. A large pistol sat in a holster belted to his hip.

He dropped his hand beside the holster while appraising me up and down. I was thinking one good kick to the gonads would bring him down to my size.

"Something I can do for you?" he asked, his dark eyes steady on mine.

"I just called about some ammo."

He stepped back and I followed him into the house. The room was set up like a retail store with floor-to-ceiling wooden shelves along the back wall, every shelf crammed full of cartridge boxes. A counter made from plywood and two-by-fours sitting on barrels ran in front of the shelves.

Bubba sat on a stool behind the counter and waited for me to say what I wanted. I searched the walls for a framed firearms license but found nothing. Bubba didn't look like the smartest bullet in a box of cartridges but, surely, he knew he had to have a federal firearms license to sell ammunition.

"I've got a Japanese WWII rifle that was handed down from some relatives. According to the internet it's a 7.7 mm caliber."

Bubba pulled a nine-millimeter automatic from his holster and sat it on the counter with his hand lightly touching it. "Back up," he ordered. "Get away from the counter."

I stepped back and raised my hands, palms out.

"Who do you think your bullshitting?" he demanded. "What's this all about?"

"What do you mean?"

"An Asian man bought two boxes of ammo that caliber this morning."

"Okay, okay," I said. "Easy man. Can I put my hands down?"

"Slowly," he said.

"Did you hear about the two missing girls last night?"

"Are you a cop?"

"If I was a cop, I'd be closing you down for operating illegally out of your house."

His demeanor changed. "Listen," he said. "I just got my license and I'm moving to a storefront this weekend. Can you keep your mouth shut that long?"

"If you'll put the damned gun down. You're making me nervous. I am a friend of the man who bought the ammo this morning. He is the grandfather to one of the missing girls in today's paper."

"Oh, Christ," Bubba said, blowing out a big breath.

"He was out all night looking for those girls and now he has a loaded weapon. I'm worried about—"

"Shoot the sons-of-bitches. That's what I'd do."

"We're afraid he might be out of control. I need to find him before he does something he'll regret. Did he say anything about where he was going? Anything at all?"

Bubba put the automatic back in its holster. "No, man. He didn't say nothing. He bought two boxes and left."

When I started for the door, Bubba said to my back, "He did say he wanted to make sure the old relic worked. I guess that meant he was going to test fire it somewhere."

I sat in my truck in front of Bubba's house trying to think through the problem. A search on my phone for rifle ranges indicated none on the island. The closest range was halfway up I-45 toward Houston. I doubted Rudy wanted to be that far away in case something broke, so I discounted the range. I thought about the large fields on the west end of the island and decided Rudy wouldn't risk getting arrested on someone's private property. So where the hell did he go?

My phone buzzed showing Sumner's name. "What's up, detective?"

"You'd better get out to San Luis Pass quick. Your friend, Rudy Aoki, is out there shooting at sand dunes. They heard the shots from the tollbooth at the bridge and called it in. Sergeant Pulley was patrolling West Beach. He's with Aoki now, but he hasn't been able to talk him out of the rifle."

Twenty minutes later, I drove by the turn-off to The Garhole and continued toward San Luis Pass at the end of the island. A toll bridge connected the island to the mainland. I exited the highway before the bridge entrance, then turned under the bridge and followed a rutted sand road to the water's edge at the pass.

San Luis Pass is a favorite fishing spot for weekend anglers. Game fish like trout and flounder move in and out between the Gulf and West Bay with the tide. But tricky currents also move through the narrow pass, posing danger for anyone wading into the water. Unknowing families bring their kids so they can play in the sand and water while the adults throw their lines into the pass. Last summer, the sheriff's office called me three times to help find missing persons swept away with the current. The last call was for a five-year-old boy who had waded into the water. Luckily, another fisherman spotted the boy struggling to stay afloat and pulled him in.

I turned and drove down the beach until I found Rudy's truck and a Galveston patrol unit sitting side-by-side about fifty yards in front of the dunes. Rudy sat on the ground holding the rifle across his body. I parked next to his truck and Sergeant Pulley approached.

"Empty cartridge box by his side and a full one nearby. Couldn't talk him out of the rifle. I hate to call for backup because of what's going on with his family, but…."

I cracked open the door and got out as Pulley stepped back.

"Give me a minute, officer," I said and turned toward Rudy.

In case he was in some kind of a trance, I yelled out, "Hey Rudy, it's me, Parker. I'm coming over."

Rudy didn't respond. I moved beside him, shaded my eyes and stared at the sand dunes, trying to find his target. I lowered my hands from my eyes and sat beside him.

"How does that thing shoot, Rudy? I mean, does it have much recoil?"

When he didn't answer, I shaded my eyes again with my hands and said, "I don't see a target, Rudy."

He didn't answer. I held my arm toward him, "Mind if I try, Rudy? I see a piece of driftwood by that first dune."

Rudy held the rifle close and gave me a hard stare. Then his shoulders slumped as if a ball of worry had lifted.

"I just came out to test the weapon," he said. "Make sure it's operating. I didn't know I was breaking the law. But I'm not giving the gun up, Parker."

I knew why he was out here practicing. It was all about his granddaughter. And that rifle was the only weapon he owned. And then I thought about Rudy with that kid last night on the beach. Thinking of his sudden rage sent my head spinning. What would have happened if he'd had the loaded rifle then?

"Rudy, I'm going to speak with Sergeant Pulley. See what I can do. I'll be right back."

I approached Pulley. "He doesn't want to give the rifle up. His granddaughter's missing. You probably understand a little of what he's feeling."

"That's what scares me," Pulley said. He sighed and

glanced at Rudy sitting in the sand.

"What exactly is the law here?" I asked.

"Unlawfully firing a weapon on public land. Usually a fine and confiscation of the weapon."

"Usually? So there's discretion involved?"

Pulley didn't answer, so I took it that Rudy's infraction might have some breathing room.

"Did you see him fire the rifle?" I asked.

"No."

"Is there a witness that said he fired the rifle?"

Pulley shook his head.

I looked toward the dunes. "There's no obvious target. I don't see how we could find a slug in that sand."

"There's the empty cartridge box beside him," Pulley said, "And I'm sure his rifle smells of cordite."

"Circumstantial though, don't you think?"

"Where are you going with this, McLeod?"

I went into a serious frown, as though I was trying to come up with an idea.

"How about this," I said. "Give him a ticket and let him keep the rifle. I'll take responsibility."

"Just how are you going to do that?" Pulley responded. I couldn't answer that,

Both Pulley and I were facing away from Rudy, and we hadn't heard him come up behind us.

Rudy said, "Officer, I apologize for shooting out here. It should have never happened. I heard what Parker said. How about it?"

"Damn it, Rudy," Pulley exclaimed. "You have me in a pickle. I know damned well why you were out here shooting that rifle. I have to stop you from doing something stupid."

Pulley blew out a breath. He turned and studied the water

behind us. The breeze had shifted from the north over the island to the southeast from the gulf. As the wind increased, rolling swells pushed toward the beach. Fifty yards out in the water squawking seagulls were taking turns diving into the water, picking off shrimp stirred up by a school of hungry trout.

I hoped Pulley turning away meant he was trying to figure a way out of the situation.

"Okay," I said. "How about this? Rudy gets a ticket and I keep the rifle. Rudy doesn't own the rifle. Neddie Lemmon's uncle brought it back from the war. You know how things tend to get lost in the property room. It'd be a damned shame if it turned up missing. It's a genuine antique."

Pulley didn't respond. I caught Rudy's eyes and nodded, signaling him to stay quiet. We waited patiently, hoping for the best.

It was then that Pulley walked to his patrol car. He reached in the front seat, pulled out a ticket pad and started writing.

After Pulley left, Rudy said to me, "Wait here for a moment."

He went out to the sand dunes, picked up the target sheet and brought it back. Most of the bullet holes were either in the bull's eye or close to it.

"I was lucky I had knocked the target off the piece of driftwood it was attached to."

"You got that right," I said. "Pulley would have confiscated the rifle for sure."

He wadded the paper and tossed it into the back of his truck.

"Just wanted to see if I could still do it," he said. Not a smile or grin on his face.

# Chapter Seventeen

## Thursday Afternoon

---

After Sergeant Pulley left us on the beach, Rudy followed me to The Garhole. The cover to the front wall was pulled up and latched to the inside ceiling, which meant Bully had finished his nap and opened for the day. Rudy parked beside me and we entered the front door. Lighted beer signs cast streaks of red and blue across the walls. The room smelled of red pepper and boiled shrimp.

Bully sat in his wheelchair on the dock, looking out over West Bay. With his back turned, he said, "About time you forkin' got here, Parker. Couple of fishermen showed up to clean their trout. Wasn't anything to feed them so I boiled up some of the live bait shrimp you caught off the dock last night."

"Good Lord, Bully," I said. "Did they see you take the shrimp out of the bait bucket?"

"Don't think so," he said. "They had a nice mess of fish. When they were at the cleaning table, I sneaked the bait bucket inside and emptied the shrimp into the sink."

I couldn't help but chuckle at the thought of customers eating boiled bait shrimp.

When Bully noticed Rudy behind me, he whirled the wheelchair around and said, "Rudy, good to see you! Any news about Akemi?"

Rudy shook his head. While they talked, I went back inside,

sliced an onion and fried the rings along with the filleted trout the fishermen had traded Bully for lunch. Not much was said during the meal, and Rudy and I avoided eye contact. After the last bite, he pushed back from the table and got up.

"Sorry for the rush," he said. "I gotta get back to town and check on things. Maybe raise hell with the cops. Something's got to give."

Bully stacked the empty plates and forks in his lap. As he rolled the wheelchair toward the sink, he jerked his head around to look at Rudy. "Wish I could do more," he said.

"I know you do, Bully," Rudy answered. He turned and went out the front door.

I approached him just as he grabbed the door handle of my truck and shouted, "Hold it, Rudy."

He looked back at me.

"I want the damned rifle."

I moved closer, hoping the confrontation wouldn't escalate. I'd had army training in self-defense and could handle myself in a bar fight. But I sure didn't want to tangle with a jujitsu expert who I'd witnessed putting Officer Kroton on the ground faster than the human eye could absorb it. I raised my palms to signal a peaceful advance and kept my voice carefully modulated.

"Can't do it, Rudy. I promised Sergeant Pulley. And I agree with him. You are in no condition to be carrying a loaded weapon around."

Rudy removed his hand from the door handle and squared his stance.

"Don't judge me, Parker. I got through the damned war without doing anything stupid and I can handle this."

Yes, and you must have done something awfully heroic to earn the DSC, I thought but didn't say. I'd read many citations of men awarded the Distinguished Service Cross and Medal of Honor. Many of their actions had happened when their buddies were trapped by enemy fire. And then impulsively, in a moment of spontaneous bravado, they had risked their lives to save others. A moment of total loss of control. I'd already witnessed an example of Rudy losing it and that's what bothered me.

When I didn't respond to Rudy's outcry, he seemed to calm himself. He ran his hand through his hair and his eyes fell to the ground.

Then he looked up and said, "For Christ's sake, Parker… it's Akemi we're talking about."

That got me. I'd never met Akemi and I don't have children, but the image of Kathy wrapped in a tight embrace with her daughter Julie flashed before me.

"Okay, listen, Rudy. I am working with Detective Sumner, and Harry Stein has a direct line into the police chief. Between Harry and me, we'll know every step they're taking when—or before—it happens."

Rudy cocked his head, "What are you saying?"

I hesitated. I knew better than to say what I was thinking, but it came out anyway.

"I'm saying maybe we can get to the kidnapper before the cops do."

That seemed to appease Rudy. He shook his head, balled his hand in a tight fist and shook it. Not at me, but more as a way to control himself.

When Rudy left, I got the rifle out of my truck and took it up to my room. I called Harry Stein, relayed my predicament with Rudy, and asked for his help through his relationship with Chief Puryear.

"Absolutely not," Harry responded. "Chief Puryear is a

friend. I won't pump him for information just so you two can beat the police to the scene. It would end our friendship when he discovered I'd betrayed his trust. And more importantly, if something went wrong—"

I cut in, "Don't say it, Harry."

We were both thinking the same thing. The girls' lives were at stake. What if Rudy and I jumped ahead of the authorities and blundered the rescue? I realized I should have thought this through before I made the commitment to Rudy.

Then the guilt hit me. I was putting Harry in an untenable situation, boxed between the chief and me, two of his best friends. What the hell was I doing, dragging Harry into a compromising situation like that?

"Sorry, Harry," I said. "Forget about what I just asked you. It wasn't the right thing to do."

"It sure wasn't. Not like you to put me in a squeeze."

"I know."

"So how are you going to handle it now with Rudy?"

"I have no idea. My scheme to keep the rifle was to promise him we'd stay ahead of the police and get to the abductor first. I'd calmed his angst by promising something I should have known wouldn't work."

Harry grew quiet, letting me stew in the mess of my own making. On top of my foul-up with Harry, I'd agreed to use information I'd gotten from Detective Sumner. I couldn't do that either. It was a high-wire act I didn't know how to balance.

After letting me suffer for an appropriate length of time, Harry said, "Are you coming to town?

"Yes."

"Good. Come by my house. I want to show you what I learned about Rudy. It might help you understand him better."

# Chapter Eighteen

## Thursday Afternoon

---

Driving down FM 3005 toward town and seeing the photos of the girls posted on the gas pumps at Red's Groceries prompted me to call Detective Sumner. She answered on the first buzz.

"I was just picking up the phone to call you," she said.

"Sure you were."

"Cool it, McCloud. I don't need attitude right now. Do you want to work with me or not?"

"Sorry, I've had a bad day."

"A bad day, huh? Well, join the friggin' club. I don't have time to hold your hand, much less be your therapist. Sergeant Pulley said you worked it out okay with Mr. Aoki. You do have the rifle, right?"

Not wanting to elaborate, I answered with a simple affirmative.

"Good. So why did you call me?"

"To see if you've had any leads from the flyers."

"Fifty calls the last I heard. I've been through this in other cases. Most of the calls are probably people squealing on neighbors they don't like. And to make it worse, we're so short of officers I had to pull a couple off the pedophile detail to work the contacts. It'll take hours just to sort through the calls."

"Sounds like you don't like the idea. Why did you do it?"

"Mixed emotions. Following up on the calls takes a lot of needed man-hours, but we might get lucky. And I'm worried about the ticking clock. The girls disappeared around six last night. It's four o'clock now. Twenty-two hours since they went missing and we don't have a single lead."

The ensued silence made me think of the worry frowns I'd seen on her face at Atticus Lott's house. No doubt she needed a break and wasn't getting one. I asked her if she thought the girls were still in Galveston.

After a moment, she said, "Depends on who took them and why. But wherever these girls are, they sure aren't out where anyone can see them. Somebody's got them holed up. You can bet on that."

"Well, I'm headed into town now. Call me if anything breaks."

"Okay," she replied. "I've got a call in for another detective I want you to meet. Stay close."

When the conversation ended, I had just merged onto Seawall Boulevard from FM-3005. At this point the elevation increases from barely above sea level on West Beach to seventeen feet behind the seawall. The seawall was built after the 1900 storm that surged across the island and killed an estimated 6,000 people. The seawall does a good job of protecting the houses near the gulf from the wind and fury of a hurricane. But any tidal surge sneaking in from the bay side floods the downtown business area and houses close to that part of the island.

Harry's home was near the middle of the island, a couple of blocks off Broadway. Even without the seawall, his house, built on pillars eight feet high, somehow survived the 1900 storm.

My friendship with Harry stretched back forty years so I

didn't bother to knock. I stuck my head in the front door and shouted down the long hallway.

"Harry, it's me."

The hallway emptied into a fully updated open kitchen area where Harry spent most of his time. A commercial-type gas stove with two large ovens hugged the side wall while a huge granite island in front provided the serving area. In front of the island sat a pine table large enough to seat eight guests comfortably. As president of the Galveston Historical Society, Harry often held board meetings at the table. The members could always gather at the Society's offices, but no one wanted to pass up Harry's lavish cooking sprees prepared especially for the meetings.

Harry stuck his head around the corner of the kitchen and yelled back, "Come on in. I just got some cherry scones out of the oven. Best when they are hot. Want some milk to go with?"

"Milk?"

I reached the kitchen and returned Harry's grin as he handed me a Shiner Bock. The homely aroma of fresh-baked pastries wafted through the kitchen.

On Harry's apron was the imprint of the tall ship *Elissa,* docked at the Pier 21 Wharf. The ship is a three-masted barque originally launched in 1877. The historical society had found the ship rusting in a Greek shipyard. They brought it to Galveston and volunteers spent the next several years repairing and refurbishing the ship as a tourist attraction.

"Have a seat at the counter," he said. He pushed tongs into the oven and came out with a hot scone which he slid across on a plate.

I took a larger than normal bite out of the scone and scored an entire dried cherry in the process. "Great stuff, Harry. Delicious, as usual."

"One of my specialties," he said. "Sorry I don't have a lot of time, Parker. I baked these scones for the *Elissa* committee members, and I still have to shower and dress before they get here. We have a lot of work to get the ship ready for the tall-ship parade. It's a big deal. Ships coming in from all over the world."

Underneath the apron was a tee shirt and shorts, something I would never have believed Harry would wear until I captured the sight with my own eyes.

"How many committees are you on?" I asked.

"Oh, several," he answered. "But this one is my favorite. One of the members is a cute widow I've been making eyes at."

"So you're working a new girlfriend, huh? What about the two casserole ladies that are hitting on you?"

"Give me a break, Parker."

"What does that mean?"

"Turns out Dorothy, the woman down the street, was playing me and shuffling dishes to two of us, a widower on the other side of her and me. Seems that he succumbed to her charms, thank the Lord. They're now an item about town. The sad thing is, she was the best cook. Her gruyere potato dish was excellent."

"And the lady across the street?"

"She's a very nice person and we partner well in duplicate bridge tournaments. But...she doesn't know when to quit. This morning she traipsed over here with a fresh-baked tuna-and-noodle casserole. The smell of canned mushroom soup almost made me gag. She brings something like it every week, obviously thinks I eat the crap."

"Harry, such language," I said with a teasing grin.

He frowned and turned back to the oven.

"So what do you do with the casseroles?"

He placed the steaming scones on a large serving plate and set it on the island. It was all I could do to keep from scarfing another one.

"I usually drop her God-awful casseroles by the Catholic Church's soup kitchen over on Winnie Street. Missy, the woman who runs the kitchen is a sweetheart. I am afraid to ask what she does with them."

I finished the goodie, licked my fingers and took a slug of the Shiner Bock.

"So what do you have for me?" I asked.

Harry reached down the counter and handed me a manilla folder. Inside was the citation for Rudy's DSC.

"How did you get this, Harry?"

"The National Personnel Records Center in St. Louis keeps the records for U.S. service men. You might remember I got a copy of Bully's Silver Star citation he received for saving his lieutenant in that mine field. All I needed was Rudy's DOB and service number and Maggie was kind enough to give them to me."

"Guess he doesn't know she is in cahoots with you, huh?"

"Stop that, Parker. We've renewed our friendship and that's it. You keep that up and there will be no more Shiner Bock in my refrigerator."

Harry handed me reading glasses as I pulled the citation from the folder.

DSC Citation:

*The President of the United States of America, authorized by Act of Congress, July 7, 1918, takes pride in presenting the Distinguished Service Cross to Second Lieutenant Rudolph Kenshi Aoki, (ASN: 30105501), United States Army, for extraordinary heroism in connection with military operations against an armed enemy while serving with Company G, 3d Battalion, 442nd Regimental Combat Team, attached to the 34$^{th}$ Infantry Division, on 28 August 1944 east of Pisa and west of Florence, Italy, near the Arno River.*

*While encountering heavy small-arms, artillery and mortar fire, all of Company G officers had become casualties except Lieutenant Akemi. Akemi's platoon was advancing against dominating enemy positions when it was suddenly pinned down by the crossfire of two machine guns. During the German bombardment and crossfire, Lieutenant Akemi grabbed a BAR and silenced a machine gun. Continuing to advance, he killed a sniper before his own gun was torn from his hands by a burst of fire. The enemy tried to close in on him, but he drove them back with hand grenades, killing several. When his platoon was ordered to withdraw, he provided first aid to several team members and volunteered to cover the withdrawal movement, making himself the target of enemy fire. He engaged another machine gun and killed three enemy soldiers. During the withdrawal, Lieutenant Akemi was severely wounded by fragments from mortar fire. His personal bravery and zealous devotion to duty exemplify the highest traditions of the military forces of the United States.*

I finished reading the award and blew out a long stream of air, thinking about what that moment must have felt like: his friends dropping all around him, bleeding, torn to pieces from artillery and mortar fire.

"Wow," I said. Meeting Harry's eyes, I knew we were thinking the same thing. Rudy had been to hell and back. He was a genuine hero, and at that moment I knew any reticence I may have felt about going to the wall for Rudy had vanished. I slipped the citation back into the folder.

# Chapter Nineteen

## Thursday Afternoon

---

I sat in my truck in front of Harry's house trying to think through my next move. Shades of gray creeping through the large oak trees that lined the street meant night was falling. I didn't know Rudy well, but his reactions to Akemi's disappearance were beginning to scare the hell out of me. I looked up the number and called Colonel Kennon.

"Well, if it isn't Parker McLeod, one of my more successfully treated patients. I wish they all progressed like you. How's it going, major?"

"Doc, you got me almost free of pain and off the pills and hard liquor. Probably saved my life. I owe you big time, but today I need your help."

"Shoot."

"I have a WWII vet friend who went through hell in Italy. He was a hero and saved his men from a German machine gun but was severely wounded during the fight and almost died."

"WWII? He must be in his eighties."

"Correct."

For the next few minutes, I related the facts of Akemi's kidnapping, Rudy's behavior with Officer Kroton, his attack on the kid at the beach and finally his out-of-control actions with the rifle on West Beach.

"So you're worried about his loss of control? What he

might have done with the rifle if you hadn't gotten it from him?"

"Yes, colonel. His anxiety level is through the roof. Is it possible he has some form of delayed PTSD from the war?"

"Interesting that you asked, Parker. Most WWII veterans who experienced traumatic battle situations never discussed them. They purposely repressed the events, trying to get on with their lives. As a result, some developed lifetime symptoms. During the war, we called it Combat Stress Reaction or Combat Fatigue. The term Post Traumatic Stress Disorder wasn't developed until 1980.

"It's possible your friend's missing granddaughter may have triggered those WWII psychological wounds, especially if he never received therapy. Let's just hope there's not another trigger."

"Another trigger?"

"Another traumatic event, either before or after this one, that he hasn't dealt with. Two might send him...well, I'd rather not discuss it without seeing him."

He was quiet for a moment then offered, "Look, Parker, I would like to help. Your friend would make an interesting case study. Please see if you can get him in. If not, I suggest you keep a tight watch. He may be close to something even more untoward."

Kennon's last couple of statements almost sent me to Panicville. Another trigger? What the hell was he talking about?

No doubt Rudy was becoming as fanatical as Captain Ahab chasing the white whale. And I didn't like the way that tale ended. What to do?

Just then, a dark Lexus sedan parked behind my truck. A petite, attractive lady, maybe in her seventies, with short but stylish gray hair and a cashmere sweater that matched the color of her hair, hurried up Harry's front steps. As she reached the porch, the front door opened and Harry stepped out. He had nixed the apron for a mauve shirt, gray slacks and matching tennis shoes. With a beaming smile, he gave her a quick peck on the cheek and guided her inside. Style begets style.

If the other committee members looked as sharp as these two, it was time to crank up my old heap and vamoose before someone wondered why a man in jeans and tattered golf shirt was lurking at the clothes horses' curb. No need to embarrass my friend.

# Chapter Twenty

## Thursday Night

---

A faint, yellow light from the single overhead bulb in the kitchen sneaked into the room as the door opened. A tall, slim man stood at the entrance; his features hidden by shadows from the back lighting. From his stature, Akemi could tell it was Juan.

"Get up," he grumbled. "Time to eat."

Akemi heard shuffling across the room and watched Sarah's tall, thin body tread in front of her to the open door. She noticed Sarah's pale skin and straight blond hair parted in the middle and combed down past her shoulders. Younger than Akemi had thought, she was probably in her late teens or early twenties.

When Sarah glanced at her, Akemi was struck by her blue eyes that once might have been pretty but were now dull and lifeless. Akemi thought of Emma, a friend of hers at school, a tall blond with blue eyes like Sarah, but Emma's eyes sparkled with youth and hope and anticipation of life.

Akemi let out a slow breath. She understood the transformation, the downward spiral, and silently vowed that would not happen to her or Maria.

The two younger girls followed Sarah into the kitchen, their heads lowered as if in a trance, their footsteps short and steady like the gait was expected. They took their places at the table.

The short man with the beard, Hector, stood in front of the back door with a scowl on his face and his arms folded across his chest like Mr. Clean on the bottle of surface spray. He was blocking the door, Akemi thought. Showing his control, his power.

Akemi's heart pounded as Juan cut the tie that bound Maria's wrists. Now it was her turn. What would Juan do when he discovered the missing zip tie?

"Su...su...sorry," Akemi mumbled. "It br...broke." Her nervous stutter was part real and part fake, and she didn't know which was which.

Sarah and the two girls had filled their bowls and moved back to the table. Lucky for Akemi, Hector was distracted by Sarah allowing him an eyeful down the front of her low-cut dress.

With a muffled voice Akemi could barely hear, Juan said, "Yeah, well, they better not break again."

Akemi went to the stove with a bowl in hand. She recognized the aroma from the pot as the same she'd whiffed from Maria's thermos at school. *Menudo*, the spicy Mexican stew made from peppers, hominy and meat. Akemi had eaten it once before when Maria invited her for dinner. She had really liked the dish until Maria told her the small strips of meat were from the stomach lining of a cow. She had almost retched at the thought.

But tonight, Akemi was hungry and when she sat down to eat, she noticed Maria was halfway through her bowl.

Maria whispered, "This *menudo* is almost as good as my mother's."

That made Akemi think about Juan. The food he served had been good so far. But they only ate two meals a day and the first one wasn't until after noon. She wondered if keeping her and Maria perpetually hungry was part of the kidnappers' plan to control their victims. No matter. She and Maria had discussed the possibility earlier and decided to eat as much as they could when food was available. They needed to keep their strength up.

Maria hurriedly finished her bowl of *menudo* and got up to go to the stove for more, but Hector moved from the door, blocked her path and pointed to her seat.

When Akemi finishing eating, Juan strapped a new tie on her wrists. Was it her imagination or had Juan put it on less tight than last time?

Hector fastened Maria's zip tie and when she complained it was too tight and cutting off her circulation, he smiled. He put his hands on Maria's shoulders and massaged slowly, his long fingers slipping down toward her breasts. When Maria twisted away, Hector laughed.

Akemi glimpsed the humiliation in Maria's eyes and wanted to give Hector a kick in his privates like Jiichan had taught her.

Juan went through the girls' bedroom and into the far bedroom while Hector stood watch over all the girls in the kitchen. Juan came back with a pair of sneakers stuffed with white socks. He dropped the shoes at Akemi's feet.

Juan said, "They're Juanita's, probably too big," he said, "but they'll work."

Then while Juan stood watch, Hector went into his bedroom and returned carrying a body over his shoulder. It was wrapped in a sheet, two naked feet sticking out the end. Blood oozed through the sheet and left a red spot on his tee shirt. He carried the body out to the garage. Sarah traipsed behind him, her face void of expression. The two younger girls followed behind.

Juanita's body, Akemi thought, the girl who killed herself. It was like she figured. The body was in the room on the other side of the door she had tried to open while exploring her room.

"Okay," Juan said to Akemi and Maria. "Follow the other girls out to the van. I will be watching you closely."

In the van, Hector slipped the sacks back on Akemi and Maria's heads and told them to lean against the side wall. The garage door opened, the van backed out and the door closed again. Akemi felt the van making turns back to the highway.

"What are they doing?" Maria whispered to Akemi.

"Remember, they said they needed to get rid of Juanita's body? I think they are really afraid of El Tigre."

"But why did they bring us?"

"Because there are only two of them and no one left to watch us in the house."

"I am scared Hector is planning to do something to me," Maria whispered.

Akemi thought the same thing, but she was reluctant to confirm Maria's fears and didn't respond.

Akemi started counting the seconds and transposing them into minutes. The van turned left and sped up. A few minutes later, it turned again and rapidly gained speed as if they were on the freeway.

Ten minutes later, Akemi heard the clicking sound of the turn signal. They left the freeway, drove on the feeder for what seemed like a mile and then turned right. After several more turns, the van slowed and turned onto what she thought was a gravel parking lot and stopped. Akemi heard Sarah get up.

"This is where we work, girls," Sarah mouthed softly.

"What is it?" Akemi asked.

"The Acapulco Cantina. You'll be here with us soon." Sarah said, laughing. "Don't do anything foolish. Mind them. Hector already screwed up by letting Juanita kill herself. You try anything, he'll hurt you."

The side door opened and Sarah and the other two girls got out, leaving Akemi and Maria in the van. Akemi heard loud brassy music and a voice singing in Spanish. The door slammed shut and the van took off.

Akemi whispered to Maria, "Work your zip tie, try to break it. We may have a chance to get free and we have to be ready."

After dropping Sarah off, the van traveled another twenty minutes. Frustrated, Akemi lost track of the turns. Finally, the van turned onto a rough road and slowed to a crawl. She felt the tires bouncing in and out of holes and heard water splashing against the van's undercarriage.

Hector said, "The road dead ends at the water. Stop here before we get stuck. We'll carry her the rest of the way."

Akemi heard the front doors open. Then the side door opened and Juan said, "Turn around girls, show me your hands."

Akemi and Maria complied, thankful the ties were still intact. The compartment was dark enough that Juan couldn't see the deep lines Akemi had cut into her hands while trying to break the ties.

Then Hector said, "Stay put. We'll be watching you."

Akemi heard one of the men drag the body across the van floor to the side door and grunt as he lifted it. The other man slammed the side door shut.

"We are alone, Maria," Akemi said. "Work hard, try to break your tie. We only have a few minutes."

Akemi had been working the tie since they left the house. She couldn't break the tie but was able to loosen it. She pulled and twisted and heard Maria doing the same. Finally, Akemi was able to slip one hand free. She removed the sack from her head and then Maria's. Maria gasped loudly, taking in fresh air.

"Quick, let me see your hands," Akemi said. She pulled on Maria's ties but couldn't set her free.

"We can't wait," Akemi said. "I will climb into the front seat and open the passenger door. You follow behind me."

Akemi climbed over and unlocked the door. Maria stood and moved toward the door, but with her hands still bound, she fell between the two front seats and cried out, "Mother Mary, help me, Akemi! I can't get up. "

Akemi tugged and pulled. "Use your feet. Push, Maria." At last, Maria broke free from the space.

"I heard one of them say water is near, "Akemi whispered. "Maybe they are going to dump the body into a creek hoping it will float away. We don't have much time. When I open the door, I will help you down."

"I can't see anything in the darkness."

"Step down and stay with me. We'll run back up the road to the pavement. Maybe a car will come by. You must be quiet. Hurry now!"

Maria tried to run, but with her hands still tied, she tripped into a hole filled with muddy water that soaked her jeans. A rock scratched her face. Akemi helped her up and wiped the trickle of blood off her cheek with her hand. She held Maria's arm to balance her as they shuffled down the road.

Akemi stopped. "We're moving too slow," she said. "We'll never make the paved road." She pointed out to the darkness. "We have to get off this road, try to disappear in the field."

"But we don't know what's out there."

"Okay, stay here. I'll check it out."

"No please, don't leave me!"

Akemi pulled her off the road into a patch of weeds. She heard Hector scream.

"Juan, they are gone! Come quick."

At the sound of Hector's voice, Maria froze, unable to move. Akemi hugged her and felt frightful shivers coursing through her friend's body.

Akemi pulled Maria further off the road into the darkness hoping to find a place to hide. As they sloshed through mud and water, Akemi realized the splashing sounds were too loud, but they had to keep going. The weeds were getting taller and providing some semblance of cover. Through the darkness, Akemi spotted a stand of trees.

She whispered to Maria, "If we can make it to those trees ahead, we might have a chance. No lights behind us, so I don't think they have flashlights."

"I've been working the ties," Maria answered. "When we get there, I think you can get me free."

Akemi kept tugging on Maria, forcing her to move faster. They reached an area where some of the smaller trees had been cut by an animal of some kind.

Maria hit a cut-off stalk and started to stumble. She slammed her foot down, trying to maintain balance. A sharp stab penetrated her sneaker into the soft bottom of her foot. She screamed a horrifying, pain-filled yell that radiated out across the prairie, breaking the silence of the quiet night.

Akemi knew Juan and Hector must have heard Maria's fearful cry. But when no sound came from their direction, she hoped they were farther up the dirt road toward the pavement. And then Hector's loud voice carried across the prairie.

"This way, Juan. We have to catch them before they get to that stand of trees."

Akemi glanced at the trees, maybe thick enough to hide in if they could make it. Maria was crying, worrying about her bleeding foot, trying to hold back the tears and keep the noise down. But it was too late. The sound of sloshing feet storming though the weeds penetrated the night air.

"Go Akemi, go!" Maria whispered. "You can make it. Leave me…save yourself."

Akemi glanced at the trees again, maybe thirty feet away. She moved a foot in that direction. All she had to do was pick up the other foot and run. She could make it. She could be free.

Another glance at her friend. Maria moaned in pain.

Akemi shrieked, "No Maria, I can't leave you!" She stepped back and tried to pick her friend up to carry her, but she wasn't strong enough. She pulled Maria up, put her arm under her shoulder and said, "We will make it together."

They took one step and a hand hit Akemi's back. Both girls tumbled into the weeds.

"You little bitch," a voice said.

Hector grabbed Akemi's arm and yanked her upright, forcing her to release Maria. She only glimpsed Hector's open palm for a millisecond before the slap hit her. She fell on top of Maria. Hector yanked her up again. His arm went back for another slap when a hand grabbed his wrist.

"Enough!" Juan yelled. "We have them now. You know El Tigre doesn't like bruised faces. Scares the customers."

"I don't give a damn," Hector responded, his face

steaming and pouring sweat through his beard, his eyes red and full of fury. Hector tried for another swing, but Juan held him fast. Hector released Akemi and she fell back into the weeds and mud.

A heavy throbbing radiated from Akemi's lower jaw to the top of her head. Her face stung as if a thousand needles were stuck in her cheek. She touched the side of her face and felt her skin, warm and pulsating. She had never felt pain like this.

Hector pointed to Akemi. "Look at this bitch," he said. "She broke her cuffs."

Akemi was hurting too much to answer. "No," Maria yelled. "They just popped loose."

Juan noticed the blood oozing from the bottom of Maria's shoe. He picked her up and started back to the van. He looked back at Hector with a menacing stare and nodded toward Akemi.

"Bring her," he said.

Hector held tight to Akemi's arm and yanked her along. Strangely, the ache in her cheek strengthened her resolve. With a slash downward on Hector's knee, she could put him on the ground and sprint for the trees. But then she looked up at the helpless resignation on Maria's face. She gave up the struggle and let Hector pull her toward the road.

# Chapter Twenty-One

## Thursday Night

---

Detective Sumner had said to stay close as she was setting up a meeting with another police officer. I had no idea who he or she was, but at this point it didn't matter. Any new train of thought was welcome. As I pulled away from Harry's house, my cell phone buzzed with a call from Sumner. Good timing.

"Parker, it's Donna. Can you meet now at the station?"

"First names, huh? Does this mean we're going to be friends?"

"Stow it."

Five minutes later, I parked behind the police station on Twenty-Fifth Street and strode into the back entrance. Sumner met me at the door and we hustled up the stairs to the second floor. Inside a small office, a man about my height, thirties, with dark hair cut close, dark eyes and a well-trimmed, close-cut beard rose from a desk. He had a gold shield attached to his belt.

He offered Sumner a quick smile, including a discernable eye twinkle. Interesting. He shoved his arm toward mine. I took his firm grip.

With a grin he said, "The famous Parker McLeod. I've been wanting to meet you."

Taken aback, I said, "Famous? I don't think so."

"You know," he said. "Breaking up that terrorist threat

last year. Sorry, I didn't mean to be flippant."

I released his hand and backed up a step.

Sumner broke in, "Parker, meet Lieutenant Julius Lott. Julius is in charge of the Sex Trafficking Unit at Galveston PD."

My heart thumped a little at the words sex trafficking. Dark fears I had suppressed about Akemi and Maria surfaced. I pushed them away.

"Lott, huh? Brother to Atticus?"

"Yes," he said. "I understand you met with Atti this morning. We were supposed to fish this weekend, but with two young girls missing, that obviously won't happen."

Lott waved us to chairs in front of his desk. He looked at me. "I understand you are helping with the case. Donna asked me to talk to you about what we do in this department."

"Sex trafficking, huh…I hate to think about that. Akemi and Maria are so young."

"You'd be surprised how many are lured in at their ages."

"Maybe, but we don't think these girls were lured. What makes you think Akemi and Maria have been trafficked?"

Julius leaned forward. "Let's start with the basic definition of sex trafficking. He read from a card on his desk: *The use of force, coercion or fraud to get someone to sell or trade sex for something of value.*"

"Simple enough," I said.

"Except it's not," Lott replied. He sat back in his chair and rubbed a hand over his light beard.

"Imagine you are a young girl living in Honduras or Nicaragua or El Salvador, all countries overwhelmed with poverty and crime. There is no work. Not enough food to feed your family. No medicine for the sick. Maybe you've been beaten by a boyfriend or husband. You see this as your life for the next forty years.

"One day someone comes to your village and regales you with stories of America, the land of plenty and opportunity, where you can earn money and send it back to your family. You are hungry, your family is hungry. You have no education, no way out. It sounds good, better than your life now.

"But the man tells you it takes much money to get there. Not to worry, he will loan it to you. You can pay him back from the job you will get through his contacts. But you have no paperwork, no documents. He will take care of that as well.

"You find yourself on a long bus ride. Then you are sneaked across a river. You are taken to a *barrio* in a large city. You don't even know where you are, totally disoriented. You have no money. You are helpless.

"A new man greets you and takes you to a cantina that advertises *Chicas* in a flashing neon sign out front. You see scantily clothed girls at the bar flirting with men twice their age.

"He feeds you, takes you to a windowless wooden shack at the rear of the property. You notice a high wooden fence surrounding the shack. There are mattresses on the floor. He gives you a small, wheeled suitcase for your belongings."

"Why the suitcase?" I interrupted to ask.

"Because they will move you often. They don't want you to bond with one of the other girls or maybe a customer. They want to keep you isolated, helpless. He tells you this is where you will work to pay off your debt. You will be a prostitute. He beats you if you resist. You are terrified. He threatens your family back home, your mother, your little sister.

Maybe he gives you a pill to ease the pain where he has beaten you."

"A pill?"

"An opioid like Oxycontin or Percocet. The pill helps, but now you need another one and then...another. Now you stay for the pills."

"Are there places like that on Galveston Island?"

Lott nodded, continuing, "They pop up on a regular basis. Busted several this year. But there's more in the county. The area on the other side of the causeway is large and spread out and there aren't enough sheriff deputies.

"Houston, of course, is loaded with them. The city is so large with so many Hispanic *barrios,* it is impossible for the police to find and monitor all the sex bars.

"The Feds estimate at any given time there may be 15,000 sex slaves nationwide. That figure is probably low. Because of its size and location close to the Mexican border, Houston is a prime location. It's the center of an interstate highway between L.A. and Florida. Plus, it has a major airport. The Feds say twenty-five percent of the nation's total number of sex slaves end up in Texas. I've seen estimates that Houston harbors a 1,000 or more. Who knows?"

Lott's spiel seemed rote, routine. "I think you've given this talk before," I observed.

"Pretty much have it memorized," he said. "Churches, rotary clubs, anyone who will listen."

"What's the answer?"

"It's not easy. We need more officers working the problem, tighter border security, heavier sentences for the sex bosses. There's also a movement to penalize the Johns—make illicit sex a felony. That might help."

He paused, looked down at his desk and then focused

back on me. "Or maybe shoot the bastards running the girls. But you never heard me say that."

He rose from his desk, a signal the meeting was over.

I said to him, "You're kidding, right?"

He nodded toward the nine-millimeter automatic in a holster on the corner of his desk. "Am I?" he said.

On the way down in the elevator, Detective Sumner checked her watch. "I can consider myself off duty," she said. "Although we both know I'm not. How about a beer? There's a Mexican Café across the street."

We sat in a booth facing each other and ordered two Modelo Darks and a plate of nachos from a heavy-set Latino woman with a gold tooth, an apron decorated with hand-painted flowers and a big smile. Too loud Mexican music with heavy brass and lots of guitars blared in the background. A couple, early twenties, entered the restaurant. The man hollered across the room at the waitress to turn up the music. I had to lean halfway across the table to understand what Sumner was saying.

The beers came, then she waited until she was sure I could hear her and our eyes were focused on each other.

"Here's the deal," she said. "I noticed the way you looked at Julius when he smiled at me. Being the intrepid investigator that you are, you've figured out the relationship between JuJu and me."

"JuJu?" I said, interrupting with a teasing smile.

Sumner frowned, "Stop it, Parker. Our relationship is not a secret, but we're also not advertising. So keep it to yourself." She tipped the Modelo at me to clink bottles in agreement and said, "*Comprende amigo*?"

We touched bottles and the nachos arrived. After finishing the plate of peppers and cheese and each of us knocking down another Modelo, she pushed the plate away. When I ordered the third beer she politely declined.

"Okay," she said. "Let's summarize. It helps me think through where we are. You remember me postulating about the Bermuda Triangle?"

I nodded, just as my beer arrived.

"The first leg of the triangle was that they ran away because of trouble at home or maybe a boyfriend talked them into it."

"Right," I responded. "But after meeting with the families I think we both agreed to drop that angle."

"Exactly," she said. "The second leg is the pedophile possibility."

"Yes…well, as you said, neither of these girls would have been foolish enough to be enticed into a stranger's car."

"Agreed," she continued. "And since Detective Moss and his team are working that angle, you and I can focus on a couple of other scenarios. If you consider the Killing Field episodes, Atticus did make a strong case for the girls being kidnapped by some other kind of sexual predator."

"And that fits with your theory about the third leg of the triangle—the girls were taken."

The gold-toothed waitress with the friendly smile arrived to take our plates and give us the check. I laid two twenties on the table and told her to keep the change.

"Now that we are on a first-name basis, I'm picking up the tab."

"Well, I am struggling on a lowly detective's salary. So thanks."

Getting the conversation back on track, I said, "What are the chances a local pimp took them?"

"Doesn't fit," she said. "Pimps like to groom their girls.

They find the runaways or girls that have been abused by a stepfather or mother's boyfriend. And there are plenty of them around in gentlemen's clubs, the malls, or just walking the street forlorn and lonely.

"In the trade, this kind of pimp is called a Romeo. The girl's self-esteem is so low she falls for the pimp's phony caring attitude. Over time, the Romeo convinces the girl that he is the only one who cares for her. Then the Romeo makes the girl repay him by prostituting herself. Strangely, the girl is so desperate for love, the scheme works."

"Man, that's some sick stuff. I've got a couple of .45 caliber pieces of lead with that bastard's name on it."

"I get it," she said.

"So what's left? The network of sex traffickers that Julius discussed?"

"My gut is leaning that way," she said. "But there's a problem. Most of the trafficked girls are from out of the country: Mexico or Central America, even Thailand and Eastern Europe."

"I see where you are going," I added. "Why would a trafficker risk kidnapping a couple of teenaged girls off the street when there is an abundant supply in the pipeline?"

"Unless..." Sumner suggested. "Unless a problem developed and an urgent need arose."

"Like what?"

"I don't have the faintest idea. But it's something to think about." She glanced at her watch. "Meanwhile...I just hope we haven't run out of time."

# Chapter Twenty-Two

## Thursday Night

---

After leaving the nachos and beer, Sumner said she needed to return to her office to check on possible new calls prompted by the flyers on the girls.

My mind shifted to Akemi and Maria. We needed a break in the case. Something to move us forward. Rudy had said Akemi was tough and she would resist. Had she tried to escape? What would her abductor do to her if she tried and failed?

I thought about the forty-eight-hour timetable the police used. We were at the halfway mark and we had nothing. Lieutenant Lott said the traffickers moved their girls often. How often? Hopefully not within the first forty-eight hours. But who knows? The thought of the kidnapper moving the girls before we could rescue them tore at my gut like a shredder ripping through a field.

It was past nine o'clock and I was on Seawall Boulevard heading west toward The Garhole. A young couple walking the promenade atop the seawall stopped to embrace. Galveston's proximity to Houston, only an hour's drive, made it a top honeymoon destination for couples who couldn't afford to travel or take time off work. Maybe this was one of those couples. The October evening was cool, and the man removed his jacket and draped it around the woman's shoulders.

I wanted that feeling for Akemi and Maria—the pure joy of first love. They have so much life ahead of them: new friends, marriage, children. But most of all, I wanted each of them to have the freedom to choose her own life's path. No one should take that away from them.

I caught the red light at Sixty-First Street. My eyes drooped and I almost nodded off. As much as I wanted to stay in the search, without rest I wouldn't be at my best tomorrow. I called Sumner and she answered on the first buzz.

"Nothing new here," she said, anticipating my question. "A few more calls on the flyers, but nothing looks good. We're running the leads anyway."

"I'm going to The Garhole. I hate to be that far away if anything pops, but I need sleep."

"Call me in the morning," she said and clicked off.

The light turned green and I started past the intersection when my cell phone rang.

"Parker, it's Maggie Peterson."

"Well, hello Maggie. Everything all right at your house?"

"Rudy wants to see you. Can you come by?"

I didn't want to, but what could I say? The stress Maggie and Rudy were going through had to be multiplied by ten over whatever I was going through.

"Sure, what is it?"

"I don't know. His behavior is so erratic. I have been trying to get him to meditate, but...."

When I arrived, Harry's Cadillac was parked in the driveway. I pulled to the curb and hustled to the front door. Maggie let me in, and I found Harry sitting on the couch in the living room drinking coffee. He was wearing the same mauve shirt as earlier, but he'd changed his pants to a pair of black wool and his shoes to dress wingtips. I should have known he would never be around Maggie without his best ensemble.

I gave her a quick hug and said, "Where is Rudy?"

"In the bedroom. I just got him to meditate. I hate to disturb him." She looked at Harry and me. "Do you mind waiting?"

Maggie offered coffee and I eagerly accepted, knowing a caffeine pop might give me some semblance of alertness.

When she left the room, Harry caught my eye. "Do you know what this is about?" he said.

I explained Rudy's behavior when he attacked the boy on the beach and his off-the-wall escapade with the rifle on the sand dunes.

"That *is* strange," Harry observed.

"I guess we'll learn more soon enough. And on a lighter note, how did it go today with your new squeeze?"

He sighed, shook his head. "Really, Parker. No need for such vulgarity. Squeeze of all things. Tsk, tsk."

"Well, I can see the mutual attraction. I mean she was dressed to the nines. A classy lady."

"Yes, her name is Elizabeth, and she certainly is," Harry replied. "And I have to admit, the idea of a squeeze certainly lights me up."

We both chuckled.

"What about the casserole lady across the street? If she spotted you with Liz, you might have gotten your last dish."

"One can only hope," Harry replied. "And Parker," he added, giving me a stern look, "The lady's name is Elizabeth."

Maggie returned with the coffee and a plateful of warm chocolate-chip cookies.

"Never knew a boy or man who didn't like these," she said, smiling.

I snatched one immediately, thinking the extra caffeine in the chocolate might help me focus.

Harry said, "Maggie has some news on the Japanese rifle. Maybe you'd like to hear it while we wait for Rudy."

I sat beside Harry on the couch sipping coffee while Maggie pulled a chair close.

"I know you have the rifle, Parker, and that's a good thing. Especially with Rudy's state of mind."

She looked at me for a response, but I just nodded, sipped more coffee and devoured another cookie, still waiting for the caffeine to kick in. Harry was also doing his part, matching me treat for treat.

"When Rudy brought the rifle home," she continued, "I copied the serial number and photographed the message in Japanese on the stock. I found a Japanese translator on the internet. Her name is Harumi Rudolph. She lives in the Dallas area, very nice lady. I just received an email from her with the translation."

She handed me a printed copy.

*Hello Mrs. Peterson, I have translated the writing taped on the rifle stock as: Second Lieutenant, Masayoshi Watanabe. Unit 7165, 32nd Japanese Army.*
*Note: The 32nd Japanese Army was responsible for the protection of its southern islands during WWII, which meant he probably participated in the Battle of Okinawa which lasted from April 1 to July 22, 1945.*
*I have contacted the Japan War-Bereaved Families Association to see if they can trace any surviving family members of Lieutenant Watanabe.*
*Sincerely, Harumi Rudolph, Certified Japanese Translator.*

I read the email and handed it back to Maggie.

"What do you think, Parker?" she asked.

"Well, first of all, good work, Maggie. You no doubt found the right interpreter. She seems willing to go the extra mile."

"I think so," Maggie agreed. "What do you plan to do with the rifle?"

"The rifle belongs to Neddie Lemmon. It's up to him."

"Well, I have an idea. What if Harumi can trace the family and, as a good will gesture, we give it back to them."

Harry chimed in, "Great idea, Maggie. After all, the war was over sixty years ago. It's also possible Lieutenant Watanabe is still alive."

"He wouldn't have given up his rifle," I offered.

"That's true," Harry added. He looked at Maggie. "But it does sound as if Ms. Rudolph will continue to try and locate the family."

Harry said, "I'll talk to Neddie about it. See if it's okay with him to return the rifle."

The room went quiet while we finished our coffee. I asked for another cup and Maggie graciously complied. She returned with the pot and refilled all the cups. We waited for Rudy to end his meditation and join us.

Harry gave Maggie a sweet smile and said, "I've been really curious about how you and Rudy met. Do you feel like….?"

"I don't mind, Harry. Let me see…well…after Ball High, I went to nursing school in New Orleans. I fell in love with a wonderful man I met there, Johnny Peterson. We married while I was still in nursing school.

"After Pearl Harbor, Johnny volunteered for the army while I finished school. He went missing after the D-Day invasion. I waited and waited but never heard. Even when the war was over and they emptied the prison camps, I had hope. But Johnny never turned up."

"One of the thousands of unknown soldiers," Harry commented.

"Sadly, yes," Maggie agreed. "But I never stopped hoping. After nursing school, I joined the Army Nurse Corps and was assigned to the Eighth Evacuation Hospital. We shipped to North Africa and then Italy.

"Rudy was in the 442nd Regiment attached to General Clark's 5th Army in Italy. They landed at Anzio in June of '44 and fought their way up the Italian coast. By August the unit had suffered heavy casualties but had made it to the Arno River. We followed behind, moving several times, and by then were set up at Grosseto just south of Florence."

"Was the 442nd close to Pisa?" Harry interjected.

"Well, yes," Maggie added. "Rudy told me he could see the Leaning Tower of Pisa from his hilltop position. That day must have been a hell of a fight. I know some of the details, but I won't go into them out of respect for Rudy. He doesn't like to talk about his combat experiences.

"I can only tell you that the shrapnel from a German mortar round blew a hole in his midsection. He was stabilized at battalion aid and transferred to the Eighth Evacuation Hospital.

"I was on triage duty when Rudy came in. None of us thought he would make it. Shrapnel penetrated his colon. He was on intravenous fluids and getting almost constant blood transfusions. Truly touch and go."

Maggie paused to wipe her teared eyes. She raised her cup to sip but her hand shook, and she lowered the cup to the coffee table. It was as though those memories had returned with perfect clarity. Maybe they had never left. Several times she glanced at the kitchen doorway as if nervously expecting Rudy.

"Maggie, it's okay," I said. "If it's too much…."

She took a deep breath and exhaled. "No, I can do this. I need to. I just don't want Rudy to hear me. Not right now with all that's going on."

Harry sat on the edge of his chair, leaning forward, as if he wanted to get up and give her a hug. Instead, he ran his hand over his beard and waited.

"Rudy developed a raging fever that spiked at times to 106. Peritonitis, an infection of the lining of the abdominal wall, set in. Drugs kept his blood pressure up, but we realized anything could happen. The infection could spread to the blood and cause sepsis. Internal organs could fail—lungs, kidneys, liver.

"I was assigned to his ward and watched over him day and night. We treated the infection with sulfonamide, a sulfa drug."

When she paused, I said, "Did they treat him on the battlefield?"

"Yes, they all carried packets of sulfa powder and were taught to pour it over wounds. It might have helped, but the dirt and grime of the battlefield were also in the wound."

"So did the sulfa drug eventually work?" Harry asked.

"No…well, maybe it kept him alive. But he was terribly allergic to the drug, broke out in a horrible rash. I thought he was a goner for sure. Then we finally got a shipment of penicillin. Thank God."

"Miracle drug," Harry said. "Saved thousands of lives during the war."

Maggie continued, "Two weeks later, he was up and walking around. The last few weeks we got to know each other well. Long walks around the grounds. Even held hands. It was a special time. No doubt we developed feelings for each other, but I was married and still in love with Johnny.

"By the time Rudy was released, the 442nd had been transferred to France. Rudy desperately wanted to rejoin his unit, but because of his rehabilitation requirements, he was sent back home.

"After the war, I stayed in the Army Nurse Corps, retired a lieutenant colonel and moved back to Galveston. I never remarried."

Maggie paused. She drank the rest of her coffee and sat back. It was obvious she had completed the story. But there was still one part I wanted to know. How did she and Rudy get together after the war? He had obviously gotten married and fathered a child.

"Was Rudy married before he joined the army?" I asked.

She sat pensively, probably trying to decide how much to tell. After a moment, she straightened and leaned forward.

"As I said, Rudy was sent home to recuperate. He married the girl he'd been dating when the war broke out. They had one child, a son. Rudy said it was a happy time of his life until his wife got cancer. After she died, Rudy moved to California to be close to his son and grandchild. Then the accident happened last June. Rudy was a truly lost soul. On a lark, he came to Galveston, found me and—"

"Any coffee left?" Rudy said from the kitchen door, holding an empty cup in his hand.

At the sound of his voice, we all stood. Maggie crossed to him. They embraced and came back to the sitting area. Rudy pulled a chair up next to Maggie. Dark circles and pouches under Rudy's eyes showed the wear and tear of the last few hours.

He said, "Thank you for coming over. I won't apologize for knocking down that detective, Kroton, but there is no justification for what I did on the beach with that boy and his girlfriend. I will certainly offer a heartfelt apology to both of them at school. And firing the rifle on the beach was out of line.

"The truth is, I lost my composure, and that is not who I am. This is no excuse, but I can't bear to lose Akemi. When my son died, I sent a prayer to him promising I would protect her, and I have failed."

Maggie started to interrupt, but Rudy held his palm up.

"Please," he said, "let me finish. I learned the ancient art of Zazen from my father. I have practiced it my entire life. Meditation got me through the war and my wife's cancer. But when I do things like my actions with the boy on the beach or firing the rifle, it seems as if Zazen has forsaken me.

"I don't understand what's happening, but I will continue to meditate to help me through this, and I will not rest until Akemi and Maria are safely home. I just wanted you to know something about what's going on with me and to thank you for your support."

No one spoke. Rudy saying he'd lost control brought me to my conversation with Colonel Kennon. Maybe he *was* suffering from delayed PTSD from the war. And Akemi's kidnapping had triggered all that repressed trauma.

But I was not a psychiatrist, and I was certainly not going to bring up my conversation with Kennon in front of Maggie and Harry. What worried me was what Kennon said about the second trigger and what that might mean. Was there something I didn't know about? Was Rudy truly in control?

Maggie got up and draped her arms around him for a hug. I lowered my eyes, admiring his candor and their obvious affection for each other.

Rudy gave me a determined stare and said, "Enough about me. You're working with Detective Sumner. Please tell me there's some movement about Akemi and Maria."

As badly as I wanted to sound a positive note, I couldn't. "A few calls into the hot line, that's all."

Rudy rose. "I'm going out again," he said.

Maggie countered, "Rudy, honey, please don't. You need rest."

He gave her a thin smile and squeezed her hand. "I have to," he replied. "Want to ride along, Parker?"

Part of me wanted to go, just to offer a buffer for his possible actions, but I was dead tired.

"I can't, Rudy. I need rest. If I get some sleep tonight, I can go all day tomorrow and through the night."

# Chapter Twenty-Three

## Thursday Night

---

Back at the house after dropping off Juanita's body, Hector removed the hoods from the girls and checked the ties on their hands. He pushed the girls into their room and told them to stay on their mats.

Akemi called out, "Maria is hurt bad. She needs a doctor."

Hector paused at the door to the kitchen. Without looking back, he pulled the door closed behind him. The room went black. The girls huddled on the mats with their backs against the wall.

Maria spoke softly, "Akemi, thank you for speaking up for me. My foot hurts something terrible, but I am more worried about you. I can't see you now, but in the light of the van before they put the hoods back on, the side of your face was all red. I think it was swelling. Does it hurt?"

Akemi wished she could see her face in a mirror. Was the heavy ache caused by a broken bone? She moved her jaw sideways and opened her mouth wide. It didn't feel broken.

"I am okay, Maria," Akemi answered. "Probably looks worse than it feels." She hated being untruthful, but she didn't want to add to her friend's stress. Maria had enough of her own.

They sat in silence for a moment, then Akemi said, "Did you hear what Juan said when Hector wanted to slap me again?"

"No," Maria answered. "I was too scared and my foot hurt."

"He said El Tigre doesn't like bruised faces, turns the customers off." She paused, then squeezed Maria's hand in the dark and said, "If my face stays red and bruised from Hector's slap, maybe they will leave us alone for a while. Maybe enough time for Jiichan to rescue us."

"Do you really think Jiichan will rescue us?" Maria asked, her voice tentative, unsure.

Akemi squeezed Maria's hand again. "Yes, he will, Maria. I know he will."

The girls sat in silence again. Then Akemi heard Maria moan softly. She asked, "What's wrong, Maria?"

"My foot is aching. What can we do?"

Maria's outcry tore Akemi's thoughts away from her own pain. "Do you think it's bleeding?"

"I don't know, but it hurts."

Akemi had to do something, but she felt helpless with her hands bound behind her back. None of the other girls were in the room. She asked Maria if she could push her shoe off the hurt foot using her other foot.

"I will try."

Maria struggled, finally managing to push her sneaker and sock off. Akemi scooted in front of Maria so that her back and her hands were by Maria's feet. She felt Maria's foot.

"I think the bleeding has stopped," she said. "But it's a puncture wound and, according to my first aid class, that can be dangerous."

Akemi instantly regretted her last comment. But they had been in a muddy field and there was no telling what nasty organisms had entered Maria's foot.

"It'll be okay," Akemi said. "We just need to get you

cleaned up. Get up and follow me."

"I can't. It hurts too much."

"Be brave, Maria."

Akemi shuffled to the bathroom with Maria leaning against her shoulder. She positioned Maria against the outside of the bathroom wall then backed to the door and opened it with her tied hands. Inside, she pressed her back against the wall searching for the light switch. She flipped the switch up with her shoulder, but nothing happened. Then she remembered Sarah telling her they had to pee in the dark. Why was that? she wondered. Did they also have to shower in the dark?

With no curtain on the shower stall, Akemi easily stepped inside. She felt her way around to find the water handle and pressed her shoulder against it. Cold water flowed gently out. She stepped back and told Maria to stand by the edge and hold her damaged foot under the stream.

After a couple of minutes, Maria tired and lowered her foot.

"Does it feel better?"

"A little."

Akemi realized Maria had become too dependent on her since they had been taken. She knew that her friend was stronger than she was acting. She remembered Maria's action the day they met in the school cafeteria. That bully had pulled her braid and Maria had slapped at him. The boy had been much bigger than she was, but Maria had stood up for herself. Akemi knew she needed to help her friend find that courage again. It would take both of their minds and hearts to escape.

"Good, now find your way back to our mats and lie down."

"I can't," Maria said.

"Yes, you can. Just do it!"

When Maria turned away, Akemi got in the shower fully dressed, afraid Juan or Hector might come in and see her. She held her face up to the rushing water. Her mind turned to home and how her mother had given her baths when she was little. She focused hard and remembered her mother's sweet face, always smiling with warmth and love. Oh God, how she missed her. Tears ran down her cheeks as quickly as the water washed them away.

She cried for a while and, finally exhausted, turned her thoughts to Jiichan and began to steel herself. She managed to turn the water off and return to the mat, her hair and clothes soaking wet. She put her back to the wall and focused on finding strength and empowerment in Jiichan and her mother's love.

She needed to meditate, to cleanse her mind of negative feelings. She assumed the half-lotus position that *Jiichan* had taught her. She sat on the mat with her back centered to allow her diaphragm to move freely and her mind to provide stability. She couldn't place her hands in the normal position because of the zip ties but ignored the restraints in order to concentrate.

Her left foot went onto her right thigh, and she tucked her right leg under. She lowered her gaze to a forty-five-degree angle, trying not to mentally focus on anything. Now she was ready.

She took a few deep breaths through her nose and blew them out slowly through her mouth. She began to relax. Jiichan had taught her that the more deeply her mind was at rest, the more deeply her body was at rest.

He had also taught her not to suppress thoughts and emotions coming into her consciousness. When they come, concentrate on breathing, he'd said. And over time they will dissipate. Twenty minutes later, still sitting silently, her mind felt like the surface of a still pond, calm and serene.

Then a loud voice vibrating through the wall broke her peacefulness. It wasn't Juan or Hector. The voice was stronger, more powerful. Akemi realized it must be the man they called El Tigre.

She woke Maria to translate. Maria put her ear to the wall and whispered the translation to Akemi.

"Is Juanita here?" El Tigre demanded. "I want to spend some time with her before I leave."

When no one answered, the kitchen door opened, and streams of light flooded into the room. A tall, powerfully built man stepped in. His head reached to the top of the door opening. A kaleidoscope of colors tattooed on both arms glistened in the ambient light from the kitchen. His black hair, pulled into a ponytail, hung below his neck. A full, black beard covered his heavily pocked cheeks, his top lip shaved clean.

He flipped a wall switch and four dull bulbs in the ceiling fixture threw weak rays of light across the room. El Tigre spied Akemi and Maria huddled against the wall. He approached the girls and stood over them, looking down.

"Who are you?" he groused.

Akemi had never seen a man this large. Her voice caught in her throat. She tried to answer but nothing came out.

A huge hand grabbed her shoulder and yanked her up. Akemi winced at the pain. Her eyes leveled just below the man's chest. He bent down and looked carefully at her face. Trying for whatever sympathy she could get, she tilted her face upward, giving him a good look at the bruise on her cheek caused by Hector's slap.

Only one eye stared back at her. Her body quaking, she tried desperately to hide her shock. A scar began above his left eye, cut through the eyebrow and across the closed lid, then bent like a quarter moon across his cheek, ending at his stop lip. The mutilation looked rough and poorly healed and was lighter in color than the dark mahogany skin hidden beneath the beard.

No pity radiated from his remorseless eye, only streaks of red like the feral eye of a wild animal caught in a trap.

El Tigre said nothing more. He doused the light and left the room, closing the door behind him. In the black stillness of the room, Akemi took in a deep breath and blew it out slowly. The terror in her soul would be a long time leaving, if ever.

Then the sound of a ferocious slap hitting someone's face emanated through the wall. Maria whispered the translation.

"*Imbécils,* both of you. Taking two schoolgirls off the street. The kidnapping is all over the television and radio. It's all they talk about. Hard to believe you two are so *estúpido,* but I guess you are. We have an unlimited supply of *puta* coming from the south. Which of you hit the Asian girl?"

The girls heard no answer. The sound of a harder slap came through the wall, followed by a sick moan.

"I know it was you, Hector, you dumb *cabrón*. We couldn't put that girl to work now if we wanted to. No customer would want her with that bruise. If fact, we can't put either of the girls out. Someone would recognize their faces from the flyers and call the police for the reward."

"Reward?" Juan asked. "What reward?"

"Never mind. Just do what I tell you."

The sound of Hector's voice came through the wall, but it was different, weak and subservient.

"Sorry, Tigre. When Juanita disappeared, we wanted to replace her for you."

"What? Disappeared? What are you talking about?"

"We went to pick her up and she wasn't there. We searched the cantina, the neighborhood. We think she may have run off with a date or maybe one killed her. We spoke with people, but no one has seen her. We…we thought we were doing the right thing by replacing her."

"The right thing? You are total fools. Every cop for fifty miles around is searching for those girls. You must get something else to move them in case someone saw this van."

"Juan checked before he got in the van," Hector said. "No one saw us."

"Idiot, you don't know that. It only takes one person to see you."

The conversation paused. No sound came through the wall.

Then El Tigre spoke. "I am going to the Acapulco to see if Sarah or the other girls know anything about Juanita. Surely, she's not so stupid to think she could switch to another cantina and get away with it. She knows what will happen when I catch her.

"I'll check some of the other places too, and then pick up Sarah and the other two and bring them back here. I'll be gone two, maybe three hours. Enough time for you, Hector, to take the van into Houston, leave it there and steal another. You had better be here when I return. Juan, you stay here with the girls."

"Why Houston?" Hector asked, his voice timid, unsure.

"You fool. If someone saw you, the cops are looking for the van. So many cars are stolen in Houston every night, no one will put it together."

"I can't do it by myself," Hector argued. "If I leave the old van in the same place as the one I steal, the cops will figure it out and be looking for the new one right away. It takes two of us. Houston is a big place all spread out. Our best chance is to steal a van on one side of town and leave this one on the other side."

Tigre ran his hand over his beard. He put his hand on his chin as if in thought. "Okay," he said. "Meet me at the Acapulco and I will tell Beto to go with you. The cantina can do without its bouncer for a few hours."

When the back door slammed, Akemi figured El Tigre was gone. Her cheek pulsated; the ache worse. She turned away, hoping Maria hadn't noticed the pain in her face.

What would happen when El Tigre returned with Sarah and the other girls? Would one of them be so frightened she would tell El Tigre about Juanita cutting her wrists and bleeding out in the bathtub? What would El Tigre do then?

Hector opened the kitchen door and stalked in, yelling, "Get up and come to the kitchen."

When they got there, Hector sat at the table holding a wet rag to his cheek. Akemi hoped Hector hurt as much as she did. If his pain got bad enough, maybe he would go to the hospital and only Juan would be here.

Her throbbing cheek forced her thoughts to her own face. She had seen the color of a bruise on a friend's arm at school when she had taken a nasty spill off her bike. She felt swelling in her left cheek and wondered if it had started to turn the dark, bluish-purple color she had seen on her friend's arm.

She moved to a place where she hoped the single light bulb would intensify the colors of the bruise. When Juan looked at her, she tilted her head slightly toward the light. Just as she wanted, he grimaced and turned away.

Akemi caught Maria's eyes shift to the pot steaming on the stove. Hector must have noticed as well. He removed his leather belt and slammed it on the table. Both girls flinched as the sound of leather hitting wood reverberated across the room.

"No food tonight or tomorrow after that stupid effort to get away. And if El Tigre asks about Juanita, you know nothing, get it? You say anything and I will lash every inch of skin off your body."

Wham! He slammed the belt on the table again.

Akemi flinched at the sound. Chills traveled though her body. Then she glimpsed the tears in Maria's eyes and the goose bumps on her arms. Akemi hardened her resolve. She would not let these bastards win.

When Hector left for Houston, Juan set two bowls of steaming *menudo* on the table in front of the girls.

"It's all I have to offer now," he said. "You should eat some before Hector gets back. You may not get anything tomorrow."

"You are so kind," Akemi said. "Thank you."

Juan took a knife and cut their zip ties loose. "Don't try anything," he said. "You've seen how mean Hector gets."

Maria asked, "Are you afraid of him?"

"No. Hector is a lot of mouth."

Akemi wanted to ask why Juan tolerated Hector if he wasn't afraid of him. But Maria changed the subject.

"Your cooking is very good," she said. "Did you work in a restaurant before coming to *El Norte*?"

They already knew Juan was from Honduras, and that he had come to the U.S. to escape the cartels. But they couldn't let him know that they had heard Hector and him talking through the wall.

Maria was doing good, Akemi thought, trying to loosen Juan up, get him talking about himself.

"My *mamá* taught me her recipes. I thought I was going to be a chef when I arrived in America, but…." Juan dropped his eyes.

Akemi caught Juan's reaction and knew they were making progress. Maybe, just maybe….

"If you want to be a chef, why are you here with Hector and El Tigre?" Maria asked.

Akemi watched Maria avoid eye contact while speaking in between bites of the *menudo*. She knew Maria was just trying to keep the pressure off. Akemi beamed inwardly at Maria's resurgence. Her self-confidence seemed to grow with each exchange.

Juan said, "The cartels were bad. I had to get away, but I had no money. I owe El Tigre for the passage. I can't leave until I've worked off the debt."

"Oh, Juan," Maria said, softly. "I am so sorry."

When Juan looked away, Akemi nodded to Maria to keep going.

"Juan, if you will help us escape, we will make sure you are protected. We have friends in the police department."

It was a lie, Akemi knew. But so what, if he agreed to help? Juan turned back to the stove. He scraped the remaining *menudo* into a bowl and set it in the refrigerator. He pulled out two zip ties. He looked at the girls and back at the ties as if debating with himself. He sent the girls into the bedroom with their hands free.

A few minutes later, Akemi heard Juan's soulful voice coming through the wall. She had noticed a guitar in the kitchen and had wondered who played it.

Akemi said to Maria, "Listen, Maria. Juan is singing and

playing the guitar. Do you understand the song?"

Maria put her ear to the wall. "Oh, yes," she said. "This one is a love song, "*Bésame Mucho.*" My *papá* used to sing it to my *mamá*. He is saying 'kiss me, kiss me a lot. As if tonight, it is the last time. Kiss me, kiss me a lot, me who fears losing you.' It is a very beautiful song," she said. And then she sang along with Juan. Her voice was strong.

"Oh, my gosh, Maria. You have a beautiful voice," Akemi said.

"I sing with *mamá*," she answered.

The kitchen door opened and Juan rushed in. "Maria, was that you? Come into the kitchen."

Juan pulled two chairs out and beckoned Maria to sit across from him. Akemi followed her in.

After they sang a couple more Mexican ballads, Maria asked, "Do you know '*La Paloma Blanca?*'"

"Of course," Juan said. "Everyone knows that one."

Maria said, "Can we sing it in English so Akemi can understand the words?"

Juan burst into the song and Maria sang with him.

When the sun shines on the mountain
And the night is on the run
It's a new day
It's a new way
And I fly up to the sun.
I can feel the morning sunlight
I can smell the new-mown hay
I can hear God's voice is calling
For my golden sky light way
  *Una paloma blanca*
I'm just a bird in the sky

*Una paloma blanca*
Over the mountains I fly
No one can take my freedom away

Akemi wanted to sing along with the chorus, but her cheek hurt too much. Maria seemed to ignore the pain in her foot.

They sang the chorus over and over, the girls laughing and giggling, not wanting to quit. Then Juan suddenly stopped and grew solemn, remembering where they were.

He said, "You must go back to your room now. Hector or Tigre will be back soon."

Akemi and Maria stood and ambled to the door. Maria turned and said, "Juan, do you believe that?"

"What?" he asked.

"That no one can take your freedom away."

# Chapter Twenty-Four

## Thursday Night

---

Two hours later, voices awakened Akemi. The door to the kitchen opened and Juan came in.

"El Tigre brought the girls back. They are all eating. You must eat again, too, before Hector gets back."

When Akemi and Maria entered the kitchen, Juan motioned them to the table. He set two bowls of steaming chicken soup down in front of them.

Sarah and the two girls Akemi had seen in their room were already at the table eating soup. It was always dark in the bedroom, so this was the first time she was able to get a good look at the girls.

She viewed Sarah up close. Her blond hair looked dirty and the roots were black. Her blue eyes had disintegrated into a blank stare. She was older, with bad acne she did her best to cover with makeup. She offered no eye contact with anyone. Every few seconds her head twitched. She swallowed a few spoons of soup and lay her head down on her arms.

Akemi thought the two dark girls were probably Hispanic. They looked maybe fifteen or even younger, their red shorts so tight she wondered if they cut off circulation. With dark eyes and straight black hair hanging below their shoulders, they looked so alike they could have been sisters, even twins. Except the breasts on the girl wearing the halter top bulged over the top. The tee shirt on the other girl showed the picture of a naked woman with her mouth open and tongue turned up.

When Akemi looked at the scar on Tigre's face, she felt a burning sensation as something foul entered the back of her throat. She choked it down and turned her head.

El Tigre yelled at Juan, "Where is Hector?"

"I don't know."

El Tigre glanced at his gold Rolex. "Three hours was enough time to steal a truck and get back."

El Tigre took out his phone and called a number. No answer. He ended the call and texted a message. Then he jerked his thumb at Sarah and said, "Come with me."

Sarah didn't move, her face still in her arms.

Juan unlocked the cabinet over the stove and took out a small vial. He shook out a pill and gave it to Sarah. She swallowed it quickly and passed in front of Tigre into the girls' room.

Tigre said to Juan, "If Hector is not here when I've finished with this bitch, his ass will be mine when I get back here tomorrow."

# Chapter Twenty-Five

## Friday Morning

---

Nature's alarm clock banged me awake early at The Garhole. Squawking seagulls had announced daybreak to people on the gulf coast for hundreds of years, even before the Karankawa Indians first paddled their dugout canoes across West Bay.

I reached for my cell phone on the nightstand and touched nothing but a thin layer of dust, reminding me to clean my room before Kathy's next visit. I had hoped for an early morning call from Sumner announcing the safe return of the girls but realized I had left the phone in my truck.

I slipped on one of the tee shirts I'd made with a drawing of a smiling alligator gar and the words "The Garhole Bar" above it. I added shorts and an old pair of running shoes and hustled down the stairs.

In the bar, Bully and Neddie sat at a table drinking beer, Bully in his wheelchair chewing an early morning cigar and Neddie across from him smacking his lips on his usual dose of nicotine gum. The scene never changed.

"A little early for even you two alkies to be at it," I cracked as I entered the door.

Neddie accepted his drinking problem, but Bully fought the idea. He sucked down the rest of the beer and crumpled the can with one hand.

I passed to the front of the room and opened the wall,

hoping a breeze would blow the stink of the cigar out the back door.

Neddie said to my back, "We figured you'd be busy, and Bully wanted me to go into town for supplies. I thought I'd come by for breakfast and then head out."

"Yeah, well, the beer delivery's coming today. Try to leave before it gets here. I'd like to see some of the brew end up in the cooler."

"Give me a break, Parker. What's a few beers to you? Besides, I brought some fresh trout to fry up if you're lucky enough to have a customer drop in."

I acknowledged his tit-for-tat sarcasm with a frown. "Pick up a few loaves of French bread and a gallon of oysters for tomorrow. Maybe po'boys will lift our spirits."

"Anything to get you off our ass," Bully quipped.

Neddie said, "Hell, Parker. I can get 'em from my buddy's oyster boat on the wharf. I can shuck 'em faster than you can fry 'em."

I found my phone dead in the truck and plugged it into a wall socket by the bar. I asked Neddie to wait to go for supplies until I finished my morning run and to come get me if there was a break in the case.

I crossed the highway and jogged up the narrow path to the beach. With good rain in Galveston this year, the lively yellow and crimson Mexican hats were still showing off in the field and the wild lantana bushes were a blur of pink. I carefully dodged the occasional prickly pear plant by the edge of the path, knowing its painful spines offered a subtle warning to stay on the track.

Thankfully, life appeared normal on West Beach. I wish the same were true for the city. I cleared the salt grass and turned left, heading for the Jamacia Beach development three miles in the distance. The wind had laid, allowing the surf to turn a warm emerald green as it moved in gentle swells toward the beach.

A steady pace put me clipping along at a ten-minute mile. During my army years, I ran seven-minute miles, but age had slowed me. The few extra pounds strapped around my belly didn't help either.

Still, my pace flushed small flocks of sandpipers into the air, disturbing their morning routine of scouring for worms and hermit crabs in the wet sand.

I made it to Jamacia Beach and back in an hour and arrived at The Garhole winded but invigorated. Two fishermen stood at the cleaning table putting the finishing touches on their fillets. Neddie had whipped up scrambled eggs and bacon for all of us, including the anglers.

After making quick work of Neddie's breakfast, I grabbed my cell phone and slipped upstairs. Seven a.m. and no calls. I showered and dressed in jeans and a golf shirt, ambled to my Adirondack on the deck, and called Sumner hoping she was awake.

"Damn, Parker. You always up with the chickens?"

"More like squawking gulls. Any news?"

"I wish. Are you coming in?"

"Yes, but I don't know what the hell to do when I get there. I have an inherent personality trait that doesn't allow me to just sit and wait."

"ADD?"

"More like thirst for cold Shiner Bock."

"Okay, stay there. I'll call you if something happens."

Just as I terminated the call, Kathy rang in.

She opened with her usual salutation of "Good morning, lover" and then said, "I work the three-to-eleven shift later today. How about I come out to The Garhole for whatever masterpiece you're cooking up for lunch?"

My mind flashed to the dust on my nightstand. "Well, uh…okay sure. Sounds great."

"What's this hesitancy in your voice?"

"Well, you know me and my bedroom."

"Yeah, well…you have time. I need to shower first."

"You could wait and do that here. I'll squeeze in with you."

I knew she wouldn't like that idea: we had tried it before and could barely turn around in my shower. I hung up and began cleaning—put on fresh bed linens, dusted the nightstand and swept the floor. Then, a quick shower and fresh clothes. Now I just needed to hit the room with a vanilla scent spray.

I took a last hard look at my phone trying to conjure up good news about the girls, but nothing happened. Damn.

Downstairs, Kathy was out on the dock gazing across the bay. The wind was still down, leaving the bay without a ripple except for an occasional swirl where fish were feeding.

Bully was plopped in his wheelchair beside her, snoring softly. Cigar ashes trailed down the front of his shirt and the stub lay on the deck by his one good foot. The eyepatch was pushed up to his forehead as though he'd been rubbing the eye socket again. Kathy turned, put a finger to her lips indicating silence, and joined me in the bar.

"I really love being out here and watching the world go by, so quiet and peaceful. I wish I could do more of it."

"I would like you to do more of it."

She smiled at my comment, took a Coke from my hand and toasted the gar head. I followed her gesture with a Shiner. We clinked bottles and I leaned over the bar and kissed her.

Minutes later, we cuddled upstairs on my clean sheets. After a lazy session, I craved a cigarette though I hadn't smoked since my first hitch in the army.

She put her shirt on, reached for my hands and pulled me to the edge of the bed. "Too early for lunch. How about a walk on the beach?"

We finished dressing, crossed the highway, strolled past the salt grass and flowers and stopped at the edge of the water. Out in the surf, a flock of terns busily bleated out their raspy calls while diving and grabbing their lunch of schooling mullet. We held hands and strolled casually along the beach, searching for treasures that had washed up with last night's tide.

"Parker, you grew up in Galveston. Did you ever build a bonfire on the beach with a bunch of kids, sing songs and drink beer?"

"Sure. New Year's Eve was our favorite. The guys would gather driftwood and build a bonfire. The girls would bring fried chicken and potato salad. We ate, shot off fireworks and drank all the beer. If a guy was lucky, he'd end up wrapped in a blanket with his girl."

I reached down, picked up a broken sand dollar off the beach, and handed it to Kathy.

"Hardly ever find a whole one of these anymore. Too many early-morning shell seekers out here."

We ambled for a while, neither of us speaking, both enjoying the day. We stopped to admire the gentle rolling surf, a sight that always seemed to soothe the soul.

Kathy squeezed my hand, "I missed out on most of my high school fun times. I was in middle school when Dad died of a massive heart attack. I worked all through high school to help support my mom and little sister. I've been working ever since."

I put my arm around her shoulder and gave her a light squeeze.

"Well, Kathy, you're a caregiver. Pretty special. You must feel good about that. Sometimes I feel guilty about sitting on all this land my grandfather gave me. I'm not helping anyone but myself."

"You could sell part of it."

"There's the rub. If I sold it, some greedy developer would cut canals in for houses and destroy some of the last virgin wetlands in Galveston. I can't do it. We need the estuarial breeding grounds for the marine life."

"So you are giving back in your own way, Parker. Helping to save nature for future generations."

"Yeah, well, maybe. But sometimes it doesn't seem like enough."

I dropped my eyes to hers, feeling a little magic flow between us. We hugged and stood wrapped together, neither of us wanting to quit. Then she whispered in my ear. "Julie's dad is picking her up Friday for the weekend. How about my house for a couple of nights?"

"I'd love to as long as I can stay loose in case something pops with Akemi and Maria."

She nodded.

We walked a while and I said, "How is Julie doing?"

"Still shook up. That's why I called her dad, to get her away from all this stress. She overheard one of the girls at school saying her boyfriend may have seen the vehicle that abducted the girls."

My pulse quickened. "What? How long have you known this?"

"Don't stroke out, Parker. Julie casually mentioned it this

morning before school. She didn't really believe it because that girl always makes stuff up."

"Where did the boy supposedly see the vehicle?"

"She didn't say."

"Damn it, Kathy! Every lead is important. We're really struggling. I wish you'd told me sooner."

"Sorry, Parker. When Julie told me about the girl, I guess I just discounted it because of the source."

I noticed the hurt in her eyes and regretted my tone. I put my arm around her.

"It's okay, I just can't get those girls off my mind."

I kissed her forehead and explained I needed to get into town and follow up on the lead.

We hurried back to The Garhole. She got in her car and started the engine. I leaned in for a final smooch and said, "Kathy, I don't know how to say this but…every minute counts finding Akemi and Maria. Whoever took them might move the girls soon and if that happens, well…."

"What are you trying to tell me?"

"I'm going to call Detective Sumner and head to the school to talk with Julie. We have to know who this boy is and what he knows. We can't wait until she gets home. Time is just too critical."

Kathy flinched. "I understand. But can you wait to call Sumner until after you talk to Julie? She's so fragile right now I don't know how she'd react to a police officer."

# Chapter Twenty-Six

## Friday Morning

---

I parked in a visitor's spot at Julie's school and entered the front door. A passing student gave me directions to the Administration Office. A brass plate on the door read: Bobbye Bennett, Principal.

An attractive, mid-fifties woman with a warm smile and friendly eyes greeted me cordially. I was taken by her alabaster complexion, so smooth she could have modeled for a Michelangelo sculpture. She acknowledged Kathy's call giving permission for Julie to meet with me. Then she graciously allowed me to use her office for the interview.

Julie came in with nervous eyes and a wrinkled brow, probably wondering what she had done wrong. She saw me and some of the tension eased from her face.

I motioned Julie to the couch and sat across from her.

"Is mom, okay?" she asked, bouncing her knee as she spoke.

"Yes. Yes, of course, Julie. Your mom's fine. I just need to visit with you about what you told your mom this morning."

"What?"

"You heard a girl say her boyfriend might have seen the car."

"Oh, that was Stacy. She's so full of BS about her boyfriend, we never believe anything she says. Makes me want to puke."

She made a face and stuck her finger into her open mouth like she was trying to gag.

"It may be important, though. Do you know the boy's name?"

"David Mendez. She brags about him giving her free vanilla cones at McDonald's."

"McDonald's?"

"That's what she said."

"Thank you, Julie. You've been a big help."

I gave her a hug and she hurried back to class. I immediately called Sumner. She arrived a few minutes later and we met at the principal's office. I introduced Sumner to Mrs. Bennett and explained the situation. Sumner asked her to keep it confidential.

"I will," Bennett said. "But you know kids. It'll be all over the school by the time the bell rings to go home."

Bennett looked up David's class and called his teacher on her cell phone. Three minutes later a small Hispanic boy, maybe five-four and 120 pounds, appeared at the principal's door. He wore his neatly combed dark hair straight back with what looked like a whole tube of grease holding it in place. His bottom lip quivered when his eyes caught Sumner's badge hanging on a lanyard around her neck.

"Hi David. Thanks for coming in," Mrs. Bennett said, her voice low and soft. She motioned him to the couch and continued in the same tone of voice. "Relax, you're not in trouble."

She smiled broadly and introduced Sumner and me. "Detective Sumner would like to ask you a few questions. I'll be right outside, okay?"

David nodded and offered a tentative, "Yes, ma'am."

Sumner sat in a chair across from the couch. I stayed back,

thinking David didn't need pressure from both of us.

Sumner smiled and leaned forward so her eyes were level with his.

"Thank you for coming in, David. You may be able to help us."

David moved his hands around and cracked his knuckles.

"You work after school at the McDonald's on Broadway, right?"

"Yes, ma'am."

"Two nights ago, Akemi Aoki and Maria Santos went missing after the school volleyball game. We think they disappeared on their way to McDonald's. It was just getting dark when the game ended. You're here David because we need your help. Did you see anything that day?"

David hesitated. He lowered his eyes momentarily, then looked up at Sumner. His lip quivered again. "I...I don't want to get into trouble with my mom."

Sumner smiled again and sat back in her chair. "David, you have done nothing wrong. What makes you say that?"

"I...I was smoking out back on my break. You won't tell her, will you?"

Sumner continued her disarming grin. "No David, your secret is safe with us."

"Okay, well...when I came out for a smoke, there was a truck up the block parked at the curb. I noticed it because it was facing toward me on the wrong side of the street. Its lights were off. Then the driver gunned the motor and took off. I stepped up to the edge of the building where I could watch him because it was so weird."

"Did you see the girls?"

"No."

"Did he turn his lights on?"

"I don't know."

"What kind of truck?"

"The kind where the side door opens."

"You mean like a van?"

"Yes, that's it. My uncle has one. The guy never slowed down. He crossed the median, made the turn on Broadway at full speed."

"You said 'he.' Did you get a look at the driver?"

"Well…not really. I mean, he hauled ass pretty quick."

"Not really? That means you noticed something, right?"

"Uh…."

"Was he young or old?"

"He was kinda old, like maybe, thirty?"

"What color was his skin? White? Black?"

"I mean, he wasn't a Black man. But his skin was more…brown like me. Coulda been a Mexican, I guess."

"Did he have a beard or any facial hair?"

"I don't know, it happened so fast."

"Okay, so what color was the van?"

"Like, dark blue or black."

"Were there any markings on the van, the name of a company or anything?"

"I don't think so."

"Did you get the make like Ford or Chevrolet?"

He shook his head. "I don't know anything about them kinda trucks."

"Did it look new or old, any dents or damage you could see?"

"I don't think so."

"Had you ever seen the van around before?"

"Not that I remember." David bit his lip to keep it still. "Jesus…do you…do you think the girls were in that thing?"

Sumner paused, as if considering her answer and said, "We don't know, David, but think about this: Is it possible someone else working at McDonald's or maybe a customer saw the van?"

David scrunched his eyes in thought, "No, I'm sure they didn't. There was no one outside and well...I'm the only smoker. They all give me hell for doing it." He hesitated, then looked at Sumner as if asking for approval and said, "Guess I need to quit."

Sumner smiled again. She handed David her card. "Will you call me if you think of anything else? Even something that doesn't seem important."

"Okay."

"David, we really appreciate your help. Do you think you could work with a police artist to help her draw a description of the driver?"

"Well, gee, I don't know. I mean he really zoomed by."

"One last question. Which way did the van turn on Broadway?"

"Left toward Sixty-First Street."

Sumner paused and pursed her lips. "Or maybe the causeway?"

The shock hit me like I'd touched a live wire. If the girls had been taken over the causeway, they could be long gone.

# Chapter Twenty-Seven

## Friday Morning

---

Akemi lay on her mat, the throbbing in her cheek seemingly worse. She gradually emerged from her painful haze not sure if she had slept or not. With the room dark as usual, she had no idea what time of day it was or how long she had been out.

She was pretty sure the locked door on the other side of the room led to the bedroom where El Tigre had taken Sarah. She wondered if El Tigre and Sarah were still in there. For Sarah's sake, she hoped not.

The bathtub where Juanita had bled to death was probably in a bathroom off that room. She cringed at the thought of a girl feeling so hopeless that slicing her wrists was her only way out. Even through her pain, Akemi vowed it would never happen to her or Maria. She would not be a victim. And she would help Sarah if she could.

Akemi wondered if Sarah was sleeping on her mat across the room. She wanted to call to her but didn't want to wake Maria or the other girls if they were in the room. She padded slowly to Sarah's mat. A soft whimper came from the darkness.

Akemi knelt close to the mat and whispered, "Sarah, it's me, Akemi."

Another whine from the darkness.

"Sarah…"

"Oh, I hurt so bad. My insides are on fire."

Akemi leaned closer to Sarah's head. "How can I help you?"

"Water…I'm…so thirsty."

"Be right back," Akemi said.

Akemi heard noises through the wall from the kitchen but no voices. Maybe Juan was alone, cooking. She went to the kitchen door and tapped lightly. No one approached. She tapped again.

Juan opened the door with a spatula in his hand. He looked at Akemi and flinched. She thought it must be her bruised face. He put his finger to his lips to indicate silence and motioned her into the kitchen.

"Hector got in late. He's sleeping in the other room. We must be quiet. I am making tacos with eggs and jalapeños."

Akemi pleaded, "Sarah hurts bad. She needs a glass of water."

"Have you seen her?"

"The room's too dark, but she's in a lot of pain."

"Go back quietly. Bring her here."

Sarah pressed her hand to her stomach as Akemi helped her stand. She draped her arm around Sarah's waist and guided her to a chair at the kitchen table. Sarah dropped her head into her hands and emitted a terrible wailing sound.

Akemi said, "Please be quiet, Sarah. We don't want to wake Hector."

Juan poured a glass of water. Sarah drank quickly and motioned for more. Akemi sat beside her. She placed her hand gently on Sarah's back and began a soft rub. She glanced at Juan and thought she saw moisture in his eyes.

"You want some eggs?" Juan asked.

Sarah shook her head. "It hurts so bad. Tigre said I didn't

please him. He kept hitting me in the stomach. I saw blood on the toilet. I think he broke something inside me."

Akemi swallowed hard. She felt terrible about Sarah's pain, but she couldn't think of anything more she could do for her. Her cheek throbbed. She desperately wanted to check her face and hoped Juan might let her look in a mirror. She rose and stood beside Juan at the stove.

"The eggs look good," she said. "I am so hungry."

"Go get Maria and I will feed you both before Hector wakes up."

"Okay," Akemi said, and then, "Juan, look at my face. Tell me what you see."

When Juan wouldn't look at her, she knew it must look as bad as she felt.

"Can I at least look in a mirror?" she asked.

"There is one in the bathroom that you and the girls use."

"But it's dark in there," Akemi said.

"Hector keeps it that way," Juan answered. "He puts a bulb in when the girls shower. He likes to watch everyone bathe naked."

Akemi thought she would vomit.

"That sicko jerk," she said softly but loud enough for Juan to hear. "Never." She sneaked into the room and awakened Maria.

"Be quiet," Akemi whispered. "Come with me."

Akemi and Maria ate two tacos each and finished with large glasses of water. They put their paper plates in the garbage sack so Hector wouldn't see them when he came in. Akemi again asked Sarah to eat, but she didn't raise her head from the table.

Akemi knew she had to say something to Juan before the other girls came in. She approached Juan while he stood at the stove with his back to the table.

"Juan, please help us. Maria's foot is hurting, and Hector may have broken my jaw when he slapped me. And…look at poor Sarah. She doesn't deserve this."

Juan started to speak, but the kitchen door opened and the two young Hispanic girls ambled in. The girl with the big breasts rubbed her eyes as though she was barely awake. She wore bright red pajamas with the picture of a prancing horse on the front. The other girl's pajamas were white with a picture of the Disney Princess Girls on the front.

Akemi almost smiled, remembering she'd had a similar pair when she was younger. The pajamas were definitely for younger girls, which made Akemi wonder if she'd misjudged their age. Could they be even younger than she and Maria were? And judging from the tight shorts they had worn last night, they were already working, hustling men twice their age or older.

When she felt herself tearing up, she stopped and gathered her resolve. El Tigre's plan was plain to see now, right before her eyes. She couldn't weaken now. She wouldn't let this happen to Maria and herself.

"We smelled the eggs," the girl with the horse on her pajamas said in Spanish. They sat at the table and Juan brought tacos.

Suddenly the kitchen door flew open and Hector marched in, his shoulders stooped, his tattooed arms glistening in the light and his large belly jiggling as he crossed the room. He stroked his mustache and eyed the scene.

"So how are you sweet ladies today?" he asked. He spotted Akemi and Maria and said to Juan. "You didn't feed them, did you?"

Juan ignored Hector's question and motioned him off to

the side. He spoke in a low voice. "What time did you get in?"

"It was late. El Tigre was still here so I drove around waiting for him to leave."

"Did you steal another truck?"

"Me and Beto thought if the cops found the one we had, they would look for another van. So we found a Suburban with a third seat and dark windows in a strip center way out on the west side of Houston.

"What about the van?"

"I ditched it in a hospital parking lot off I-10 east, must be fifty miles from where we stole the Suburban. Hospital lots are always full, so no one will notice it for days."

"El Tigre is pissed at you for taking so long to steal that Suburban. I don't know what he will do when he returns."

"I'm not worried. He needs me," Hector declared.

"You better hope so," Juan added.

Hector focused on Sarah, her head down on the table. "What's wrong with her?"

"El Tigre beat her up."

"Damn! I wanted to spend some time with her before she went back out."

"She's too sick," Juan said firmly.

Hector looked over the table. "Well… I've never had an Asian girl."

When Akemi heard Hector, she almost panicked and dashed for the back door. No way she would allow that freak to touch her. No way. She would fight. She would use what Jiichan had taught her. She would throw that fat prick Hector to the ground.

But she was so small. Could she do it? What about using some outlawed moves, the ones too dangerous for tournaments, like *Do Jime,* the trunk squeeze. But that would never work with Hector's round belly, even if she could get him into that position.

Jiichan had told her, "If you're in real danger, go for the eyes. A finger in his eye will give you time to get away."

# Chapter Twenty-Eight

## Friday Afternoon

---

Out in the school parking lot, Sumner's cell phone rang.

"Hi JuJu, what's up?"

I couldn't hear Lieutenant Lott's end of the conversation, but I could tell by the grimace on Sumner's face it wasn't a personal call.

"We're five minutes away, can you wait for us?" She terminated the call and looked at me. "A fisherman found a girl's body in one of those bayous that run into Clear Creek. The forensic team is on its way. We'll ride with Julius."

"Damn," was all I could say. I grimaced, ran for my truck, and followed Sumner as she sped out of the parking lot with her emergency lights on. We spun into the back parking lot of the police station and found Lieutenant Lott waiting for us. We jumped into his car, raced over the causeway up I-45 and turned right into the bustling scene of League City.

The image of Akemi and Maria from the flyers tormented my consciousness, two beautiful teenagers stripped of innocence. I could only hope the body in the water wasn't one of them. I lost track of all the twists and turns we were taking. We finished on a narrow dirt road saturated with mud-filled potholes. At the end of the road was an old pickup and several police cars parked single file behind the truck. A maroon Tahoe with letters printed on the door that read Galveston County Medical Examiner was last in line.

The road ended at a barbed-wire fence at the edge of a narrow strip of water. Just this side of the fence, a knot of people looked down at a naked body. A woman was bent over a girl's head examining her eyes. A patch on the back of her black jacket read "Medical Examiner" in big white letters.

Sumner said to me, "Do you know Sandra Lillich, the County ME?"

"Haven't had the pleasure."

When Lillich heard her name, she rose, arched her back to relieve tension and turned. She greeted Lott and Sumner. Sumner introduced me.

She looked mid-fifties, attractive, with short gray hair and large brown and appraising eyes. Lillich pushed her hand toward mine and smiled.

"Nice to finally meet you, Parker. After I read last year that you won the gumbo contest I've been meaning to come out and try a bowl. Harry highly recommended it."

I gave her hand a quick squeeze. "Thank you, Dr. Lillich. Harry says you are the best M.E. we've ever had in Galveston, and he's known them all for the past forty years."

Lott chuckled, "Okay, enough kumbaya for one day. What you got, Doc?"

Lillich stared at Lott. She looked down, pursed her lips then raised her eyes to him again. "Lieutenant Lott, when you've seen as many dead bodies as I have, you'll understand the need to occasionally lighten the load. Until then, don't give me any of your shit, got it?"

Perfect I thought. A carefully crafted combination of scorn and reckoning. Coming up through the ranks, Lillich had obviously honed her responses well. It appeared she didn't take grief from anyone, especially males.

Lott's face displayed a splotch of red. Sumner narrowed

her eyes at him like she wanted to put a foot in his groin.

Lillich ignored his reaction and turned to Sumner. She pointed to two men standing by the fence.

"Those two fishermen found the body washed up in the weeds next to the bank. The water is more of a ditch than a bayou. The fishermen say it works like an overflow when Clear Creek is high. They think the body floated down from the creek and got stuck in the weeds." Lillich scrunched her eyes when she finished.

"But you don't think so. Right, Doc?" Sumner asked.

"I think she was dumped here. The water's not deep enough for her to have floated in."

"Can you take a guess as to the cause of death?"

"Both wrists slashed. Looks like suicide, but I'll know more when we get her on a table."

I said, "If she killed herself, she sure didn't get up and drive here and then throw herself into the ditch. Why would someone not call it in instead of dumping the body?"

"We figure that out and we'll be on the way to solving this tragedy," Sumner added.

One of the responding officers spoke, "Is it okay to release the fishermen?"

Lott glanced over his shoulder at the men, "What were they doing here anyway?"

"Casting for bait," the officer replied. "They sell mullet and mud minnows to the marinas."

When the officer confirmed they had their statements and contact info, Lott let them go.

"Can we check the body," Sumner said to Lillich.

"Okay. The fishermen carried the body here so the scene's already compromised. We'll get her fingerprints and a DNA sample as soon as we get to the morgue. Maybe we'll get lucky and find her in the system.

"The black roots beneath her peroxided hair as well as her pubic area, her brown skin tones and deep brown eyes, all tell me she is probably Hispanic. Plus, the big tat across her shoulders looks like a poor rendition of the Virgin Mary. The dark circles and pouches under her eyes belie her age. Probably early twenties. Whoever this poor girl was, my guess is, she had a rough life."

Lillich paused, then, "Do any of the tattoos on her arms look familiar, maybe gang tats?"

Lott and Sumner both shook their heads no.

Sumner said to Lillich. "Any guesses on how long she's been in the water or when she died?"

"Well," Lillich mused, "the cool water this time of year slows the deterioration rate. Rigor has already dissipated and bloating has begun. My guess is she's been in the water around twelve hours or so and has been dead two to four days."

"So someone must have kept her for a while before they dumped her here," Sumner said.

"Exactly," Lillich added.

I tossed a thought into the conversation, "Would a spouse or boyfriend have gone to the trouble to bring her here? Or even a friend or relative?

Lott said, "Plenty of weird people and strange happenings in this crazy world."

"But if Parker is right," Sumner added, "think about who that leaves."

"Her pimp?" Lott mused.

"Most likely."

I turned away, feeling the officers' and ME's expertise in dealing with a dead body were beyond my limits. I could add nothing and my roiling stomach was giving me fits.

A piece of me dies each time I view death. The vision of this poor girl's young body sent another stake through my heart. But I would be remiss if I didn't admit the relief that coursed through my bones knowing it wasn't Akemi or Maria.

***

We returned to the island where I offered to buy Sumner's lunch, but she begged off claiming paperwork. A few minutes later I pulled to a stop at Harry's house and found Rudy's truck parked by the big oak tree.

I hurried to the front door, knocked lightly and entered, not waiting for a response. Harry and Rudy sat at the kitchen table munching a fresh batch of apricot scones and listening to the police radio bleating out calls.

Harry said, "Parker, glad you came. I spoke with an officer who was at the scene and he said you were there. When the call came on the radio about the body, I don't mind telling you it scared the bejesus out of us. Thank God, it wasn't Akemi or Maria."

"Did you hear anything about who she was?" Rudy asked, searching for any information he could get.

"No, but Dr. Lillich will take prints and DNA at the morgue."

"Oh, good," Harry said. "Lillich is a friend of mine. I'll get the scoop later."

I grabbed a Shiner out of the refrigerator and took a swig, wondering if there was anyone on the police force or associated with it—other than Woolly Kroton—that Harry didn't know. He'd probably done free wills and/or divorces for half of them.

Harry said, "Rudy and I have been discussing what we could do to help find the girls. Galveston Crime Stoppers set up a $50,000 reward. Rudy and I contributed another $25,000 each, so it's now up to $100,000.

"I hope that rattles some bones," Rudy added.

I said to Rudy, "Increasing the reward was a good move. Someone must know something. Any other thoughts?"

"Nothing really, damn it." he answered. "Best idea so far is to keep listening to the police traffic on Harry's radio. See what the cops find out. This is really frustrating. I am used to running with the ball, not just sitting and waiting."

Rudy turned to me with a bit of hopefulness. "So what have you and Detective Sumner learned?"

I mentioned the meeting with the kid at Julie's school and the van he said he saw.

Rudy's eyes sparked. He dropped the half-eaten scone on his plate and stood, his hands nervously flexing at his side. I would have thought he was getting ready for a karate chop, but he was a jujitsu man.

"Have they found the van?"

"Not that I know of."

"A dark van, no signs, maybe several years old. Anything else? License plate?"

"That's all I know."

"I'm outta here," he said, already halfway to the hallway.

After Rudy cleared the front door, Harry said, "Well, at least he has a new tact to follow, driving around searching for that van. Anything to keep him busy. I thought I was going to have to fight him for the radio."

"Maybe you should turn it off for a while. Tell him it's broken and being repaired."

"Really, Parker. I've been an attorney for sixty years. Never once told a falsehood and I'm not starting now."

"Want me to take it out on the sidewalk and drop it?"

# Chapter Twenty-Nine

## Friday Afternoon

---

On the drive out FM 3005 to The Garhole, I glimpsed a man mowing a field with a large tractor. Grackles and cattle egrets swooped behind the mower, eagerly grabbing the newly disturbed grasshoppers.

The simple life: a man taking care of his pasture, his property. I wondered if he ever thought about the sixteen young girls who had gone missing on I-45 South in the seventies and eighties or if he even knew about the all-hands search for Akemi and Maria.

My first priority was to see Akemi and Maria safely home, back in their daily routine with their mothers and friends at school. That done, I could return to *my* simple life: dinners with Kathy and Julie, bantering with cankerous Bully and Neddie, and sitting on my deck enjoying the sudden cracks of lightning and swirling wind as a thunderstorm moved over West Bay.

When Sumner buzzed, I put my phone on speaker and set it on the dash.

"What's up, detective?"

"I could have strangled Juju for that crappy kumbaya comment to Dr. Lillich. He knows how hard I've worked to get where I am. And the same for Dr. Lillich. Wait 'til I get my hands on him."

"He'll enjoy that."

"What?"

"You getting your hands on him."

"Parker, you smart ass."

She paused.

"I've got good news and not so good news."

"Give me the good news first, I need a lift."

"We put a BOLO out on the van the kid described, and Houston Police found one like it in the parking lot of a hospital out on I-10 East. The security man riding around in his golf cart got suspicious and called it in."

"That was quick."

"We aren't always that lucky. The plates were stolen, but the police ran the vehicle ID number. It was boosted two weeks ago in Southwest Houston. The van belonged to the owner of a flower shop. The guy wanted to know if his magnetic signs were still on the van, said he paid over $500 for them."

"So how do you know it's the right van?"

"Police found a broken zip tie in the back."

"Aw, shit…I guess that's the not-so-good-news."

"Right. The girls could be in Houston or headed anywhere, to parts unknown."

"Aw, shit again."

"The van's on a trailer enroute to Galveston. We'll go over it tire to roof looking for prints and DNA."

"How long will that take?"

"Chief Puryear's got a fire under everyone, so the rush is on. You can help."

"How?"

"You know Señora Santos and Maggie Peterson well enough to scoot by their homes and pick up some things with the girls' fingerprints and DNA on them. Hairbrushes work well. Sometimes the brush pulls out a strand with the follicle attached. Get them to me ASAP. I could send a cop, but I don't want to scare the families."

***

I stopped at Red's Grocery, picked up another treat for the dog and called Alicia Santos to verify she was home from her house cleaning job. I turned the truck around and a few minutes later crossed Broadway on Forty-Sixth Street. A few blocks up, I passed the store where the same men loitered outside, this time hugging quart bottles of beer in paper sacks.

The girl with tight shorts that I'd seen before strolled casually down the block. She looked my way and gave a friendly come-on wave. The bedraggled woman with the grocery cart wasn't on the block. Curious, I pulled to the curb.

The young girl glanced back at one of the men at the store. He seemed to nod. She crossed the street to my truck.

"Hi," she said. "My name's Rhonda. Wanna party?"

Beneath the tight shorts and sagging halter top was a walking pencil, a hundred pounds of loose skin including a rash on her neck she'd tried to cover with heavy makeup. The rash was either psoriasis or caused by meth. I'd put money on the latter. Her dilated pupils bounced around like ping pong balls in play, a sure sign of increased dopamine in the central nervous system. Her smile showed blackened teeth on her bottom jaw. My guess about her meth use was probably correct. Heavy methamphetamine use causes dry mouth. Users tend to suck on a lot of sugary drinks, rotting their teeth.

"Well thanks, but I was looking for the woman who pushes the grocery cart. I may have a job for her."

"Joy? She's in the hospital. Passed out on the street yesterday."

I shoved twenty dollars into Rhonda's palm for her trouble. As I pulled away from the curb, she walked toward the man at the store waving the bill.

Luckily, my old truck splashed through the mud holes in the alley without crushing a bottle and blowing a tire. The big pit bull raced to the end of the chain again, but this time the dog greeted me with a soft whine and wagging tail. I tossed my new best friend another pork chop.

Señora Santos greeted me on the porch wearing a red housedress with a picture of a pretty young senorita in a flowing skirt as if ready for the Sunday promenade at the Zocalo. Red blush on her cheeks matched her dress.

Santos wore her hair in the same two columns of braids that hung to her waist. It appeared she was doing everything she could to stay upbeat. New candles on the Our Lady of Guadalupe shrine were lit, a sign of the hope that she never let go out. But still, perhaps preparing for bad news, her eyes teared when I entered her home.

"Good afternoon, Señora," I said in Spanish.

"Please come in, Señor Mcleod. Have you brought me news about my Maria?" she replied in her language.

"I hope I didn't interrupt your prayers."

"My prayers are continual."

"Señora Santos, do you know about fingerprints and DNA?"

Her hand went to her mouth, "No, no, don't tell me, please…."

After kicking myself for being so indelicate, I said, "Please forgive me, Señora. I didn't mean to upset you. I came to tell you the police may have found the van Maria was kidnapped in, and we just need some help from you."

I explained about the fingerprints and DNA and asked for

Maria's hairbrush. I followed her to the bathroom and gingerly placed the brush in one of the plastic bags I'd picked up at the convenience store.

I left the Señora sitting at the shrine and weeping softly.

***

I crossed back over Broadway and drove to Rudy and Maggie's house, relieved that Rudy's truck was not in the driveway. Maggie invited me in.

She said, "Rudy called. I am so relieved the body wasn't Akemi or Maria. I heard it was a young woman. Sad…so sad. I'll pray for her."

She guided me to a chair while she took the couch. I explained about the police finding the van in Houston and the fingerprint and DNA samples.

"So finding the van was good news?"

"Yes, if the fingerprints and DNA are in the system, we will have our first good lead. We can search the perp's record and known associates. Maybe find the bastard."

When I apologized for the language, she chuckled. "Don't fret, Parker. I heard a lot worse than that in the army. I could probably match you word for word."

I followed her to the bathroom and placed Akemi's brush in the other plastic bag. I thanked her and turned to leave.

"Parker," she said, her eyes boring into mine. "You *will* keep me informed? If it's bad news, tell me first so I can comfort Rudy when I tell him. Promise?"

"Maggie, I…I…will do what I can, but Rudy is making contacts all over, so…."

She nodded like she understood.

***

I met Sumner in the station parking lot and handed off the brushes.

"What now?" I asked.

"You know the drill. The van is here and there're already dusting it. We'll run the prints immediately. Should have DNA results by morning. Cross your fingers."

I held up crossed fingers on both hands.

"Get some rest," she said. "I'll call if anything breaks."

On the way back to The Garhole, knowing Kathy was at the ER, I called her on her cell.

"Hey Kathy, sorry to bother you. Did EMS bring in an unconscious homeless woman yesterday? I think her first name is Joy." I explained how I knew about her and waited for Kathy's reaction.

"Parker, everything I do is ruled by HIPAA laws, strictly confidential. You know that."

"Of course, sorry. Take care."

I ended the call thinking I would have to ply her with wine for the answer.

Not knowing if the beer truck had made it yet, I stopped back at Red's for a sixpack of Shiner Bock. For some reason, his cooler seemed to keep beer colder than mine, or maybe that was just an excuse to take a break and catch up on West Beach gossip.

Sure enough, two women in front of me in line were carrying on about someone named Ed cheating on his wife. Fortunately, I didn't know anyone named Ed. When the ladies realized I was listening, they gave me a disgusted look like I'd been purposely eavesdropping and they changed the subject. How did they know?

Out in the truck, I cracked open a cold beer and slipped it into a brown paper sack. I knew every cop that made rounds on West Beach but there was no sense in testing my newfound fame. I cranked the engine and my cell buzzed.

Sumner spoke before I opened my mouth, "Have you passed the Sea Isle exit yet?"

"No, just stopped at Red's. What's up?"

"Detective Moss and his team are busting a pedophile. If you hurry, you might make it. Keep your fingers crossed."

"What's the address?"

"Bay Street. You'll see the patrol cars."

The sun was over the yardarm by the time I pulled out of Red's. I turned on the headlights and pressed the gas pedal.

Patrol cars blocked both ends of Bay Street. Sergeant Pulley stood by his car and waved me over.

"They caught the bastard red-handed," he said.

"Any sign of the girls?"

"Haven't heard yet."

"Well, at least it's one more piece of garbage off the street."

"You got that right."

"Sergeant Pulley, I meant to tell you, I really liked the way you handled that situation with Woolly Kroton in Rudy and Maggie's front yard."

"I didn't really do anything," he answered.

"I know, that's what I liked about it." We both laughed.

"Have you considered getting assigned permanently to the West Beach patrol? Not much crime out here except a few potheads. And I cook up some pretty good stuff at The Garhole."

"I rotate and get West Beach some. Like when Rudy had the rifle out by the sand dunes."

"How about for your regular beat?"

"I'm getting close to retirement and I'm kinda tired of separating two drunks having a domestic. Seems peaceful out here, that's for sure. Ever catch any fish off that dock of yours?"

"Yes, and it would be a nice place to take your afternoon coffee break. I might even fry up some donuts."

He patted his stomach. "Like I need that. Anyway, I don't have the pull."

"Maybe Harry Stein can help?"

"Harry did my will, didn't charge me a dime. Good man."

Wow, I thought. Another good deed by Harry.

Pulley said, "I've been married to my sweetheart, Thelma, for twenty-three years this weekend. It's been good, really good."

I smiled.

"Is Harry still playing pinocle with the chief on Friday nights?"

"Yes, want me to mention it to Harry?"

"Well," Pulley said, rubbing his neck. "If there's some way to keep me out of it. I can't be seen going around protocol."

"Let's swap phone numbers. I'll call you when I hear something."

"Sounds good," Pulley said. He glanced at his watch, grimaced, "Damn. The first forty-eight are almost up."

We both knew what that meant. Trying to lighten the load for both of us, I said, "You've been watching too much TV."

"God, I hope so."

Two officers came down the stairs, one carrying a laptop and the other holding what looked like a stack of photographs. A police photographer with a camera strapped to his neck came out behind them, shaking his head in disgust.

When the detective came down, I introduced myself as working with Sumner on the missing girls' case. His nametag read "R Moss."

"Yeah, Detective Sumner told me you were on the way," Moss said. "We tossed his house. Did a quick search on his computer. Loaded with kid porn but nothing on the missing girls. I'd sure like to see the prick stumble down the stairs and break his sorry neck. Between the photos on his bedroom wall and the computer, we've got enough to smother him under the jail for a long time. The bastard probably used them for whacking material, if the asshole could even get it up."

I envisioned a short, squirrely man with thick glasses and pimply face. A guy who missed his high school prom because he was too embarrassed to go alone. But to my surprise, the man who eased down the stairs with his hands cuffed behind him was anything but nerdy. He appeared about thirty, well-built and sharply dressed in slacks and golf shirt. Professional type. He could have been a banker or lawyer or Indian chief. But he chose to be a pervert.

The officer behind him refused to help him down, probably wishing the same thing as Detective Moss. I was hoping for a little push by the cop, myself. No one would have noticed in the gathering darkness.

"One thing this search for the girls has done," Moss said. "With extra men on the team, this is our second pedi in two days. I'd like to see more."

***

Back at The Garhole, the fishing lights were going full blast. It wasn't quite dark, but Bully was already on the dock in his wheelchair with a rod and reel in his hands and the afghan over his lap. October was always a good fishing month as the shallow waters of the bay cooled down at night and kept the trout moving around. If fishing was good, a few customers would come from town to try their luck, which increased beer sales.

Neddie was wiping down the counter trying to make himself look useful. He paused and shoved a fresh stick of gum in his mouth. I wanted to tell him to at least keep his mouth closed when chewing but decided not to waste my breath. At his age, admonitions passed over his head like darts thrown at a board.

I glanced in the trash bin at the end of the bar. Not surprisingly, at least twelve miscellaneous beer cans filled the bin. One of Neddie's old tricks was changing beer brands to make it appear several customers had come in, a ploy to disguise his insatiable thirst. Of course, I'd figured out his game long ago, and as usual I smiled to myself and let it go.

I grabbed a couple of beers and climbed the stairs to my Adirondack chair to watch the moonrise. I finished the beer and sauntered inside my private sanctuary. It was too early to sleep so I turned on the lamp by my bed. I put my arms behind my head, lay on the pillow and stared at the ceiling. With the cool October breeze outside, I left the window open, hoping to hear the comforting wail of my buddy the coyote somewhere out on the lonesome prairie.

I thought about the first forty-eight hours having passed. What were Maggie and Rudy feeling? Maybe Sumner had been right not to dash their hopes because of the clock. But it didn't help me, and it sure didn't help Akemi and Maria. Where were the girls and what was happening to them? I closed my eyes and felt a slow drain of energy, as though my body was emptying of all thought and emotion. I struggled to keep what was left but couldn't. And then I was out.

# Chapter Thirty

## Friday Night

---

When Hector announced he'd never *had* an Asian girl, Akemi caught Juan's eye in a plea for help. Juan responded by sending Hector into Texas City for groceries.

As soon as the door slammed, Akemi's stomach started to settle. She mouthed a silent "thank you" to Juan. He ignored her response. She hoped the contorted lines on his face meant he was still wrestling with what to do about her and Maria. At least the ice was beginning to melt, she told herself.

After Hector left, Juan shuffled the girls out of the kitchen into their room. He followed behind, locked the kitchen door and crossed into the extra bedroom. He came back with a small rolling bag and flipped on the overhead light.

Akemi glimpsed the two Hispanic girls on their mats watching Juan. Sarah lay on her mat rolled into the fetal position, facing away from them.

Juan rolled the bag to Akemi. "This was Juanita's," he said. "The clothes may be too big, but there are things you can use. There is soap and shampoo, a hairbrush. I will get you both toothbrushes and pick up another bag so each of you have one. Get you more clothes too." Juan left the light on and stepped back into the other bedroom.

As soon as Juan left the room, Akemi scooted over to check on Sarah, still in the fetal position. She was holding her stomach with both hands and moaning. When she mumbled something, Akemi leaned in close.

"I…can't…sleep," Sarah said, her voice so low Akemi could barely hear her. "It…hurts too much."

Akemi placed her hand on Sarah's forehead and almost freaked out at her clammy skin. Sarah huffed in short, rapid breaths and her lips showed a bluish tinge. Akemi lifted Sarah's blouse. She swallowed hard as she saw the dark blue and purple bruise that ran across the entire width of her midsection.

From her health class, Akemi remembered clammy skin and rapid breaths could be a sign of shock, deadly if left untreated.

Juan came back with towels for all the girls. "You best shower while Hector is gone," he said.

Maria said, "But what if he comes back when we are—"

"He won't," Juan broke in. "I know him. He will steal enough from the grocery money to shoot pool and drink beer at one of the cantinas."

Juan put a bulb in the bathroom light socket then stopped at the kitchen door. "I will leave the bedroom light on for you. Don't worry," he said. "I will be here cooking dinner."

Akemi said to Maria, "I think Juan is beginning to soften. He knows Hector likes to watch everyone shower, but he's letting us do it while Hector is gone."

"We should keep working on him," Maria answered. "Let's talk to the other two girls and see if they will help."

"And Sarah too," Akemi said.

After the two other girls traipsed to the bathroom, Akemi went to Sarah and tried to get her up so she could shower too, but she refused to move. Akemi went back to her mat and waited for the girls to finish.

A few minutes later, they came out freshly showered. The

scent of soap and shampoo wafted toward Akemi as they passed. She noticed the girls were dressed in the same tight shorts and shirts they'd worn the previous night.

Akemi grabbed the rolling bag, hoping she and Maria could shower before Hector returned. While Maria showered, Akemi studied her face in the mirror for the first time since she had been captured. Just as she feared, her left cheek had turned a strange combination of red and purple. A throbbing pain still radiated across her jaw.

After Maria finished showering, Akemi stepped in. She held her upturned face to the shower stream and luxuriated in the lukewarm water. It felt like heaven. She didn't want the feeling to end. But worrying that Hector might return any moment, she hurriedly washed her hair twice and scrubbed every part of her body.

They found clean panties and shorts and shirts in Juanita's bag. All the clothes were too large, but they put them on anyway. Akemi knocked on the kitchen door and Juan came in and removed the bathroom light bulb.

Sometime later, the kitchen door flew open. Hector marched in, scowling that the bedroom light was on. He pounded his hand against the switch, turned it off and went back into the kitchen. His voice carried through the wall.

"Damn you, Juan. I told you I control the lights. Never touch them again."

Juan said, "I had to check on Sarah. If she dies, El Tigre will blame us. She doesn't look good. We should get her to a doctor."

"That's impossible and you know it."

"We could drop her off at the front of the hospital."

"And she would lead the cops straight here. No. We will let her die if she's going to. It's Tigre's problem. He's the one who beat her, not us."

Maria translated for Akemi and then added, "We cannot let Sarah die, Akemi. We must do something."

"I agree," Akemi said, proud that Maria was getting her courage back. "Maybe the other girls can help us too."

She padded over to the girls sitting on their mats. Akemi whispered, hoping the girls spoke enough English to understand her.

"Come sit with us."

The older girl said, *"No habla Inglés."*

Akemi waved Maria over and explained what she wanted. Maria spoke Spanish to the girls and back to Akemi in English. They all trod back to Akemi and Maria's mats and sat down. Akemi asked their names.

"My name is Gabriela," said the older girl in the halter top. She put her arm around the younger girl. "And this is Sayda."

"Hello, Sayda," Akemi said in English. "You have a very pretty name."

When Maria translated, Sayda lips broke into a partial smile that faded quickly. Akemi had noticed their brown-toned skin and long black hair before but not their huge brown eyes, high cheekbones and slightly rounded faces.

"You look so much alike," Akemi said. "Are you sisters?"

"Yes," Gabriela answered, a proud inflection in her voice. She straightened, causing her breasts to bulge in her halter top.

"I am sixteen and my sister is fourteen," she said.

Sayda sat silent and expressionless as if in a daze, holding Gabriela's hand.

Nana had told Akemi that girls started to grow and fill out more after puberty. She subconsciously moved her hands to feel her own breasts. She dropped her hands.

"Where are you from?" Akemi asked.

"Guatemala," Gabriela said.

Akemi remembered photos in her social studies book of pretty Guatemalan girls wearing brightly colored dresses with stick figures on them. The teacher had told her they were copies of ancient drawings.

"Do you have one of those pretty Mayan dresses?" she asked.

"We each had one our *mamá* made for us," Gabriela replied. "Mine was blue. Sayda's was red. But we had to leave them in Guatemala."

Gabriela teared up. Akemi wondered if the memory of her mother had flashed through her mind. Gabriela said something to Maria that Akemi couldn't understand.

Maria said to Akemi, "They don't like to talk about their home. It was bad for them. They lived in a small mountain village. Their parents were murdered."

Akemi reached out and took Gabriela's hand. "I am so sorry, Gabriela."

A tear ran down Gabriela's cheek.

"We just want to be your friends," Maria said.

Gabriela lifted her eyes. "After our *mamá* and *papá* were killed, we didn't know what to do. We have an older sister, but she is very poor and lives with her *esposo* and four little ones in another village. She could not help us. A man came by our village. His last name was also Lopez, like ours. He said he was our cousin and he would take care of us. In *El Norte* we would be safe, away from the gangs. He brought us here."

"How long have you been here?" Akemi asked.

"We don't know. We asked Sarah. She said several weeks.

But we started making money for El Tigre pretty quick."

Akemi's heart sank. What did *pretty quick* mean? This was Maria and her third night here. Were they getting close?

"We noticed you have rolling bags. Are all your clothes in the bags?"

"Yes, we have night clothes for when we go out and sleep clothes for here. We keep all our things in the bags. Juan taught us how to use the washing machine in the back room. Hector gave us red paint for our cheeks and lipstick to make us pretty at night."

"Did Hector give you the bag because you are getting ready to leave here?"

"We don't know. Sarah said everyone gets a bag and El Tigre moves girls when he is ready. She said we will all move soon to a place with rooms in the back. Maybe to the *cantina* where we go at night."

Akemi glanced at Maria. She could tell by the fear in her eyes that she'd gotten the message. The word *soon* had scared them both. What did that mean? How much time did they have?

Sayda sat transfixed as though she were somewhere else. Gabriela said, "Sayda never laughs anymore. She doesn't eat much and barely talks to me."

Akemi decided this was the opening she needed. "Have you thought about escaping, getting free?"

"Free?" Gabriela said. "Juan and Hector take care of us. The man who said he was our cousin brought us to them when we had no place to go, no food to eat. We give them the money we make, and they feed us and give us a place to sleep. They are our friends. Hector taught us how to attract the men. They like these."

She put her hands under her breasts and pushed them up.

"Sayda told Hector she cries when the men poke her. It hurts. He taught her how to use her mouth. Sayda says the men like that."

Akemi sat stunned. She turned her head. 'Be brave,' she told herself.

"You seem worried about Sayda," Akemi observed.

Sayda continued to stare across the room with vacant eyes. Gabriela lowered her head and cried softly.

"We heard El Tigre talking about flyers with mine and Maria's pictures on them and a reward for letting the police know where we are. Have you heard about this?"

"Reward?" She shook her head. "What is reward? I don't know this word."

Maria said, "It's money you get for telling the police how to find us. All you have to do when you go out tonight is dial 911 on the telephone. Sarah saw the flyers too. She said the reward is $50,000."

Gabriela said, "I don't know how much that is."

Akemi paused to think of a way to explain the value of $50,000. Frustrated, she pointed to Sarah moaning on her mat and changed the subject.

"Aren't you worried that could happen to you?" she asked. She pointed to her cheek. "Or what Hector did to me?"

"That happened because El Tigre and Hector got mad at you," Gabriela said. "You were mean to them."

Gabriela pulled two small caramel candies wrapped in wax paper from her pocket. She gave one to Sayda who eagerly took it from her sister's hand.

"See what they do for us?" Gabriela said. "Hector knows what we like. He loves us."

# Chapter Thirty-One

## Friday Night

---

I had just dozed off when my coyote friend awakened me with his harrowing howl. I checked my watch. It was still early, so I meandered out to the deck.

Fish were popping all around in the beams from the lights. Bully's line was out in the water, but was he fishing or dozing? I edged to the railing and looked down to see his chin on his chest. I knew Bully didn't care if he caught a fish or not. As long as he was able to smoke cigars and gaze out at the peaceful water, he was a happy camper.

I moved to my Adirondack chair and lay my head back to listen to the coyote and gaze at the moon. I thought about howling myself just for the hell of it. But the stress of the hunt had worn me down. I lay back for a while, thinking about the girls and where they were. And then it hit me.

How could one man grab two girls, stuff them in the back of a van and drive off? Not unless he had more than two arms. And the way Rudy described Akemi, she wouldn't go without a fight. There had to be two perpetrators, maybe three including the driver.

I hustled down the stairs and reached for the wall phone to call Sumner then realized I didn't know her number. I got my cell phone from the truck and punched 'send' as her name appeared. She answered on the first ring.

"Parker, I'm in my favorite bar at the Tremont House

having an atrociously expensive glass of cabernet sauvignon. This better be good."

"On a detective's salary?"

"Lieutenant Lott is on his way to pick up the tab."

"Lieutenant? What happened to JuJu?"

"After his faux pas with Dr. Lilly this afternoon, he is trying to make amends. If he's lucky, after a Grey Goose martini or two and pecan-crusted redfish at Rudy and Paco's, he may get to Julius again, but probably not JuJu. Now why did you call? What brilliant idea has passed through your foggy brain tonight?"

"Two men."

"What?"

"It took at least two men to grab Akemi and Maria. One couldn't have gotten them both in the van and driven off. There had to be a driver and at least one in the back to watch them."

"Damn," she said.

"I know. You're wondering why you didn't think of it."

"Shut up…here comes Lott. We'll wrestle with it and call you back."

Five minutes later, my phone buzzed.

"Well, you've ruined my first night off in a week. But you're right, it makes sense. Which brings up another point."

"What?"

"Pedophiles sometimes share photos with each other, but they normally work alone. I think we can narrow down the kidnappers to…."

"To what?"

"Hold on, Lott is trying to tell me something."

I waited for her to come back on the phone.

"Okay, Lott says it sounds like traffickers except they

don't normally kidnap school girls off the street. There are plenty of runaways to pick from. They also like to bring their own girls in from Mexico and points south. Unless...."

"Unless what?"

"There was a special situation like...."

"Like one of their regular girls committed suicide and they needed a quick replacement for some reason."

"Exactly. But what reason?" she asked.

"I have no idea."

"Well, you've already ruined my night, so I'll call that David Mendez kid at McDonald's and see if he's remembered anything more, maybe enough for a sketch. Can you call Kathy and see if she's available?"

"Okay call me back. That is, when you've finished with Juju. Did you get the hot-sheet rate at the Tremont?"

"Screw you, McLeod."

***

I buzzed Kathy. "Do you mean tonight?" she asked. "I'm at the hospital working."

"Time is critical, Kathy."

"Well, Julie is at a friend's house, so I don't have to worry about her. Call me back when you know something for sure."

A couple of minutes later, Sumner called back.

"I got hold of David at McDonald's and told him to hang tight. Did you get Kathy?"

"Yes, but she's on duty at the hospital."

"I can handle that. Meet us at the station."

***

I jumped into some clothes and pulled into the police parking lot thirty minutes later. Kathy was just going up the steps still dressed in her green scrubs, her hair tucked under a ball cap. The scrubs fit just right. I thought about plans for the next couple of nights with Kathy and smiled.

Detective Sumner met Kathy at the top of the steps. She gave her a big hug and said, "Thanks for doing this on short notice."

"The chief himself called the hospital administrator with the urgency of the situation. I moved as fast as I could, but I still had to go by the house for my sketch pad and pencils."

"We'll have to wait a few minutes for David," Sumner added. "His boss at McDonald's said he was short a couple of workers and needed him. I wanted to go over there and whack the prick on the head. Fortunately, David called back and said he told the boss he knew the girls and was coming anyway."

The three of us moved to Sumner's office, everyone's nerves on edge. Sumner strummed a pencil on her desktop, Kathy wrenched her hands and I was about to go nuts. I didn't know how a sketch artist worked so I asked Kathy.

She thought for a moment. "Well, the first thing I learned was that no image done from memory is ever precise. But if it helps identify and catch the perp, then an imperfect sketch becomes perfect."

"You must be really proud of your work," I said.

"The national success rate is thirty percent. Mine's a little higher so, yes, that makes me feel good. I keep a copy of every sketch. If the perp is identified and arrested, I compare his mug shot to my sketch. Seeing my mistakes allows me to improve my work.

"The toughest ones are when the witness was the victim and was severely traumatized. I have to make myself focus and not start bawling."

"How do you start?" I asked.

"It almost always begins with the witness saying something like, 'It happened so quick. I don't remember much.' I hear a lot of that kind of equivocation.

"But if I let the defeatist attitude get to me, I could never do a sketch. No witness thinks I can draw the likeness. A lot of the cops think that too, but I just plug along."

David arrived and Sumner escorted him to an interview room. They visited for a moment and she came out.

She said, "I was just trying to get him relaxed. He looked like a Mexican jumping bean, couldn't sit still."

When Kathy entered the room, David had already sucked down a soda and was chewing on an ice cube. Sumner and I watched and listened through a one-way mirror. Kathy spoke so softly; I thought I would have to pinch myself to stay awake.

She introduced herself and said, "It's okay David, just relax. We'll do the best we can. No one expects a perfect image but anything you remember helps."

She invited David to talk about himself, sports, his job at McDonald's, his girlfriend. The tightness in his face calmed and he began chatting amiably. Soon they were both laughing.

Then Kathy said, "Thank you, David, for coming in to help us."

"It beats cleaning toilets at McDonald's," he said. They both laughed again. David added, "I don't know why you think I can do this. I only saw him for a second and it was kinda dark out."

Kathy smiled. She positioned her sketch pad on an easel and picked up a pencil. Not wanting David to be staring at the drawing while she worked, she placed the easel at an angle. She situated her body far enough away to not invade his personal space.

She asked a few questions about the shape of the suspect's face. Then she asked David to close his eyes so he could visualize better.

He twitched. "Do I have to?"

Kathy continued her soft voice and gentle smile. "It really helps sometimes, David. Just try it, okay? Keep them closed for a few moments and then we'll start the drawing."

David nodded and closed his eyes.

"Did he have any facial hair, like a mustache or beard?"

David paused, then said, "I…I…don't think so."

"How would you describe his hair?"

"Uh…pulled back in a ponytail, I think. When he drove by, the tail was hanging down in the back like to almost his shoulders."

"Did he look at you?"

David flinched, but kept his eyes closed. "For a second, enough to scare the crap out of me."

"Earlier, you told Detective Sumner you thought his skin was kind of dark."

"Sorry," he said, opening his eyes, "Was that a question?"

"Oh, sorry, David. Yes, that was a question."

"I don't think he was a white guy or a black guy. I mean his hair was black. Maybe a Mexican like me. I already told that to Detective Sumner."

When David started to fidget in his chair, Kathy stopped the questioning and said, "I'm getting thirsty, David. How about another Coke?"

"Okay," he said. "But I'd rather have a Dr. Pepper."

David's shoulders seemed to drop, tension easing. He added, "Do they have any cookies in that machine out there?"

"I'll be right back," Kathy answered. On her way to the

vending machine, she stuck her head in our room. "I think it's going well," she said. "The key is patience."

After a short break with more laughter, Kathy resumed the interview. She asked about the face: Was it round, long, skinny, wide? Then his nose, ears, eyes and mouth. She showed him FBI drawings for each part of the witnesses' face until he agreed on one. He remembered nothing about his clothing.

She put a few final touches on the drawing and then turned the easel so David could see what she'd done.

"Does this resemble the man driving the van?"

David stared at the drawing. "I…think so," he said.

"Any changes?"

David shook his head no.

# Chapter Thirty-Two

Friday Night

---

After the interview, Kathy offered to take David home. She said she felt close enough that she could ask more questions to test his memory.

I caught her at the door. "Earlier you said Julie was at a friend's house. I thought her dad was picking her up for the weekend. I was coming over tonight."

"Oh, Parker. I am so sorry. With all this going on I completely forgot. Julie's dad called and canceled. Some kind of emergency. One of his usual antics, either a blond or a redhead. I am as disappointed as you. How about taking us both to lunch tomorrow?"

"That's a deal."

"And just so you know, Donna is really pissed at you about the crappy remarks you've been making about her relationship with Julius. You'd better cool it if you don't want to get black-balled off the team."

"Can't take the teasing, huh?"

Kathy thoughtfully continued, "There is something you need to know. When Donna was a teenager, she used to babysit her seven-year-old cousin, Charla. One night, Donna wanted to go to a football game and, in desperation, Charla's mother turned to a neighbor who'd been friendly with Charla. The guy was a pedophile—abused the little girl. The father stormed over to the man's house and shot him dead."

"What happened to the father?"

"Got off, self-defense."

"Really?"

"His attorney said, 'Hey, it's Texas.' But Donna took the blame, never forgave herself. She still carries the guilt."

"That why she's a cop in Juvenile?"

"Quick thinking, Parker."

That left me feeling pretty low. I'd been out of line teasing Sumner. She had a big enough sack of rocks to carry without me dumping more in.

I stopped back at Lieutenant's Lott's office and found him holding a copy of the drawing.

"This is being printed as we speak," he said, handing me the copy. "I called the head of Crime Stoppers as soon as Kathy got here. He's been gathering volunteers. A bunch of them are waiting downstairs: off-duty firemen, cops, Rotary Club members, Red Cross, you name it. Folks are going all out. The sketch will be plastered in every convenience store and bar in Galveston County by midnight."

A detective working on Lott's team knocked on the outside of the door and entered the room.

"We got the fingerprints back on the van found in Houston. Prints from the van match the prints on the girls' hairbrushes."

The news hit hard. The deflated look on Sumner's face told me what she was thinking. If the girls had been taken to Houston, the chances of finding them in that jungle of Hispanic *barrios* had just dropped precipitously.

"What about the other prints in the van?" Lott asked.

"Several sets on the steering wheel and passenger side but none are in the system. So many of these traffickers are up from Mexico and Central America, we can't keep up with them."

"But," I interjected, "all the more reason to suspect the girls were kidnapped by traffickers. What about a fast, hard check of the cantinas? Maybe we can learn something. Isn't that where most of the girls work?"

"Hell, there must be a thousand of them in the Houston metroplex," Lott said.

"I know you're exaggerating, lieutenant."

"Maybe," he said, rubbing his beard. "But not by much."

"Still," Parker added, "there's a chance they dumped the van in Houston to throw us off. Akemi and Maria could be at some hidey-hole in Galveston County."

Sumner looked at Lott, "It's worth a try. Up for a late-night swing through the joints around here?"

"Are you asking me for a date?"

"It's cheaper than the dinner you were going to buy me."

Lott said they would take the ferry to Bolivar Peninsula, hit the bars there first and then come back to scour the island.

When Lott and Sumner left to change clothes into something less obvious, I thought, what else do I have to do? But I didn't want to search by myself, and asking Rudy was out of the question. Atticus Lott had said he'd help anyway he could, so I called him and explained the situation.

"If they're checking Bolivar and the city, that leaves a hell of a lot of Galveston County on the mainland," he said. "Come on by, we'll take a looky-loo. Listen to some good music, maybe a twirl around the floor."

# Chapter Thirty-Three

## Friday Night

---

I passed over the causeway and eased into Atticus Lott's driveway in Bayou Vista. He met me downstairs dressed in jeans, a faded blue work shirt and a Houston Astros ball cap. He'd pulled the cap low over his brow.

He noticed me staring and said, "Most of the guys in these bars are big Astros fans. Hell, half the team members are from somewhere in the Caribbean."

He got closer and continued, "Take a good look at this face." He pointed to an area just in front of his nose and made a circle with his finger.

What the hell was this about? His eyes were still brown and his dark hair wavy. His beard with the gray flecks still covered his cheeks.

"Okay, so you haven't trimmed your beard today. So what?"

"Don't be a smart ass. I'm talking about my skin color. I spend a lot of time in the sun fishing and working outside. I'm dark enough to pass."

"Pass for what?"

"A Hispanic.... Damn, McLeod, get with it! Take a good look in your truck mirror. Yours is the last Anglo face you will see tonight. Thanks to you, they'll spot us for cops as soon as we hit the door. Best if you don't go in anywhere."

"Okay, okay," I said. "Enough of your ragging. We're past

forty-eight hours since Akemi and Maria were taken. If there's a chance the girls are still in the Galveston area, we need to do what we can and fast."

"Are you carrying?"

"Forty-five in the glove compartment."

He raised his right pant leg and showed a small, nine-millimeter automatic strapped to his ankle. He looked at me. "You got any cash?"

"Maybe a hundred. Do we need more?"

"Probably," he said. "We don't want to use a credit card in these joints, and I might need some for a snitch."

We took my truck because he said he didn't think his would make it. He only used it for grocery and beer runs with an occasional stop at Home Depot. Plus, he said his air conditioner didn't work, and the October night was unseasonably humid and he was already sweating. I told him my A/C didn't work either but by that time he was already in my truck.

We stopped at the convenience store in Bayou Vista and each of us got the maximum allowed out of the ATM.

We sat in my truck outside the store while Atticus made a couple of calls on his cell phone. The first number was no longer in use. The second call seemed to hit paydirt as he got into an extended conversation.

After the call he said, "We got lucky. Izan, or Izzi as he's known here, will meet us at the Valero station at the corner of FM 1764 and Highway 6. He's been my CI for years. Always dependable."

As we pulled out of the parking lot I said, "Izan? That's a different name. I think it means 'host' in English."

"Then it's perfect for him," Atti said. "Izzi grew up in Ciudad Acuna, the Mexican border town across from Del

Rio. He learned English before he was ten, working the streets, hustling Texas college boys to the whorehouses in Boys' Town. One of the more popular brothels was the Blue Agave where Izzi's mother worked as a…."

"Got it," I said, grinning. "So the name Izan served two purposes. One for his name and the other for his occupation. His mother must have been a real businesswoman."

"Hey, everybody has to make a living. Anyway, because of his green eyes, Izzi has always suspected his father was one of the Air Force jockeys stationed at Laughlin Air Force Base outside Del Rio. Izzi said the brass regularly warned new servicemen about the dangers of disease and robbery at the bars in Mexico, which probably only made them salivate more about going."

We approached the Valero cautiously. Atticus spotted Izzi's old Chevy sedan parked on the dark side of the station. We got out and slipped into the rear seat of his Chevy.

Atticus glanced at the worn Astros shirt Izzi wore and said to me, "See what I mean?"

Izzi was thirtyish, small and clean shaven with one gold tooth in front which gleamed when he smiled nervously at Atticus. Neither of them thought it important for Izzi to know my name or why I was there.

Atticus unfolded a flyer from his shirt pocket and handed it over the seat to Izzi. "We're looking for these girls," he said.

"*¡Ay, caramba*!" Izzi screamed. "*Mucho dinero*! Can I get it?"

"Find these girls," Atticus said.

"Why you think I know?" Izzi asked.

"They were taken off the street in Galveston on the way home from school. They were trafficked. We found the van with the girls fingerprints in it."

"Where?"

"Houston."

Izzi sighed, shook his head. "Holy Mary," he said. "They could be anywhere."

"We know that," Atticus answered. "But they may also be somewhere local. Maybe one of the cantinas."

Izzi rubbed his chin, thinking. "I can tell you where some of the trafficked girls are, but I can't go with you." He looked at Atticus as if he'd understand it was too dangerous for him.

Atticus didn't respond.

"The two cantinas near here are the Bougainvillea Club, couple of miles farther up Highway 6, and the Green Parrot over by the I-45. My fave is the Acapulco Cantina on the other side of the freeway. I'll draw a map, but you probably can't hit them all tonight." He glanced at his imitation gold watch. "It's already midnight and they close at 2:00 am."

Atticus slipped him several twenty-dollar bills.

"Be careful," Izzi said. "The way you guys stick out, you could be two of those Arizona Rangers totin' the 'Big Irons' Marty Robbins sang about." He laughed as we got out of his truck.

The Bougainvillea Club stood back off Highway 6 in a grove of tallow trees. Behind the cantina were a couple of small huts put together with plywood. Brassy *Tejano* music, with strong trumpets and loud guitars, pounded out of the open windows. A dozen old cars and pickups littered the gravel parking area. We checked the lot looking for a van or other vehicle that could transport several girls but found nothing.

We pulled to the side so we could see the back door. A fiftyish Latino with a big stomach and cowboy boots came out with an arm drooped over the shoulder of a young, heavily tattooed girl wearing lots of makeup. His other arm swung a beer bottle while he walked. The girl wore tight black pants and a white push-up halter top. Both laughed as they entered the nearest hut.

Atticus pointed to a couple of trash bins by the edge of the trees and said, "Why don't you hide behind those dumpsters and see who comes in and out of those shacks behind the cantina. I'll see what I can find out inside."

Thinking about a quick getaway, I backed the truck into a slot close to the dumpsters. I got out to get a better view of the buildings in back. During the next few minutes, another couple went out the back door to one of the huts.

I was about ready to go in and fetch Atticus when a voice in broken English behind me said, "Hey, Gringo. What you doin' here?"

I turned to find a big Mexican with a large mustache holding a club similar to a baseball bat.

I raised my hands with palms out, showing I was not a threat. I spoke in Spanish. "Waitin' for my compadre to come out. We're just leaving."

"You a cop?"

"Are you kidding?"

He motioned to the back entrance. "Let's go there," he said. "*El Jefe* wants to see you."

"Sorry, I can't do that. We're on our way to work at the refinery."

He held the club with both hands and raised it to just off his shoulder. "Go that way," he said, pointing to the back entrance.

"Okay, okay," I said and turned toward the back of the building. When I sensed he had dropped the club to his shoulder, I pivoted and hit hard with a balled fist into his solar plexus. He grunted and folded toward me. I sliced down on his kneecap with my foot, aiming to knock his kneecap off. He collapsed to the ground, squirming in pain.

He reached into his back pocket, I assumed for a knife or a gun. He came out with a push-button blade and sliced at me. I jumped back and his swing missed. While his arm was still moving through the stab, I kicked the back of his elbow, and the knife went flying. I smashed his nose with a solid right hand, and he fell back onto the shell parking lot, moaning.

I jumped in the driver's seat, started the truck and whipped in close to the front door. I gave the signal we'd agreed on, two long honks separated by a short beep.

Atticus barreled out the front door like he was being chased by a pack of wild dogs, two large Hispanics hot on his tail.

He opened the door and slid in. We spun out of the parking lot to the sound of pistol fire, ducking and hoping the shooter would miss.

I reeled onto Highway 6 and pressed the pedal to the floor. The old rust bucket's engine sounded as if we were only hitting six cylinders. It wouldn't take much for someone to catch us.

"Anyone following?"

Atticus glanced out the back window. "No headlights… coming…out of the driveway."

He was puffing hard, spilling out words in between breaths, leaning forward in the seat as if his back hurt.

"Holy shit…that was a close one," he said. "I guess I was wrong about my dark tan camouflaging me. I'd just got in a few questions to a young thing at the bar when those two came over. They made my ass and started asking questions…lucky to get out of there alive. I was already easing to the door when your horn went off. Thank God you came in time."

"Do you think Akemi and Maria could be in there?"

"Possible I guess, but I didn't see them. Only one girl came out from the back with a date while I was there."

"Date? Is that what they call it?"

"Hell if I know. That's what they called it in the old days in the cathouses on Post Office Street. One thing for sure, they don't like gringos in that joint."

We drove on and I asked, "Did you learn anything?"

"I'd slipped the girl a couple of twenties when I first got there. She said all the girls live in those shacks behind the cantina. She knows them all and she's never seen anyone who looks like Akemi or Maria. She said she was sixteen and the youngest one there. She came up from El Salvador last year with her 'protector.' He sold her to the guy who owns the cantina."

"How come the cops don't know about that place?"

"They probably do," Atticus said. "Can't get anyone to squeal. She said if they told the cops anything, someone would kill their parents and siblings back home. I told her about the reward, her eyes got big as pie plates. Those girls can't fathom that kind of money. Maybe the more we spread the word…."

He turned to me as he spoke and, still huffing, his voice grew louder than it needed to be. "Why were you in such a hurry to leave?"

I told him about the big Mex surprising me out of the shadows. "Looked like a security type," I said.

"How bad did you hurt him?"

"Probably broken kneecap and elbow. Maybe nose."

Lott squinted at me. "You some kind of bad ass, Parker?"

I ignored his question. "Think they'll report us?"

"Oh, hell no," Atticus replied, calming down now that no one was chasing us. He laughed, "They don't want cops lurking around."

I glanced at my phone. "We got time for a couple more."

Atticus looked at me. "On a roll, huh, Parker? Ok. The Green Parrot first, then the one Issi liked, the Acapulco Cantina across the freeway."

# Chapter Thirty-Four

## Friday Night

---

Akemi heard Juan and Hector's voices seeping through the kitchen wall.

"I just checked on Sarah," Juan said. "I'm telling you, it's not good. We need to do something."

"And I am telling you it's El Tigre's problem," Hector replied.

"She's totally out of it, like in a coma or something, rolled up in a ball. I…I think if we help her…."

Akemi heard the back door open. El Tigre's rough voice sounded through the wall. "Gabriela and Sayda were at the Acapulco. Where's Sarah?"

Akemi whispered to Maria to feign sleep. Akemi lay on her side on her mat with Maria in front of her, both facing the far wall. Akemi had positioned herself so that her head was just above Maria's, giving both a view of Sarah.

The kitchen door burst open, and the overhead lights flashed on as El Tigre stormed in. Akemi peeked enough to see the horrible scowl on his face.

Tigre stood over Sarah, who lay tucked in the fetal position and holding her stomach.

"Get up and get dressed," he yelled. "Time to work."

Sarah emitted a painful moan.

Tigre kicked her leg with his boot.

"No, please," she cried. "I hurt too much to go tonight."

To Akemi's surprise, Maria got up and limped over to Sarah. She put her body between Sarah and El Tigre's foot. She felt Sarah's cheek and turned to Tigre.

"She is very sick," Maria said in English. "I think she will die if we don't get her help."

Akemi brimmed with pride at Maria's newfound courage, but worried what Tigre would do. She started forward to support her but stopped when Tigre spoke. He grinned, the scar on his face moving as he spoke.

"How would you know that, little girl?"

"My mother is a nurse," Maria lied.

El Tigre studied Maria for a moment as if trying to decide whether or not to believe her. Then he turned and quickly left the room, slamming the door but leaving the lights on. Akemi and Maria hurriedly put their ears to the wall.

In the kitchen, Tigre's voice boomed, "That bitch Sarah is in bad shape."

"What do you want to do?" Juan asked.

"Nothing."

"She's made you good money," Juan said. "We could drop her at the hospital."

"Are you loco?"

"We could tell her we know where her family is and we'll kill them all if she squeals."

"Do we know where they are?" Tigre asked.

"No, but Sarah doesn't know that. In her condition, she'll believe us."

"I don't give a shit how good she's been for business. She's easy to replace. It's time we moved anyway. I'm going back to Houston to make a spot for everyone. Juan, you pick Gabriela and Sayda up later while Hector stays here with Sarah and the new girls."

Akemi's stomach churned at what she'd just heard. She had to stifle a gag to keep from throwing up. All she could think of was Hector saying he'd never had an Asian girl. And now, for the first time, he would be alone with them.

She started shivering and held her arms around her body to contain herself. Then Maria's arms enveloped her in a tight hug and she began to calm.

Akemi took her friend's hand and said, "Thank you, Maria."

"No, it is me who thanks you," Maria said. "I couldn't have made it this far without you. You helped me through my weakness and fear. We are one now. Together we will fight this through. We'll never give in, no matter what they do to us."

When El Tigre left, Hector told Juan he was going to his bedroom for a shower. Hector stalked through the kitchen door. He went to Akemi and Maria and leered down at them, saying nothing.

They glared back at him, defiant and unblinking, trying to send a message that he would pay a high price if he tried anything. He sauntered into his bedroom and shut the door behind him.

Akemi didn't know if he got their message, but if he came after her, she would fight with every ounce of strength she could muster. Nothing was off limits: gouging, biting, whatever it took. She vowed she would die before she let the slimy bastard violate her.

Maria said to Akemi, "Juan is alone. We don't have much time before Hector comes back in and Juan has to leave to pick up the other girls. We've got to convince him to help us."

"What are you thinking?"

Maria paused, bit her lip. "We know Juan is not here by choice. Maybe he's good but got caught up in bad things. Let's remind him of what he has done for us."

They went through the unlocked kitchen door and found Juan at the counter stacking groceries in the upper cabinet.

"Hi Juan," Maria said demurely. "Can I help?"

Juan shook his head no. Maria poured Akemi and herself a glass of water and they moved to the table. Juan grabbed a beer from the refrigerator and sat across from them.

Maria said, "Juan, we are really afraid of Hector. The way he looks at us.... What he said to Akemi that he'd never had an Asian girl."

Akemi caught Juan's eye, hoping he would see the fear in her face. The glass shook in her hands. He glanced at her, then looked away. The response she wanted.

"We're glad you're not like that," Maria added. "You have done so much for us."

Juan drank some beer and focused on the far wall across the room. It was obvious to Akemi he was trying to avoid them. But he didn't get up, so she hoped this was a sign he was on the verge of cracking, of coming around to them.

Akemi took over for Maria and said, "You saved me in that field when you stopped Hector from hitting me again. I couldn't have taken another hit. Look how my cheek is still swollen."

He swallowed more beer, glanced at Akemi's face and turned away. Akemi nodded to Maria to keep going.

"You saw my bleeding foot and carried me to the truck," Maria said. "You fed us when you weren't supposed to, and you let us shower when Hector was not here. We wanted to thank you for all you've done."

Juan took a big breath and let it out. He still wouldn't look at them. No one spoke for a couple of beats. Juan finished his beer then rose and reached into the refrigerator for another. He popped the top and took a swig. He turned toward the cabinets and started arranging the shelves again.

After a moment, Maria said to his back, "Juan, you told us that the cartel killed your *papa.* Was that in Mexico?"

"No. Honduras," he answered, his back still turned.

"And you had to leave. But what about your brothers and sisters? Did they get out?"

Juan turned to face them and leaned against the kitchen sink, the beer in his hand. "I had one sister, Elina," he said. "She was beautiful. Big round dark eyes, long black hair to her waist. I loved her so much."

"What happened to her?" Maria asked.

"She wanted to be a dancer. She was only sixteen when the cartel took her. I tried for three months to find her, traveled all over Honduras, but she had disappeared. I can only pray she is okay." Juan's eyes gathered tears. He turned away to wipe them.

Akemi feared his sister was not okay. She thought he knew it too. Elina was either working for the cartel, in Honduras or maybe somewhere in the US, or she might be dead.

"Let us pray for her now," Maria said. "Will you pray with us?"

Juan nodded and sat down. Maria put her hand on his.

"Lord God, I pray for Elina. I pray that under your wings she can find refuge. Protect her from trouble wherever she goes and keep evil from her. Amen."

Juan repeated the Amen.

Maria kept her hand on Juan's and squeezed it gently. He opened his eyes, pulled his hand back and said, "Thank you, Maria."

Akemi looked at Maria and nodded. They moved quietly into the bedroom, leaving Juan at the table with his thoughts.

Back on the mats, Akemi said, "You got Juan to talk about his sister. That was smart. And your idea about the prayer worked. Maybe he will see your kindness and help us."

"I wasn't trying to trick him," Maria shot back. "I meant every word. My mother and I say that prayer every night for my grandfather who is still in Mexico. We miss him so much."

"I am so sorry," Akemi said. "I hope your grandfather is well."

Feeling a little chastised, Akemi turned away. But then she thought, 'We are both under so much stress, I have to ignore Maria's outburst and just be proud she has regained her strength.'

Sometime later, Hector left his bedroom, locked the door behind him and went through their room into the kitchen.

Through the wall, Akemi and Maria heard him say to Juan, "It's time to pick up Gabriela and Sayda. You should leave."

"I guess so," Juan said. "But I'm busy here in the kitchen sorting the groceries you brought. Would you pick them up?"

"No," Hector fired back. "Tigre told you to do it."

Akemi's throat started to close at his words, making breathing difficult. She fought down the feeling of panic.

A cell phone buzzed. When Hector answered, El Tigre screamed through the phone so loud that Akemi and Maria heard him through the wall.

"You dumb asses. If Juan is there with you, put the speaker on. So no one saw you take the girls, huh? Juan? Beto just called me. Some *gringo* just delivered a drawing of you to the club."

"What are you talking about?

"Someone saw you, fool! Don't show that ugly face of yours nowhere. We have to close the house and get the hell out."

"Oh, Christ," Juan said, disgusted that he'd let Hector manipulate him into stealing the girls. And even more foolish, he thought: Why had he driven the van?

El Tigre screamed again, "Hector, you pick up Gabriela and Sayda tonight. Juan is done in Galveston!"

# Chapter Thirty-Five

## Saturday Morning

---

Daybreak arrived bright and cool, confirming that October brought the best weather of the year for West Beach. I stepped out to the deck and took in a deep lungful of fresh fall air.

I gazed along the shoreline to take in the still bay water, unruffled by wind or tide. The crisp morning brought back memories of wade fishing with my grandfather along that hard, sandy bottom, the only sound an occasional cork popping to imitate the sound of trout feeding at the top of the water. We'd spent many Saturdays gracefully gliding along the tranquil water, snaring a fish or two and sharing the joy of a peaceful morning.

Toward the gulf, the sun was just peaking over the horizon, soon to be majestic in its offering of continuity, tranquility and hope. For a moment, it seemed as though all the anxiety and worry of the last few days would be sucked into that great ball of life-giving warmth and whisked away into the endless sky. One could only hope.

Bits of conversation drifted up from the dock below. Neddie was standing beside Bully in his wheelchair, both of them gazing out at the bay.

I wondered what the two old friends were discussing. Maybe the 1940 Ball High football game when Bully, slim and powerful as the tight end, caught Neddie's thirty- yard pass and ran it in for the game-winning touchdown. That game propelled the team to the state quarter finals. While reveling in their momentary fame, neither knew that a madman in Europe would soon have such a devastating effect on their lives.

After a few quick stretches to ease the pain in my lower back, I hurried down the stairs, hoping Neddie had put something on the stove for breakfast. Not disappointed, the aroma of sizzling bacon hit my olfactory senses as I entered the back door.

I turned the bacon, then shouted out to the dock, "I guess you two gluttons were hoping to finish off that pound of heart stoppers before I woke up, huh?"

"Oh man," Neddie exclaimed, already making his way to the door. "Glad you got there before it burned, Parker. I plum forgot about it."

He checked the bacon, saw that I had things under control, then grabbed two cold beers out of the cooler and moved with Bully to a table.

While the bacon began to crisp, I moved a spoonful of grease to another skillet, sauteed a handful of onions and jalapenos and dropped in a dozen eggs.

Like a vacuum cleaner on a rug, Neddie and Bully sucked their eggs down without pause, maybe without a breath. I was working on my last piece of bacon when Bully wiped his mouth and said to me, "So you got in late last night. Anything new?"

I brought Neddie and Bully up to date on the search for Akemi and Maria, including last night's soiree into several bars including the rhubarb at the Bougainvilla.

"Damn," Bully said. "Twenty years ago, I woulda gone with you, knocked some heads."

"Yeah," I said. "Except now they all carry handguns and AR-15s in their pickups. We were damned lucky to get out of that joint with our teeth intact."

Bully grunted, finished his beer and tossed the empty can into the trash can behind him. He lowered his eye patch, rubbed his bad eye socket and slid the patch back in place.

He said, "What can we do to help, Parker? We've been sitting around here with our hands in our pants, waiting. I don't like it. It's not me."

"Best thing is for you and Neddie to run The Garhole while I search for the girls. I can't afford to shut it down."

Neddie came back to the table with a fresh beer out of the cooler and a wry grin on his face. "No problem," he said.

I went out to the truck to find my cell phone unplugged and out of juice. I plugged the cord into the cigarette lighter and called Sumner. The phone buzzed several times before she picked up.

"Mercy, Parker. Is the sun up?"

"The rooster crowed hours ago."

"Horny bastard."

Joking aside, I got to the point. "Any luck last night?"

"I figured we needed a Hispanic cop, so I called Sergeant Guerra. He rounded up his partner, Officer Morales, thinking he needed a female. They made the rounds. Even made it to the dance floor a couple of times."

"Probably belly rubbing," I quipped. "Think there's something going on there?"

"Oh, my God, Parker. You really do need a weekend somewhere with Kathy."

"I can't argue that, detective."

Sumner said, "Julius and I, along with Guerra and Morales, hit every joint we could find on Bolivar and then

Galveston Island. Guerra and Morales didn't learn much. But Guerra said the flyers with the sketch of the perp and $100,000 reward were displayed in some of the bars. Several patrons mentioned they had their eyes out. Need the money."

"You and Julius didn't go in?"

"We hung close as backup. You and Atticus do any good on the mainland?"

I decided not to say anything about the little rhubarb we'd stirred up last night at the Bougainvillea Club and hoped Atticus wouldn't tell his brother Julius. I didn't want Sumner to find out and kick me off the team this late in the game.

"We hit a few," I said, "including the Acapulco Cantina. That one looks promising, complete with a couple of mobile homes in back. I didn't go in, but Atti managed to take a girl named Camila to the back. He plied her with cash, and she was so excited she didn't have to perform, she willingly rattled out answers to his questions. He asked about young girls who worked there and she spilled about two of them. They worked last night but had gone by the time we got there. Young ones, she said. Too damned young, she admitted. Atticus said his ears pricked up, but then she said both girls were from Mexico and had worked there a while."

"What's that got to do with Akemi and Maria?"

"Camila said some of the girls get dropped off and picked up every night…and get this…by some Hispanic dude driving a dark van."

"Holy shit!"

"I thought you'd like that."

"Why didn't you call last night? We could have got SWAT rolling."

"Because it was 2:00 am, and the girls weren't there."

Sumner paused, then said, "I'll get with Julius and make a plan for tonight."

***

My phone read 11:30 am when I parked in front of Kathy's bungalow. The houses on the street were all built post-war, funded with G.I. loans. The shiplap siding on her bungalow looked freshly painted. The mint-green, pastel color reminded me of pictures of homes on a Caribbean island.

The large front porch, where folks used to sit on hot summer evenings, sip iced tea and visit with their neighbors, was gone. Air conditioning and television brought them inside and the porch was taken in for an extra bedroom. Now there was only a small stoop flanked on either side by the dozens of yellow and purple pansies Kathy had worked so hard planting.

She opened the door with a welcoming smile, wearing jeans and a pastel blue shirt. Julie followed her out, her long brown hair falling almost to her waist. The minor puffiness under her eyes underscored her worry.

Kathy glanced at my truck and said, "Still no A/C?"

She guided me toward her several-year-old Toyota sedan in the driveway. We all climbed in with Kathy behind the wheel. She started the engine and cranked the A/C to high.

"Julie wants fried shrimp. Okay with you?" she asked.

Five minutes later we sat next to the railing on the upper deck of The Spot, a popular tourist haven on Seawall Boulevard with a clear view of the Gulf of Mexico. The wind had calmed, which settled the sandy water and turned the surf green. Across the boulevard on the beach, a young couple wearing sunglasses and swimsuits relaxed under a red-and-blue umbrella while a young boy and girl dug holes in the sand.

When Julie went downstairs to talk to a friend, I said to Kathy, "Okay, you're away from the hospital. What can you tell me about the homeless woman Joy?"

Kathy tightened her eyes. "Parker, rules are rules. You want me to get fired?"

I looked at her with surprise on my face, "Hey, Kathy. It's me, Parker. Not the FBI."

She sighed, looked around, leaned in, "I checked after you called. She's in detox. Probably will be for a while. Meth is tough stuff. It'll take a lot of rehab and determination on her part. She can beat it if she's strong enough. But…few do."

"Oh, man, seeing her on that sidewalk pushing that grocery cart put my heart in my throat. I hope she makes it."

Julie returned and the conversation turned to small talk, mostly about her friends and favorite subjects in school. Anything to avoid what we were all worried about—Akemi and Maria. The food came and we chowed down.

After a quiet pause, precocious Julie blurted out, "Parker, are you going to marry my mom?"

Kathy gave her daughter a stern look. "Julie, really!"

Julie's face turned red. She said, "Sorry, Parker."

I smiled broadly to ease the tension. "Hey, hey, please. Really, it's okay, Julie. I care a great deal about your mom. And I think she feels the same way about me. We are enjoying each other's company, and you and I are getting to know each other. Marriage is a big step, and we are taking our relationship one day at a time. I hope you can understand that?"

Back at their house, I gave Julie a hug and she went inside. Kathy stood on the stoop eyeing me with a big smile. Then she chuckled.

"What's so funny," I asked.

"Sorry, Parker. I can't help but laugh. You should have seen your face when Julie asked if you were going to marry me. You looked like you'd just been caught stealing a piece of cake off your mother's counter."

"That bad, huh?"

"Come on, Parker. Do you really think I'm ready to rush into another marriage? We're having fun, what's wrong with that?"

I didn't know what to say so I smiled and kissed her.

***

Part of me wanted to go back to the Acapulco and set up surveillance. Hang there all day and into the night. Whatever it took to find the girls. But Detective Sumner and Lieutenant Lott were busy formulating a plan and I didn't want to take the chance of screwing it up.

Plus, now that the kidnappers had dumped the van, we had nothing but speculation to tell us what their next move would be. What kind of vehicle were they driving now? Were they nervous with all the publicity, the reward and the police sketch of the driver? Did the man in the drawing know every cop in the county was looking for him? And what about the reward? Surely $100,000 was enough to motivate someone to call in.

No doubt it was going to be a late night, so I decided to call Harry and see if I could nap on his couch. He encouraged me to come over and said I was welcome to his spare bedroom.

When I arrived, he greeted me at the front door wearing a well-pressed pair of light-green linen slacks, matching golf shirt and boat shoes. His hair looked recently barbered, goatee trimmed to perfection and his fingers perfectly manicured.

I looked him over. "Hot date today?"

"If you must know, Elizabeth and I are having lunch at the Yacht Club. And by the way, if you're lucky, you may get to meet the casserole lady from across the street. When she observed your truck, she called and said she needed a new yard man and would be over to meet you."

Harry never stopped with his playful digs. I said, "Gosh, Harry, I appreciate the opportunity to inhale an intoxicating whiff of a fleshly baked tuna-noodle casserole. But what I need more is a nap. I hope Elizabeth is not the jealous type if she drops by when the lady across the street is here."

He frowned and sent me to my room.

# Chapter Thirty-Six

## Saturday Morning

---

Akemi heard pots rattling in the kitchen. She put her ear to the thin wall but heard no conversation. Feeling as though she'd slept several hours and it was probably morning, she nudged Maria and spoke softly into her ear.

"Are you awake?"

Maria moaned, "I haven't slept. My foot hurts so much. I'm hot, Akemi. Something's wrong."

"I think Juan is alone in the kitchen, maybe Hector is asleep or out somewhere. I'll turn on the light so we can look at your foot."

She got up and flipped the light switch, hoping Hector wouldn't suddenly come into the room. The dull overhead lights in the middle of the room flickered on. The sound of shifting covers drifted over from Gabriela and Sayda's pallets as they moved to avoid the light in their sleep. No sound came from Sarah's pallet.

Akemi gently lifted Maria's foot. "It's so hard to see in this light," she said. Then she flinched.

"What's wrong," Maria asked.

"Your foot is really red around where the stick went in and there's some ugly pus coming out." Akemi paused to look closer. "A bunch of tiny red spots surround the red and tiny red streaks are creeping up the sides. Does it hurt when I push around the hole where the stick when in?"

"Owww!" Maria yelped. "I told you it hurt all night. Let me look at it."

Maria grabbed her foot with both hands and twisted it so she could see.

"Holy Mother! It looks really bad. Feel my face, Akemi."

Like her mother used to do, Akemi placed the palm of her hand on her forehead and then felt Maria's.

"You're burning up, Maria. We need to tell Hector."

"Get Sarah to look at it," Maria said. "Maybe she knows more than we do."

Akemi scooted over to Sarah and found her wrapped in her sheet. She whispered, "Sarah, Sarah, it's Akemi are you awake?"

No response. Akemi poked Sarah's back with her finger and repeated, "Sarah? Sarah?"

Sarah's arm was cold to the touch. Her face was pale, almost white, eyes open, but still. She felt Sarah's face.

"Oh, my God," Akemi yelled. "She's…she's dead. Sarah is dead!"

Akemi collapsed over Sarah's body, weeping.

She knew she was responding to more than finding Sarah dead. All the pent-up emotions she'd harbored deep within herself from the moment she was kidnapped poured out like water boiling over in a pot. Feelings she'd bundled up inside so she could be strong for herself and for Maria. She couldn't stop crying; and she didn't want to stop. Somehow, deep down, she knew she needed the release.

Other memories flooded in too. The accident in California. Screeching tires. The hurting sound of metal crushing metal. Blood. Both her mother and father. She'd repressed all memory of that tragedy. But now she couldn't stop it.

And then Maria was there, her arm around Akemi's

shoulder, not speaking, not crying. Stoic. Akemi felt the heat from her body.

Maria stayed a moment and limped back to her mat.

Akemi wondered if the pain from the infection had silenced her or if death had become so routine for Maria that she could simply bury the hurt and move on. She knew Maria had seen discarded bodies, tangled and stiff, left to rot by the cartel in her village. Even some on her torturous trek across the border into Texas.

But this was different, Akemi thought. Someone they knew and liked had died in the same room where they slept. Someone who might have helped them. Someone they'd tried to help.

Awakened by Akemi's scream, Gabriela and Sayda moved to stand next to Sarah, their arms wrapped tightly around each other, tears streaming down their cheeks. Akemi studied the sisters' faces. She saw more than grief, more than their feelings of loss for Sarah. In that passing instant, Akemi realized the girls wept not only for Sarah, but for themselves. Two young women they knew had died within a matter of days. Were they next?

The kitchen door flew open. Juan rushed in. "What is it? What is going on?" he shouted. He pushed past Akemi and Maria and knelt at Sarah's body. He closed her lifeless eyes and covered her face and torso with the sheet.

"There's nothing we can do," he said. "She's been dead a while."

Juan stood and made the sign of the cross on his chest. Gabriela and Sayda crossed themselves. Juan began a prayer in Spanish and Gabriela, Sayda and Maria softly repeated his words.

"Eternal rest grant unto Sarah, O Lord, and let perpetual

light shine upon her. May her soul and the souls of all the faithful departed, through the mercy of God, rest in peace. Amen."

Akemi gazed at him and said, "Juan, what do we do now?"

Juan embraced her. "So sorry," he said.

Just as he released her, Hector stormed in from the other bedroom. He shouted at the girls.

"What's all this racket?"

"It's Sarah," Juan said, pointing to Sarah's body wrapped in the sheet.

Hector glanced down. He turned toward the kitchen door and said, "I'm hungry. Let's eat."

Juan blew out a breath. He lowered his head in a moment of seeming hopelessness and followed Hector into the kitchen.

Sayda and Gabriela returned to their mats, lay down and whimpered, the sound gradually fading as they drifted off in exhaustion.

Maria said to Akemi, her voice weak, intermittent, "We must…look to ourselves now. If they…take us to Houston, we may…disappear. We…have to do something."

Akemi felt Maria's forehead and leaned in close. "You need a doctor, Maria. That is our first priority."

Voices came through the wall speaking in Spanish. Maria translated for Akemi.

"I don't think El Tigre will move them in the daytime," Hector said. "Probably late tonight, less chance we will be noticed."

"What can we do with Sarah's body?" Juan asked.

"I'll call Tigre."

"Put him on speaker," Juan said as Hector dialed.

Tigre answered, "What?"

Hector said, "Sarah is dead."

Silence. No response.

"What do we do with the body?" Hector asked.

"Put it in the other bedroom. I will deal with it tonight when I come."

"Are we moving tonight?"

"Yes."

"Should Gabriela and her sister go to work?"

No response. Then, Tigre said, "Take them to the Acapulco now. We won't move until late, and they might as well make some money. We'll pick them up on the way to Houston. Is Juan listening?"

"Yes."

"Juan, you *cula*. Do not leave the house. The drawing of your face is everywhere on those damned flyers."

When the conversation ended, Hector stormed past the girls into his room.

Akemi felt Maria's face again.

"Oh, my God, Maria. You are getting worse. We must do something."

Maria didn't reply, but instead rolled into the fetal position and moaned softly. Akemi ran to the kitchen door and knocked loudly, yelling, "Juan. Juan. Help!"

The door opened and Akemi screamed at him, "Maria is worse. She needs a doctor."

"I can't leave the house," he said.

Akemi quickly spun and ran to the back door to escape. Juan caught her around the waist just as she reached the door. He lifted her. She kicked and struggled until she realized she could not free herself from Juan's strong arms. She began to calm herself.

"I thought I could trust you, Akemi. I will have to put the zip ties back on."

"No, please, Juan. I'll be good, I promise. I won't leave Maria."

Juan set her down.

Akemi got close to Juan and whispered, "She needs help, Juan. I know you're not like Hector. Help us!"

Juan handed Akemi a glass of water and two aspirins. "Give her these," he said. He took a bowl down from the cabinet, filled it with cool water and grabbed a kitchen towel off the rack.

Akemi got Maria to take the aspirin and drink the water. She sat back against the wall, moved Maria's head to her lap and began bathing her face with the cool water. She thought about how Sarah had looked last night and now, this morning. She wasn't going to let that happen to Maria.

She didn't know what she was going to do, but she would do whatever it took to save her friend.

***

Late that afternoon, after falling asleep with Maria's head in her lap, Akemi awakened to find Juan leaning over them with the back of his hand on Maria's cheek.

Juan removed his hand. "You are right about, Maria," he said. "When I was a young boy in Honduras, me and my friend went around with no shoes. One day, we were exploring an old hut. He stepped on a nail. It didn't bleed so we didn't think much of it. He didn't even tell his *mamá*. We lived in a small village. The closest doctor was fifty miles away. When the fever started, his *mamá* made poultices from *bairorin*, a desert plant. Our people used the poultices for hundreds of years."

"And…," Akemi asked.

"They…they didn't work," Juan said. "My friend he…he went to live with the angels."

Juan wiped his eyes with his hand and looked away.

Akemi reached out and put her hand on his.

She gave him a moment, then said, "Juan we have to take Maria to the hospital. We just have to. She is worse, I can't wake her. You are her only hope."

Maria moaned softly as Akemi spoke. It was as if she'd made a sound on cue to Akemi's plea. But Akemi knew better. Her friend was really sick. Her hand on Juan's arm began to shake. She released her grip and her whole arm shook. She took hold with her other hand and held it still.

Juan rose to his full height but never took his eyes off Maria.

"Are you going help us?" Akemi pleaded.

He went into the kitchen and locked the door.

Akemi lay Maria's head down gently on the mat and covered her with a sheet. She pounded again at the kitchen door, shouting Juan's name.

He opened the door, went back to the table and sat down with a bottle of Tequila and a half-full glass.

Akemi asked, "Where is Hector?"

"He took Gabriela and Sayda to the Acapulco."

Juan took a good slug and looked away from Akemi.

"I'm not going to stop until you help us," Akemi said, her voice strong, determined.

Juan turned the glass up to his lips, finished the Tequila and poured another.

# Chapter Thirty-Seven

## Saturday Afternoon

---

A speckled trout big enough to win the West Bay Fishing Contest chugged the line off my reel almost to the end. I was already thinking about the first prize of a boat and motor when my cell buzzed.

Oh, man, I only need another couple of minutes…maybe not even that long in a dream. As my mind cleared, my first thought was I should have left the phone in the truck.

"Hi Maggie. What's up?" I asked, my voice still dragging from sleep.

"This is the first chance I've had to call you since Rudy got in. He's sleeping now and…."

"Got in from where?" I asked.

"Jail!"

"Jail? What happened?" I was wide awake now, sitting up straight, in the bed in Harry's spare bedroom.

"When I told him what you said about the police finding the kidnappers' van in Houston, he went searching for the girls. He got into trouble in some bar. All I know is, Harry called a lawyer friend in Houston and he got a bail bondsman and…."

"I was just with Harry. He didn't say anything about it."

"Rudy made him swear not to tell anyone but me. Getting into a fight and being arrested was scary enough. Then I found out he had the rifle with him."

"The Japanese rifle? Are you sure?"

"He doesn't have another one."

"Did the police confiscate it?"

"No, he had it stashed behind the seat in his truck. The problem is, he left the truck in a no-parking zone and a wrecker towed it to one of those private lots. Probably cost a fortune to get it released. I went to an ATM this morning and got all the cash I could. He told me to let him sleep for a couple of hours and then call you. He needs a ride to get the truck and I don't drive on the freeway. Neither does Harry."

"How did he get back to Galveston?"

"The Houston lawyer's secretary brought him."

"Why didn't he pick up the truck then, save the secretary the trip?"

"Rudy is a proud man," Maggie said. "He wouldn't ask the attorney for money, he didn't have the cash, and he doesn't own an ATM card."

"Okay, Maggie. I'll be right over."

I hung up and immediately called The Garhole.

"Garhole Bar, where the elite meet to eat!"

"Neddie, where do you get that stuff?"

"Old radio show from the forties. Before your time, Parker."

"I need you to do something. Go upstairs and look under my bed."

"What am I looking for, a dead mouse?"

"Your rifle. I'll hang on while you check."

Minutes later, Neddie was back. "It's gone."

"I was afraid of that. Has Rudy been out there?"

"He took it? Must've come last night when Bully was asleep and you were out honky-tonking."

I let his sarcasm pass. The less he knew about what I did

last night, the better. I also didn't say anything about Rudy going to Houston because he'd asked Harry not to tell anyone.

Me and my big mouth, telling Maggie the police had found the van in Houston. I'd caused this whole problem. Damn. Sumner had called me "the intrepid investigator," but I felt more like the bumbling Inspector Clouseau.

I didn't mind taking Rudy to Houston to get his truck as long as I could get back before dark. If Sumner and Lieutenant Lott were planning on hitting the Acapulco Cantina tonight, I didn't want to miss the chance to find Akemi and Maria.

***

When Maggie answered the door, I smiled and gave her a quick hug. I tried not to notice the extra makeup she'd used to cover the dark circles under her eyes. The stress was beginning to pound everyone involved.

"Sorry to ask you to do this, Parker. He didn't have anyone else to call."

"Glad to help, Maggie."

She motioned me to the couch. "I'm really worried, Parker. Rudy taking that rifle with him…."

Her voice faded. I looked away, trying to think of the right response, when Rudy walked in from the bedroom. I stood and took his firm grip.

"Thanks for helping, Parker. I know it's a pain, but I really need my truck."

He kissed Maggie, and we went out and climbed into my truck.

I grinned and said, "This heap hasn't made a trip this long since my last visit to the V.A. I hope it makes it."

He didn't respond. My obvious attempt to diffuse the

tension failed. I never was good at chit-chat.

During the hour drive to Houston, I waited for Rudy's explanation about last night, but he sat quietly staring out the window. He appeared stoic, but I could only imagine the turmoil rattling his gut with Akemi and Maria missing, and a desperate trip to Houston that had gotten him nothing but trouble.

Rudy had bucked enormous odds during the war and had received a medal for his incredibly brave but audacious actions. Did he still think he was bullet proof? Or was he just so incensed that nothing mattered except finding Akemi?

We exited the freeway and turned north onto the 610 Loop, exited again at Harrisburg and turned onto Navigation, the street that paralleled the Houston Ship Channel.

A couple of blocks more and he directed me into a driveway where the sign read "Martinez Vehicle Storage." We entered the office, a small room with a couple of chairs and a man sitting behind a sheet of bullet-proof glass that had a slot under it like a bank counter. Rudy shoved his license in the slot while asking the man about his truck.

The man was maybe forty, but his sagging jowls and acne-scarred face made him look sixty. His cheeks were covered with stubby black hair that matched the stringy mess that fell to his shoulders. He took a deep puff from a hand-rolled joint, held the smoke in for a moment and blew it out. With the joint still in his lips, he picked up the license and studied it with squinty eyes.

He punched keys on a computer and said, "Looks like four hundred and ten dollars."

"Are you shitting me?" Rudy said.

"Not if you want your truck," the man answered. "Two-fifty for towing and one-sixty for storage."

He managed one more deep drag before he dropped the joint on the wooden floor and stepped on it.

"Thief," Rudy said, his pale face growing red. "Care to step outside that fortress you're in and talk about this?"

The man emptied his lungs of smoke and stood, bringing a baseball bat to the counter. He was built like a TV wrestler and was well over six feet tall. He leaned close to the glass. "If that's what you want, buddy."

Rudy stood his ground and waved him on. I stepped in front of Rudy, facing him with my back to the glass.

"You don't need any more trouble, Rudy. It's a screw job, but there's nothing you can do except pay. Give me the money. We've got things to do."

Rudy huffed and withdrew a wad of folded bills from his pocket. I counted it out. "You're ten dollars short."

He shrugged. I dug ten dollars from my wallet, added it to Rudy's bills and shoved it under the glass. I never looked at the man, knowing I would feel the same as Rudy and then we'd both have problems.

A young Hispanic man drove Rudy's truck out of the gate. Rudy climbed in and said, "I'll park up the street. We'll ride together. I want to show you the last place I hit last night."

He drove a couple of blocks and parked on the side of the street. I pulled in behind him. He got out and opened my passenger door.

Before he climbed in, I said, "You forgot something."

His raised his eyebrows in a quizzical look.

"The rifle."

He climbed in and slammed the door. "You know, huh? This time I'm keeping it, Parker."

"Damn it, Rudy. That rifle is going to get you in trouble."

"Yeah, maybe, but nothing compared to the trouble Akemi is in."

He stared at me, his eyes steeled, unblinking. I shook my head in disgust and drove off.

He directed me over the ship channel on Old Highway 90 and then turned onto Market Street.

"How did you determine where to go last night? Houston's a big city." I asked, still steamed about the rifle but trying to calm down.

"I checked the internet. You can't drive far in Houston without finding yourself in a Hispanic neighborhood. I drove several areas. Must have checked a dozen bars in several parts of the city—Airline Drive, the southwest area down around Sugarland, west toward Alief—nothing. I was about to give up when I decided this area looked promising because of the number of cantinas that showed on the net."

Rudy turned a corner and slowed down. He glanced at me. "It was past closing time when I discovered this street. I got dirty looks in the first two joints and then I found this dive."

He pointed to a cantina on the corner on the right. The sign read: *El Soledad*, and in smaller letters, *Chicas*. The building was constructed of unpainted cement block with two large windows on either side of the front door. The windows were painted black so no one could see inside. Two pickups as ragged as mine sat in front. A high wooden fence surrounded the back side of the building, with a couple of beat-up mobile homes tucked inside it.

Outside the fence on the side street, three men sat in folding chairs with their shirts off, drinking beer in the afternoon sun. We turned on the street and passed by, getting a killer stare.

"Hold it," Rudy exclaimed. He pointed toward the men. "The fat guy in the chair on the end was the bouncer. He had a club that I took away and jammed against his neck. But those other two jumped me, pinned me down. Someone called 911 and I ended up in jail, arrested for assault."

"Damn, Rudy. Assault is a serious charge."

"Right, except the fat man didn't press charges. I think the bar owner didn't want the possible trouble. I spent the night in jail, but this morning Harry's lawyer friend got me released and said I was good to go."

Before I could stop him, Rudy bounded out of the truck and was halfway to the sidewalk. The three big Hispanic men got up off their chairs, including the fat bouncer.

I murmured, "Oh, shit," to myself, grabbed my Colt 45 automatic out of the glove compartment and stuck it in the back of my pants. Rudy faced them while I stood behind.

"Ok, big boy," he yelled to the fat one. "It's me and you this time, if you have the *cojones* to tell those other shitheads to back off."

As they started to close around him, I whipped out the Colt and waved it around, hoping they wouldn't miss the sun glaring off the chrome. All three men stopped.

I yelled, "Get in the damn truck, Rudy!"

He glanced around to see me holding the automatic and started to back away. The bouncer stepped toward Rudy. I cocked the hammer and pointed the gun at his fat stomach. He stopped.

The other two moved toward me. I pointed the gun in the air and pulled the trigger, hoping the bullet wouldn't come down on someone's head a mile away. The hammer snapped, no bullet in the chamber. Having no cartridge in the barrel was a safety feature for me, but in the adrenaline rush, I'd forgotten to jack one in.

One of the men coming at me laughed. I quickly racked the slide to move a cartridge into the chamber and leveled the gun at the man's head. He stopped and raised his hands. Rudy moved behind me and climbed into the passenger side of the truck. I jumped in, cranked the engine and hit the gas, hoping the sudden acceleration wouldn't kill the engine.

As we sped away, Rudy scowled, "Parker, you had no right to interfere. I could have taken all three of them."

I thought about Rudy's age and his slight five-foot-seven frame facing those lunkers and wondered if he was all bluster. But then I remembered him in action with Kroton, the Galveston cop who'd put his hand on Maggie.

We drove back to Rudy's truck without another word between us. I waited for him to get out.

He put his hand on the door handle and looked at me. "Sorry, Parker."

I sighed heavily, "Houston's a big city, Rudy. You could have searched for a month and not found the girls."

"Ok, but don't rag on me. I got enough going without it."

"Right," I said. "But I gotta tell you, Galveston Police don't think the girls are in Houston."

"What? Why?"

"They think the perps dumped the van in Houston to throw us off. They probably stole another vehicle to replace the van, and the problem is we have no idea what kind. Dozens of vehicles are stolen every day in Houston, half of them probably headed immediately to Mexico. The perps know the Galveston Police have more to do than routinely search for cars stolen in Houston."

Rudy bit his lip. "So I wasted time in Houston last night. Are the cops searching the bars in Galveston?"

Still hot about him keeping the rifle, I laid into him with sarcasm.

"Yes. Last night while you were fighting off drunks in the Houston jail, Galveston cops were out checking cantinas. They got a good lead at one of them. Several nights ago, an informant watched some girls get dropped off from a dark van. That was before Akemi and Maria went missing, but the vehicle fits."

Rudy's face lit up in anticipation. "Which bar?" he asked.

I gave him a hard stare. "Not until you give up the rifle."

# Chapter Thirty-Eight

## Saturday Afternoon

---

During the return from Houston, I realized Sumner hadn't called me about tonight's plan. Were they going to raid the Acapulco or just surveille it? Either way I needed information.

Sumner's silence got me wondering again if her plan all along was to just use me for what I was worth as a substitute detective. Someone to ride with and maybe as backup—and then cut me off from the final takedown. Well, maybe. But now that I knew about the Acapulco, it was kind of late for dumping me. Which gave me an idea.

Sumner's cell phone beeped twice and then, "Parker McLeod, how's your hammer hanging?"

"Now, who's got sex on their mind?"

"I wish. What's up?"

"I just called to let you know I'll be staking out the Acapulco Cantina tonight if anything pops on the search."

Silence.

"Okay," I said. "I'll check with you later."

"No, wait," she countered, the strain in her voice obvious. "I wasn't going to tell you, but we're hitting the Acapulco with SWAT tonight. Arrest everyone there. Get some damned answers."

"Doesn't sound legal," I offered.

"I don't give a damn," she said, exasperated. "We're out of time to find those girls."

"Might mean your job."

Sumner chuckled, "Yeah, well I aways wanted to be a fishing guide."

I smiled at my phone and said, "Okay, so why didn't you want your *new* partner to know about this raid?"

Sumner waited a beat, then, "I couldn't take the chance you'd inform Rudy. We damn sure don't need him there."

"Jesus, give me *some* credit for a brain. He's the last person I'd tell."

"Okay. Sorry, Parker. Meet me at the station about 9:00 pm tonight. We'll go sometime after that."

# Chapter Thirty-Nine

## Saturday Afternoon

---

Rudy couldn't believe Parker had slipped and told him that Galveston PD got a tip about the bar where two girls had been dropped off. Finally, he thought. A solid lead. Like a dog chasing his tail, he'd run all over Galveston and half of Houston desperate to find Akemi and found nothing. He only hoped he could keep his jumbled mind together until he learned more. Something was happening inside him he didn't like.

He made it to the front of his house and parked. He knew he needed to meditate to try and calm himself, but he couldn't seem to focus. What the hell was going on with him?

His mind flashed to his dad sitting on a mat with his eyes closed, his legs crossed and his arms resting on his thighs. The scene was the bedroom of his family's wooden shack beside the pineapple fields, high in the hills of Maui.

Then the image switched to blood splattering his face as his best friend's arm flew by him, torn loose by a mortar shell.

His muscles twitched. Uncontrollable tremors spread through his hands and arms. He was on a mountain road in California, a truck veering into his lane, the horrible sound of screeching tires and crashing metal.

He shook his mind clear and wiped the sweat out of his eyes with his hand, then laid his head on the steering wheel.

A splitting headache woke him, the top of his head about to blow off. How long had he been out? His mind was back, but would this out-of-control behavior happen again?

Rudy's gut told him Galveston PD would raid the bar tonight. He needed to find out which one. He figured Parker would go along on the search and he could just follow him. But he had no idea where Parker might be. He decided the safe approach was to stake out the police station.

He thought the cops would probably make the raid after dark when the cantina was hopping with customers, and it was more likely Akemi and Maria would be there. He had mixed emotions about finding Akemi and Maria at a place like that. He wanted desperately to find them but hated the thought they may have been violated. He wanted to kill everyone involved with their kidnapping. Suddenly, the pain in his head came rushing back. He winced, rubbed his temples, and hoped Maggie had some powerful drug that would give him relief.

When he found Maggie was not home, he rummaged through the medicine cabinet himself, finding nothing but aspirin. He took four and lay on the couch. The pain subsided slightly, but his mind wouldn't quit whirling.

If he was going to follow Parker and Detective Sumner tonight, he certainly didn't want to be detected. The smart move was to use Maggie's five-year-old Honda Civic. He had never driven the Civic to The Garhole Bar, and he was sure none of the Dead Peckers or Parker had ever seen the car.

The aspirin must have kicked in because, when he awoke on the couch, he was surprised no sun came through the blinds. He opened the front door and almost panicked at the dark shadows on the street. He had to get going.

Maggie came in, her lined face alive with concern. "You needed rest. I didn't want to wake you."

"God, Maggie. I wish you had."

She reached out for his hand. "Rudy, we need to talk. What's going on with you?"

"Four days, Maggie. Is she even alive?"

Maggie touched his cheek. "Don't give up, honey. The police will find her. You'll see. You've been out every night, please stay home tonight and rest."

"Can't Maggie. Something is going down tonight. It may be our last chance."

He explained about the cantina and the possible raid. He told Maggie his plan to follow the police from the station and explained why he needed her car. Maggie didn't say anything. She just stood with her hand over her mouth and her eyes full of concern as he walked to the garage—where she knew he'd stashed the rifle.

# Chapter Forty

## Saturday Evening

---

I cruised over the causeway, beating myself up for my slip in telling Rudy that Galveston PD had found the bar where the dark van had been seen. If he could find out the name, he'd be there for sure with that damned Japanese rifle. Thinking Rudy's main source of information may be the police radio Harry Stein monitored, I decided to swing by Harry's house.

The front of his house was amazingly clear of vehicles—no good-looking widow, not even a committee meeting of some kind. Of course, that didn't mean the casserole lady from across the street wasn't visiting.

I parked in front, bounded up the stairs and knocked. He opened the door wearing an apron with the imprint of the tall ship *Elissa* across the front and a surprised look on his face.

"Parker, how nice to see you."

"Got a minute, Harry?"

"Actually, you're in luck. I was about to pull two roasted Cornish game hens from the oven. I was planning to keep one for lunch tomorrow, but I'd much rather share with you. I've already whipped up a nice spinach salad with my special warm bacon dressing. Come join me."

I followed Harry into his kitchen, thinking I had a couple of hours before meeting Sumner at the station so why not enjoy a gourmet meal. The food was so tasty I didn't want to distract Harry with questions about Rudy. Being a wanna-be chef myself, I asked him about the recipe.

"Not difficult," he said. "Baste the birds with a mixture of olive oil and honey, some fresh herbs, then stuff the cavity with carrots, celery and fresh rosemary. Roast until the inside temperature is 165 degrees. That's about it."

The birds were delicious, as is the case with anything Harry prepares. After the main course, Harry brought out two pieces of key lime pie he'd baked that morning and two cups of his special-blend Arabian coffee. I waited for him to swallow his second bite of pie.

"Harry, we need to talk about Rudy."

He put his fork down and studied my face. "Sure, Parker. What's on your mind?"

Harry knew Rudy had spent the night in the Houston jail, but I doubted if he knew the details. I filled him in on Rudy's sojourn and our trip this morning to retrieve his car.

"He's deteriorating quickly," I said. "He almost got into it with the guy at the car compound. Then when we arrived at the cantina where he'd gotten into the fight last night, the same bouncer was there and he challenged him again. We barely got away. Add in the fact he won't give up the rifle…well, I'm worried, Harry."

Harry picked up his fork to cut another bite of pie, then put it down again and pushed the plate away.

"You want me to do something, Parker. So out with it!"

"You read me well, Harry."

"I've known you since you were sixteen years old."

"It's about your police radio."

"That's interesting. Rudy called and said he wanted to come over tonight. I'm sure he wants to listen to the radio."

"That's the problem."

I told Harry about an informant at one of the cantinas seeing the van, but I didn't mention the bar's name. In case Rudy asked for the name, it was best Harry didn't know.

"Galveston PD is setting up surveillance tonight, maybe even a raid. Could be fireworks and we don't need Rudy there."

"So what do you want me to do?"

"Tell him the radio's broken."

"I won't lie, Parker."

"Okay, Harry. Well then, I need the radio to follow the case. Will you please let me borrow it?"

Harry retrieved the radio from the bar and set it on the table in front of me.

He said, "I understand your concern, Parker. I feel the same way about Rudy. I thought his meditating would keep him under control but…."

I related my conversation with Colonel Kennon about the possibility of Rudy suffering from Delayed PTSD. Kennon had speculated his granddaughter's kidnapping might have been the trigger that set him off.

"And then Kennon sent my gut reeling. He asked about a second trigger, some other traumatic event that, combined with his missing granddaughter, would send him…well, he didn't go into detail, but the way he said it left me panicked."

"A second trigger, huh?" Harry commented. "Like maybe his son's and daughter-in-law's deaths in the car accident?"

"No, I mentioned that to Kennon. He said it had to be something he thought was his fault and he's been consumed with guilt about, but not letting it out. Something he'd repressed and never dealt with."

Harry thought for a moment. "What do you know about the accident?" he asked.

"Rudy, his son and his son's wife and daughter—Akemi—were going to a baseball game. A truck in the other lane veered into them. It was a head on. Rudy's son and his wife died at the scene. Somehow neither Rudy nor Akemi was seriously injured."

Harry took in a big breath and blew out a stream of air. He scrunched his face. "Did Rudy tell you he was driving?"

"What? Oh, Christ, Harry!"

***

I stashed the police radio on the floorboard of my truck and drove to the seawall to sort out what I'd learned about Rudy. I found a parking spot and sat on a concrete bench overlooking the beach. Night had fallen but, as always, the full moon continued to spread its consoling rays over the calm surf. A few tourists lazily strolled the quiet beach below and even the drivers in the cars on the boulevard seemed to be moving casually, enjoying the peaceful evening.

It was Galveston like it was supposed to be on a cool October evening, except it wasn't. Two teenage girls were missing, and a worried grandfather was toting a rifle determined to save them. At the police station, cops were huddling, making a plan to raid a suspected trafficker's den.

The big clock on the seawall said 7:00 pm. Seventy-three hours past the kidnapping. We were making progress, but there was no certainty tonight's raid would produce results. The girls could still be anywhere.

Since Harry told me Rudy was coming to his house tonight, I thought it safe to call Maggie. She answered on the first ring. I brought her up to date on what Colonel Kennon had said about the possibility of Rudy's Delayed PTSD and the danger of something triggering his long-buried trauma.

I asked, "Did Rudy ever mention getting treatment for his

suffering and pain from the war?"

"No, Parker. I'm sure he didn't get treatment. Most of the returning veterans kept that stuff bottled up. They just wanted to get back to their friends and family and have a normal life.

"Rudy still has nightmares of bombs going off nearby, friends killed, even blown up before his eyes. How do you get treatment for that?"

I could feel the empathy in Maggie's voice. I needed to learn more about the accident in California.

"Harry told me Rudy was driving the car when the head-on happened that killed his family."

"Yes, Rudy won't talk about that either. I'm sure he's carrying a load of guilt. He did say he thought it was his fault."

"But the other vehicle veered into his lane."

"Yes, but Rudy blames himself. He says he should have avoided it, didn't try hard enough. 'There is always a way,' he said."

I thanked Maggie and terminated the call. The car accident had occurred last summer. If Rudy believed he was responsible for his son's death, that could be the first trigger Colonel Kennon was worried about and Akemi's kidnapping the one that finally set him off.

# Chapter Forty-One

## Saturday Night

---

I arrived at police headquarters to find the SWAT team assembling in the parking area. Eight officers dressed in helmets and flak jackets stood confidently checking their Colt M4 carbines. Along with infrared laser sights, each weapon carried a 30-round magazine. The M4 is similar to the AR16 I carried in Desert Storm, except the M4 barrel is shorter and easier to maneuver. The 5.56mm round used in the M4 and AR16 is only slightly larger than a .22 caliber squirrel gun. The difference is the size and weight of the bullet and the amount of powder. The SWAT officers also carried Sig Sauer 9mm P226 automatic sidearms each holding ten rounds. These guys weren't fooling around.

Detective Sumner greeted me in her office wearing utility pants, a black shirt, steel-toed leather shoes and a somber face. I nodded to Lieutenant Lott standing beside her dressed in a similar outfit. Sumner introduced me to Sergeant Guerra and his partner Officer Morales.

She said, "Guerra and Morales are the officers that went with us last night. They work undercover in Vice. Tonight, they volunteered to go in and reconnoiter the cantina."

Both Guerra and Morales appeared to be mid-thirties. Officer Morales looked sexy in her tight-fitting jeans and an expensive-looking blouse with silver-threaded embroidery of the Aztec calendar on the front. Her black hair fell past her shoulders and matched her dark eyes, which lit up when she smiled. I imagined they could fire up quickly if needed. Her bright red lip gloss matched the blush on her cheeks.

"Fine-looking blouse," I said, gesturing to the silver calendar.

"It better look good," Morales answered. "Cost me a week's pay." She batted her eyes. "Think I'll pass as a high-price madam?"

"No doubt," I said.

"If one of those drunk Mexicans spills beer on my blouse, I'll cram a beer bottle up his…."

I think she meant it, too.

Guerra wore tattered jeans, scuffed cowboy boots and a faded green Western shirt with phony pearl buttons. His wore his long hair swept back along the sides ending in a ponytail and a ball cap that said "Fish Whisperer" on the front. A several-days-old dark beard that needed trimming covered his cheeks.

Sumner said, "Both Guerra and Morales are wired so we can listen. Lott and I will handle back-up outside. SWAT will station around the corner with less than a minute ETA. You're not an officer. You can go with us but stay out of our way."

I followed Sumner and Lott to his vehicle and couldn't avoid patting the back of my pants for reassurance that my .45 was safely tucked away. If any of this involved Akemi and Maria, I'd be ready.

# Chapter Forty-Two

## Saturday Night

---

The entourage of police vehicles left the station a little after 9:00 pm and crossed the causeway, spacing themselves between other traffic to not attract attention. Guerra led the way in an old pickup that had garnered almost as many rust spots as mine. Morales followed in a two-year-old black Ford Mustang.

Making Morales appear to be a successful business woman was part of the plan. She would go in first and gather as much attention as possible to distract attention from Guerra when he entered. The thought of Morales attracting attention would be like witnessing a school of hungry trout attacking a pod of baitfish. It would happen. No doubt all eyes would be on the attractive woman, along with thoughts of who she was and why she was there.

Sumner, Lott and I followed discreetly in Sumner's unmarked black Ford sedan. The SWAT team's "rescue vehicle" lagged behind, complete with bullet-proof armor, protective vented windows and roof-mounted cameras with thermal imaging capability. The team's commander said the police department also had a front plow they could attach if needed to clear obstacles.

We headed north and exited the freeway to the right between the City of La Marque and League City, two small municipalities that hug northbound I-45 toward Houston.

After a few more turns, we ended up on a seldom-used dark road. Several paved streets intersected from the left, but only a couple of homes dotted the area, the residue of a failed housing development. The developer had probably gone bust during one of the real estate downturns.

On the right, a water-filled ditch paralleled the road. A wide culvert allowed access over the ditch to a poorly lit gravel parking area. In the rear of the parking lot, an old wooden building sat nestled in a mott of scraggly trees.

As we entered the parking area, we could see large windows held open with wooden poles. The openings allowed air flow through the front and sides of the building while ceiling fans creaked slowly overhead. Neon signs touting *Corona* and *Tecate* decorated the walls. A wooden fence surrounded the back of the building. The fence was obviously designed to camouflage the two mobile homes Atticus Lott and I had noticed during the previous night's visit to the cantina. Only small portions of the roofs showed above the fence.

Mexican music, with the sound of lively accordions and trumpets, blared out of what was probably a jukebox inside. The sounds floated out the open windows and across the parking area where old cars and pickups jammed the lot. A red neon sign atop the building read, "Acapulco Cantina," a smaller light below blinked, *"Chicas."*

Before leaving the police station, Sumner and Lott had donned bulletproof vests with POLICE stamped in large white letters on the backs. I put mine on as we entered the parking lot. We now sat sweating in the hot vests, waiting for the signal from Guerra and Morales to move in. The SWAT vehicle had backed into a side street a couple of blocks away. We wore ear buds tuned to Guerra and Morales' microphones, with me acting as translator if needed.

Morales and Guerra were to reconnoiter the bar, learn what they could, if anything, about Akemi and Maria and report back to Lieutenant Lott. Guerra hoped to talk with Camila, the girl Atticus Lott had spoken to last night who'd given him the information about the dark van dropping off two girls. Based on what they learned, Lieutenant Lott would make the final decision for a raid, including potential SWAT actions.

Our ear buds crackled with Officer Morales' voice as she approached the front entrance. "The parking lot is crammed full, but a pickup close to the front row is leaving. Try to grab that space for a good view and quick access."

Sumner quickly maneuvered her car into the vacant spot, giving us a direct view through the open windows into a large room with a long bar at the back. I handed Lott and Sumner binoculars from the back seat. Sumner got out and checked the parking lot to be sure no one was moving around who could squeal on us.

When she gave the "all clear," Lott and I followed her out. The three of us leaned over the car's roof to steady the field glasses. When a patron left the bar, or a new vehicle entered the parking lot, we ducked low behind Lott's car to avoid discovery.

We used the same binoculars favored by Army Special Forces and Navy Seals. The gyro-stabilization systems powered by two small batteries allowed a steady vision for their fourteen-power magnification, giving us clear views of everyone in the cantina.

Officer Morales entered the bar and immediately attracted attention from the dozen or so men standing around drinking beer. She smiled at those closest to her and paraded to an open spot at the far end of the long bar.

A Latino with bulging chest and muscled arms got up from a table near the front entrance and followed Morales to the bar. A heavy black beard covered his face, and various colored tattoos snaked along his arms from his wrists to above his powerful biceps. When the other male patrons viewed who was approaching Morales, they backed away. Their actions made it obvious the man was some kind of *jefe* at the cantina. Judging by his size, I pegged him as the bouncer.

Morales' task was to keep attention on her so Guerra could slip in and get information from Camila or one of the other girls at the bar. Morales didn't turn away when the man approached.

"You're new here," the big man said in Spanish, his eyes squinched and his top lip curled up on one end into a nasty sneer. He casually laid the back of his hand on Morales' shoulder and eased it down her sleeve to her elbow.

With a bored look, as if she was used to being hit on, Morales turned to the bar and ordered a shot of tequila. The *jefe's* arm slipped away. She downed the shot quickly and ordered another.

"I'm Beto. Security," he said. "Looking for work?"

She gazed around the room, finally letting her eyes drop to him. It was as if he was the last person of interest in the room.

"Heard about the Acapulco and came down from Houston to check it out."

Beto said, "Things getting tight in the big city?"

"Couple of girls I need to place. Young, but experienced."

"I can help you," Beto said, grabbing her elbow. "First, we go to the back. You can show me what you taught the girls."

Morales pulled her arm back. "Bring me your boss and we'll talk," she said.

"He'll be in later," Beto answered.

Morales turned back to the bar. "I'll wait," she said and cocked her head in the opposite direction from Beto making it obvious their conversation was over.

In the parking lot, Guerra heard Morales' conversation with the bouncer. He decided to go in. Not wanting to bring attention to himself, he waited for two new patrons to approach the entrance. He slipped behind them and entered with his head down and brushing dust off his jeans as if tired from a long day of work. He strode straight to the other end of the bar away from Morales and close to the hallway.

He sat next to a young Latino girl sitting on a stool and sipping a Coke. He ordered a beer.

I had a good view through the binoculars and focused on the girl's round face, rouged cheeks and fiery lipstick. She couldn't have been more than fifteen or sixteen. She leaned into Guerra, parading her ample bosom and spoke in Spanish. I translated for Detective Sumner and Lieutenant Lott standing beside me.

"My name is Gabriela. Want to party?"

She seemed nervous, constantly glancing around as if someone was watching her.

"My God, so young," Sumner murmured softly beside me.

When Guerra didn't respond, the girl moved closer. She reached down to his crotch and said, "I can make you happy."

"Where?" Guerra asked.

She cocked her head toward the hallway. She took Guerra's hand, slipped off the stool, and led him down the hallway toward the mobile homes in back.

# Chapter Forty-Three

## Saturday Night

---

As soon as darkness fell, Rudy found a parking lot crowded with cars and pickups across from the police station's back entrance where the SWAT vehicle was parked. Using the vehicles in the lot as cover, he settled in to watch. Maggie's powerful 8.5x40 bird-watching binoculars offered a clear view of the entrance and part of the police parking area.

At 8:00 pm, Parker entered the lot in his old truck. Nothing else happened until 9:00, when several heavily armed SWAT officers came out and stood by their vehicle. When Parker and Detective Sumner appeared a few minutes later, Rudy knew he had guessed right. Then a man and woman, both Hispanic and dressed in civilian clothes, huddled with Sumner and Parker. Two undercover cops, Rudy figured. He got a good look at both.

A little after 9:00 pm, the male undercover cop drove out in a beat-up pickup. The female followed in a black Mustang and then Parker and Sumner in a black Ford, finally followed by the SWAT vehicle.

Rudy followed the group over the causeway, being careful not to be detected. After some twists and turns, the SWAT vehicle slowed and backed into a side street. He couldn't see the other vehicles any longer.

He drove past the SWAT behemoth, hoping the team inside had been busy positioning themselves and hadn't gotten suspicious. Two blocks ahead, the cantina appeared on the right with a neon sign saying "Acapulco." Cars and trucks crammed the parking lot in front.

He turned onto a dark side street directly across from the parking lot, drove a block, turned around and came back so he would be facing the cantina. Maggie's binoculars gave him a clear view through the cantina's large open windows.

Inside, a dozen or so men dressed in jeans and wearing ball caps or Western hats mingled around a large room. He focused on the bar at the back. At one end he saw the woman cop who'd driven the Mustang.

It appeared Detective Sumner wasn't just surveilling the cantina: she had a plan. But where were she and Parker?

Rudy scanned the counter toward the hallway at the other end of bar. The man at the end was the cop he'd seen driving the pickup out of the police parking lot. His heart thumped. A young teenager, about the same age as Akemi, leaned toward the cop, her boobs pushed up in a halter top. She took his hand and led him down the hall toward the mobile homes in back.

Rudy understood it now. This is what traffickers do: capture young girls and turn them into sex slaves. What were the cops waiting on, he wondered? If Akemi and Maria were in there, they needed to move!

# Chapter Forty-Four

## Saturday Night

---

Akemi didn't know how long she had slept, but the pain in her cheek from Hector's slap still hurt like the devil. She felt the swelling with her hand and worried it was getting worse. Wanting to check her face in the mirror, she found her way to the bathroom in the dark and flipped the light switch. Nothing. Hector had continued his nasty game of removing the bulb so he could replace it when the girls showered. Just the thought of Hector staring at naked girls sent Akemi's stomach into a whirlwind.

Back at her pallet, Akemi heard voices in Spanish coming through the wall. She could only understand a few words, but she did hear Hector ask for the time and Juan replied, "Eight o'clock."

At least now Akemi knew it was nighttime. El Tigre was coming tonight and time was running out. Was Juan going to help them?

The buzzing sound of a cell phone drifted through the wall.

"El Tigre, what is the plan?" she heard Hector ask. For some reason he spoke in English.

El Tigre's rough voice came through loud and clear. Akemi thought Tigre must have told Hector to put his phone on speaker so Juan could hear and respond.

"Beto, the bouncer at the Acapulco, called me. He said last

night a big gringo, masquerading as a Latino, was talking with Camila at the bar. Beto said he thought at the time the gringo was probably a cop. He said he can smell them. But then he had to handle a fight in the parking lot, and he didn't see the gringo take Camila to the back. He only learned it happened from the bartender when he came on shift tonight."

Juan responded, "So maybe the gringo just wanted to get laid. Camila is good for that."

"The gringo showed Camila one of the flyers with the bitches you two donkeys kidnapped. Wanted to know if she'd seen them."

"What's the problem?" Hector asked. "Akemi and Maria have never been to the Acapulco."

"It took a little *persuasion* from Beto, but Camila finally admitted what she'd told the gringo. She said she'd never seen the girls in the flyer, but for some reason she told him a dark van dropped Gabriela and Sayda off each night. Camila said the gringo seemed real interested in that."

"Holy Christ," Hector said.

"It's a good thing you got rid of the van. The cops will be watching the Acapulco. I hope you haven't taken Gabriela and Sayda there yet."

"Well…I mean…well, you told us to."

"Goddamnit! We are moving everyone to Houston tonight. Go to the Acapulco now and pick up the girls. But first make sure no cops are watching the place. I'll be down as soon as I can get there. Don't screw this up!"

Akemi felt chills up her spine. She started shaking. She wrapped her arms around her body to calm herself. This was it. If Tigre took them to Houston, Jiichan would never find her. She had to do something.

Maria's moaning had stopped. Akemi felt her cheek, now cool and dry. Not good, she thought. She had worried about turning on the bedroom light because of what Hector would do if he caught her, but she had no choice now, she must get a closer look at Maria. She eased to the light switch by the door and flipped it up.

Akemi knelt close to her friend and saw Maria's eyes rolled up so only the whites showed. Her whole body twitched—arms, legs. Her skin was turning blue. She vomited. Akemi quickly turned Maria to her side so she wouldn't choke.

Akemi had to act! There was no time to wait; she must save her friend. She felt her hurting cheek again and gathered her courage. Maria was more important than anything that could happen to her. She ran to the kitchen door and pounded heavily.

Hector stepped in, noticed the light was on, and raised his hand to hit her. Juan was right behind and jammed his fist into Hector's kidney with a powerful blow. Hector went down. Juan stood over him, yelling.

"Leave her alone. You've hurt her enough."

Hector tried to get up, but Juan kicked him hard in the ribs. Hector rolled over, moaning, holding his side.

Akemi shouted, "Juan, it's Maria, she's...she's dying!"

Juan went quickly to Maria, folded her in his arms and strode to Hector.

"Get up," he yelled. "We're leaving."

Hector, woozy, stumbled to his feet while holding his rib cage. Juan herded him out ahead of him. While Hector stumbled into the passenger seat, Juan lay Maria down gently on the back seat.

He took zip ties from his pocket. "I am sorry Akemi. I

must bind you. If I let you get away, Tigre will kill me."

"What about Maria?"

"We'll take her somewhere, but I will tell Tigre she died and we dumped her body."

"We don't have time to do that," Hector mumbled, wheezing as he spoke. "Tigre ordered me to pick up Gabriela and Sayda. If the cops get them, they'll know where we live."

"I've already seen Juanita and Sarah's dead bodies," Juan said. "I won't let that happen to another girl."

Juan secured Akemi's zip ties. He fitted the cloth hood over her head, guided her into the back seat, and positioned Maria's head in her lap. He opened the garage door, climbed into the driver's seat and started the engine.

"Hurry," Akemi screamed through the hood. "Maria is having trouble breathing."

Juan looked back to see Maria's chest expand as she arched up, her lungs crying for oxygen. Akemi's tears flowed from the bottom of her hood and fell on Maria's face.

Juan made the turns out of the subdivision and stopped for traffic at the intersection with Highway 6. Hector reached for the handle of the driver's door with his right hand while pushing Juan with his left, attempting to open Juan's door and shove him out.

Juan grabbed Hector's neck with his right arm and rammed his left fist into Hector's face hard three times. Blood splattered from Hector's nose down into his mustache and onto the man's face on his tee shirt. Before the blood could get to Juan's shirt, he pushed Hector back to the passenger side.

"Try that again, Hector and I'll beat you unconscious."

"El Tigre will kill us both if you do this," Hector cried, wiping his nose with his shirt.

"I will handle Tigre," Juan answered. "And you damned well better keep your mouth shut when we meet him."

Hector whimpered, then lay his head on the seatback and closed his eyes, pinching his nose with his hand. When Juan turned onto the highway and sped past Bayou Vista, Hector opened his eyes and pointed to the freeway.

"You missed the turn to I-45 North. What are you doing?"

"Going to Galveston."

"What? We have to get Gabriela and Sayda. We've moving to Houston tonight."

"First I have to take care of Maria."

"Take care? What are you talking about? The hospital has outside cameras. They'll nail us."

"If we drop her in Galveston, the cops will think Akemi is held some place close to where we leave her."

Juan drove onto the freeway toward the causeway, carefully staying below the speed limit. He drove onto the island and turned right on Sixty-First Street, remembering an Urgent Care Clinic a few blocks up. He slowed as he passed the building.

"You see any cameras?" he asked Hector.

"No, but what if someone comes in the parking area while you're there with the girl?"

Juan ignored Hector's plea. He hoped the one car in the lot belonged to an employee, thinking that person wouldn't come out until after closing. All he had to worry about was a new patient showing up while he carried Maria to the front door.

He turned right at the end of the block, parked on the corner and turned the engine off. He took the keys and got out. He checked the traffic flow on Sixty-First[t] Street and determined that cars were stopped at the light a block away.

He had to hurry. He opened the back door of the car and gingerly lifted Maria. Checking that the traffic was still stopped at the light, he quickly hustled Maria to the front door of the clinic and lay her in front of the door. He pounded the door several times, ran back to the Suburban and sped down Sixty-First.

He U-turned and entered the causeway, heading north to the Acapulco Cantina.

"Jesus, I hope we get to the Acapulco before the cops," Hector cried out.

"Stop it," Juan replied. "We don't know the cops are coming tonight. That's just what El Tigre thinks."

Juan said that just to calm Hector. In truth, he had a feeling the cops *were* coming. So what if the cops caught him at the Acapulco loading the girls? Part of him hoped they would. At least the nightmare with El Tigre would be over. If the cops didn't show, he would have to tell Tigre that Maria had died and he had dumped her body. And he had to worry Hector might squeal and tell Tigre what really happened. And what would El Tigre do to him then?

But then, what if the cops caught him and Maria died? Would they blame him? Would Akemi help him? And what if he picked up Gabriela and Sayda before the cops got there and Tigre took them and Akemi to Houston? What would happen to Akemi? She didn't deserve this.

He'd helped Maria get free. Should he help Akemi escape? Maybe he should have left her with Maria. But Akemi had heard Hector say they were going to the Acapulco Cantina. If he had dropped Akemi with Maria, she could tell the cops everything. They'd for sure be waiting for them at the cantina.

Juan swallowed hard and drove on. He thought he'd done

the right thing so far, but he had some thinking to do and not much time to do it.

Akemi, with the hood over her head and her hands bound, lay quietly on the cold back seat thanking all the gods she could think of that Juan had taken Maria for help. But was it too late? What could she do to help Maria now?

At Maria's mobile home, she'd watched Maria's mother pray at her shrine to Our Lady of Guadalupe. Maria had said Our Lady of Guadalupe was the most important saint in Mexico: the patron saint. Maria had told her she also prayed at her mother's shrine. Akemi decided Maria's God was her best hope. She had never prayed before and didn't know what she was supposed to do. She lowered her head and asked Maria's God to please see that someone would find Maria in time.

# Chapter Forty-Five

## Saturday Night

---

Sergeant Pulley sat at the counter in the Waffle House on Sixty-First Street, finishing his second cup of coffee and last bite of peach pie and chatting with the gray-haired waitress he'd gotten to know over the last few weeks. As she rattled on about her day, Pulley was thinking about how hard her life must be and how fortunate he and Thelma were to have had so many good years together.

His usual routine when an evening shift ended was to stop for coffee and a slice of pie and two pieces to go. He knew Thelma would be waiting up for him and together they would enjoy the late-night snack while reviewing their day. Of course, he never told Thelma about the first piece he'd already scarfed down.

He'd just dotted his lips with a napkin and laid the money on the counter for his snack, including a heavy tip, when the call tone on his radio blared across the empty restaurant.

"Injured girl at the Urgent Care location on Sixty-First Street. Officers responding."

Pulley knew he was only a couple of blocks away. He answered, "329 enroute, two minutes."

Pulley realized the report of an injured girl could mean anything from an accident to an assault. He tried to shake off the negative vibes and raced to the scene, lights flashing. In less than a minute, he pulled into an open spot at the clinic, making sure to leave room for the ambulance. Inside the front door, a doctor leaned over a gurney with a stethoscope pressed to the injured girl's chest, his tight jaw signaling his concern. An assistant beside him held a bottle of saline above the girl's arm. The sound of an approaching EMS siren pierced the quiet night.

"My God," the physician said as Pulley hurried in. "Someone just left this poor girl in front and banged on the door. We were closed and just finishing up. Lucky we heard the noise."

Pulley looked down at the girl's pale face, closed eyes and shallow breaths. He thought about his beautiful granddaughter and said a quick prayer for the girl. He stepped out to his patrol car, removed the small poster from the front seat and returned to the gurney. He glanced from the poster to the girl and back several times.

Pulley stepped away from the gurney and clicked his radio.

"329 to Dispatch."

"Go ahead 329."

"I'm at the scene of the injured girl on Sixty-First Street. EMS is pulling in now. The girl is alive. Could be Maria Santos, one of the missing teenagers. Suggest calling the officer in charge, Detective Sumner, to arrange verification."

An ambulance screeched to a stop in front and began backing to the door. The physician had already notified EMS of the patient's condition, so the paramedics wasted no time loading the girl into the back. Seconds later the ambulance sped off toward UTMB, the island's "Level One" trauma center, lights flashing and siren blasting.

Pulley turned to the physician standing forlorn at the door. He said, "How is she, doctor?"

The doctor paused and bit his lip. "Critical—totally dehydrated. We started a drip line. She has a raging infection. Her foot is turning gangrenous. I hope they can save it…Christ, I hope they can save *her*!"

Pulley jumped in his vehicle and squealed out, lights flashing. Thelma answered on the first ring.

"Are you almost home?"

Pulley explained the situation and that he was enroute to the hospital.

"Oh, my goodness," she said. "Prayers for the little girl."

"I think she needs them," Pulley answered.

Pulley had met Maria's mother, Señora Santos, earlier with Detective Sumner at Santos' mobile home. Thinking the Señora would remember him, he notified Dispatch of his intent and raced to her home to break the news and offer an escort to the hospital.

# Chapter Forty-Six

## Saturday Night

---

After the woman's rebuff, Beto stalked off to his table by the entrance to the cantina. His phone pulsed in his pocket.

He grabbed it. "Beto."

"Hector and Juan are coming to pick up Gabriela and Sayda," El Tigre's gruff voice announced. "Have them ready. We're moving tonight."

"Are *you* coming here?"

"Why?"

"A hot *mamacita* at the bar says she came down from Houston to place two of her girls. She wants to meet you."

"You didn't tell her my name."

"Of course not."

"From Houston? That's never happened before. Doesn't make sense. The bitch is a cop, get the girls out now."

Beto glanced back at the woman still at the bar, drinking. Nothing seemed unusual. Still El Tigre suspected….

He turned to the bartender, "Where is Gabriela? Sayda?"

"With customers," the bartender replied.

"Gabriela was just here. Who did she go with?"

"Some new dude, haven't seen him before."

A picture of El Tigre's face flashed before Beto. What would he do to him if things went wrong? He turned and strode quickly down the hall.

# Chapter Forty-Seven

## Saturday Night

---

Morales turned from the bar and spoke softly into her microphone. "Beto was on the phone then he hurried down the hallway. I think he's following Guerra and the girl."

"Be careful," Lott replied.

Morales asked directions to the *baños* as a feint to follow Beto. I knew what she was doing and hoped she hadn't created suspicion in the bartender.

Her voice sounded again two minutes later. "I checked the restrooms in the hall. Nothing. I'm worried about Guerra. I'm going to the back."

I looked at Lott, "This sounds bad. Let's go in."

"No, wait— "

A shot sounded over the din of his voice, not loud enough to have come from the cantina.

I yelled into the microphone, "Morales? Are you okay?

Silence.

Lott screamed into his radio to the SWAT team, "Shot fired! Shot fired! We're going in!"

We broke from the vehicle and raced toward the front door. Men streamed out the entrance, passing on either side like we were parting the Red Sea.

I trailed close behind Lott and Sumner as they broke through the front entrance with both hands wrapped around their 9mm Glock automatics, the ambient light reflecting off the word "POLICE" emblazoned on their flak jackets.

Behind us the SWAT rescue vehicle careened into the parking lot. Officers jumped out. Half of them began corralling the fleeing cantina patrons outside while four officers followed us in.

The SWAT leader ordered the remaining patrons to line up and interlock their hands on top of their heads. The other officers began zip tying their hands behind them.

From the looks on their faces, I figured every man in the room was probably worried one of the heavily armed SWAT team would shoot him. The room went eerily quiet.

Sumner was closest to the hallway and took the lead, followed by Lott and then me and the SWAT leader.

A single low-watt bulb cast a dim light ahead of us. Procedure demanded that we check every room as we went. No one wanted to be shot in the back.

The sign on the first door to the left read "*Damas*." Sumner kicked the door open and barged inside, weapon out front ready to fire. She hurriedly checked the stalls and yelled "clear" to the hallway. Lott kicked in the *Caballeros* door next to it and repeated "clear."

That left me in the lead with the SWAT officer close behind. The only other room down the hallway was ahead to the right. Past that was the door to the outside that led to the mobile homes. Before I could reach the door, the SWAT officer brushed past me. He kicked the door in and rushed inside, with the flashlight on his M4 leading the way. I halted at the entrance.

The small ten-by-ten room was obviously for storage. Cases of beer and miscellaneous supplies sat stacked to the ceiling at the rear and on each side of the room. The SWAT officer repeated the clear signal and stepped behind me.

Again in front, I moved quickly to the rear door.

Outside, two covered walkways led right and left to the mobile homes. A single bulb in the ceiling of each walkway cast a dim light to show the way. The open space to each mobile home looked about twenty feet. No doubt someone could be hiding in the open area and waiting to spring a trap on whoever came through.

But there was no time to consider risk. If Sergeant Guerra and Officer Morales were okay, they would have come out to greet us. Something wasn't right.

They had to be in one of the mobile homes. But which one? I signaled toward the right and raced toward the small porch on the front of the mobile home. The SWAT officer followed close behind. Sumner and Lott took the other path.

I moved cautiously up the steps to the porch. The SWAT officer waited at the bottom watching for anyone coming out of the cantina. With my .45 in a firing grip, I eased the door open and peeked inside. The living room and small kitchen appeared empty. I slipped into the eerily still scene and checked the hallway to the two bedrooms, both doors open.

Moving slowly, I pressed my ear to the wall just before I reached the first door. No sounds. I stepped into the doorway ready to fire. The big Latino, Beto, held Officer Morales with his left arm around her neck. His right hand pushed his weapon against her temple.

Sergeant Guerra lay on his back on the floor. Blood oozed from his chest. Gabriela sat on the bed holding her hand to her mouth, eyes wide, terrified and frozen in place.

Morales' eyes bulged and gurgling sounds emanated from her throat as she tried frantically to breath.

Beto spoke quietly, "Lower your weapon or I'll blow her brains out."

I held my .45 even with Morales' chest. I'd heard of a Mexican Standoff, and now I was in one. My only chance was to distract Beto so I could get off a shot. The timing and aim would have to be perfect. Only half of Beto's face peeked around Morales' head.

Concentrating on Beto's eyes, I spoke in Spanish to the girl on the bed.

"Gabriela, come to me now. Get off the bed and come to me."

A soft moan came from the bed.

Beto, with his eyes steadied on me, said, "Do not move, Gabriela."

A few seconds passed, both of us in a stare down.

I said in Spanish, "That's it, Gabriela. Keep coming."

Beto's eyes flashed to Gabriela. In that half-second, I raised my .45 and fired. The sound echoed around the room, causing momentary deafness in my ears. The bullet tore through Beto's right eye and blew a hole out the side of his head behind his ear. Blood splashed Officer Morales' cheek down to her expensive blouse. Beto collapsed to the floor taking Morales with him.

I quickly leaned over the crumpled but still-entwined figures and gingerly moved Beto's arm off Morales' neck. She rolled over face down and gasped for breath, her chest heaving in frantic moves. I stuffed a pillowcase onto Guerra's wound and held pressure.

Gabriela fell back on the bed emitting an out-of-control banshee-like wail. The banshee's howl foretells death. Did that mean the present or future? I could only hope.

I'd had enough death for one night.

# Chapter Forty-Eight

## Saturday Night

---

Rudy heard a shot and immediately people stampeded out the front entrance. He spotted Parker and Detective Sumner through his binoculars, forcing their way up the steps through the crowd.

The SWAT vehicle careened across the culvert into the parking lot and slammed to a stop just short of the door. Officers in flak jackets and helmets poured out and herded the patrons together as they fled the cantina.

Rudy grabbed the Japanese rifle from the seat and shoved the car door open to make a dash for the cantina. The rifle shook in his hands. He grabbed the door to steady himself. If Akemi and Maria were there….

He paused and mumbled to himself, "No…. Leave the rifle. You're running toward a team of highly trained SWAT officers, their adrenalin peaked."

He dropped the rifle on the seat and sprinted across the culvert toward the cantina.

An officer pointed his M4 carbine at Rudy's chest, "Stop or I'll fire!"

Rudy slowed to a walk, shouting, "I'm Akemi's grandfather."

# Chapter Forty-Nine

## Saturday Night

---

Officer Morales had wiped Beto's blood from her face and now, still shaken, sat at a table in the bar with her head down in her arms. A newly arrived detective from Internal Affairs sat across from her, drumming his fingers on the tabletop, waiting to begin the initial interview.

I wanted to slap his face. I got close enough to Morales to see splotches of dried blood on her expensive blouse. I swallowed hard, knowing it was my hand that put the blood there.

When the detective spotted me leaving, he rose and stopped me at the door.

"I'll take your weapon, McLeod," he said to my back.

I turned and gave him a hard stare. "Not going to happen."

"What do you mean? You were involved in a shooting. Your weapon is evidence in the investigation."

"Except the shooting may not be over."

"What? Give me your damned weapon or I'll arrest you as a material witness!"

"Better check with Detective Sumner or Lieutenant Lott before you get your pants in a wad. Better yet, call my attorney Harry Stein."

At the mention of Harry's name, the detective sighed heavily, shook his head and stalked off.

Sumner and I went out to the ambulance where two paramedics tried desperately to stabilize Guerra with saline infusions.

"Blood pressure eighty over fifty," the older paramedic said. "Where is that damned bird?"

A Life Flight helicopter, blowing dust across the parking lot, landed in an empty spot close to the road. As soon as it settled, paramedics lifted one end of the backboard holding Guerra while two SWAT officers grabbed the other end. They were out of the ambulance in seconds, rushing Guerra across the parking area. A minute later, Life Flight lifted up and banked toward UTMB Galveston.

Sumner turned to me, her eyes misty and red. She shook her head. "God, I hope Guerra makes it. It was my idea to use him and…."

There was no need for words. I stepped forward, gave Sumner a hug and listened to her quiet sob on my shoulder. Then she backed away, dabbed under her eyes with her hand and straightened her shoulders.

Someone yelled at Sumner from the parking lot.

"Detective, I'm Rudy Aoki, Akemi's grandfather. Is she…is she here?"

Sumner and I moved closer to him. Rudy's eyes were wild, darting in all directions.

"Mr. Aoki," Sumner said. "What are you doing here?"

"What about Akemi?"

"Akemi and Maria aren't here. Please Mr. Aoki, go home. Let us handle the search. I promise we'll find your granddaughter."

Lieutenant Lott came out of the entrance following two EMTs with a young girl strapped to a backboard. The EMTs hurried to a waiting ambulance.

I got a quick glance as she went by and she didn't look good. Her nose was bent and her lips were puffy. Purple bruises splotched across her cheeks indicated a terrible beating. A small cut creased her forehead and a white bandage covered one eye. My heart sank. If I could just have two minutes with whoever did this, a little interrogation of my own.

Lott eased to the side of the door, leaned against the outside wall and threw up. He wiped his mouth with a handkerchief. Sumner and I waited, giving him time to gather his composure.

He turned to Sumner with mournful eyes, "That's the girl that told my brother Atticus last night about the dark van dropping off two girls. Her name is Camila. That bastard Beto did that to her as punishment for talking to Atticus."

He looked at me, "You did the right thing, Parker."

When he said that, it hit me for the first time that I'd taken a man's life. No doubt a worthless piece of dung, but still.... Then I remembered Gabriela's terrified face while sitting on that bed and the vision of Sergeant Guerra on the floor, his life blood pouring out.

A moment of quiet validation passed through me. My shoulders slumped and I exhaled a long breath, releasing the tension of the last hour. I had wondered if I would carry the guilt of taking a life and now decided. No, not for that man. I wouldn't waste my grief on evil.

Sumner put her hand on Lott's shoulder and squeezed, "Sorry, JuJu."

Lott and Sumner closed to a quick embrace. I turned away hoping no one but me noticed.

They parted and Lott said, "How is Sergeant Guerra?"

"Life Flight just took off," Sumner answered. "Go on to

the hospital Julius, we can handle this."

Lott nodded and headed toward one of the newly arrived officers to commandeer a ride to the hospital.

Sumner turned to me, "I have to go inside and interview Gabriela and the other girl. I'd like to question them separately, but they won't leave each other."

"The other girl?"

"After the shots were fired, a SWAT officer brought out a terrified girl from the other trailer. Maybe fourteen. Jesus…."

"I'll go with you," I said.

"Absolutely not!" she replied. "I don't want Gabriela to see you. Damn it. Think, Parker. She just watched you blow a man's brains out. Stay here."

Detective Sumner entered the bar and approached Gabriela and a younger girl at a table drinking Cokes. The officer sitting beside the girls had found a couple of light blankets and draped them over the girls' shoulders to offer comfort to their half-naked torsos.

Gabriela sat with one arm around the other girl, and their hands were clenched so tightly their fingers showed white. With her head down, Gabriela didn't see me slip around the table behind her.

Sumner mouthed, "What the hell are you doing?" I ignored her gesture.

The officer's tag read 'J Peña.' She was speaking to the girls in Spanish. Sumner took a seat across from them.

Peña said, "We know you came to America without permission, but don't worry, you are safe now. Detective Sumner and I will take care of you."

When neither girl responded, Sumner said, "Gabriela, I am so sorry you had to witness that bad man getting shot. It must have been really scary."

Peña repeated her words in Spanish. A moment of silence and then Officer Peña shifted to the other girl and asked softly in Spanish, "What is your name?"

More silence. Then, Gabriela spoke, her voice so soft we could barely hear her. "She is my sister. Her name is Sayda."

"Sayda is a pretty name," Peña said, hoping Sayda would answer.

"She doesn't talk much," Gabriela said, pulling Sayda closer. "Juan and Hector are coming for us," Gabriela continued. "We will go with them."

My pulse zoomed and I could see Sumner's eyes light up. We both realized these could be the two girls that Camila told Atticus about last night. The ones dropped off here in a dark van. Maybe the same dark van that took Akemi and Maria away.

"Oh," Sumner said. "So Juan and Hector are coming for you in the van?"

Officer Peña repeated Sumner's question in Spanish. It was a smart question as we already knew the van had been found but were unsure what the kidnappers were driving now.

"Yes, they are our friends," Gabriela answered. "They give us money to send to our sister in Guatemala." Gabriela pulled two one-dollar bills out of her bra and held them up for Sumner to see. "But they don't have the van anymore. El Tigre made Hector get a new car.

"Really," Sumner said, acting excited at the news. "What did they get?"

"Not a van, a long car with more seats."

"You mean like a Suburban?"

Gabriela shrugged.

"Is El Tigre coming, too?" Sumner asked, her voice soft.

"No. He will meet us at the house to take us to Houston."

"Really? Where in Houston?"

Gabriela shrugged again.

"Do you want to go to Houston?"

"Yes," Gabriela answered. "Hector said we will like it there."

"Are you and Sayda the only girls going to Houston?"

Gabriela hesitated briefly. She dropped her eyes momentarily then raised them again.

"Well, maybe Maria and Akemi too," she said. "But Maria is really sick, so I don't know…."

Bingo! There it was! I wanted to grab Sumner and hug her. It was obvious her interview experience during years of working with juveniles had paid off. We were so close.

Sumner continued, "Gabriela, you say Maria is sick. What is wrong with her?"

She waited for a response, but Gabriela didn't say anything.

"Well, how about this, Gabriela," Sumner continued, concern in her soft voice. "If your friend, Maria, is sick, we must help her. We can't wait for Juan and Hector, and we can't leave you and Sayda here alone. We'll take you to your house and wait for them there."

Gabriela didn't respond. Sumner stepped away from the table and called Lott on her cell phone.

"Where are you?" she asked.

"Almost to the hospital."

"How is Guerra?"

"I don't know yet."

Sumner heard the anguish in Lott's voice. She wanted to say something comforting. All she could think to say was, "Prayers for Guerra."

"He needs them," Lott said.

"We've had a breakthrough here," she said anxiously. "The two girls at the cantina are sisters being run by a man they call El Tigre. They say he's from Houston. Can you check him out and get back to me ASAP?"

"Will do," Lott said.

"We think the girls are the ones that Atticus said got dropped off in the van. And get this…one of the girls mentioned Akemi and Maria's names."

"Holy Christ!" Lott exclaimed.

"I know," Sumner responded. "We also have the names of two of the girls' keepers, Juan and Hector. We're taking the girls so they can show us the way to their hidey-hole. This could be it!"

"Need more officers?"

"No. Four SWAT officers will follow us. We're good."

"Things are popping here, too," Lott said. "An ambulance is bringing in an unidentified girl that may be Maria Santos."

"Holy cow, Julius. That's good news. Do you really think it's Maria?"

"I don't know, but I'd better stay at the hospital in case it is Maria so I can interview her. If it's her, Akemi may be alone at that house. Think you can handle the raid?"

Total silence, then Sumner said, "You'd better not have asked that question because I'm a woman, or it's back to roses, fine wines and expensive steak dinners for your bony ass."

# Chapter Fifty

## Saturday Night

---

A SWAT officer instructed Rudy to stand with the group of men from the cantina. When paramedics rolled two gurneys by, he couldn't get a good view of either. One gurney went to the waiting Life Flight helicopter and the other into an ambulance.

"Damn," he said softly to himself, hoping it wasn't Akemi and Maria on the backboards. Then he remembered Detective Sumner telling him the girls weren't there. He sighed heavily, wondering what to do now.

Just then, McLeod and Sumner herded out two young girls with blankets draped over their shoulders. One was the teenager with the halter top who'd gone down the hall with Guerra. McLeod put the girls into the back seat of Sumner's sedan and drove out followed by the SWAT vehicle.

At first, Rudy thought Sumner was transporting the two girls to the police station. But then, why had half of the SWAT team loaded into their vehicle and followed Sumner, leaving a parking lot full of patrons with their hands on their heads and only a couple of officers watching them? It didn't make sense.

As soon as the SWAT vehicle turned onto the blacktop, Rudy sneaked back across the street and cranked up Maggie's car. Before he rolled out to follow Sumner's car, a Suburban drifted by on the street, barely moving. Even with the darkened windows, he could see the driver and passenger were studying the scene at the cantina.

He knew the kidnappers had dumped the van and, chances were, they didn't want another one. Still, they had to have a vehicle that would transport several girls. Could the Suburban be their new vehicle?

Rudy debated whether to go with the Suburban or follow Sumner and the SWAT vehicle. If he tracked the Suburban and it turned out not to be the kidnappers, he would lose Parker and the cops for the night. Decision time.

As soon as the Suburban was safely down the street, Rudy sped toward Sumner and McLeod, hoping he hadn't lost them.

# Chapter Fifty-One

## Saturday Night

---

Before they'd left the house to take Maria to the clinic, Akemi had heard El Tigre say he thought the cops would raid the Acapulco tonight. He'd ordered Juan and Hector to pick up Gabriela and Sayda at the Acapulco and, along with Akemi and Maria, take off to Houston as soon as possible.

Realizing this could be her last chance for freedom, she lay on the back floorboard of the Suburban desperately trying to think of a way to escape. At least Juan had zip tied her hands in front this time. With her hands in front, she could easily remove the hood, but decided only to do it when she knew she could get away. This was not the time to make Juan mad. He'd just saved Maria; maybe he would save her. Whatever was going to happen, it had to be soon. Once she was in Houston, she knew she'd be lost forever.

Akemi could tell they'd turned off the freeway. She remembered when they'd dropped Sarah at the Acapulco, the cantina was only a few minutes away.

After a few twists and turns, she heard Juan in the front seat say to Hector, "Look at that monster truck making the turn in front of us."

"Holy shit," Hector said. "It's one of those damn SWAT trucks."

"How do you know?"

"Seen 'em on TV."

"There's a black car in front of it, hauling ass. Both in a big hurry."

"Looks like they came from the Acapulco."

"Jesus, man. We're in trouble."

A couple of minutes later Juan said, "Parking lot's full of flashing lights and cop cars."

"El Tigre was right," Hector added. "Better slow down. Maybe they won't notice us go by. Stay down, Akemi."

***

Akemi decided this was the time. She removed the hood from her face, raised her hands over her head and found the door handle. Maybe she could open the door and roll out. She would hit the ground hard, but they'd slowed. It was her only chance. She was close enough to the cantina she could run toward it screaming and someone would hear her.

She pushed the handle up and shoved the door preparing to bail out. Nothing. Too late she realized the door was locked.

The palm of Hector's hand hit the top of her head. She fell to the floorboard.

"Stay there," Hector yelled. "Get up and I'll hit you again."

Akemi still felt the sting on the top of her head. This was the second time he'd hit her. She felt her bruised cheek, still swollen. She would get even somehow, someway.

Akemi noticed Juan hadn't responded to Hector's threat like he had after Hector had slapped her in the field. Had she lost him?

# Chapter Fifty-Two

## Saturday Night

---

When Kathy Landry arrived for her late-night shift in the ER, she noticed most of the previous staff had voluntarily stayed over. The entire ER buzzed with the anticipation of Life Flight and an ambulance arriving at the same time. She saw it in their anxious faces. It was strange, she thought. Everyone seemed to be sharing a mixture of apprehension because the patient in the Life Flight was a police officer tempered with hope that the arriving ambulance contained one of the missing girls.

The Life Flight helicopter transporting Sergeant Guerra landed and waiting attendants whisked the wounded officer straight from the Helo pad through the ER to the operating room.

In the waiting room outside the ER, a dozen or more Galveston police officers with drawn faces gathered in small groups and quietly murmured their concern for Guerra. Galveston PD was a small force and everyone knew the injured officer. At the entrance, a pathway opened between more arriving officers as Chief Ryan Puryear hurried through the door.

Puryear, in his full-dress dark-blue uniform with braided hat and four stars on the epaulets, nodded to the other officers as they came to attention. At six-two, powerfully built and square-jawed, the chief projected a commanding image of police authority. He headed straight for Kathy at the entrance to the ER rooms.

"Any word?" Puryear asked.

"He's in surgery, chief," Kathy answered. "Fortunately, Dr. Andrew Hardy, the head of surgery, was on call. He's the best. Sergeant Guerra has lost a lot of blood. The bullet entered just below his clavicle. He's critical but at least no vital organs were hit."

"Thank God for that," Puryear said.

Puryear asked directions to the surgery waiting area and trailed off to wait with the officer's family.

Kathy stood just inside the door to UTMB's Emergency Department nervously waiting for the ambulance transporting the girl from the Urgent Care on Sixty-First Street. The notification from Sergeant Pulley that the girl could be Maria Santos had everyone in the ER pulsating with excitement. The ER physician had called in the hospital's top infectious disease specialist, Dr. Martin Evan, who now stood beside Landry, already gloved and masked.

Just then the ambulance pulled into the drive. The doors opened and two hospital attendants quickly lifted the gurney to the ground. With the ER physician at Maria's side, checking her pulse and vital signs, the attendants rolled the gurney inside to a treatment room.

Kathy recognized the two paramedics from the ambulance. She cornered them with cups of black coffee. "What do you think?" she asked.

"Touch and go," the lead paramedic said. "We thought we'd lost her enroute, but she's a tough little girl."

A nurse came out of the treatment room and spoke to Landry.

"She's still unconscious, in shock. She has a nasty

puncture wound on the bottom of her right foot. The lab's doing a rush job on the blood samples. Dr. Evan is waiting for the results to start the antibiotic infusion."

Kathy knew different antibiotics reacted to pathogens differently and Dr. Evan wanted to be sure he was using the correct one for the girl's infection.

The outer doors to the ER waiting room opened and Sergeant Pulley, with two women in tow, hurried through the door. Kathy stepped up and met the trio just outside the entrance to the treatment rooms.

Pulley moved ahead of the women. He asked Kathy in a soft voice, "What do we know?"

"She's in a treatment room now. Dr. Evan is with her."

Pulley put his hand lightly on Señora Santos' elbow and brought her forward. The other woman followed.

"This is Alicia Santos, Maria's mother," he said. "And Señora Gonzalez, her cousin."

"I want to see her," Santos said to Kathy. She spoke in broken English, her pale face a maze of worry lines from her furrowed brow to her tight jaw.

"We are not sure it's Maria," Kathy said. "And there are laws…."

Santos didn't respond, a quizzical look on her face. Pulley gave Kathy a look like, *What the hell? Do something!*

Kathy excused herself. She hurried to the treatment room and stood outside motioning to Dr. Evan. After Kathy's explanation, Evan thought for a moment.

"Exigent circumstances," he said. "If this is Maria, we need to know her medical history and drug allergies. Mask and glove Señora Santos and bring her in."

Minutes later, Maria's mother emerged from the treatment room weeping. She dropped her mask and took several deep breaths, collapsing into Kathy's arms. Kathy helped her to a chair in the waiting room. Santos dropped her head and continued to weep.

Kathy mouthed to Pulley, "It's Maria."

After Kathy escorted the two women to a room down the hallway, she stepped outside and called Harry Stein on her cell phone.

"Harry, it's Kathy. Maria Santos has been found alive. She's in the ER. Can you notify Maggie and Rudy?"

"Of course," Harry answered, excitedly. "Tell me what you know."

After Kathy's quick explanation, Harry said, "If Rudy's not home, I'll bring Maggie to the hospital."

Lieutenant Lott was harboring in the surgery waiting room with Puryear and Guerra's family, but closely monitoring his radio and cell phone. When the call came in that the girl was Maria Santos, he hurried to the room Señora Santos was using and knocked on the door. He stepped inside and noted Maria's mother, uncontrollably distraught, unable to stop weeping.

Lott stepped out and found Kathy at the ER entrance.

"It's imperative I interview the girl. Akemi Aoki is still out there somewhere. We have no time to waste."

"Impossible," Kathy said. "Maria is still unconscious."

Frustrated, Lott bit his lip, then stepped outside and called Sumner on his cell phone.

"Señora Santos just identified the girl the ambulance brought in as her daughter, Maria."

"Oh, man, that is great news!" Sumner responded. "How is she?"

"Very sick, unconscious. At least we've got her. Now find Akemi!"

# Chapter Fifty-Three

## Saturday Night

---

Juan drove a few blocks, turned onto a darkened street and stopped in the parking lot of an abandoned strip center. He dug his cell phone out of his jeans.

"El Tigre, you were right. The cops hit the Acapulco. They've got everyone lined up outside."

"What? You're just getting there? What the hell have you been doing?"

"The girl died from the infection. We had to get rid of her body."

"Why didn't you just leave her at the house? Sarah's body is still there. What's one more? We're ditching the house anyway, moving to Houston."

"I didn't think of that."

"You never think. Where did you dump her?"

"In a ditch, far away from the Acapulco."

"Did anyone see you drive by the Acapulco?"

"I don't think so, but…."

"We can't take the chance. We'll leave Gabriella and Sayda at the Acapulco. Maybe we can get them later. Meet me at the house. We'll leave the Suburban there and take my truck to Houston."

# Chapter Fifty-Four

## Saturday Night

---

Sumner ended the call from Lieutenant Lott and slapped the steering wheel, a broad smile on her face. She turned.

"Great news! They found Maria Santos. She's in the hospital, unconsciousness with an infection of some kind, but alive. Damn, damn, damn." She slapped the wheel several more times.

"Man, that *is* good news." I reached over and high-fived Sumner. "We're halfway home. What about Akemi?"

Sumner shook her head.

From the back seat, Gabriela asked in Spanish, "You said Maria and Akemi's names. Are they okay?"

I spoke in Spanish, "Maria is at the hospital. We don't know about Akemi."

"Maria stepped on a stick," Gabriela continued in her language. "It got bad. Juan was worried. He took her somewhere."

I told Sumner in English. She nodded, wanting me to continue with Gabriela.

"So, Juan helped her?"

"Yes, Juan is good. Cooks us *posole.* He tried to help Sarah, but she went to live with Jesus."

"Sarah?"

"She was our friend. El Tigre hit her in the stomach. El Tigre is scary, but Juan looks after us."

"What about Hectòr?" I asked

Gabriela shrugged.

After a moment I said, "Gabriela, how do we get to the house?"

"I don't know from here. We were on a freeway."

"Do you know the way from the freeway to the house?"

Gabriela shrugged again.

Sumner's cell phone buzzed. "Julius, what's up?"

"Houston PD sent the rap sheet on El Tigre. He's one bad mofo."

"I'm putting you on speaker so Parker can hear."

"Real name is Pablo Cortez. Age thirty-five, American citizen, born in Brownsville, Texas. Mean looking dude, 6'4", 260. Body like a Greek God. Got that working out during a four-year stretch at Federal Social Readaptation Center No. 1, a high-security prison near Mexico City. They call it 'La Palma.' I'm sure that's tongue in cheek."

"What was he in for?"

"Knife fight in a bar. During his prison term, the man he cut up arranged a hit. Hitman cut Cortez's face with a homemade shank. Of course, Cortez killed the guy. The prison ruled self-defense. The prison doctor who sewed it up didn't do a class job, pretty rough. So Cortez wears a heavy beard to help cover the scar that runs from his brow, across his eye, and around his cheek to his lip. Downright nasty looking. Meet him in a dark alley, you'd probably pee your pants. His shoulders and arms are covered with crude tats, too. Probably done in prison."

"So, born in Brownsville, how did he end up in Mexico City?" I asked.

"His mother had six kids, four different fathers. Cortez never knew his. Pushed dope in high school, got caught, kicked out, drifted into Mexico. Worked his way up in the drug gangs. Word is, he killed over twenty people in Mexico as the enforcer for Héctor Salazar, the drug lord of the Sinaloa Cartel."

"Jesus," Sumner murmured.

"No shit," Lott said. "Be careful with this bozo if you find him."

Lott paused, then continued, "Doesn't drink or do drugs, hobby is working out. Likes women, but rough. HPD hasn't been able to nail him. He was arrested in Houston for killing a man, broke his neck. Charges dropped because no one would testify against him."

"Thanks for the info." Sumner said.

"Where are you now?"

"Enroute to the hidey-hole."

"Good luck. Stay safe."

The call ended.

I blew out a big breath, looked at Sumner. "As Chief Brody said, 'We're gonna need a bigger boat.'"

We made the usual twists and turns until the I-45 overpass loomed ahead.

Continuing in Spanish, I said to Gabriela, "Which way when we get to the freeway?"

Gabriela shrugged as usual. Then her sister, Sayda, whispered in her ear.

"Sayda says Hector stopped at that store on the corner for *cervezas*. She says go under and turn left onto the freeway."

# Chapter Fifty-Five

## Saturday Midnight

---

Not knowing how close they were to the house, Sumner and the SWAT vehicle cut their flashing lights.

She rubbed the back of her neck. I was feeling some of that tension myself, nerves jumbled, hands not steady. I'd already killed one bad guy and would have to face the consequences. But if that's what it took to rescue Akemi….

I grabbed my .45 and checked the chamber. Loaded and ready, knowing if I got into a tête-à-tête with El Tigre, it would take more than one 230-grain beauty to stop that big humper. But's that's okay. I started the day with seven in the magazine and one in the chamber. I had gifted one round into Beto's head and in all the excitement, forgot to reload. That left one in the chamber and six in the magazine. Should be enough. And I wouldn't mind putting every one of them into the bastard's thick skull.

My heart thumped against my chest, my pulse rate zooming. I took a deep breath and exhaled slowly. Jeez, what's happened to me? All I wanted after coming home from twenty years in the army was to run a quiet bar, cook some decent food and mind my own business. How do I get involved in these things?

I realized we only had two more exits before we entered the causeway. Was it possible we were going into Galveston? I didn't think so, but still….

Sumner slowed and moved to the right lane, anticipating—maybe hoping—this was the exit. The sign said Highway 6 and Bayou Vista. We'd just visited Atticus Lott in Bayou Vista. So much had happened, that meeting felt like a year ago.

I said to Sumner, "Do you think the hidey-hole could be in Bayou Vista?"

"Probably not," she answered. "Too much activity, people and traffic."

Sayda whispered again.

"Turn here," Gabriela said in Spanish.

Past the exit ramp, the road split. To the left, Highway 146 passed through the City of La Marque and Texas City, two decent-sized municipalities with subdivisions that could easily harbor the bad guys.

To the right, Highway 6 began and dissected several small towns—Hitchcock, Santa Fe and Alvin. We passed the turn to 146 and stopped at a light. To the left was Bayou Vista; Highway 6 straight ahead.

Gabriela pointed to a store just inside Bayou Vista. "Juan stopped there for groceries. He gets us cherry popsicles. Go straight here."

Sumner radioed to the big SWAT vehicle lumbering behind us. "Heads up. We're close."

We rolled past the bridge over Campbell's Bayou, a waterway that empties into West Bay. We passed Louie's Bait Camp on the right, a café and boat launching dock.

Another couple of miles and Gabriela directed us into a subdivision that looked like "the land time forgot." Abandoned houses, weeds for flower beds. Ditches full of water breeding mosquitos. We passed an old car on blocks with its wheels off and a camper with a power cord connected to the house next door for juice.

Sumner said, "Half of the folks that lived here left after the last hurricane. No insurance and not enough help from FEMA. Many of the people who stayed had to make the repairs themselves. Tough to do with no money. There're so many empty houses, El Tigre could have easily rented one on the cheap. Local cops say it has its share of crime and dope. It's one of those areas where people mind their own business and ignore nefarious goings on."

"Nefarious? Pretty big word for you, Sumner." I mused.

She gave me a look that said *"Get a life"* and shook her head.

The area was dark as pitch. No streetlights, the moon hidden behind clouds. We inched ahead, our headlights off, not knowing which house was the target. A house on the left doubled as a church.

"Looks like the good folks here still have hope," I said, trying to find a positive.

We wound slowly through several streets following Gabriela's direction.

*"Aquí,"* Gabriela said. She pointed to a house in the next block that backed up to the bayou. The house was one of the few in the subdivision not on pilings, which meant it probably flooded with seven or eight feet of water during the last storm. Amazing that it was not completely washed away. A large board nailed across the front door made the place look abandoned. Perfect for a trafficker's nest. The garage faced a side street, the overhead door closed. A door out of the garage led to the back entrance of the house.

We parked a half block away, the SWAT team behind us. Sumner faced me. "You stay in the car, Parker."

"What?"

"Someone has to watch Gabriela and Sayda and you've seen enough action for one day, don't you think?"

As much as I wanted to go in, she was right. I'd killed a man, albeit a scumbag. I'd had dubious authority to be on scene, much less use a weapon. I wasn't a cop or member of any branch of law enforcement. I had no idea how my actions would shake out. In the end, I was just a concerned citizen searching for two kidnapped children. I hoped that would be enough.

But at the moment, I didn't really give a damn. I wanted in on the action. I started to bolt for the house in defiance of Sumner, but one glance at Gabriela and Sayda's innocent faces and I knew I couldn't leave them without protection. What if one of the traffickers broke loose from the house?

Sumner folded out of the driver's side for a powwow with SWAT. They quickly formulated a plan and sprinted to the house. Two officers guarded the front and side of the house while Sumner and the remaining officers approached the garage. The lead officer peeked over the fence between the garage and the back door and gave the all-clear.

The team entered the back yard through an unlocked gate. Inside the yard, one officer opened the side door to the garage and signaled another all-clear. The other officer passed by him, hustled to the back door and crushed the lock with a sledgehammer. Sumner shoved the door open and rushed inside, gun in firing position.

Her voice came though the police radio in her car. "Kitchen clear."

The sound of an officer kicking open a door.

Sumner, "We're in a bedroom, several mats on the floor. A bathroom. Clear."

Another door breeched. Sumner again, "House clear."

A moment later she spoke again, "Christ! We've got the body of a young woman wrapped in a sheet. Heavy black and blue bruises across her abdomen."

Silence, then, "Dear God, what kind of animals are these people?"

I said through the car radio, "That must be the girl who went to live with Jesus. El Tigre's work."

Suddenly we heard the sound of slamming brakes. A block away, the driver of a black Suburban backed into a driveway and peeled out.

I couldn't see the occupants, but it could have been the bad guys on the way to the house, maybe with Akemi. I scooted to the driver's seat, put my hand on the keys. I paused. What was I thinking? I couldn't chase after the Suburban with two girls in the back seat.

A gray Honda Civic roared in from the other direction and slammed to a stop beside Sumner's car.

Rudy yelled through the open passenger window, "Get in, Parker!"

What the…?

"The driver of that black Suburban is the guy on the flyers."

I piled out and shouted to one of the officers at the front of the house, "Watch the girls!"

I jumped into Rudy's car and he burned rubber.

"You'll never catch them," I said.

"We have to," Rudy answered, his eyes hard on the road ahead.

# Chapter Fifty-Six

## Saturday Midnight

---

Hector checked through the rear-window then turned to Juan, screaming, "Hit the gas. Those cops back there might have seen you turn around."

He pulled a small revolver from the back of his pants and rotated the cylinder, checking the ammo.

Juan's eyes went wide. "Holy shit! Where did you get that?"

Hector held the pistol up, closed one eye and aimed it at the windshield.

"Bought it off some drunk *güey* at the Acapulco who needed money. Nice thirty-eight, big enough to blow a hole in someone."

Juan shook his head. "You're gonna get yourself in trouble."

"Yeah, well, I can handle it." He aimed again and made sounds like shots.

Juan said, "Did you see the size of that SWAT tank? Those guys are tough mothers. Maybe we should give up."

"You cross Tigre, he'll track you down, put a shiv in your gut."

Juan called Tigre and put him on speaker, "Where are you?"

"Highway 6 exit."

"SWAT's at the house."

"How?"

"Don't know. We barely got away."

Silence.

Tigre, "Meet in Houston."

"What about Akemi? We could dump her."

"No, bring her. My bouncer likes Asian girls."

When Akemi heard Tigre's words, she thought her heart would stop. Bouncer? She said to herself. What is a bouncer? Some big fat slob? What would he do to her?

The image sent shivers through her body; her insides twisted into knots. "Please no," she mumbled. She wrapped her arms around her chest trying to calm herself.

Her worst nightmare—Houston. She imagined bars with Tejano music pounding and scantily clad girls lurking by the windows. Would she be one of them?

Jiichan would never find her. Tears trickled down her cheeks into the corners of her mouth.

A new picture formed in her mind. Jiichan sitting still as a rock, his legs crossed, hands folded. His eyes half lowered. His lips weren't moving, but his message came through.

"Find your courage," he said.

Thankful that Juan had tied her hands in front, Akemi removed the hood and wiped the tears from her cheeks. She spent a few moments counting her breaths, emptying her mind, letting all thoughts pass through without judgment, practicing the ancient art of Zazen as best she could. She felt a warmness course through her body, her strength returning. She opened her eyes: new purpose, new strength.

Her attempt to unlock the door and roll out from the back floorboard had failed. But she would never give up. Never quit.

# Chapter Fifty-Seven

## Saturday Late Night

---

When we rolled out to Highway 6, the Suburban was nowhere in sight. Which way to go? Right toward the small towns further up the highway or left to the freeway?

I said, "One of the girls spilled they were going to Houston tonight."

Rudy turned left toward Bayou Vista. He cut to the freeway and sped north. The speedometer hit eighty-five.

I blurted out, "Talk to me, Rudy. What are you doing?"

"I know where they're going."

"Where?"

"You said Houston…It has to be *El Soledad,* the place with the big bouncer we hit this afternoon. I burned the layout in my brain—wooden fence behind the cantina, two mobile homes. The hallway by the bar at the back. Even the word "*Chicas*" on the sign. It's the same set up as the Acapulco. Tigre must run both."

When we hit ninety, I could only hope the cops' radar wasn't working.

"Probably another dozen just like it in Houston," I said.

"Come on, Parker. I scouted at least fifteen bars and cantinas when I was searching for Akemi. None of those are like The Acapulco."

"It's a long shot."

"You got a better idea?"

I didn't reply.

"If Akemi's not at *El Soledad,* we'll hit every damn bar in Houston until we find her."

By the gleam in his eye and tight jaw, I think he meant it. We caught a traffic slowdown and Rudy laid on the horn, tailgated, swerved between lanes, anything to find a hole. I tightened my seatbelt and steadied my hands against the dashboard. My arms ached from the tension.

"Rudy. Slow down for Christ's sake."

More horn blowing, the sounds blaring across all lanes. People honked back, lowered their windows, cursed, made hand gestures.

He bullied his way through the slowdown, never flinching, never giving. The traffic cleared and he raced on.

My cell phone beeped. Detective Sumner. I showed Rudy the call.

He shook his head no. The call went to voicemail. I checked the message.

"Parker, where the hell are you? Officers said you blasted off chasing a Suburban with Rudy Aoki. Damn it, Parker. You are not authorized for this kind of stunt. This guy, Tigre, is a killer. Way too dangerous for you guys. If you don't call me immediately, I'm putting a BOLO out for that Toyota. Already got one out for the Suburban. You'd damn well better call or I'll have you and Aoki arrested."

I erased the call and stared hard at Rudy. "She may be right. SWAT trains for rescues. They know what they're doing. And Sumner can bring in a trained hostage negotiator."

"Negotiator my ass," Rudy said. "Akemi's my only granddaughter. I'm doing this with or without you."

I wanted to say more about the risk to Akemi, but at this

stage Rudy wouldn't listen. He was still fired up, but something had changed. No shaking or fidgeting, no outward nervousness. Didn't seem out of control, just determined. Eyes filled with purpose, teeth clenched.

At this point, the only way to stop Rudy was a one-on-one confrontation and, after witnessing him in action, that idea was easy to nix.

Well…what the hell, I thought. Go for it. My heart pounding, I faced him and said, "Okay, Rudy. I'm in."

As we approached Loop 610 I said, "Better slow to five over the speed limit. You don't want to get pulled over this late in the game."

He slowed, turned east on the Loop, passed over the Houston Ship Channel and exited at Market Street.

"We should reconnoiter first. Make sure they're here," I said, trying to improvise a plan.

"Reconnoiter, huh," he answered. "I made a few *volunteer* reconnaissance patrols in Italy. All they did was cost us good men. Always some damned colonel trying to make general. You can stay behind for backup if you want. I'm going in full bore."

I checked my phone: 1:10 am. I hoped this late at night *El Soledad* wouldn't be crowded. I was wrong. Pickups and old cars crammed the parking lot. At the sight of the cantina, my shoulder twitched and gut tightened.

My body's reaction sent me back to my army days and a particular night in East Berlin. We were surveilling an East German spy. I had the same twitch in my shoulder and knot in my stomach. We never knew when one of those go-for-broke bastards would come out firing.

Rudy eased past the parking lot and turned on the side street. "There it is, Parker. There it is." He slammed the steering wheel with an open palm.

The black Suburban sat nose in, its grill almost touching the wooden fence that surrounded the mobile homes. Rudy doused the headlights and backed in beside the Suburban, positioned for a quick exit. He pulled a large folding knife from his jeans.

"First things first," he said, opening the blade. He stepped out and sliced the air valves on the Suburban's front and back tires closest to him. The tires settled into the gravel with a whooshing sound,

"Insurance," he said.

We approached *El Soledad* with no plan, which was against everything the army had taught me. Even the Boy Scout motto was "Be Prepared."

Rudy retrieved the rifle. He eased open the bolt and checked the chamber. I did the same with my Colt.

We peeked over the fence into the small backyard. Just like the Acapulco Cantina, two mobile homes sat side-by-side, their entrances facing each other only ten feet apart. As Yogi Berra had said, "It's *deja vue* all over again."

Light shown through the windows on the mobile home closest to us, the other was dark with a padlock on the door. Business must be off. The good news was we only had to worry about one.

Unlike the Acapulco, there were no covered walkways from the cantina to the mobile homes, giving us a clear view to the back door of the cantina.

We debated options. Neither of us would pass for Hispanic which meant, if we went in the front door, we'd stand out like a strutting tom turkey at mating time. And assuming Akemi was in there, we'd probably have to blast our way out, putting her in more danger than necessary.

We decided to go in the back way, hoping Akemi was in the mobile home. I wanted to grab her and get the hell out of Dodge. I wouldn't mind putting a few slugs into Tigre along the way, but if we could vamoose before all hell broke loose, all the better.

We moved along the fence at the side of the mobile home. Rudy used the tire tool from the Toyota to pry off three boards. He passed through, while I made one last check around the outside. No one in sight.

With only a foot between the fence and mobile home, we squeezed through to the front of the home. We waited at the corner to see if anyone in the building had heard us and sounded an alarm.

All quiet. Rudy slipped around to the front and climbed the three stairs to the landing outside the door. I waited by the corner, close to the fence, gun in hand, hoping no one would come out the back door of the cantina.

Rudy eased the metal door open and stepped into a small living area furnished with a tattered couch, two armchairs, and a dim lamp that threw just enough light to see.

He moved carefully toward the small kitchen to the right of the living area and peeked in. No one. He crept along the hallway at the other end of the living area. Two bedrooms, one on either side with a bathroom at the end of the hall. The bathroom door stood open; the room appeared empty.

Rudy put his ear to the left bedroom door. Not hearing anything, he turned the handle and peeked inside. Vacant. His heart sank. Only one room to go. What the hell would he do if Akemi wasn't in the home?

He stepped across the hall and listened at the door. He heard a commotion, rustling, possibly a struggle. He threw open the door and stepped in.

Two figures wrestled on the bed. Akemi's long black hair trailed off the side of the bed. She squirmed under a man twice her size, his shirt off, his bulging stomach pushed against her body. Sweat dripped off his face. He'd pinned her arms and legs, but she bucked and snarled, her mouth open, teeth ready as if trying to reach his face.

Rudy stepped forward; the man looked up. Recognition in both their eyes. It was the bouncer, the same man who'd put Rudy down when he got arrested. The fat bouncer rolled off Akemi, trying to get his feet on the floor. Akemi rolled off the end of the bed. Rudy glanced at Akemi, saw her bruised face and went ballistic. His adrenalin spiked and blood rushed to his face, turning it beet red.

He slammed the bouncer's forehead with the rifle butt. The bouncer fell backward on the bed. Rudy moved in and hit him again with the butt, this time on his nose just below his eyes. Blood poured from the bouncer's broken nose, one eye already puffed and closing. The bouncer vainly held up his arms, trying to protect himself, as if saying 'Please, no more.'

Rudy jammed the stock into his fat stomach. The bouncer dropped his arms. Rudy slashed across his face with the rifle barrel, cutting a gash in his cheek. More blood streamed out, falling to his naked chest. He slumped against the wall beside the bed. Eyes closed. No movement.

Akemi stood, hugging Rudy and saying "Jiichan, Jiichan, you came."

Rudy wrapped an arm around Akemi in a tight embrace. He put his mouth to her ear and whispered, "We're going home, Akemi."

The man on the bed raised his hand to his head, moaning a terrible sound. Rudy raised the rifle again and butted him full force in the forehead.

I heard the fight going on inside and ran for the door. Just as I reached the steps, the back door of the cantina opened. A Hispanic man holding a beer bottle came out. When our eyes met, I pointed the big Colt at his chest. He threw the bottle at me and ran back inside. I knew that was trouble. Someone else would be coming out, probably with a gun.

Rudy came out of the trailer, one arm around Akemi and the other holding the rifle. We made it to the corner of the mobile home when a short, fat man came out of the cantina with a pistol in his hand. Another man, much taller, behind him.

Akemi yelled from behind me, "Juan! Hector has a gun! Help us!"

Juan glimpsed Akemi and moved toward Hector. Before Juan could stop him, the short man she'd called Hector raised his pistol and fired.

Then Rudy shot Hector. The shot knocked Hector to the ground. He lay on his back unable to move, blood seeping out of a hole in his chest.

Something burned in my side. My hand came up soaked with blood. I collapsed to the ground and put pressure on the wound as best I could.

The tall man, Juan, sprinted for the cantina. Rudy raised his rifle but didn't fire. Juan came out with a bar towel and ran to me, bypassing Hector. He pressed the towel to my wound.

A figure appeared in the door. His head reached the top of the frame and his body blocked all light from the cantina.

Akemi said, "Jiichan, it's El Tigre, the leader. He killed Sarah."

Rudy didn't know about Tigre's ruthlessness, but I did,

having just gotten the report from the Houston police.

Tigre surveyed the scene and stepped outside. Fiery eyes, the scar on his cheek pulsating. He glanced at Hector, stepped past him, cut his eyes at me for a half-second and moved cautiously toward Rudy. I rolled to my side, searching for my automatic, hoping I could get off a shot.

My Colt was four feet away, out of reach. I got Juan's attention and pointed to my gun. He dropped the towel and handed me the Colt. More blood oozed out. I fought hard to keep my eyes open, to stay conscious. Raise your arm and shoot, I told myself. But I couldn't: too weak.

I heard Juan behind me calling 911.

I tried to shout, to warn Rudy, "Shoot him, Rudy. Shoot him." But the words wouldn't come out.

Tigre's didn't need a weapon; his formidable size said it all. He crept slowly toward Rudy, like the tiger he was, plotting his pounce. He seemed to ignore the rifle aimed at his head.

An eerie silence fell over the scene. Even the jukebox and people noise from the cantina had quit. Tigre and Rudy seemed to sense the significance of the confrontation.

Then Rudy did the unthinkable. He handed the rifle to Akemi and gently pushed her back. What the hell was this? The final test: mano-a-mano. I wanted to scream out to Rudy to stop. To think about Akemi.

Tigre stopped, stood up tall. Smiling now. They circled, each one looking for his best chance, like two big-horned mountain rams stalking each other, readying the charge.

I could see Rudy focused on Tigre's every move, every slight change in his hands, in his feet. But mainly his eyes. Tigre's eyes would tell Rudy when he would strike.

And then, only steps away, Tigre charged. His hands

reached for Rudy's neck. Rudy ducked under his arms and sidestepped. He stuck his foot in front of Tigre's leg and grabbed his shirt to help propel him forward. Tigre started falling, but Rudy grabbed his foot in midair and in an incredible show of strength, flipped the big man to his side. It was like a scene from a kung fu movie, except it was the real thing. Amazingly, Rudy stepped back and allowed Tigre to get up.

"That was your first mistake," Tigre said, sneering.

I couldn't believe Rudy was allowing this behemoth a second chance. I wanted to shoot the bastard. I held the automatic with both hands, trying to get a shot, but I was getting weak from blood loss, I had trouble lifting my arms.

Rudy and Tigre circled again. Tigre moved in. Rudy dived low, trying for Tigre's legs. This time Tigre sidestepped. He grabbed Rudy's midsection and flipped him over to his back, then fell on him. He balled his fist and hit Rudy hard in the face. Blood spurted. Tigre laughed, hit Rudy again.

Akemi ran to the fight, jumped on Tigre's back and tightened her arm around his neck, trying desperately to cut his air. Tigre sputtered. He reached back with his arm, grabbed Akemi's shirt and flung her off. She rolled to the ground.

Akemi's move gave Rudy the chance he needed. Tigre had made a big mistake and left Rudy's legs free. Rudy grabbed Tigre's shirt with his left hand and pulled him down. He raised his right leg, bent it over the back of Tigre's neck and pulled him closer. Then he folded his left leg over his right ankle making a firm choke hold that compressed Tigre's carotid artery.

I'd seen this jujitsu move demonstrated during army training. The victim would be unconscious in ten seconds, followed by death shortly after if the hold was not released. Rudy didn't seem to want to quit.

Tigre fought to loosen Rudy's hold, but with no blood passing to his brain, his struggle lessened. His eyes rolled back and his head flopped forward. Rudy held the hold. And held. And held.

# Chapter Fifty-Eight

## Saturday, Three Weeks Later

---

Cars and pickups overflowed the VFW parking lot. Two TV mobile units had commandeered spots, their rooftop antennas reaching toward the satellites. The boys from Rudy's jujitsu class were busy valeting cars with Kevin in charge, the boy Rudy had attacked at the beach.

A large banner over the front door read, "Happy Birthday, Maria!"

Inside the large hall, where Friday night bingo games were usually the most exciting events of the week, colorful fiesta lanterns hung from the ceiling and garlands of yellow, blue and red were strung around the walls.

A *mariachi* group played lively Mexican favorites, complete with violins and trumpets, the men in huge sombreros, black vests and pants embossed with gold trim.

Local restaurants had donated food and drinks all served buffet style from the kitchen. Tables were set up around the walls, leaving room for a dance floor in the center.

Maria had spent a week in the hospital recovering from her infection and receiving trauma therapy from a psychologist. She was now fully recovered from her illness but was still attending weekly sessions with the therapist. Akemi was seeing the same psychologist.

Maria's mother had wanted to celebrate her *quinceañera* a week earlier, but Maria insisted they wait until Sergeant

Guerra had recovered and could attend. Tonight, Sergeant Luis Guerra, still in a wheelchair, sat at a table with Chief Puryear, Officer Sylvia Morales, Detective Donna Sumner, Lieutenant Julius Lott and Sergeant Ken Pulley. Puryear had insisted all the officers appear in dress uniform.

Another table included several of Maria and Akemi's teachers including the school principal Bobbye Bennett. Behind them were two tables of students from the school including Kathy's daughter Julie and David Mendez and his girlfriend Stacy. David was the boy who'd spotted the kidnapper's van and had given the description of the driver to Kathy to help her draw the flyer.

A table of local dignitaries and politicians, who everyone tried their best to ignore, sat tucked in the corner.

The entire night shift from the ER at UTMB were there along with Doctor Hardy and Doctor Evan and the county medical examiner, Dr. Sandra Lillich. The physician and his assistant from the emergency clinic where Juan had dropped Maria off and the two paramedics who had cared for her enroute to the hospital sat at another table.

Maria Santos sat at the main table up front with her mother, Alicia Santos, and her cousin, Patricia Gonzales. Akemi sat on the other side of Maria with Rudy and Maggie next to her. Akemi had wanted me at the table, but I had politely declined.

Across the table were two special quests: Gabriela and Sayda. The sisters were now in the custody of the state welfare department and lived with an approved foster parent in Galveston. With Rudy and Harry's approval, Crime Stoppers had awarded the $100,000 award to Gabriela and Sayda. Harry suggested setting up a trust for the girls: the juvenile judge in charge had agreed and appointed Harry trustee.

Maria and Akemi desperately wanted Juan to be there but he was still in jail, the Galveston DA trying to determine charges, if any. Hector had just been released from the hospital and was sitting in the Harris County Jail in Houston charged with trafficking and attempted murder.

I was only hospitalized a few days, but the bullet had nicked my liver. Like a fool, I had removed the hot flak vest when I'd climbed into Rudy's car. The doctor cautioned no alcohol for at least a month which left me drinking Diet Dr. Pepper with Harry Stein.

Kathy Landry sat beside me along with Harry and his new girlfriend Elizabeth, both of them dressed like they were attending the Academy Awards. Across the table were Bully Stout in his wheelchair and Neddie Lemmon. As a retired officer, Atticus Lott hadn't wanted to dress in uniform, so he sat with us.

For the first dance, Maria asked me to be her partner. She was absolutely stunning, with her long black hair flowing over her special red *quinceañera* dress with the puffy skirt and bright sequined top her mother and cousin had made. Unconditional love going into every stitch. She also wore the silver tiara designed by her grandfather for her mother's *quinceañera.*

I escorted her to the floor, and we danced to the soulful rhythm of "Las Mañanitas," Maria's favorite Mexican birthday song. Halfway through, Maria waved to Akemi. Rudy escorted her to the floor to the rousing applause of the guests. Akemi glowed in the green "Cinderella dress" Maggie had made for her.

When Rudy and I left the floor, all the young people got up to dance. A handsome boy moved to Maria and danced every number with her, holding her closer with each dance.

I glanced at Maggie, my palms up, asking who is the boy with Akemi?

Maggie said, "Akemi told me his name is Carlos Garcia. He sat next to Maria at the volleyball game before they were taken. Akemi said he visited Maria every day in the hospital. She said his mother named him after Carlos Fuentes, the celebrated Mexican writer."

I nodded to Maggie thinking: first love—so special. And how close Maria had come to not experiencing that feeling. Life is so damned fragile, every minute counts. I caught Kathy's eye and whispered....

On the dance floor, all the girls looked pretty in bright party dresses and the women in colorful *rebozos,* delicately placed over their shoulders. The young boys and men all wore traditional white *guayabera* shirts.

After the *mariachis* entertained us with a number of rousing Mexican favorites, the VFW post commander rose to speak. He stood at the podium where the bingo caller usually turned the wire basket and spoke from the microphone.

He welcomed everyone to the celebration, wished Maria a very special birthday and delivered a well-prepared—if too long—soliloquy about Post 176 of the Veterans of Foreign Wars, ending with a pitch for Friday night bingo. After scattered applause for the commander, the room got totally silent.

Maria came to the microphone, so filled with emotion she couldn't speak. Akemi rose and put her arm around her friend's waist. Maria tried again.

"I...I owe so much to everyone here. I don't know where to begin. First, I want to say to you Akemi, I couldn't have made it without you. Your strength and perseverance carried me through. I love you so much."

She hugged Akemi to enthusiastic applause from the floor, then turned back to the microphone.

"I want to thank my mother. Please stand *mamá*."

As Señora Santos stood Maria said, "I felt your love during the whole time. You never left me. You prayed at our small shrine to Our Lady of Guadalupe and never gave up. Love you, *mamá*." She blew her a kiss. "And special thanks to Mr. Aoki and Mr. McLeod."

She asked Rudy and me to stand, but we just waved when she said our names. She continued with thanks to the Galveston Police Department, Galveston EMS and the nurses and doctors at UTMB.

In closing, she thanked Juan for saving her life by taking her to the emergency clinic. She explained how singing with Juan had given her courage.

Maria said, "I dedicate this song to Akemi and my friend Juan." Akemi joined Maria and they harmonized with the accompaniment of the *mariachis.*

When the sun shines on the mountain
And the night is on the run
It's a new day
It's a new way
And I fly up to the sun
I can feel the morning sunlight
I can smell the new-mown hay
I can hear God's voice is calling
For my golden sky light way
*Una paloma blanca*
I'm just a bird in the sky
*Una paloma blanca*
Over the mountains I fly
**No one can take my freedom away**

When Maria and Akemi sang the chorus, everyone in the hall stood and joined in. They continued the chorus over and over. It turned out this was more than a birthday party. It was a celebration of life, and no wanted the evening to end.

# Chapter Fifty-Nine

## Monday Afternoon

---

The Harris County Grand Jury no-billed Rudy and me, thanks to the efforts of Harry Stein and his attorney friend in Houston. The Galveston Grand Jury was still considering my shooting of Beto, the scumbag bouncer at the Acapulco Cantina, but I wasn't too worried. After all, I was still somewhat of a local hero for my actions last year in foiling a terrorist plot. But that's another story.

I don't like getting caught up in these dramas, but things just seem to happen. Kind of strange, considering I live twenty miles from town on an isolated stretch of West Galveston Beach and like to mind my own business.

Today was a typical Monday at The Garhole Bar. I'd latched up the cut-out wall in front to cool the inside. Bully had spent the morning trying to teach his new dog how to heel to the side of his wheelchair. So far he hadn't had much luck.

Someone had anonymously reported the chained pit bull next to Maria's mobile home to the Humane Society. (I can't imagine who would have done that.) The dog was picked up, given the proper shots, fed and bathed. I'd mentioned it to Bully and the first day the canine was put up for adoption, he came home with him. He had named the dog Marvin after his friend who'd choked to death at the donut shop.

I hadn't mentioned how much the dog and Bully favored

each other. Both with a pug face and the occasional growl. And I wasn't the only one who'd noticed it.

Sarah's mother came in from Arkansas to take her body back home. A special go-fund-me page collected over $10,000 for her burial.

Harry had called a meeting of the Dead Peckers' Club to install me as an honorary member. Kathy and Maggie had come out for the special occasion.

We had finished off the last batch of crab gumbo for the season, and were all sitting around a table, Harry and me with Dr. Peppers and the rest with cold beers, Neddie already on his third one.

Kathy and I sat in shorts and tee shirts enjoying the breeze. Rudy sat next to Maggie trying to keep his beer off the new Garhole Bar tee shirt I'd given him. Neddie Lemmon sat across the table dressed in one of his gaudy women-repelling tee shirts. Bully Stout, in his wheelchair next to him, fiddled with his eyepatch and chewed on an unlit cigar. He quit with the eyepatch and began massaging the stump of his missing leg.

Harry, his hair perfectly coiffed as usual, sat tweaking his mustache while complaining his perfectly pressed linen pants would get unduly wrinkled in the afternoon humidity. His girlfriend Elizabeth was a picture of style and grace, her blouse alone must have cost in the hundreds.

Before the final initiation, we toasted the gar head hanging over the bar, pleased that it seemed to be smiling at us. Harry said a few words and they all welcomed me as the newest member.

"Honorary," I confirmed. I winked at Kathy, secretly pleased to see her smiling as if she understood my message.

Maggie went out to the car and brought in the Japanese

rifle. She handed it to Neddie. She said she'd received an email from Harumi Rudolph, the Japanese interpreter who'd been trying to track down the relatives of Masayoshi Watanabe, the Japanese Army lieutenant who'd owned the rifle and was presumably killed during the battle for Okinawa in 1945. Maggie read the email from Harumi:

*I just heard from the Japanese War-Bereaved Organization. They said a staff member of a USA-based NPO called OBON Society will help in the investigation. I provided your email address to pass onto the NPO.*

Then, Maggie said, "It appears we are making progress returning the rifle. The OBON Society is based in Astoria, Oregon. Their purpose is to facilitate the return of war memorabilia brought home by American soldiers whose families now want to return the item to the Japanese soldier's family. The organization is named after the OBON Festival, an annual holiday when the Japanese people pay respect to their ancestors and loved ones who have passed away. During this time Buddhists believe spirits are able to return to Earth and be with their families.

"OBON's website indicated the process may take months, even years. I thanked Harumi and invited her and her husband down to stay with us for a weekend in November."

Her report left everyone smiling at the thought of something good happening after the turmoil we'd all been through.

Out in the bay two fishermen in a small outboard puttered toward the dock. They tied up and hurried in for cold beer. They took the beers out to the dock and began filleting their trout at the cleaning table. Life seemed back to normal at The Garhole Bar. At least for a while.

# Japanese Rifle

The Japanese rifle story in this book is based on fact. My uncle, Doug Walsworth USN, won the rifle in a dice game from a GI on Doug's ship. The ship was returning American servicemen to the U.S. following the end of the war. Uncle Doug gave the rifle to my dad who passed it down to me.

I was fortunate to find Harumi Rudolph, Certified Japanese Translator, who interpreted the characters on the rifle. The rifle's owner, Second Lieutenant Masayoshi Watanabe was attached to the 32nd Army of Japan responsible for guarding Okinawa and the surrounding islands. We speculate that Lieutenant Watanabe was killed in the battle for Okinawa during the last few days of the war.

Harumi also graciously agreed to help find family members of Lieutenant Watanabe with the idea of returning the rifle to his relatives. She contacted the Japan War-Bereaved Families Association and the OBON Society based in Astoria, Oregon. We are anxiously awaiting the results of the search.

# About the Author

## A. Hardy Roper

As a fourth generation Texan and Galveston resident, A. Hardy Roper writes from a wealth of knowledge about the island's storied past and vibrant present. Mr. Roper's great grandparents arrived from Germany in the 1852 and entered through the Port of Galveston, at the time, second only to New York for immigrant destination.

Today's Galveston is an eclectic mixture of 'old money' and Victorian mansions checkered among indigent neighborhoods of African Americans and Hispanics, all weaved tightly together, as if huddled against the onslaught of the next storm like the epic 1900 hurricane that claimed 6,000 lives.

From its 19th Century past of pirates and buried treasures, to its 20th Century lifestyle of bootlegging, bawdy houses and gambling, Galveston Island offers an endless setting for mystery and intrigue.

A. Hardy Roper has studied its culture and its history. His Parker McLeod thrillers weave an intricate path of deceit and mayhem as the city struggles to balance its colorful past with the inevitable collision of sleepy 'island life' and the hurried weekend rush as the playground of Houston's wealthy baby-boomers.

Contact Hardy on Facebook
www.facebook.com/TheGarholeBar

## More Books by the author:

The Garhole Bar™

Assassination in Galveston™

Saving Jake™

Bad Moon Rising

Girls Lost

## Children's books:

Gullet the Mullet

Ma Skeeter

**Reviews for *The Garhole Bar*** **November 4, 2007**

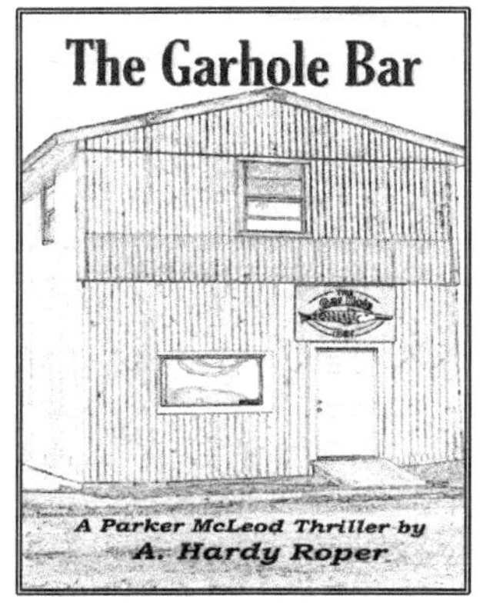


**From the *Galveston Daily News***
**Captivating and Engrossing,**
By **Margaret C. Barno**
**"story weaver" (Pflugerville, TX)**

How long has it been since you've stayed up to the wee hours of the night so engrossed in a book so that you could read just one more page? It happened to me last night, or rather, this morning.

*The Garhole Bar* is a thriller, full of suspense, unexpected turns and many of these events unfold on the West End of Galveston Island. Its author, A. Hardy Roper, who called that location home for over twenty years, sets the novel, his first, at a bar owned by Parker McLeod. Named after the skeleton of an alligator gar jaw he had found and pried open, it is displayed prominently, hanging from the ceiling behind the bar counter.

The story's plot is complex; depth of character development, covering a sixty-year time frame. The scenes initially shift from Germany and Galveston, eventually covering three continents.

Parker McLeod, a 19-year veteran, is struggling to get his life back together. While attempting to help an old friend and his granddaughter, Parker discovers skills learned during his military service come in handy in his new career as owner of a small bar on the west end of an island in the Gulf of Mexico off the coast of Texas.

The story is well presented and kept my heart thumping to the last page. I hope that next thriller involving Parker McLeod is ready for press soon. My hunch is that A. Hardy Roper has a new venture as author that will keep him busy and his books in demand for years to come.

**Review Written by wilhelmlette (Houston, TX USA)**

Well done...had my interest from start to finish!

December 11, 2007

Having been to Galveston Island many times, this book was especially fun to read. This novel will clearly be just as much of a page turner for those who don't know the island at all. A. Hardy Roper does a nice job of character development and successfully weaves the various storylines into a truly entertaining novel of intrigue. The book was an easy and entertaining read.

**Review for *"Assassination in Galveston"*** **Dec. 3, 2011**

**From the *Galveston Daily News***
**by Margaret C. Barno, story creator**
**"Island thriller is a page-turner."**

Military veteran and former spy Parker McLeod had all intentions of settling in Galveston's West End to fish and run a quiet restaurant, *The Garhole Bar,* after his medical retirement resulting from the Gulf War.

Those plans have been only partially realized. He has gotten involved in solving crimes. This book is another of those unanticipated adventures when a dear friend and lover Of Kemp's ridley sea turtles is murdered and her home set ablaze. The plot is multi layered, involving assassinations initiated and orchestrated by Fidel and Raul Castro, of Cuba. The long-range goal is instigating an uprising in Venezuela, resulting in a coup in which a friend and ally hopefully will become ruler, enabling the flow of much-needed oil to go to the desperately impoverished nation of Cuba.

Where there's life and danger, there's usually romantic intrigue. The author has placed a realistic variety of such interludes throughout the book. The scenes are descriptive yet not graphic. For that I was grateful.

It's another page-turner that, on a couple of evenings, I set a chapter limit to read no further before going to bed. Roper's characters are well-developed, like the "bad guys" to the folks at the VA hospital and residents on Bolivar Peninsula and Galveston's West End. Perhaps the best descriptions were the Galveston landmarks, particularly the areas around the ferry landing. I could hear the waves hitting the boat, the ever-hungry gull cries and occasionally see the dolphins racing the ferry no matter who was going where for whatever reason.

I've deliberately not mentioned the ending. If Ii had, you'd not read the book. You'd miss a thriller by doing so. I'm going back to read it again to see what I missed during the first time through.

*Review for "Assassination in Galveston"* **– 5 out of 5 stars! by Saucer**

This is another of the Parker McLeod thriller series I couldn't put down until finished. The author's descriptive writing style puts you right in the Texas Gulf Coast area. The beaches, seasonal storms, old restored homes, and other sites bring Galveston alive, right at the seaside.

The protagonist, Parker McLeod, is an ex-army Intel officer who inadvertently gets involved in a plot to murder a South American presidential candidate. When a good friend of Parker's is murdered, he begins his own investigation and meets a cast of nefarious characters and a beautiful Cuban ex-patriot who he teams with to attempt to solve the mystery.

*Review for Saving Jake* – **5 out of 5 stars!** **Nov. 3, 2015**

**From the *Galveston Daily News***
**by Margaret C. Barno, story creator**

The book begins with the simple act of picking up a boy and woman at a stop in Lake Charles, La. Both look emaciated. The woman only asks to be driven west. One of the few bits of information former Army Intel officer, Parker McLeod, gets is their names, Jake, a boy about 14 and his mother, Joy. The way Joy clutches a duffel, Parker suspects there is more than clothes in the bag. He drops them off just east of the bar he owns at the far western end of Galveston Island. The more Parker learns, the more he is determined to save Jake from the life he has been forced into by his mother's habits as a junkie. Things go from bad to worse when the people who own the bag of drugs Joy has stolen arrive in Galveston. Meanwhile a very wealthy man in Boston has hired a P.I. to learn the truth behind the death of his son. Where there is fire, gun smoke that is, there will be killings and severe injuries, often involving innocent people who are hospitalized unable to talk. That means the only person who knows the location of the drugs is Jake, and he's disappeared. What happens next will keep you, the reader on the edge of your seat. You may even forget to eat, as I did, more than one meal. There's much more, I've not mentioned. You'll need to find those events and personalities when you read the book. If you like thrillers, this is one you can't miss reading.

**Format: Kindle Edition, verified purchase**

"Saving Jake" is an excellent read! As soon as I finished the book, I immediately bought the other two books by this author. Extremely readable and filled with the sights and feel of Galveston.

**Amazon: verified purchase**

"Saving Jake" is a great story. I finished the book in two evenings. This is the third book by Hardy Roper that I have read. His knowledge of Galveston is amazing and his other experience makes him a must-read author.

**Format: Kindle Edition, verified purchase**

Exciting. Interesting character development. Great Plot.
January 14, 2016

**Format: Paperback – verified purchase**

Hardy Roper's stories get better and better. This is the best writing he's published. Exciting. Interesting character development. Great plot. And I love the setting of this and all his books, the west end of Galveston island. People often say that the first few words of a book are important. I was caught in the story from the first few paragraphs of this book:

*Review for Bad Moon Rising* – **5 out of 5 stars! Nov. 3, 2015**

**By: Sharan Zwick Galveston Bookshop**

"A. Hardy Roper, Bad Moon Rising is your best story yet!"

If you have read A. Hardy Roper's three previous thrillers set on Galveston Island, then you know Parker McLeod. The easy-going owner of The Garhole Bar, Parker is at his best with a cold beer in his hand and a beautiful woman at his side. While he never goes out looking for danger, somehow it seems to find him. Bad Moon Rising, Hardy's latest book about this enigmatic but likable character is no exception. Parker's beloved grandfather had used the phrase "bad moon rising" as a warning when a dangerous storm appeared on the horizon. Parker now claims ownership of the expression as the "bad moon" of terrorism comes to the island.

Characters in this fast-paced novel are exquisitely drawn: A beautiful scientist from Germany who is the new Assistant Director of the Gulf Coast Level 4 Biological Lab; the Secretary of Homeland Security, in Galveston for a routine inspection; Islamic terrorists intent on revenge against the Secretary; and Parker—a former Army Intel officer with a personal vendetta against one of the terrorists. Add the FBI, NSA, CIA, Secret Service and local police and the intensity ratchets up with every page. The terrorists will use any means available including kidnapping, coercion and threats, to kill the Secretary. When the first attempt fails, the terrorists devise a scheme to use a deadly pathogen. During a raging winter storm, Parker must race through flooded streets and dark alleyways to try and prevent a cataclysmic event for the usually sun-filled city of Galveston.

**If you like thrillers, Bad Moon Rising is a must read!**

**Verified Amazon Customer** **5.0 out of 5 stars**

A. Hardy Roper's Best Book in a Great Series!

*Reviewed in the United States on July 10, 2019*

I waited for this latest Parker McCleod novel by Hardy Roper since I put down his last book. It is the best in the series. The wait was worth it. In each book the image of the Garhole Bar and it's owner becomes clearer in my mind. I can see Parker walking down the beach as a storm heads his way. It makes me want to buy an old pickup and drive to Galveston in it to find the bar on the West end of Galveston Island and stop by to have a bowl of gumbo. Or a reason to take a trip across the bay and tie up at the dock. In this book Parker has put many of his past demons to rest, but still fights those remaining. He is a believable hero. While each book stands on its own, after reading this book you will want to start with the first book and read or re-read them all.

**Verified Amazon Customer** **5.0 out of 5 stars**

Roper's best McLeod Thriller!

*Reviewed in the United States on July 7, 2019*

I finished Roper's latest Parker McLeod thriller a few days ago. After reading his third McLeod thriller I said that it was the best. I was wrong. Roper has raised the bar another notch and produced his best book. A terrific story with great plot and character development. In keeping with his previous books, Bad Moon Rising is fast paced and is indeed a "page turner". The book builds to a action packed ending, and perhaps leaves an opening for a another McLeod adventure. And, Roper manages to weave into the text some interesting bits of Galveston history. I highly recommend Bad Moon Rising.

One person found this helpful

**Verified Amazon Customer** **5.0 out of 5 stars**

An exciting, action-packed novel that could really happen

*Reviewed in the United States on July 26, 2019*

Bad Moon Rising, Hardy Roper's latest book, is a page-turner if ever there was one and has "movie" written all over it.

Hardy has really done his homework on jihadist mentality and bioterrorism, two of the scariest realities of our time. He has also done what good authors who write about special places do: describe a location in terms of its history, importance and geography. For those who know Galveston, Texas, they can close their eyes and follow Hardy's protagonist, Parker McLeod, and the book's other fascinating characters as they traverse this unique island city that is part of Texas folklore.

The book's characters — quirky ones you would want to know to establishment types from the FBI, NSA and UTMB's medical research complex — along with plot twists Daniel Silva and David Baldacchi would likely appreciate make the fourth Parker McLeod thriller one you will not forget.

**Verified Amazon Customer** **5.0 out of 5 stars**

Wanted to read from cover to cover in one setting.

*Reviewed in the United States on July 7, 2019*

A strong storyline that was weaved together for a very smooth read with excellent dialogue and well defined characters. Parker McLeod has been established as a character that you are anxious to read his next challenge. A. Hardy Roper continues to grow as evidenced by research, knowledge of locale used and characters he creates to enhance each new offering. If this type of story is what you read I urge you the read this new book by A. Hardy Roper!! It's suspenseful and entertaining.

**Verified Amazon Customer** **5.0 out of 5 stars**

Parker McLeod at his best!

*Reviewed in the United States on July 30, 2019*

Could not wait for Mr. Roper's latest book – and it is his best effort yet! As with all his work, the plot in this book is a "cannot put down" page turner. Bad Moon Rising has great characters and when you add the historical charm of Galveston Island – you're already looking forward to his next novel.

*Review for Girls Lost:* **– 5 out of 5 stars! Feb 16, 2023**

**Publishers Review**

Hardy Roper's latest book, Girls Lost, begins on a fearful note when teenage friends Akemi and Maria are kidnapped by sex traffickers looking for new recruits for their prostitution ring.

Knowing that time is critical in rescuing the girls, the feisty, female police detective in charge of the case recruits ex-army intel officer Parker McCloud to aid in the search. Parker—well known to readers from Roper's four previous books—takes to the streets to find them. Tension builds as the scenes move quickly between the innocent captive girls and the brutal kidnappers.

Roper does an excellent job of developing the characters through sympathetic views into the hardships the girls have already experienced in their young lives and the ugliness of the sex/slave trade represented by their captors. The reader experiences the sense of urgency facing Parker and the police as time rushes by without word of the girls.

Girls Lost is an easy read, filled with the author's usual cast of eclectic characters, as well as his familiar vivid descriptions of Galveston Island.

This is A. Hardy Roper's best Parker McCloud book yet. Don't miss it!

*Review for Girls Lost:* – **5 out of 5 stars!** **Feb 12, 2023**
by --Saucer

Parker McLeod, a retired U.S. army intelligence officer, now owner of the Gar Hole bar on west Galveston beach is on a roll again.

As in all of Hardy Roper's thrillers, Parker comes to the rescue again in the author's new book, *Girls Lost*.

Parker is always willing to help ladies in distress, especially when the ladies are two young innocent teenage girls that have been kidnapped, presumably by sex traffickers. He teams up with old friends from the Gar Hole bar, and with some new friends at the Galveston Police Department.

Never a dull moment as Parker overcomes one obstacle after another in his search for the girls. It's another of Roper's fast-paced books I couldn't put down until the end.

The setting is Galveston, Texas, and Roper's vivid descriptions of the island makes me want to buy a house and retire on West Beach.

*Review for Girls Lost:* – **5 out of 5 stars!** **Feb 12, 2023**
By --Anne Sloan
**Author of Her Choice, a historical novel set in 1928**

For the fifth volume in his Parker McLeod's series, Roper crafts a compelling page turner which deepens our understanding and awareness concerning the trafficking of children.

Galveston's proximity to Mexico provides the stage, and Roper's finely drawn characters enable the reader to witness the tragedy of this crime from multiple points of view. The girls, their parents, the community, and law enforcement officers combine to provide suspense and gut-wrenching anxiety about the fate of the abducted victims.

CPSIA information can be obtained
at www.ICGtesting.com
Printed in the USA
JSHW032148160323
39015JS00001B/3